Seven Archangels:
Dedication
of the Stars

Seven Archangels: Dedication of the Stars

Jane Lebak

Philangelus Press
Boston, MA USA

ISBN: 978-1-942133-55-1

Cover art by Charlotte Volnek
Editing by Michaela DeToma

Prologue

Gazing at Lucifer, Gabriel hungered for fire.

Long after the Second Coming, ages after Lucifer and his host had been locked inside Hell, Gabriel sat on his heels, a wingspan away from the only angel stronger than himself. His library balcony felt like the nexus of eternity, and two impulses dominated his heart.

First, that engaging with Lucifer was wrong. Dangerous. Frightening.

Second, that it was entirely right. Intoxicating. And exactly what Gabriel must do.

God had granted the fallen seven days out of Hell for the Heavenly banquet. At the same time, Gabriel had been presented a plan. A plan, and a long shot hope.

Lucifer met Gabriel's eyes with light dancing in his own—that light, that light—and Gabriel reached for God. *Steady me.* A week ago, this would have been unthinkable. It still was unthinkable. Danger tingled in Gabriel's mouth, and an impulsive smile overtook him as he regarded Lucifer in motion. He was beauty itself with twelve wings of bright feathers, the platinum hair, the sheer brilliance of his mind, and all the potential of the Seraph-Cherub bond they should have had.

The bond they still could have.

Lucifer caught Gabriel's impulse, and he leaned forward. Had he realized how hard Gabriel was holding back?

It took more willpower than Gabriel thought he possessed, but

God gave him strength to turn away. Gabriel's balcony looked out on three cedars, tall, firm as faith. They reminded him of the last time Lucifer had attempted a full-on seduction of his soul.

Israfel. He should train his mind on Israfel, who with her own fire had urged Gabriel not to get close to Lucifer.

Abruptly Lucifer was right behind Gabriel, his breath over Gabriel's wings. He murmured, "What are you thinking? Don't tell me it's nothing. You're so deep inside yourself."

Gabriel riveted his gaze to the trees. "I'm thinking about your plant."

He wasn't thinking about only the plant. A tree had been Gabriel's salvation from his own arrogance when he fell from it. A tree had saved humanity when the Son of God hung from it. Now Lucifer had a plant of his own, a thirsty heather that hungered for light it couldn't comprehend.

From Lucifer's thoughts, Gabriel detected confusion and deception and loathing, and all aimed at one leafy being. They were a lot closer to bonding than Gabriel should be comfortable with—and he wasn't comfortable at all.

Lucifer only said, "Why do you care about that plant?"

"Because you cared about it." That plant was a life preserver Gabriel might toss into the storm surge, perhaps to pull back a drowning soul, but there had to be a hand on both sides.

Eyes closed, Gabriel focused again on the plant that could absorb Lucifer's light without guilt. Plants don't know when they're in the hands of the father of lies. Gabriel remembered having his hands in the soil, separating the plant from the dust. He'd been coaxing the roots free of the useless ground, the sunless Earth now stale with the scent of ash. He'd extended his heart into it, and by reflex he extended his heart now toward Lucifer, then yanked back. Behind him, Lucifer's heat surged.

Focus on the plant. Gabriel murmured, "I wanted to save it."

Lucifer said, "Tell me why."

Was his voice softer? Was he open?

That should be frightening. Instead, it was just as enticing as it had been three thousand years ago in a shepherd's field. Gabriel's name meant "God's Strength," but he was so weak.

Gabriel breathed, "I knew I could."

He didn't know anything anymore. Or rather, he knew what he'd been instructed to do, but he didn't know anything further.

Lucifer stepped closer, and Gabriel's senses snapped to attention. Lucifer said, "You, the plant messiah, redeeming the greenery?"

The Earth was dead. One more or less dead plant wouldn't have mattered. Would one more or less fallen angel?

It wasn't too late to retreat. Instead...the mission. His instructions. Gabriel pressed forward.

"Tell me..." He kept his voice dusky. "...what do you think..." His library was at his back, his trees before him, and God within. "...of redemption?"

Gabriel detected Lucifer's psychological chess game, calculating thousands of moves until every option ended in checkmate. In a voice equally dusky, Lucifer said, "Not now, I don't want it."

That was—unexpected. Would he? Had he ever? But since that was how Lucifer expected Gabriel to respond, Gabriel said, "What *do* you want?"

The answer had always been, "I want to unseat God," but that wouldn't be the answer now, not when as both a Seraph and a tempter, Lucifer would be angling to offer Gabriel whatever he wanted.

Lucifer's voice was a breath at odds with the roaring emotions. "I want to want to repent."

Gabriel's eyes widened.

Lucifer's words floated through Gabriel's mind. "I've never experienced that craving to be forgiven. But I wish I could feel it. Just once."

Oh, if only for a minute— What God could do with a minute!— with even a second.

Lucifer's heart and flame were wide open. Gabriel could move things around, sift the thoughts and aim light at the shadows.

Lucifer made his voice softer, more breathy. "I don't want to return." He'd be standing with his wings relaxed, his eyes closed, his own soul focused on his fire within himself. That same light had sustained a plant amidst darkness and starvation. "I want what I've lost. I want not to ask for it."

Lucifer's relationship with God was ruptured, but his fascination with the possibility of repairing it swirled through Gabriel's awareness. Gabriel's soul ignited with the heat Lucifer was ejecting. It was time to meet it with icy steel. Now was the moment to draw out the frenzy so Gabriel could flood the empty spaces with calm.

Lucifer had committed. Their souls were exchanging fire and ice, as paired as an inhale and an exhale.

His power was overwhelming. Gabriel had no idea how to handle this much. Raphael had urged Gabriel that if he got this far, he needed to run before he got burned. Instead, Gabriel asked, "If you had a way back, would you take it?"

Lucifer replied, "There is no way back."

Gabriel lowered his voice. "You didn't answer my question."

Gabriel trained Lucifer's thoughts like a spotlight into his heart. Lucifer was aware of Gabriel's presence the same way a human immune system was aware of exposure to a bacteria, responding but without recognition.

Lucifer began absorbing tendrils of Gabriel's calm, and Gabriel threaded them through the Seraph's soul like a network to join ideas with notions with desires with new questions.

Terrifying, indeed. But also thrilling. "Want to want to repent"— that was a start! He'd done the impossible. While Lucifer thought he was seducing Gabriel, Gabriel had reversed the playbook.

Run? There was so much good to be done here. Just a few seconds more.

The answer kept coming up: yes, Lucifer might want to return. If he could do so without humiliation. Without admitting defeat. Except, relenting meant defeat because victory lay in nothing less than unseating God.

A few seconds more. Gabriel coiled in tighter, twisting the question around. This was what every Cherub had been designed to do—inverting frameworks, challenging assumptions, pressing on unanswered issues. Did there have to be humiliation in walking back a decision? Lucifer had felt no shame about reversing his early decision to love God.

A geyser of flame and anger scorched up, and Gabriel yanked back from the shame: shame that Lucifer had loved God at all, shame that he'd been tricked by the Almighty during those early, new moments. When he'd been soft and pliable, he'd attributed so much wonder and glory to God, when God only wanted him as a tool.

Gabriel soothed the shame so Lucifer could keep focus. If only Gabriel could present this beautiful fire to God. Just a little more—

Lucifer's attention snapped onto the Cherub coiled around his soul, tempering it with Cherubic clarity and calm—and he realized.

Gabriel pivoted to find Lucifer with his wings flared. His green eyes went black like a shark's.

Fire lit up Gabriel's world, lit up his heart, lit up his eternity—lit him up with terror.

Eternally bonded. Gabriel was trapped.

Chapter One

SATAN STRODE THROUGH HELL with his heart crackling, hands clenched, sword at his side. The monkeys crumbled like charcoal, and whenever one got in his way, he kicked it aside. Most moved to the corners on their own. Some of them couldn't, so he flared power ahead of himself like a flamethrower clearing the underbrush.

There was no way out. None he could find, and none his Cherubim could find. The Second Coming of the Son of God had sealed the Pit, and here they were stuck for eternity.

Staying in Hell had never been part of the plan, not when they could sprawl through the plane of Creation and seize whatever they wanted. Now, their best bet was to break open the walls of Hell so they could expand toward the Void and annex the area that used to be Sheol. Except so far, none of their avenues of escape had panned out. Asmodeus and Belior had worked on a tunnel, but even with Satrinah's assistance, they could drill only so far. Mephistopheles had even less success using the thread method Gabriel had devised to break into Sheol.

Still, eternity was a long time. The key was persistence. If they didn't give up—and he would never give up—they could crack open even the hardest stone and make everything as it should be.

Satan stopped at the Lake of Fire, admiring the work the army had done toward taming it. A team of Virtues had created a channel between the ice fields and the lake, and they were working to temper the extremes. The area wasn't pleasant, but being able to use this space might alleviate the overcrowding.

The head of the Virtues approached. Bowing, she said, "Sir, what did you think of the Guarded spheroid?"

Satan tilted his head. "The Guarded spheroid?"

"Has Belior not shown it to you?" The Virtue's eyes gleamed with an implication that she'd anticipated exactly this response from her master—and she knew where the true authority lay. "I wanted to deliver it myself because it was such a curious find, but he seized it to study and then present to you as a mystery solved."

Satan's mouth tightened. "How long has Belior been 'solving' this mystery?"

The Virtue smirked. "Long enough that I'd anticipated its delivery by now. I apologize for not allowing him enough time."

Satan called, "Belior," and then pulled him through space from wherever he was—which, it felt, was behind a Guard. Behind a doubled Guard, and the doubling felt like the strength of Belior's bonded Seraph Asmodeus.

With a bow, Belior took form before Satan. "Yes, sir?"

"I'm informed you encountered an anomaly while tunneling." Satan folded his arms and shifted his stance. "An egg-shape under a Guard. Report on it."

Belior kept his expression and voice flat. "Given that my other assignment was your top priority, I've focused on the tunnel instead of what seems like an unimportant, though tantalizing, mystery."

Satan frowned. "In the interests of keeping you tantalized, I want that object now so we can examine it together."

Belior remained impassive. "Surely it's not worth your time if someone lost something small in the ice."

The Virtue folded her arms. "It was buried a mile and a half down an ice shaft, and the Guard itself carries a repulsion field."

That...was very interesting. "Now you've got me tantalized, too. Belior, retrieve the object."

Belior flashed away. Was that fear in his wake?

He returned with the Cherub Satrinah, who had her hands

cupped around a shimmering cocoon. She never took her gaze off it, not even when she presented it to Satan at arm's length.

Both of these had primary bonds with Asmodeus, and it was the work of a thought to lasso him as well. As Asmodeus arrived, Satan plucked the egg from Satrinah's hands.

It made his skin crawl. He wanted to toss the slippery thing away and not think of it again. "That repulsion field is plied right into the Guard. How many individuals could create such a thing?"

Satrinah kept her wine-dark eyes trained on the egg. "Realistically speaking, anyone could if they were highly-motivated and had a sufficiency of time to dedicate to the task."

"That was a non-answer of the highest caliber, and it's as good as a sworn confession that you have far more information than you're admitting." It paid to commend your underlings for work well done, but it also paid to keep them uncertain as to how much noncompliance you'd tolerate. "How many individuals are currently capable of creating this?"

This was the correct question, proven by how neither Cherub moved to answer. He fixed his eyes on Belior.

Mephistopheles appeared, Beelzebub at his side. Satan hadn't summoned him, and none of the others would have done so. Mephistopheles bowed, his voice a soft tenor. "Sir, I need to consult with you as soon as possible."

Satan handed him the egg, noting how Mephistopheles recoiled before taking it. Satan asked, "What is this?"

Mephistopheles' blond curls obscured his face as he cradled the object in his palms. Beelzebub made no effort to hide his disgust, but Mephistopheles raised his head, entranced. His words were like wind through the boughs of dead trees. "I don't know, sir. I can't scan past the Guard, and it's sealed in a way to make itself all but invisible. Given the way it deflects attention, I'm surprised to be holding it at all. Are there others?" He glanced at Belior. "If they haven't succeeded in unspooling it, I would be grateful for the opportunity."

Belior sparked with irritation. Satan said, "The project was Belior's, but as yet he's made no breakthroughs." Likely because he hadn't tried. "Why did you want to consult with me?"

Mephistopheles looked at Belior. "Have you been reading into the Divine Will? This feels urgent, but I don't want to interrupt your conference if you've already brought up the matter to our master."

What could be urgent in a sealed-off Hell? Satan said, "Belior has mentioned nothing."

Belior and Satrinah both adopted the thousand-mile stare Cherubim got when peering into a mystery. Asmodeus said, "Quit teasing and spit it out."

Mephistopheles said, "We're being released."

Satan flared with fire. Asmodeus spun toward his two Cherubim. The Virtue grabbed her sword.

What madness was this? Was God organizing a prisoner parade before the ranks of Heaven?

Mephistopheles expounded on and on, his voice a twin to the roar of the lake's flames. "From what I can read of the Divine Will, we've been...invited, I suppose...to a banquet. In Heaven. It's mandatory, though, so a better word would be 'subpoenaed.'" Mephistopheles had better get on with it, because Satan was about to roast him where he stood. "The Godhead announced a seven-day banquet, only Abraham refused. He objected that some of his 'offspring numerous as the stars' were in Hell, and he would not celebrate without them at the table."

Satan huffed. "That's—"

"—preposterous," Mephistopheles interrupted, "but every time I challenged what I saw, I encountered the same scenario. A banquet. A refusal. A negotiation."

Asmodeus muttered, "Why are you reading the Divine Will?"

Beelzebub folded his arms. "When you were our lord's top advisors, you should have been probing it, too. Maybe you wouldn't have gotten demoted."

Mephistopheles inclined his head. "It pays to have intelligence on their intentions. They haven't forgotten us."

Hell's continued flames and the interior pain of every damned soul indicated as much. Satan said, "We'll never be forgotten. I made sure of that."

"Granted, sir, but that very remembrance opens us to the possibility that the Creator may decide to snip off the dangling ends."

Mephistopheles meant unCreation. At some point, with no reason to keep Satan around as a reminder of His failure to bring them all to heel, God might wipe them out. Part of escaping Hell and establishing their own domain was to minimize that risk.

Belior snapped to. "Sir, he's correct!"

Satrinah still hadn't refocused. Satan said, "When will this happen?"

From outside Hell's carapace, his forces might be able to blow it open. They might be able to drill toward the tunnel that couldn't break out from inside. He might be able to establish an alternate plane from within Heaven and move everyone there, then seal it off from the inside.

After all the ages, their own kingdom.

Barring that? One last invasion of Heaven. One final attempt to oust God from His throne.

He needed to prepare. "Mephistopheles, when?"

Mephistopheles said, "Soon."

Belior's eyes widened. "Not soon. Now."

Michael stood aside as the Apostle Peter unlocked Hell's outer gate.

I trust You, Michael prayed, *but this feels like a terrible idea.*

Allowing the damned into Heaven so they could enjoy one final week-long spree of spitting in God's face was...well, not a thing Michael wanted to endorse. Fortunately for him, he didn't have to endorse it. He just had to deal with it.

Michael signaled the Archangels behind him to tighten their ranks to prevent the inevitable flood of souls the moment the gate opened—only then, no one exited.

Had Satan tied them all down? Given the fight the angels had getting everyone inside, it had been a sure thing the demons would surge out in a torrent, scratching at the doors and thrusting from the other side.

Instead, with the silence deadly, Michael's team proceeded into the entrance. At the bottleneck where Satan always clocked everyone in and out of Hell, they found the entire Maskim.

Resplendent, Satan stood with his arms folded. A diadem of light encircled his head, its gleam enhancing the green of his eyes. Dressing for the occasion hadn't occurred to Michael, so he had to face Satan in full regalia while wearing only his standard gear.

Adjusting his armor now would only make Satan smirk harder, so Michael chose to ignore it.

The moment before Michael would have spoken, Satan cut him off. "We know about your miserable banquet. I'm uncertain why we should attend."

Again, not what Michael had expected. Satan continued, "We need to negotiate the terms of our attendance. Can I speak to someone in charge?"

"That would be me, and my orders are non-negotiable." Michael hadn't missed dealing with Satan, that was for sure. "You and yours must be evacuated. We've prepared a place for you, and we will enforce this. You have to go, but you don't have to participate. Step aside."

Satan said, "Follow me," which accomplished the same without any appearance of capitulation. Image management was always the top concern of the fallen angels. Michael walked right past the Maskim, following Satan to Hell's great hall where millions of souls were lined up in ranks, in silence, in anticipation of orders.

He's so practiced at delivering a threat, Michael prayed. *Why bother telling me he has an army when he can show me, instead?*

God replied, *You know exactly what he has.*

He doesn't have You, which is the important part. Michael said, "Thank you for not putting us through the trouble of waiting."

Satan sounded irritated. "Many don't want to go, but I've got them in hand. You'll have a harder time convincing them to stay in Heaven, but that's not my problem."

It won't be my problem, either, since apparently I'm not in charge. All Satan's forces wore armor—and most of them looked eager. How was Satan keeping them still when they wanted so badly to escape into the movement of time? Yeah...fear. Michael had interrogated enough demons to know Satan wasn't restrained about punishing those who failed him—nor especially particular about figuring out whose failure it was. If he got it wrong the first time, he'd likely get it right the next.

Speaking of fear, there were far fewer humans in those ranks than there should be.

Saraquael took his place at Michael's side, discomfort crawling off him. Raguel joined on the opposite.

Michael turned to Satan. "To keep everyone's expectations clear: we're hosting a week-long festival. Your people will have free range of the outermost layer of Heaven. Everyone will be assigned personal quarters. Anyone wishing to access Heaven's deeper layers may do so if and only if they have a one-to-one escort."

Satan's eyebrows raised, but his Cherubim made no response at all. Michael continued, "I'm not going to ask you to behave. We have measures in place in case anyone gets out of hand."

Satan glanced aside as if bored. "You can force us out of our domain for whatever frippery your Tyrant desires, but we see no requirement to participate."

Michael shrugged. "My orders were to evacuate Hell, not to ensure you have a good time."

Satan snorted. "You're no worse a host than I would expect, but to reiterate, we intend to comply."

Of course he did. Michael said, "We've arranged for passage, but you can handle that if you prefer."

Oddly, he did. Satan looked in turn at each of the Maskim, who then focused on their own underlings and began deploying each division. Standing to the side, Michael caught himself analyzing the formation as though it were an invasion, but their order didn't have strategic value. Satan wouldn't attack now. He'd wait until he had everyone ensconced in a defensible position within Heaven.

The more ranks moved out, the more it became obvious the humans weren't present in sufficient numbers. Michael turned to Saraquael. "We're going to need additional teams to sweep the corners. You're going to find humans hiding in any niche they can, and they're not going to trust us, either."

Saraquael inclined his head. "Our seekers are ready to go." He vanished.

Outside Hell's entrance, the Principalities had established a portal linking to the outer layer of Heaven. It had functioned as Limbo for a while, but with no further need of it after the Second Coming, the elect souls had mostly abandoned its gentle hills and sweet breezes. When God had agreed to admit the fallen for the banquet, that had seemed the best location. Anything they did to defile it wouldn't matter quite as much, plus they'd be contained on one layer.

With the evacuation under way, Michael sent to Saraquael, *Will you need additional help locating the stragglers?*

Saraquael replied, *We may. As predicted, humans are hiding everywhere. Take a look at the Lake of Fire when you get a chance. Satan's been doing upgrades, and it's impressive.*

Michael replied, *Have you checked the ice fields?*

My other assignment can wait. I didn't want the Maskim to wonder why I went there first.

Michael forced his shoulders to relax. Hell's units were filing past as though they didn't want to go. Jittery. Scared. Some were wounded, and Michael called into the air, "Raphael, we're going to need medical assistance at the landing site."

Beelzebub drawled, "How sweet." When Michael glared, he added, "They're weak. You locked them away with creatures dozens of times stronger who hated them. It's hardly our fault some of them got damaged."

Satan said, "Enough. Keep them moving," and then did another thing Michael didn't expect, flashing among the ranks and singling out anyone in need of assistance. Asmodeus joined him, and momentarily Moloch appeared at his side, then flashed to another area.

Michael didn't take his eyes off Satan. He was all over the ranks by now—not just bilocating but in dozens of locations simultaneously. For all that the damned were in hell for resisting authority, he had tight authority over all these. He wasn't just ordering them out, though. He was getting them moving on their own, and in some cases getting them carried out. By angels, of course. Why not order Michael's forces around while he had the chance?

Saraquael returned with ice chips melting on his teal feathers. "I've deployed teams into the ice fields to look for humans."

Michael prompted, "And the other—?"

Saraquael shook his head.

Michael shuddered.

"That's a credit to how hard we worked to hide it in the first place." Saraquael gave a rueful smile. "Just because we built the trap doesn't mean we know how to open it again."

To be fair, that was by design. If Michael ever got tortured to reveal what he'd done, he couldn't give up information he didn't have.

Saraquael departed again, then returned, then left again, then returned a third time—only now with a puzzled expression. "Are we sure my target isn't already uncovered? Seeking it keeps leading back here."

Michael scanned the demons. "This is your specialty. If you think it's close, I trust you."

Saraquael closed his eyes, swiveled, then flashed away—reappearing beside Mephistopheles. Michael joined him before Beelzebub could get in between, and he immobilized Mephistopheles while Saraquael's hand shot into a pocket in the demon's cloak. Momentarily, Saraquael was holding an ovoid casement that Michael wanted to run from.

Before they could react, Beelzebub pushed Michael away from Mephistopheles, then Satan had clamped his hand on Saraquael's wrist. "Unhand my officer."

Michael said, "You're not allowed to transport contraband."

Satan twisted the egg from Saraquael's palm. "You're under orders to take our people, not our playthings."

Mephistopheles protested, "I'm still examining it."

Belior appeared. "Actually, it's mine."

With ferocious eyes, Satan looked at the object, all the revulsion transforming to hatred, and the hatred to strength. He squeezed down on the Guard the same way Michael had once squeezed down on a similar Guard, and now, as then, with a shower of sparks and a scream, the Guard collapsed.

An angel tumbled out of thin air, and Michael shot forward to catch him. He was soft, pliable, and confused.

Michael's voice cracked. "Hastle? I've got you."

Hastle spun about, face to face with the entire Maskim—and streaked away. Asmodeus leashed him in midair.

Hastle thrashed. Maybe two thousand years had robbed him of his words because he only projected terror. He recognized Michael, but Michael wasn't the threat.

Asmodeus reeled Hastle back, and Satan seized him by the neck. "Explain this."

Michael spoke quickly. "No explanation necessary. We're taking custody of—"

Asmodeus yanked Hastle's chains tighter. "You have no jurisdiction over my—"

"I assure you, I do." Michael raised his voice. "Your petty grievances can wait until after the banquet."

Satan coiled new chains of will around Hastle, hand and foot. Hastle finally set his eyes on Michael, and betrayal washed out from him: Michael had promised he wouldn't be found, and he thought Michael had led them straight to him.

Satan dropped Hastle and studied the residue on his hands. "Belior, how did you make that egg?"

Belior sounded unnerved. "I didn't make it. That technique isn't mine."

Wings curved, Satan towered over Hastle. "Am I to believe this technique is his?"

Michael swallowed hard. "You can question him later. We're

removing him to Heaven, the same as everybody else."

In a voice practically a growl, Asmodeus said, "We're not evacuated yet. Surely I have time to ask a few questions."

Belior added, "At least twenty minutes' worth."

Unable to stem the terror, Hastle kept shivering while the residue of a shredded Guard evaporated off him.

Satan rubbed his chin. "I have to admit to a certain curiosity myself. Hastle..." He murmured the name, eyes glinting. "You disappeared right when Belior attempted to spring a deathtrap on me. Were you its incompetent inventor, or just its first test subject?" Before Michael could speak, Satan waved him off. "It's wonderful, whatever he did, and Belior was attempting to re-invent that type of Guard as recently as two hours ago." He looked to Michael. "Thank you for alerting me to the true nature of the artifact."

"On the contrary, you figured it out by destroying it." Michael side-eyed Belior. "I'm remanding Hastle to our custody until we can assess him for injuries. Release his bindings." That sounded as though Michael knew what he was doing. "Raguel, take him."

Asmodeus flared his wings, but Satan murmured, "I'm letting him go. Unless you'd like me to question him myself," after which a jittery Asmodeus stood down. Raguel flashed Hastle to Heaven, and Michael returned his attention to Satan—who'd vanished. He was once again moving through the ranks of the damned, making sure everyone proceeded in an orderly fashion.

Smirking, Beelzebub shifted his stance and quipped, "Doesn't this feel like a terrible idea?"

Michael clenched his teeth and went back to work.

Chapter Two

GABRIEL KNELT IN PRAYER at the Ring of Seven, head bowed, wings cupped, arms crossed over his chest.

Emptying Hell made no sense.

The banquet did make sense. The Word was human, and humans—all of whom had been resurrected into their bodies—celebrated with food. During the year Gabriel had spent as a human, he, too, had experienced the way celebratory nutrients rendered human events more festive, and therefore it seemed fitting that on the tail end of Creation, they would employ food to celebrate. The "wedding feast of the Lamb" would be, in fact, a feast.

Abraham's protest, likewise, made sense. He'd always been a proponent of mercy, as when he'd advocated for sparing Sodom (whereas Gabriel had advocated for its destruction).

But God's seeing fit to bargain with Abraham now, after Hell had been locked up and the damned consigned to eternal fire? That made no sense.

Making sense of the senseless was a Cherub's job, so instead of joining the revelry, Gabriel had returned to the Ring directly before God. He had no desire to see any of the fallen angels again, whereas he did desire to be with his Father. Dressed casually in a silver-trimmed tunic, cotton pants and ankle-high boots, Gabriel prayed, *I thought we were done.*

A loop appeared in the air before him. It shimmered like light, and when Gabriel extended his fingers through it, it became a silvery string. Standing, he peered into the heart of God. *What should I be doing?*

The Holy Spirit replied, *What do you think you should be doing?*

The string seemed ordinary, so Gabriel wove the circlet into the paired slingshots of a cat's cradle.

The thread tightened as invisible fingers pulled and twisted, flipped the string about, and created a new design in the open air. Gabriel took the next step, a stage he'd overheard a young child calling "pinkies."

He looked back into God's face, settling his heart. If God wanted him to play a child's game, Gabriel would assume all fretting was unnecessary. This week would come and go, and afterward, the elect could enjoy eternity as they'd been created to do.

The cat's cradle got raveled back and forth between the Cherub and the Creator, with each step becoming more complicated. As Gabriel worked, he improvised a song to a tune Israfel had written, lyrics about thread and webs and the fingers of the Divine. God could play with string, and Gabriel could play with his voice.

At intervals, Gabriel would find the string too tight around his fingers, so he'd gaze into God's eyes, and then the string would lengthen so he could make the next move. He invented new steps to keep the lines crossing. At last, though, when the Holy Spirit twisted it off his fingers, Gabriel had no clear path forward.

A holographic duplicate appeared in the air, and Gabriel swiveled it, inverted it, and ran through every possible conversion. Anything further meant the cat's cradle would collapse. Unless—

Raphael?, he sent.

His bonded Seraph appeared, then blinked at the cat's cradle and projected a question.

Deflecting with a question of his own, Gabriel frowned. The Holy Spirit had wanted to take Gabriel's mind off the de-facto God-ordered invasion of Heaven with a game...except God had driven the game too far for it to be just a distraction.

Gabriel needed Raphael's hands. Fixing points in midair would have worked, too—well, he could have made it work. He could have altered his subtle body to give himself extra hands, for that matter. The more important thing he needed was Raphael's zeal, and as he studied the structure, Gabriel overflowed into Raphael's mind, allowing him to feel the process and sense the progression.

Flames sparked in Raphael's eyes. "Let's do this. I want my hands here and here—no, wait, rotate that—"

Their hearts merged as they worked the piece simultaneously, the string significantly longer as they drew it into new configurations. They'd work one change, and then the Holy Spirit would take the next so they could puzzle out the best transformation for another switch.

Thinking deeper, Gabriel sang no longer. This had to be an object lesson, but the lesson felt as contorted as the string, and with every twist, the riddle grew.

By now the cat's cradle crossed over itself so many times it could have strained seawater. The Holy Spirit plucked several strings from the middle, tugged, twisted, inverted—and it looked like a lovely mess.

Even so, Gabriel murmured, "This is familiar."

Raphael grinned toward God. "If Gabriel did the same crossword puzzle twice, he'd probably remember that, too."

Gabriel lit up several different points. "Place your fingers there, and hold still. I'll do the twisting."

He went in, tugged, turned his hands—and it wasn't right, except it was right. They had a pair of pyramids, point to point, with their bases flared and everything crossing through one spot in the center. One of the strings crossed over itself the wrong way, though, so Gabriel flipped it back, and again, that still felt almost right—but not quite.

Augmented by Raphael's mind, Gabriel pattern-matched with everything he knew of creation: every molecule, every crystal, every cellular structure. None matched exactly. Raphael projected that maybe the apparent familiarity came from the way so many other constructions had a similar form, but Gabriel balked. He'd seen this. He'd mapped it. Thousands of years ago, perhaps, but he'd done it.

Flip back. Flip forward. Everything was the same except for that one cross, but neither one worked, and he couldn't find a third way.

Raphael sent him energy. *You're thrashing. Pick one.*

The second format looked more stable, but it lacked familiarity. The first—Gabriel flipped it—had the familiarity, but without the stability. It needed to cross itself *here*, but it didn't, and the lack of this crossover eliminated one point—

Gabriel jerked back, breath and heart still.

Raphael sent fire into him. *Hey, it's okay.*

It's not okay. These are the choirs of Seraphim and Cherubim, a diagram of the primary bonds. Gabriel swallowed. *This is how we're connected. You and I.* He lit up a point at the center. *Me and Israfel. You and Ophaniel. You and Sidriel.*

Raphael was burning by now, so Gabriel absorbed the flames to see his hands better. The smaller side represented the damned. He identified Asmodeus and Belior, then Asmodeus and Satrinah.

Raphael peered at it closer. "That narrow juncture is because only six primary bonds were broken between our side and theirs?"

Brittle, Gabriel whispered, "And we're missing a Seraph because Lucifer isn't here at all."

In the unstable configuration, that was. In the stable configuration, there were more crossovers. Using string crossings alone, there was no way to represent a Seraph who hadn't bonded.

Gabriel tightened his wings to his back. "When paired up, the Cherub and the Seraph supported one another. In all but six cases, when one fell, both fell."

Shadows chilled Raphael's heart. "So you're saying...because Satan never primaried someone, he wasn't fixed in place?"

Like uranium at critical mass, Lucifer's energy had become more uncontrolled the longer it built. A Cherub would have pulled that power and given it focus. Lucifer had always refused.

Correction. Lucifer had refused exactly once, with a curt, "You have nothing to offer me."

At the time, Gabriel had agreed: "You're right. You're complete on your own."

Gabriel yanked his hands from the cat's cradle and dropped to his knees, head bowed, fingers pressed to his eyes. He started vibrating as Raphael knelt at his side. *I should have insisted.*

You should have done no such thing, said the Spirit. *You did exactly what you were created to do.*

Then why show Gabriel this? Why show it *now,* when all the decisions had been made? *"You have nothing to offer me"* had been a statement of fact. When Lucifer had turned down Gabriel's proposition to bond, Israfel had gotten angry, but Gabriel hadn't. At the time, a young, female Gabriel had been the one to reassure Israfel. "You and I aren't as strong as he is. We need to work together to understand God because we have so many gaps in our understanding. Lucifer's so far above us that he doesn't need anyone."

Unless what Gabriel was realizing now was—he had. Lucifer had needed Gabriel in a way neither had understood, and which neither had understood in the thousands of years since.

As with the cat's cradle, Gabriel grasped the situation in his mental hands and twisted it, flipped it, challenged it. Had there been another way? What if he changed his presuppositions? What if A and B happened in reverse order, and what if A-prime and B-prime happened in public rather than in private? What if the suggestion had come from someone else? What if Gabriel had forced the issue? What if Lucifer had forced it?

Could the fall have been Gabriel's fault?

He knew what he was doing. Did that thought come from God or from within Gabriel? Or did it arise from Raphael, whose unconscious mind still served as the reservoir for Gabriel's overflow thoughts? No one went to Hell because of someone else's decision. Even Lucifer couldn't break that law: the choice to deny God had to come from the individual. Back at the Winnowing, Lucifer couldn't coerce Gabriel to leave. Ergo, back at the Winnowing, Gabriel couldn't have forced Lucifer to stay.

Shivering, Gabriel absorbed Raphael's fire. It had been close. Gabriel had been able to submit and worship only because

Raphael had been there as an anchor. Testimony, then, to the stability of the bonds. Testimony to Raphael's single-hearted love of God and to the depth of his trust.

Gabriel back then had so many thoughts, so many concerns. Only one had been necessary, and Raphael had it emblazoned on his heart.

You could have lost me. Gabriel shivered. *And I lost Lucifer.*

"You have nothing to offer me," Lucifer had said, an assertion for which Gabriel still would have no answer.

A hand on Gabriel's shoulder startled him, and he snapped to. Raphael was standing, and before them was Uriel with a summons.

With Hell nearly empty, Michael returned to Heaven. Standing guard outside the secure room where he was detaining Hastle, Raguel muttered, "I thought Satan wasn't going to find your time capsule."

Michael tried to squelch the bitterness in his voice. "It wasn't my time capsule. And it sounds like they only just dug him up."

Raguel folded his arms and leaned against the wall. "Asmodeus wants in, and he's unrelenting. Right now, our best bet is to move Hastle off this layer of Heaven and into a place Asmodeus can't follow."

Michael hummed. "I've been looking for a reason to get Remiel off the outer layer, since every second she's out here is one second longer that she's vulnerable to Camael."

Naturally, Remiel had no intention of retreating from the main action, even if that exposed her to her fallen twin. When chaos was happening, she wanted to be riding the storm.

Raguel said, "Do it. Then Asmodeus can deal with his master."

Michael hadn't checked on Satan since turning him loose at the main complex of buildings. The most likely scenario had Satan grilling Belior and Satrinah in his new headquarters, determining what that Guard was around Hastle and how to use it against the angels. Also possibly (most likely?) beating them senseless for not divulging it two thousand years ago. Because no matter what they said, he wouldn't believe it.

Michael sighed.

Raguel projected agreement. "This is a lot of work, to no good end."

Remiel arrived with her cheeks windblown. "I've broken up six fights already, and our fallen brethren are doing their best to destroy the Hilbert Hotel."

Raguel said, "The what?" which made Michael feel better inasmuch as he didn't have to ask.

Remiel raked a hand through her choppy blonde hair. "One of the fallen Cherubim called it that to mock us, but it caught on in a heartbeat. Turns out, 'Hilbert's Grand Hotel' is a paradox posed by a human mathematician—one assumes, named Hilbert—where, if you have an infinitely large hotel that's filled to capacity, and you get one more guest, you can accommodate the new guest by putting him in Room One and moving the guest in Room One into Room Two, and so on, infinitely."

This sounded a lot like something a Cherub would devise. The only shock was that Gabriel hadn't coined the name himself. "Why are they trying to destroy it?"

"Demons. If they can't pervert it, confuse it, condemn it, or blaspheme with it, they break it." Remiel half-leaned against a desk while raising her wings. "The point is, I haven't had so much fun busting up fights since the Second Coming, and now I have an infinite hotel full of them."

"While I'm happy for you," Michael said, "I have an assignment that's going to take you off the outer layer. We have a demon who needs protection."

Remiel narrowed her eyes. "What demon needs a bodyguard?"

"The one Saraquael helped me bury in the ice fields. Satan found him two minutes before we did, and Asmodeus never forgot that vendetta."

Remiel snorted. "The one who stuck me and Zadkiel on Earth? Maybe he needs a good beating." Before Michael could object, she raised her hands. "I know, I know! I'll take him so the big-bads can't get to him." She snickered. "Everyone else will think you pulled me off duty because I'm semifallen."

Michael gaped. "Who would think that?"

Remiel shrugged, a motion that shifted her six golden wings. "Do you want a list? Scores of demons have been asking how I tricked God into letting me stay in Heaven."

Michael frowned. "You got hit with Belior's weapon. You weren't sinful."

She glanced at the ceiling. "It's about how my twin fell and I didn't. Obviously, that means I bought my way into Heaven, since the real reason can't in any way be that I submitted to God's will and loved Him with my whole heart."

Raguel snorted. "That would never occur to them. It has to have been deceit."

Michael said, "Camael hasn't bothered you, has he?"

"He's summoned me a few hundred times, and I'm ignoring him. Babysitting a demon in the third Heaven may insulate me from his badgering." Her mouth twitched. "I'll try not to miss the throng of demons who keep soliciting me as a semifallen benefactrix who can smuggle them through God's back door, and then I guess hide them in the scullery."

Hastle hunched in the corner of the holding cell, wings around himself, knees to his chest, head down, as if he were still ensconced in an egg that simultaneously trapped and protected him.

Remiel crouched at eye level. "Hastle, do you remember me? I'm not going to hurt you, and if you'll come with me, I'll keep you safe."

Raguel said, "He hasn't responded to anyone."

Remiel raised her wings. "I need you to agree to come."

Two thousand years in an eggshell prison hadn't left him capable of that. Michael said, "Take him now. Talk to him later."

Remiel kept her eyes on Hastle. "You don't understand. I can't.

As security at the Hilbert Hotel discovered, they have to consent to be taken off the outer layer."

Michael and Raguel both flared their wings. "Why?"

"You'd have to ask God, but it makes sense that a one-to-one escort requires mutual consent from both of the *ones*." She rested a hand on Hastle, who flinched. "I can't transport him. He needs to agree."

Raguel turned to Michael. "I haven't been able to get him to respond, but maybe you can? You used to know him."

Used to. Used to be friends. Used to love and serve God together. And then back when Hastle had been harvesting Sheol material, it turned out Michael hadn't known him at all because Hastle could manipulate him like a screwdriver. Michael prayed, *Raguel's got a point, but I don't know that he'll want to talk to me.*

Michael knew for a fact he didn't want to talk to Hastle. Even so, he squatted alongside Remiel. When attempting to flash Hastle away failed to budge him, Michael said, "Listen. We need to keep you safe. If you go with Remiel, we can hide you where Asmodeus can't access. We didn't intend for them to find you at all, so this is the best we can do."

Saraquael might be able to re-create Hastle's Guarded eggshell of protection, but eternity was a long time. Once the fallen were all back in Hell, Asmodeus would take up ditch-digging as a hobby. They'd find him.

Hastle hadn't projected all that, but the sense of defeat flowed off him nevertheless. The pain would continue forever, so whether it started now or a week from now or a month from now, it was all the same.

"Will you let me take you?" That wasn't a long-term solution. Michael would need to return to the outer layer, but maybe once Hastle felt safe, they could transfer his escort to another angel.

The feelings flowed from Hastle like water through a colander. Michael had betrayed him. Michael let them find him. Satan had said as much.

Blast it. Dealing with lies all the time didn't make demons any better at detecting them, especially when some of the lies were things they already believed. After twenty centuries in the egg, Hastle might have begun blaming Michael for his isolation. Rather than thinking, "You know, I chose this," Hastle would have been thinking, "Michael did this to me." Then, once he was free, he wouldn't think, "Michael freed me," but rather, "Michael dug me up and handed me over to the torturers."

Assuming he could think coherently at all, which maybe he couldn't.

Michael stood. "Another one of Hastle's former friends may be able to take him, or at the very least may have other ideas."

In the next second, Michael stood alongside a black-uniformed Archangel in the lobby of the Hilbert Hotel. (Michael hoped the hotel's name made God smile, too.) Special Ops Officer Miriael was sorting out an argument among three damned humans and one demon, and it was so full of invective and nastiness that Michael couldn't tell if one party was at fault or if all of them were.

The soldier at the Archangel's side had two-toned wings and kept himself between the humans and the demon.

A momentary despair rippled through Michael. It was as Hastle thought: they could prevent violence right now, but eternity was a long time. If there was a vendetta, it would continue forever.

Michael didn't interfere with the officers' handling of the issue. Why give the aggrieved parties a chance to re-express their anger and argue again over settled points? The Archangel gave a few orders and sent two of the humans off with another angel. Only then did he turn to Michael. "Sir? Is there something you want?"

Michael said, "Can I borrow you from Special Ops? We have a situation."

The Special Ops officer said in a lower voice, "Let's talk outside the hotel. Tabris also has a problem for you to deal with." When the two-toned angel started, Miriael looked stern. "Yes, this has to go to Michael. I have no idea how to handle it."

Usually it was only during a war that Michael had to daisy-chain his crises. He hadn't missed this. He flashed all three of them to his office in the second layer of Heaven, where Tabris immediately walked to the window.

Michael said to Miriael, "We have Hastle in custody, and he needs protection."

He delivered the entire story with one bundled thought so all the information could bloom in Miriael's mind simultaneously: the eggshell prison, the recovery, the Maskim's vengeance, the silence.

Miriael blew off a breath, projecting agreement as well as futility. "I'll try because he was my friend, too, but I can't see I'll have any better effect than you did."

"But you're clever." It went with Special Ops: they did everything sideways, oftentimes even when a straightforward approach would have worked. "You may be able to break through the wall of silence, or you may figure out how to skirt the consent issue."

Miriael grimaced. "I'll do my best." He turned to Tabris. "Your situation is a lot more puzzling."

Unease in his eyes, Tabris glanced at Miriael, who sent him a burst of support. Tension curled through Michael because he knew what Tabris had done.

Tabris lowered his gaze. "I've had incidents with several demons that are more than a little disconcerting."

That sounded open-ended enough that Michael's sword sparked in its scabbard. "If they're harassing you, we'll either consequence them or else transfer you to another station."

Tabris shifted his weight, raising his wings to compensate. "It's not harassment, or at least, if it is, it's passive-aggressive."

Demons didn't typically go for passive-aggressive, favoring aggressive-aggressive.

Miriael said, "I witnessed the last incident, and I don't think they were baiting him."

Tabris said, "That's why I wasn't even going to report what was going on."

They were going to drag this out, weren't they? "Describe the last incident."

Tabris stared at the carpet. "A demon asked what I did to get back in God's favor after I killed my human charge."

Cold inside, Michael stayed still as a deer hearing the first gunshot of hunting season.

"They all ask the same thing, and then they don't like my answer, that it wasn't me who restored my relationship with God." Tabris's voice was thin, but Michael had gotten used to that tone from people who described their past lives. They never glossed the crimes that led them to their knees before God, but then they focused on the grace that had brought them onto the front porch to knock on the door, and the mercy that wrenched them inside once they did. "They keep asking if I offered a service or if I got off on a technicality, or if maybe I wasn't guilty from the start."

Miriael said, "That last one unambiguously thought there was a means of buying his way back. He demanded to know the price."

Michael frowned.

Tabris said, "How should I answer them?"

Startled, Michael looked up. "It's your relationship with God, and therefore it's your story."

Tabris folded his arms. "They're not accepting that. They're looking for a back door because they think I'm semifallen."

Again, semifallen. Remiel, tainted because her twin fell. Tabris, tainted because he committed murder.

"Several of them? All in the first day?" Rubbing his chin, Michael looked at Tabris. "Hang on a minute."

Across the layers of Heaven, Michael reached for Remiel. She felt excited, and he sensed she had just finished tussling with a pair of demons. He sent, *I need an opinion. A second angel just reported demons are approaching because they think he's semifallen.*

He felt Remiel startle, then prompt him to continue

Help me think this through. Which other angels would demons consider semifallen?

An image appeared in Michael's mind: Gabriel. Remiel added, *Unless Gabriel's the one you're talking about.*

Michael's feathers flared, and Miriael faced him, but Michael shook his head.

Remiel was right. If the demons thought Tabris semifallen, who hadn't been kicked out of Heaven, then absolutely they must think it of Gabriel. He'd need to be warned before he came to the outer layer.

Remiel projected, *I wonder if any demons would be considered semifallen.*

Michael couldn't quell the shudder that ran through his heart.

Remiel returned an apology, along with the thought that if any of the demons weren't fully committed, they'd have had the sedition tortured out of them long since.

Michael projected, *I was thinking of a demon who'd removed himself rather than continue to participate.*

Remiel paused, then sent two images with a request for clarification. One was Hastle. The other was a demon Michael hadn't seen since the Exodus. No one had.

Rahab? Didn't Satan destroy him?

Remiel sent, *The demon whisper network claims Rahab destroyed himself. His self-destruction might seem like an attempt to get out of continuing.*

Michael replied, *Those are just rumors. We need to deal with reality.*

He turned back to Tabris, simultaneously speaking to him and projecting to Remiel. "We need to work with the demons who are approaching you. Satan's had unrest in his kingdom before."

Miriael said, "Even if we were able to start a revolution, they're still fallen. Unseating Satan wouldn't accomplish anything."

Hearing that through Michael's ears, Remiel sent, *You're thinking there's a larger purpose to this banquet than just appeasing Abraham?*

"I have no idea what I'm thinking, but we're going to work every angle we can." Michael pointed to Miriael. "Find a way to transport Hastle." Back to Tabris, and including Remiel, he sent, "Record the name and rank of every demon who asks for advice."

Remiel replied, *Gotcha, boss,* and Tabris projected an affirmative.

Michael continued, "After a sound defeat by Christ at the Second Coming, they've had time to think. Keep telling them the way back is to repent and worship God. Maybe something good will happen."

He dismissed everyone, then stood at his window, staring out at Heaven.

It was so peaceful out there, and for the next seven days, Michael's work would be nothing but chaos. *I'm trusting You,* he prayed, *but I'm going to need help.*

God warmed him inside.

What are You up to?, Michael added, although whenever he'd asked this question before, God always answered with, "Wait."

Behind him, Raguel appeared. "We've been summoned."

Michael sighed. "Something especially horrible?"

Raguel shrugged. "I hope not. It's Mary."

Chapter Three

IN MARY'S ROSE GARDEN, Gabriel tried to relax his wings and not look like someone who'd just walked across his own grave.

Raphael sent, *I can't imagine the Holy Spirit meant you to be this rattled.*

Gabriel couldn't hypothesize what else the Holy Spirit could have intended. All that time playing their history back and forth—*praying* their history back and forth—and Gabriel still couldn't come up with a way to have prevented Lucifer's rebellion. Lucifer had said, "You have nothing to offer me," and Gabriel had respected his refusal. How could that have been wrong?

Except—possibly—every wrong thing had followed it.

The garden sprawled between two hills, one of which had Mary's house at its peak, a replica of the home in which Jesus had grown up. A single path wound through the rose bushes, and the peace of Mary's prayers clung to them all. Gabriel visited sometimes when Mary was elsewhere, walking and praying, counting his steps, admiring the multitude of rose varieties arranged in clusters. She'd caught him once. "You like it here?" she'd said. "I linger in the mornings, praying and treasuring all those moments from my life with Jesus. I've been so blessed by God."

Today, she only glanced at Gabriel with a shy smile, then averted her gaze.

As with all humans, Mary could change her appearance and relative age. Today she looked like a woman in early middle age, her black hair glossy, her eyes dark and quick, her beige skin vibrant against her loose cotton blouse.

On the bench beside her, Uriel sat, knees up and to the side, ankles tucked, creating a fabric of rose petals. A flower would come apart in Uriel's hands, and the Throne would suspend the petals mid-air, sorted by shade. Then one at a time, the petals would get rejoined like a quilt, linked in shapes that rippled with the movement of the air and emitted a fragrance that was equal parts sweetness and softness. By now the fabric was a wingspan long, and Uriel sat coiled in its length.

Other angels joined them. Remiel. Saraquael, who kept finding more ash to preen from his wings. Israfel's appearance sparked a flurry of concern over Gabriel's disquieted heart, but he dampened her fire to settle her. Her curly hair rippled like a black river between her wings, and when he reached through their bond, she smiled. At last Raguel and Michael arrived, and now they were all assembled in the breezy pergola.

Given who was in attendance—and who was not—Mary might as well have put a target on Gabriel. Fingering the stitching of his tunic, he reached for God.

"Thank you for coming." Hands folded, Mary looked at her lap. "I've been praying, and I think we may have a chance to do a lot of good."

Uriel projected steadiness to Mary, which again Gabriel found curious. Whatever came next, Mary didn't want to say it.

Mary looked up. "How are the fallen settling in?"

Remiel said, "Plenty of dust-ups over at the Hilbert Hotel, but for the most part, they're keeping to themselves."

Gabriel burst into unintentional laughter. "The Hilbert Hotel?"

She winked. "I knew you'd love that."

He said, "Grab me something with the logo on it."

Remiel snickered. "That's not the *official* name, although I don't see why it can't be."

Michael said, "Regardless of the name, most demons are sticking close to wherever we've left them, and we've only had a few requests to explore the other layers. Plus, there's one demon we need to transfer to an inner layer, but at the moment, he's not yielding."

Saraquael said, "Our seekers are still flushing out a few humans who've hidden themselves. I'll head back as soon as we're done here."

Mary said to Remiel, "Have you met Camael?"

Remiel's wings tensed. "I can't see that it would do any good."

Michael folded his arms. "I don't see that any of this is going to do any good, unless Abraham had another endgame he failed to bring up during his negotiations."

Mary offered a tense laugh, and Gabriel tilted his head. That felt like a question about to be answered.

She wove her fingers. "As it turns out, we have another goal, but it needs your support."

About to assent, Gabriel stopped himself. In ordinary times, Mary shared the same detached calm as Uriel. Even when there had been danger—by Raphael's report, even when Gabriel had been on the verge of death—she'd maintained a collected demeanor and a steadfast trust that God would work it all out to His glory. Only here she was, now, nervous.

Unnerved himself, Gabriel kept silence.

Still joining flower petals into a stole, Uriel brushed a wing against Mary's arm.

Mary raised her head. "We're hoping to convert some of the lost. If even one soul were to return to loving God, that would be an amazing blessing. Abraham and I, and Peter, and Paul, and Isaiah, and Priscilla, and Moses, and Mary Magdalene, and so many others—we've been praying and planning and hoping."

Michael's brow furrowed. "It was only Abraham who asked."

"We believed Satan wouldn't object to Abraham's intercession, whereas he absolutely would have objected to mine." Mary's eyes crinkled. "A human asking for mercy on a demon—? He'd never countenance that. But a human asking for mercy on the human progeny God awarded him as a condition of their covenant? That would seem like a matter of pride. And then our extending that condition to the rest of the damned, too, as though we were too lazy to sift one from another? We thought that would work."

Remiel exclaimed, "You played him! But to what end?"

Mary looked mischievous. "I said it. To bring some of them back."

Gabriel stared at his hands. "We don't know that it's possible."

Bright-eyed, Mary turned to him. "Only because it's never been tried. It's the question the Cherubim couldn't answer: *Can't, or won't?*"

Raphael rested his hands on Gabriel's shoulders, thrumming with possibility.

It was just—after everything—

Mary grew animated. "We'll lead up to the banquet with a festival. Our people will mix with theirs. Some souls' rebellion was tenuous from the start. We can hunt for a foothold. We can tell them all the great things the Almighty has done for us. We can show the fallen souls the greatness of the Lord and how He remembers His promises of mercy. After so long, they might want that, too."

Michael shifted his weight. "We're already getting questions along those lines." When Gabriel tilted his head, Michael said, "They're zeroing in on any angels who've ever had an apparent rupture in their relationship with God. You're going to get asked, as well."

Gabriel nodded. "I barely squeaked into Heaven as it was, so that makes sense."

Raphael murmured, "I think he means because of the year you spent as a human. They know you returned stronger than before."

Michael added, "They're going to gloss over all your soul searching and want to know how you paid off God. They're not going to wonder where they went wrong."

Raguel squared his stance. "They don't think they went wrong. I can't imagine God would let them back into Heaven in exchange for performative worship. That wouldn't even have worked for a human, let alone a demon."

Gabriel raised his hands. "If it would work at all. We'd need a demon on his knees, expressing heartfelt sorrow for all the evil he'd done and searching for a way to make it right. That would be the test."

Israfel burst into flames. "Have I lost my mind? Am I hearing the same conversation you're all having?"

Gabriel reached with his heart to calm her, but her eyes flashed like lightning.

She squared her shoulders. "Do you think souls this thoroughly steeped in evil should get restored for mewling 'I'm sorry' because they got sick of being locked up? Absolutely not." Israfel's flames weren't diminishing. If anything, they were ramping up. "Jesus paid the debt of any living human who would accept that gift, but our kind weren't included. Think about what you're saying. Maybe if some small-minded human created petty annoyances for another human—maybe if the people he harmed ended up in Heaven despite all that—maybe apologizing would be enough. But evil has a knock-on effect. Evil creates suffering, which creates more evil. They can't undo what they've done. Justice requires they stay where they are."

Gabriel extended a hand to Israfel, but with a good burn going, she sparked at the contact. She said, "Imagine a man who convinced his brother to suicide-bomb a building, and they both went to Hell. How could we justify letting the instigator out just because he said, 'Oops, sorry,' while his brother is still paying for their shared crime? What about the people whose lives he stole and who maybe ended up in Hell themselves?"

Michael raised his hands. "Israfel, stand down. We're not making the decision."

Remiel snorted. "It's a good thing we're not making the decision because I wouldn't let the demons back in, either. Even the minorest of the lowest order has harmed thousands of humans. Whether humans died because of the wars they started, or whether humans suffered because of malnutrition or illness or systematic injustice, they're at the back of it. I don't want them here."

Gabriel stared at the ground. "I felt the same. I wanted justice. Visible justice. But—"

Having experienced justice—experienced it in the full? How

could he wish that on anyone?

Except, for Gabriel, justice and mercy had been one and the same. The harshness of God's decree had been crushing and breathtaking, and Gabriel had been certain at times he wouldn't make it through to the other side. In the long view, however, that had been the most merciful thing God could have done to him. God had allowed Gabriel to experience the effects of his own decisions, and in fighting to survive, Gabriel's need had exceeded the limits of his strength. He'd begun to rely on God's. Without that justice, Gabriel would never have learned humility.

One of the human liturgies exclaimed, "O fortunate fall" because the fall of Adam had set in motion the events leading to the paschal mystery. *O felix culpa!* There was no "O fortunate fall" for the demons. They'd never been ground under the millstone that spit out humility.

Detecting the turn of his thoughts, Israfel glittered with sparks. "Look at reality, not at what you want."

He forced a smile. "Aren't you the Seraph?"

"Why should I have to remind a Cherub to analyze the facts? Demons aren't redeemable. Everything they've lost is something they deserved to lose, and if they can lose even more, God should take that, too."

Remiel folded her arms. "If God were to allow a return, I'd shut up and let it happen, the same way I shut up when God opened the banquet to the fallen. But from where I stand, I see them hating God and taking delight in causing harm. There's no coming back from that."

Mary raised her hands. "None of us can march up to a fallen angel and unlock the cuffs around his heart. That would have to be the work of my Son."

Israfel said, "The just judge."

Gabriel replied, "The merciful savior."

She pivoted, gaze boring into him. "Don't try to make this happen."

Mary's voice went soft. "Gabriel is the only angel who can."

Ice cold, Gabriel felt Israfel's fire wash outside him, unable to gain a foothold. Inside, Raphael rang with alarm.

Mary arose and took his hands. "Gabriel, I would never ask this of you except we think it's the only chance. We have one week, and then the Father will close off the pit."

A cat's cradle. Two final forms. And someone to whom Gabriel had nothing to offer.

Mary said, "Would you be willing to form a primary bond with Lucifer?"

He couldn't hear anything after that, but he knew. He knew Israfel detonated. He felt Raphael's horror, and he knew Michael negated it outright. Cross-bonding didn't happen.

Or rather, it hadn't ever happened. *Can't, or won't?* Lucifer had tried to bond Gabriel back during those human days, when he'd believed Gabriel temporarily winnowable. It wasn't enough to have taken down a third of the stars from the sky. When one more star swung close to his grasp, Lucifer had tried to pluck that one, too.

Mary was spinning out a plan, though. Once Gabriel had access to Satan's heart, he could identify any good still in him. With a Cherub's insight, he could breathe love into whatever parts of Satan remained capable of responding to love. As an advocate, Gabriel could give Satan hope and show Satan humility. Hadn't Michael just said the demons would look at Gabriel's ejection and subsequent return—his 'semifall'—as an indicator that they could do the same?

Gabriel couldn't get on top of the storm. The very suggestion—? Who had come up with this? And why hadn't they immediately consigned it to the bin of bad ideas? Cherubim did that all the time. Suggest it, deem it unworkable, and discard it. Don't suggest a means of testing it.

Especially not a destructive test.

If Gabriel could sift through Lucifer's heart and highlight parts of it—then Lucifer would do the same to a completely vulnerable Gabriel. No limits. No boundaries. No protection.

Finally something came clear in the maelstrom: Raphael. Raphael was urging Gabriel that he should refuse. Mary had no authority to order this, and at any rate, she was only asking. Yes, Gabriel loved her, but that put him under no obligation to follow this scheme.

Gabriel grasped that pillar of strength, and he emerged from his shock to find Mary had backed away, and instead Remiel stood with her arms and wings around him. Israfel had her fists clenched and stood screaming between Gabriel and Mary, surrounded by blue flame.

"—would consign Gabriel to untold amounts of pain, and for what?" Israfel had tears in her voice. "So a gang of demons who've spent all of history being hateful can spit in God's face one more time, only from closer in? So they can fill Gabriel with grief and agony?"

Raphael also stood in a battle stance with his wings lifted. "Haven't you heard what happens when a demonic Seraph scorches his own Cherub? Their hearts are burnt to husks."

Israfel gestured toward Remiel. "You see what losing Camael did to her. You want Gabriel to step into the same heartbreak! Satan will get ripped away from him, and that wound will never close."

Remiel clenched Gabriel tighter. "I'm begging you before God—don't ask him to do this."

In the face of all these objections, Uriel curled against the armrest, wrapped in the scented fabric, of petals joined to petals. Peace illuminated those lavender eyes, and Gabriel instinctively tried to connect with it.

Making an overture to convert Lucifer...? To go that far, Mary wasn't hoping for just one or two souls. She had a creation-sized plan, one she'd said Paul was a part of. Paul, who had written to the Corinthians, "*so that God may be all in all.*" For that matter, Paul had written to Timothy that the Father desired for all to be saved, and for all to have knowledge of the truth—knowledge of Jesus, who'd said that when He was lifted up from the earth, He would draw all to Himself.

Were Abraham and Mary and Peter and Paul aiming for no less than universal restoration? Did they think a reformed Lucifer could bring back everyone who'd pledged to serve him?

Even Michael looked unsteady. "I can stop this right here. Gabriel can't force a primary bond. Most bonds are lower-level."

Gabriel blinked hard. "That, at least... I should have been Lucifer's primary."

Israfel tossed her head. "Except he turned you down flat."

Gabriel rested a hand on Remiel's. His fingers were wet with her tears. "Most Cherubim have three or four primaries. I have two. I've figured for a while he should have been my third." His throat was so tight. Israfel was throwing energy like a supernova, and he absorbed some to prevent his emotions from shutting down. "If we were to attempt it, that much, at least, would work to plan."

Israfel snapped, "And the rest would fail, so you won't."

Envisioning the cat's cradle, Gabriel turned to Raphael. "What we just saw... How can I refuse?"

Raphael vibrated. "You refuse by saying no. This is the most dangerous thing you've ever contemplated, and that includes diving into Hell to rescue Israfel."

Remiel covered her face with her hands. "You don't know what you're playing with."

Gabriel paced away from them, then turned back. Uriel kept fingering that sweet-scented scarf.

Gabriel reached for God. *Would You approve of this? I would never consort with Your enemies if it would displease You.*

Lucifer had made a reluctant offer to bond back when Jesus had died. In pragmatic terms, a bond would have enhanced their united power so they could blow open the walls of Sheol. It hadn't been necessary, but unconsciously, had Lucifer's heart responded to the nearness of Cherub steel and Cherub focus?

Gabriel bit his lip. "I have to pray about this."

Israfel flared again. "You don't have to pray about this! Even if we try to cull a few stragglers from the herd, there's no reason to do this for Satan."

Uriel spoke for the first time. "It's his only chance."

Israfel threw out her hands. "I don't care."

Gabriel closed his eyes.

Israfel said to Gabriel, "Would you even want him back?"

After all this time…after Lucifer had attempted to seduce him, attempted to destroy him, attempted to contort Gabriel's soul into a mockery of love…would Gabriel want him back?

Israfel positioned herself in front of him. "Don't get lost in the potential of who he could have been. Focus on who he is. Catalog the decisions he's made. Tally up the damage he's done. He's probably in his Hilbert Hotel room right now, beating Satrinah into a sticky stain on the carpet. Bond him, and he'll do the same to you. Is that a soul worth redeeming?"

"I said I need to pray about this." Gabriel took Israfel's hands. "I need you to pray with me."

They transported to the Heavenly Temple where a multitude of white-robed angels and humans conducted the hourly liturgy. Mid-morning? Gabriel hadn't paid attention to time since the cat's cradle.

Israfel surged with flame. Gabriel called it into his heart, then filled her empty space with his steadiness.

As they knelt, she gripped his hand hard enough to hurt, projecting, *You don't want to do this.*

He didn't.

She sent, *It won't happen, anyhow. The instant Satan realizes you want to bond, he's going to withhold it.*

Gabriel's own smile surprised him. *So I can scuttle the plan by telling him a bond would make me happy?*

Make starry eyes at him like the heroine of a romance novel. He'll take off like he's got afterburners. She bowed her head. *I'm sorry. We came to pray, not to make snarky remarks.*

They settled, wings tucked, wrists crossed over their chests. Gabriel closed his eyes, and his form discorporated. *Father, I don't know.*

God's presence rippled through him. This was what Gabriel

wanted: to be with his Creator.

But he also wanted to do God's will. He wanted to please God. *I want to be the second pair of hands on Your cat's cradle.* Him to God, God back to him, him to God. It was a game, and it was real. It was love, and it was deadly serious.

I don't want to displease You.

Gabriel didn't say that he didn't want to get hurt. If there would be pain, but God intended his pain to achieve something... That, Gabriel could endure. He'd try.

Raphael wasn't wrong about fallen Seraphim burning out their Cherubim. Eight centuries ago, Raphael had come across a husk of a Cherub in the desert, hollow and brittle, with no clue how long it had been there. All the way in the Ring of Seven, the aftershocks of Raphael's horror hit Gabriel like a gut-punch. He arrived to find Raphael with both hands on whichever Cherub it was. They couldn't tell. They wouldn't identify their patient for days.

In Heaven, Gabriel had converted one of the holding cells into a convalescent chamber where Raphael did his best to heal the burns, both interior and exterior. It was so crisp, so painful. The Cherub eventually awoke, only to curl up in fear, wings tight, unwilling to bear a Seraph's touch even though that Seraph was trying to help. Instead, Gabriel tried to channel Raphael's healing power. He kept picking up images from his fallen counterpart. Violation. Humiliation. Fire scorching through the soul's core. Waves of terror and betrayal and self-loathing.

Raphael had called for Uriel, who'd soothed the demon until eventually sleep came. Uriel made sure the demon would sleep for weeks, after which Raphael visited every day with his healing light until the time they arrived to find the chamber empty.

What could a Cherub do to merit that? But these were demons. Snickering at a Seraph's mistake might be enough provocation.

Most primary pairs were equal in power. Gabriel had a little more than either Israfel or Raphael. Gabriel wasn't even on the same scale as Lucifer. If Lucifer wanted to burn him out, it would happen.

Had Israfel meant that about Lucifer even now beating Satrinah into nothing more than a stain on the carpet?

Who would Lucifer's other primaries have been? Probably not Satrinah. Her temperament didn't complement his well enough. Belior? Almost certainly, and even more certainly when Gabriel considered Belior's jealousy. He'd been operating within inches of his heart's desire for millennia and never been gratified.

Possibly Mephistopheles, except he was so bound up in Beelzebub. Gabriel couldn't even guess about Rahab, now destroyed.

If Gabriel and Lucifer did bond, then afterward, when Lucifer refused to repent and the demons returned to fire, at least he'd be able to avail himself of one or two other primary bonds.

Inside Gabriel, Israfel scolded him: this wasn't about Satan's comfort.

If it's about his redemption, then it is about his comfort.

She retorted, *I want what's best for* you, *and that can't be offering yourself to him.*

Gabriel offered a small smile. *How would I even make the overture? Should I begin with humorous small talk?*

Shedding sparks, Israfel smothered a laugh.

Thanks.

Smirking, she sent, *Oh, this is going to be a show. I cannot imagine you flirting.* Given the penchant Seraphim had for imagination? That was quite the insult. *You'd flirt by saying, "Do you want to see a pretty rock I found?"*

Gabriel struggled to squelch his own laugh, and then Israfel flashed him out of the Heavenly Temple.

They sat on the steps, periodically breaking up in giggles. Israfel said, "I'm sorry. We were going to end up disrupting someone."

Gabriel folded his arms. "How is it that we went into the temple to pray about a very serious question, and suddenly you're insulting my ability to flirt?"

"You have never, not once in your entire existence, flirted. For that matter, has anyone ever flirted with you?" Israfel snickered. "You can't answer because you don't know. You wouldn't recognize flirting unless the individual approached you from the front, bowed, and said, 'I shall now proceed to flirt.'"

Gabriel frowned. "From which I could conclude that the next sentence would be flirtatious, but what about the sentence following that?"

"There's no telling. A top-tier flirt would advance and recede like the tide. So, as I was saying—you haven't a chance."

Relief bubbled up. "If this is God's will, I can get the credit for trying, and then fail."

Israfel tossed her head so her curls sprang around her shoulders. "I can't see how this could be God's will."

Gabriel sent her his memory of the cat's cradle. Israfel flinched.

"I can't come up with a way I could have done things differently." Gabriel bit his lip. "Lucifer turned me down by saying I had nothing to offer. That was a trap, though. I did have something."

Israfel breathed, "Your loyalty."

Gabriel rested his elbows on his knees and tightened his fists.

Israfel added, "But you never were good at subtext, so instead of trying to prove yourself, you agreed that his status wouldn't be enhanced by the addition of yours."

Raising his wings, Gabriel swallowed. "I've run through every possibility. If I'd offered him my loyalty, then when he rebelled, I'd have fulfilled my obligation by going with him. If I'd badgered him to accept me, then I'd have rationalized that I owed him my support. If I'd begged him, then I'd have gone because I would have thought I needed him."

A cold wave rushed through Israfel.

It left Gabriel shivering. "The only way we could have bonded and not lost me was if he'd approached a bond as an affirmation of our friendship rather than as a transaction."

Israfel opened her hands. "Which—it is."

"That's not how I explained it. I explained it transactionally." Gabriel pressed his fingers into his temples. "I would take his fire so he could expand his thoughts, and he would give me zeal so I could implement my theories." When Israfel didn't reply, he fought nausea. "That's who I was back then. Lucifer saw no reason to bond, and the answer was always education, so I gave him reasons."

Israfel touched a wingtip to his. "We've all changed a lot. Although based on our conversations, you still love to educate."

Gabriel allowed himself to smile.

She said, "If he'd approached you as a friend and bonded without encouragement, then what? He'd still have resisted when God asked for submission. You'd still have resisted, too. You might have reinforced one another in resisting."

"Lucifer might have let his concern for me overrule his concern for himself. That's a bond at its best." Gabriel's wings sagged. "When I got so upset at God for inverting the order of creation, Lucifer might have helped me rediscover my trust the way you and Raphael did. He might have led the way just because I needed him to do it—because whatever else can be said about Lucifer, he's got leadership skills."

"Which is unfortunate," Israfel murmured.

"We all had a place in creation." Gabriel kept pressing his fingertips at the pressure points that kept him calm during his year in a human body. They did nothing for him in his angelic form, but just the position triggered a memory of discussions with his mentor and the relaxation of being safe.

If he and Lucifer bonded, there would be no safe place ever again. Lucifer would be able to reach him from across the divide to Hell.

Israfel grabbed his hand, and her prayer erupted like champagne from a shaken bottle, spraying toward God and carrying Gabriel's thoughts in her rush. Even though Gabriel was at her side on the steps, he met God face to face inside Israfel's fiery heart. His thoughts rotated around hers like clockwork while at her core she burned with the steadiness of an engine. God moved between them.

What should I do?

God wouldn't answer that. Gabriel tried again. *Is even discussing this offensive to You?*

Reassurance welled up. Gabriel wanted to please God, and

wanting to please God was itself pleasing to God.

But is it Your will that I bond him?

God's will was always more complex than that. Gabriel felt his attention drawn toward all the ways his life had unfolded, all the choices he'd made, all the decisions he'd avoided making, and the evils he'd averted. Finally God drew his mind toward all the times Gabriel had weighed one good against another, eventually settling on one even though that meant the other dissipated on the wind.

God had loved him in every one of those circumstances, every one of those choices. Gabriel wanted to please God, and God was pleased. He would continue to be pleased.

I need more direction than that. This was a tremendous decision—something Gabriel had never considered.

Could doing this cause him to fall?

No.

Gabriel tried to relax. *To be clear, the worst won't happen?*

Yes.

He prayed, *But I would be vulnerable the whole time. Perhaps forever.*

God didn't reply. That was a statement, not a question.

Gabriel held the feelings clinging to the outside of the facts, and the longer he held them, the more he realized God was already in the same situation. The right word wasn't "vulnerable," but Gabriel wasn't sure what word would convey it. God was love, and God hadn't created anything He didn't love. His love had given His creatures the ability to consent or not to consent, to decide this and not that, and to not only find themselves but to forge that self. He'd foreknown some of them would leave, and that their leaving would be painful, and yet at no point had He held back His love.

Gabriel's potential bond and almost certain separation from that bond were, from one perspective, the same as God's decision to love into being so many creatures who would choose to separate from Him.

Mingled in Gabriel's thoughts, Israfel shuddered with her objection: God didn't suffer. Gabriel would.

Gabriel prayed, *But I want to be like You.* God had given Gabriel a very stern correction in the form of a year apart, and Gabriel's response at the beginning had been...unfortunate. Later, he'd re-read his journals and burned them because...the angel he was at the start...he'd have thrown himself out of Heaven, too. But Gabriel's response by the end had been to crave being more like his Father. More empathetic. More merciful. More conscious of how God had created him to be, and how all of that was an unmerited gift.

Except— Gabriel had been hurt. He'd been hurt at Sodom. God's protection had prevented much worse, but opening up to Lucifer meant permitting "worse" to happen. There wouldn't be a divine hand extending into this rancid alleyway to halt the chain reaction of harm.

Israfel urged God to forbid Gabriel from moving forward, but then Gabriel felt her evaporate from his prayer while she dealt with God one-on-one.

She's made her opinion clear, said the Holy Spirit. *I want you to make your own decision.*

Gabriel settled into himself, completed by Israfel's fire and balanced enough to delve into his own thoughts. *I need to analyze the risks and benefits, accounting for the minuscule likelihood of a successful outcome versus the certitude of pain and the probability of disaster. At the same time, I have to weigh the overwhelming good of a changed state against the tragedy of an unchanged state.*

The Holy Spirit didn't disagree.

Emotionally, I should feel through my personal trajectory during my experience as Your child and juxtapose it against whatever is of the greatest benefit to the Kingdom. Gabriel paused, wrinkling his nose. *I'm not adept at the emotional part, even still. It sounds clinical.*

The Holy Spirit smiled inside him. Clinical analysis was fine. God wasn't unaware of Gabriel's inclinations when He brought him to a crossroads.

It would be easier if I could just pray for Lucifer from the Ring.

Gabriel's eyes flared open, and his feathers stood out.

Pray for Lucifer.

For thousands of years, once a week, Gabriel had gone through a mental checklist of every situation and condition that required his prayers, to make sure he'd covered everything. Peace. Injustice. Famine. Anything anyone had asked him to pray about. Souls in need of conversion. Bodies in need of healing. And there, snuggled into the list for two thousand years, for so long it had risen to the top as others dropped off, was one perennial item: *Pray for your enemies.*

Gabriel had asked Jesus if that included all their enemies. Their first enemy. Was he supposed to pray for Lucifer? Why would Gabriel want good things to happen to an enemy who would leverage those good things to destroy even better things?

Gabriel didn't want it. In the cold clarity of thought, though, no one wanted good things for an enemy. That was why Jesus had to tell everyone to do it. Once humans had begun praying for their human enemies, Gabriel had examined the overall needs of creation and concluded he ought to follow Jesus's directive by praying for their preternatural enemies. It would have been dangerous for humans to do it—and thank heaven, they didn't—but spiritual warfare was well within the angels' purview.

Except, as the Book of James had pointed out, praying that a homeless man should be warm and well-fed meant nothing unless the pray-er also acted within his capacity to provide warmth and food.

Here was Gabriel, having prayed for his enemy for two thousand years, with a chance to do good to the one who'd harmed him and bless the one who'd cursed him.

Be warm and well-fed.

Build up the hearth. Bake the bread. Usher the cold, hungry soul inside. Hand him a loaf and tuck your cloak around his shoulders. Then it's up to the soul if he eats, if he stays.

Gabriel closed his eyes. *It's not all up to me.* That was the humbling part, the part that kept him from committing. *If my sacrifice guaranteed success, I'd do it. I might take on this burden, though, only to get pierced and drained and buried, and he still might not turn.*

Faced with the same situation, Jesus had made a decision. Gabriel's hands tightened because he, too, had to make a decision.

Chapter Four

SATAN SUMMONED THE MASKIM to his quarters, then made them wait while he fielded questions from minor functionaries.

The oddest thing about the "hotel" was seeing his officers while he consulted them. In Hell, they all had their offices in impenetrable darkness, and while it had taken time to appreciate the benefits of lightlessness, there were many. Satan had learned to move in silence, keeping them off-balance as to where he was at any point in the conversation. He could, with steadfast focus, shine just enough to be glimpsed when he wanted. Unable to be seen, they occasionally forgot they could still be observed.

In Heaven's hotel, he'd lost a few advantages.

The angels had made their hotel pleasant, although the designers had gone overboard with the mirrors. Every hallway had mirrors. Every room had mirrors. The stairwells had mirrors.

It was Belior who'd first called it a hotel rather than a prison or a compound. Mephistopheles had murmured, "The Grand Hilbert Hotel?" which Beelzebub had found inexplicably funny. For the next hour, whenever issuing orders to his underlings, he'd worked "the Hilbert Hotel" into every sentence until that became its name. If God had given it a name to begin with, no one remembered it, which was the way with most demons, as well.

When the Maskim's two bonded pairs finally began exchanging thoughts with one another, Satan said, "Are there any status updates?"

Asmodeus said, "This," and shattered the mirror at Satan's back.

He turned in time to watch the mirror shimmer and pull itself back together. "That's unexpected."

Belior said, "The mirrors are the most oppressive feature of this hotel, and while they're less annoying than darkness or fire, I wanted them gone. The hotel itself begs to differ. We cannot break them and cannot remove them."

Mephistopheles approached the nearest mirror. "Have you studied the mechanism?"

"The building regenerates, and they're part of the wall. And yes," Belior snapped, "I attempted to remove a wall. The wall and the mirror regenerate exactly as before."

Asmodeus said, "Doubtless the enemy believes the regenerative properties will keep us from destroying it, but instead they've gifted us a stronghold that repairs itself in response to battle damage."

Before Satan could ask whether that would hold during a fight, Mephistopheles said, "Our first priority, then, is to establish whether the building regenerates after one of the enemy fires on it. They may have keyed the regeneration to only our signatures."

Belior huffed. "Easily circumvented. After an angel destroys a wall, a demon would fire on it to trigger a regeneration. But yes, establishing the limits of its regenerative ability should be a consideration prior to counting on it as a defensible position."

Mephistopheles said, "Speaking of defense, the hallways cannot be Guarded, but the individual hotel rooms are well-suited to holding a Guard."

Beelzebub added, "That's for the enemy's use. Michael has already threatened to confine any misbehaving individuals to quarters for six hours."

"Will he also send us to bed without supper?" Satan kept watching the four through the mirror. "Determine whether the other buildings have similar regenerative properties."

Asmodeus said, "I've dispatched scouts to reconnoiter this level of Heaven. They're going to get us an analysis of the size, terrain, and any other defenses."

Mephistopheles said, "In addition, I've commissioned a team of Dominions and Virtues to analyze this level's attachment to the inner layers in case it's possible to detach it from the rest of Heaven. If we can't effect a complete detachment, we may still be able to segment it off in a way that throttles the enemy's passage between their levels and ours. We could potentially eject them, seal ourselves in, and retain this level for ourselves."

Half the time, Satan didn't need to give orders. The Seraphim had enough strategic intelligence, and the Cherubim the tactical know-how, that they'd anticipate anything he could request long before he requested it, and all in an attempt to impress him.

"We haven't identified a way off the level other than with a one-to-one sponsor," Beelzebub said. "While it's not hard to find make an angel agree to serve as escort, it's not possible to leave the escort. If they get too far apart, our operative automatically returns to his quarters in the hotel. If our operative does something the escort finds offensive, the escort can terminate permission, and again, our operative snaps back to quarters."

Satan said, "About our quarters: can these room assignments be changed?"

Belior folded his arms. "As befits a Hilbert Hotel, we can change our assigned spaces, but a homebase is required."

Satan snorted. "So in the Father's house, there are many hotel rooms?"

"In effect," said Belior, humorless as expected. "While two souls can arrange for adjacent quarters, they can't both assign themselves to the same one."

Asmodeus said, "It's also not possible to create permanent access from one room to another."

"Since, however, there's no issue with travel between the rooms, I don't see that as an impediment." Belior scowled. "Quarters for the monkeys are equipped with furniture for eating and sleeping. Quarters for angelic souls are not, but those features are easily added."

Beelzebub said, "The rooms aren't all the same size. They change to accommodate the need, and your suite seems to be as large as they can get."

Was this heaven's acknowledgment of Satan's status? What if the hotel, in addition to regenerating itself, shifted around the different demons like a living thing, showing deference as appropriate?

Satan strode to the windows. The grounds outside the hotel sprawled with a nauseating gentleness, dotted by ponds and the occasional copse of trees. "How many hotels are there?"

Belior said, "I'll get you a final number when the scouts finish their survey."

Heaven's layers expanded exponentially, with the closest and tightest being the smallest, and every successive sphere larger than the last, to encase it. Creation had at one time been the outer layer of Heaven, but that had been detached after humanity's fall. This one had come into being sometime after.

If Satan could detach this level, which shouldn't have existed in the first place, Heaven would still retain all their original levels. With enough time, Satan's forces might be able to establish passage back to the Void, crack Hell open, and grow their territory —and all in a way that didn't inconvenience God. Heaven might see fit to remain uninvolved.

Satan said, "Have our forces scout the other layers as much as possible. We need to figure out ways of remaining off this plane without an escort, or if possible, escorts who will allow us to act with impunity."

Beelzebub muttered, "Who would allow that?"

Satan's eyes narrowed. "If you'll back up the conversation three seconds, you'll recall I said we need to figure out which escorts would allow it, by which I'm indicating you would be well-advised to investigate the possibility." He shifted his stance. "Are any of them discontented? Can they be made discontent? Can any of them be brought to our side? Are any especially gullible? I shouldn't have to point out these avenues." He turned to Asmodeus. "As for the matter of the demon who hid in that egg, question him and re-create the technique. A nearly-invisible Guard with a repulsion field would be invaluable for entrenching our forces."

Belior's expression remained flat, but Asmodeus seemed unnerved. Good. Hastle's disappearance coincided with Asmodeus's most scintillating act of treachery, and when both Satan and his underlings knew something of that nature, it tended to inspire performative loyalty.

He stretched his wings and ran his fingers over the window. "Be aware we may provoke our hosts into locking us in our playrooms, or even terminating our visit, so use good judgment. But don't miss any opportunities." In the glass, he caught the green glint of his own eyes. "I am not going to regret for all eternity that we had one final shot and didn't take it."

Bilocation meant Remiel could be making bread while simultaneously kneeling before God in the Ring.

The humans didn't technically have to make bread. They could have summoned bread or asked Jesus to multiply bread, but these humans and their guardian angels had responded to a holiday with the specifically human impulse to cook.

Every culture had festive foods, although Remiel couldn't always tell what made food festive as opposed to functional. Why was goose more festive than chicken, or mashed potatoes more festive than roasted potatoes? What linked cakes and birthdays, or dumplings and the turning of a new year? Why not cakes for a new calendar year as for a new human year?

With human chatter surrounding her, Remiel pounded balls of dough into discs that one of the community members would cook up in a skillet. Simultaneously, silent in the Ring, she looked up into God's face.

God loved her. Always, always, always, always she would hold onto that. God loved her and loved her and had made her for joy, and sometimes she even believed it. Like now, when her hands were rolling out flatbread rounds and her eyes were gazing into God's and hungering for His appreciation and approval.

The dough was stiff, and rolling it involved her shoulders and wrists. Anguish: here on her knees. Controlled movements: here with the humans. Eyes on the bread and eyes on the Bread of Life.

She hated bilocation because it was too close to being Irin again —but it hadn't been quite like this, either. She hadn't shared her brother's perceptions at the moment they were happening. When they were apart, they'd existed separately until they'd returned to one another, and then they reshaped one another when they mingled their experiences.

Which—now that it was all over? After all the things Camael had done and said and experienced? She didn't want to mingle with that. If Mary's plan worked and they reunited, she'd have to put up walls. They'd still be twins, but no longer identical.

She prayed, *If that's the case, then why would I want him back?*

God replied, *You've loved him for so long.*

Her hands clenched. *Love can die.*

Remiel handed her flatbread to one of her human companions and reached for more dough. She prayed, *This community acts as though we alone are responsible for seven days worth of bread for all humanity, with no one else contributing.*

God chuckled. Remiel added, *I haven't made bread for a while. This is good.*

Around her in the Ring were only flames indicating where the other six angels of the Presence would stand. Michael might not be back for the rest of the week. Raguel would be just as busy. Instead of here, Gabriel had gone with Israfel to the Temple to pray his discernment over Mary's outrageous request.

Remiel resumed rolling dough. *I can't believe Gabriel might agree to a bond. Would You tell me his reasoning?*

She expected God to refuse, so her wings puffed (in both locations) when God said, *Love.*

Remiel stopped rolling. *He loves Satan?*

Did I not say to love your enemies?

Well, yes. But knowing someone had ruptured Heaven, sought

the eternal demise of billions, and blasphemed to God's face didn't prompt Remiel to say, "This individual needs a little love."

If a little love were all it would take to reverse this, then the oceans of love back before the Winnowing should have prevented it.

Tell him no, Remiel wanted to pray, but she clamped down on that impulse because God didn't need to take her dictation.

God's love for Remiel had manifested in so many ways: in patience, in support, in jokes, in the friends who surrounded her. In the first moments post-Winnowing, when she'd been spiritually disemboweled and her soul was spraying the equivalent of blood and bile, He'd held her and given her a name. Then given her a title. He'd given her Uriel to cry all over, given her a job, and finally, given her time.

He'd given her the means of stitching herself back together so eventually she could feel like something other than a freakish half-made thing for every other angel to pity.

He'd accepted her pain. He'd accepted her rejection and her criticism and her anger, and later he'd accepted her apologies. This was how God had loved her.

Bread. Focus on the bread.

Another angel arrived, her uniform drab and her eyes quick to take in their surroundings. She settled on her knees before Remiel and took a ball of dough. "How are you holding up?"

This was Nivalis, the founder of Heaven's grief squad. They were angels who ministered to any guardian grieving the loss of a human charge, and also to human souls grieving the damnation of their loved ones. The Second Coming and the end of the world had left the squad less to do, but they were still active.

Remiel pounded at the dough until it reached the right consistency. This stuff was stiffer than most bread doughs she'd seen, but since she hadn't been the one to mix it, she assumed the humans had done it correctly. "How should I be holding up?"

Eyes on God, she wondered if God would answer instead of Nivalis, but He didn't.

Nivalis said, "There isn't a 'should.' Our team is checking in with anyone who's had a loss because it's such a confusing time."

Remiel sat back from her flat bit of bread. "Camael's been summoning me. I've been ignoring him."

Nivalis nodded.

"Aren't you going to tell me I should be taking advantage of these hours to achieve closure?"

Nivalis's mouth twitched. "I just said we're checking in with everyone because it's a confusing time. What part of that makes you think I know what anyone should do?"

Remiel tilted her head. "How can you not know?"

Meeting her gaze, Nivalis had a hollow expression. "I know folks need help. I have no idea what that help should look like."

Remiel didn't reach for another ball of dough, and she dissolved her second self in the Ring. Monolocating once more, she said, "You need help, too."

"I thought the grief was settled. It had been a while." Nivalis swallowed hard. "I was okay until it became obvious that the guardians who saw their fallen charges were devastated all over again, and then I saw how the guardians who avoided their fallen charges were likewise devastated."

Remiel looked at the dough in her hands. "It's hard to choose between such attractive options."

"At the moment, we're advising not to contact." Nivalis tightened her pearly wings around herself. "I've avoided Judas. As far as I know, he hasn't wanted to see me, although there's no reason he would. He didn't know me as his guardian." Nivalis rolled out the dough a bit too hard, so it got thin in the middle. One of the human bakers would quietly return that flatbread into a ball and re-shape it, so Remiel said nothing. "That's the thing most guardians find hardest, that they loved this person for so many years, lost the person, grieved the person—and now when they check in on them, not only is the soul twisted by its time in Hell, but the soul doesn't recognize them."

Remiel muttered, "That's better than being blamed."

"Oh, some of them do get blamed. *Why didn't you keep me from falling off my horse? Why didn't you warn me I shouldn't poison my nephew?* And on and on and on." Nivalis stretched the dough in her hands. "We're left with the prospect of meeting them briefly, seeing the devastation that became of souls created so beautifully in God's image, and then losing them a second time. Hence our advice: unless you know for sure you can't live with yourself if you don't see them...don't."

Remiel murmured, "There's a chance of mercy."

Shock exploded off Nivalis. Wings raised, she stared Remiel in the eyes.

Several Angels turned and stared, so Remiel projected quickly, *We have no idea if it's possible, but Mary has a plan.*

Nivalis tried to project, but the questions didn't escape her heart.

The closest Angel flashed to Nivalis, hand on her shoulder. "Is everything all right?"

Remiel's wings tightened. "Nothing is all right. Nivalis wanted to console me about my fallen twin, and I said something absolutely shocking even to someone who's worked with grief for two thousand years." Clenching her hands, Remiel turned to Nivalis. "I'm sorry."

The Angel offered Remiel a smile. "I can listen. I won't mind if you're absolutely shocking."

Ninth choir Angels were so generous about being supportive. They usually felt that urge toward the humans, being closest to them, but they found ways to offer assistance whenever they could. Their charity was boundless, and at the moment, it was completely unhelpful.

Nivalis blinked hard. "No, it's fine. Thank you. We'll be okay, and I need to talk to Remiel alone."

After the Angel left, Nivalis balled up the bread she'd been rolling. "You didn't have to take the blame for my reaction."

"Every single thing I said was true." Remiel's past did routinely bring everyone up short in conversation. Nivalis was one of the few who'd never been horrified into silence.

Nivalis clenched her fingers through Remiel's. *You can't leave that there. If souls try to return, has God said they'll be accepted?*

Remiel shook her head. *Nothing definitive.*

Even the potential changes everything. Nivalis raised her head, her projection churning with fear and hope. "Still...six and a half days to accomplish what we couldn't in a lifetime...?"

Remiel said, "Now there's clarity. Before there was fog."

Nivalis nodded. "Although for Judas... Clarity means full knowledge of what he did."

Remiel squeezed her hand.

Nivalis looked her in the eye. "You may want to stay away, regardless. Camael always had clarity."

With her eyes on the dough ball she'd half-flattened, Remiel shook her head. "Eternity is a long time. As you said, the question is whether I can live with myself if I don't go."

Chapter Five

ON THE LAWN OF the Hilbert Hotel, Michael confined two demons to quarters, and they vanished. Ridiculous, like squabbling toddlers.

Although not many demons were out and about, the humans had begun taking advantage of their visiting privileges, reconnecting with friends and family they'd known during their lives. Some were meeting their ancestors for the first time while others were meeting their descendants. Without children or parents, Michael could only imagine the curiosity of investigating one's origins or seeing how parts of oneself manifested in other beings.

Saraquael joined him at a gazebo overlooking a pond. He'd cleaned up his armor, but his hair smelled of brimstone. "I believe we've emptied Hell." Flecks of ash mixed with melting ice on his wings. "Our seekers have combed everything, and although there were human souls hidden in every crag, now we're not getting even the faintest signatures."

"That sounds reasonable." It wouldn't be good enough for Saraquael: his next stop would be heading to the Ring of Seven to pray that God would reveal what was hidden.

Raguel checked in. Michael asked, "Has Miriael had any luck with Hastle?"

Raguel tilted his head. "I thought you knew. Miriael called in a friend, Danel."

Michael's wings flared. "Danel?"

"Ministering angel. White robes."

"I know who Danel is. I'm surprised Miriael involved him." Danel had also been Hastle's friend, but given Danel's vocation as a temple minister, Michael would have guessed that was the last angel Hastle would have responded to.

And yet...

Michael flashed to Danel's side. Instead of arriving in the holding cell, he found himself in the Heavenly Temple.

They were between liturgies. At the very back, Danel sat with Hastle.

In God's temple.

Hastle didn't raise his eyes. He was curled tight, but he was here.

Danel put into Michael's head, *I coaxed him to return with me, but he still isn't speaking.*

Thank you. Michael shivered. *You've gotten further than the rest of us.*

But, of course. Danel had never been a soldier. Peace clung to him, and Hastle had experienced enough hostility for a thousand lifetimes.

Why did you bring him here?

Danel gestured toward the front: apparently he was going on duty.

Although no newcomer to the realm of bad ideas, Michael found this one especially breathtaking. A demon in a church was bad enough. A demon in God's holy temple was going to hear the opening praises and blow out the windows while committing any screaming sacrilege he could manage.

Danel looked at peace. Even so, Michael summoned two soldiers and indicated they should remain on alert.

Back on the outer layer, Michael found Saraquael seated at the gazebo with a fallen Seraph looming before him, all six bronze wings flared and both hands clenched.

This entire week would consist of one fight after the next after the next. Michael strode forward in time to hear the Seraph saying,

"You are, by all accounts, the best of seekers."

A demon...praising an angel?

Saraquael turned toward Michael. "You remember Ataf. He wants me to seek out Rahab."

Michael went cold. "Wasn't Rahab destroyed?"

Ataf's eyes glinted with the same bronze as his feathers. "The last we saw, he'd drowned himself in the Lake of Fire. We believe he's still there."

Whatever was left after three thousand years.

Sadness flitted across Saraquael's bright eyes. "I'm willing to try."

Michael frowned. The only possible answer was yes. God had ordered them to evacuate every soul from Hell. On the other hand, deploying Saraquael into Hell with a former member of the Maskim sounded like a recipe for Saraquael getting chained in the lake while an ambitious demon lobbied to get his old job back. Michael said, "Since you need seekers, let's send you down with a team," which would at least give them all a fighting chance if Ataf arranged an ambush.

Ataf's wings shivered. "I would appreciate that."

His appreciation had to be performative. Ataf wanted a service, and he had a Seraph's manipulative skill to achieve what he wanted. Snapping his fingers and issuing Saraquael an order would undermine his goal.

Michael left Saraquael in charge of the search effort, and he tried not to flinch when Saraquael asked for the name of Hell's best seekers so they could work together. Michael paged Miriael to join them, since Special Ops had any number of tricks for locating individuals and objects within Hell. Not to mention, they were fantastic escape artists.

That settled, Michael turned to find himself face to face with Satan.

Naturally, Satan had positioned himself a little too close, and he was a little too tall. Sounding disgusted, he said, "Weren't you supposed to provide us with tours?"

Ataf had already surprised Michael by being polite, and by all accounts, that exceeded the amount of good surprises Michael could expect. It felt much better this way, to have Satan behaving with predictable arrogance. "I haven't checked your ticket, but I believe your tour begins in an hour, unless you'd like me to make arrangements with another guide."

"I've always admired the way you think on your feet." Satan's eyes sparkled as he looked around. "This place is...*nice*." Hundreds of iterations of the word "nice" got bundled into that one pronouncement, somehow rendering it into an insult that meant "dull" or "so stupid as to be beneath notice." "I'd never stopped by Limbo, and it turns out that was a wise choice. I find I've already tired of it."

Michael said, "Then it's time for you to visit other areas, and I would add that someone of your stature deserves an escort befitting his station," which sounded elevated and would serve to get Satan out of his way. "Raphael?"

Raphael appeared immediately, and he just as immediately smothered his smile when he saw Satan. Michael said, "Satan needs a one-to-one."

Satan folded his arms. "He'll do. But with your typical myopia, you've misinterpreted my intentions."

Camael appeared at Satan's side. Reflexively armoring his heart, Michael endured Remiel's familiar eyes boring into him.

Satan said, "He's been requesting passage off the level from the other Irin, who so far has not responded."

Michael shrugged. "That sounds like a refusal."

Satan frowned. "Then summon her, because he wants her to escort him."

Michael studied Satan. "At any point in this process, were you guaranteed unfettered access to specific individuals? No."

Camael grimaced. "We're allowed to roam Heaven, so you need to grant me access to my sister's homebase."

If he took all seven days to do it, Michael still would not be able to find enough words to say how absolutely that was not going to happen. "You aren't guaranteed access to locations, either. If you've requested a meeting with Remiel, it's up to Remiel to grant or deny the meeting. If you've requested access to her home, it's up to Remiel to grant or deny access to her home."

Satan shook his head. "Those weren't the initial terms."

No, not playing this game. "The best I can do is to get a message to Remiel that you requested a visit. Since you've already done as much, you're out of options."

Satan sighed. "Surely you have influence over her."

"If I didn't respect when she said no," Michael said, "then I wouldn't be worthy of having any influence at all."

Given how disconcerting it was to stand next to an inverted Remiel within the premises of Heaven, Michael couldn't imagine how awful it would be for Remiel herself. He'd never ask that of her. In some ways, it felt like Mary asking Gabriel to bond with Satan.

Michael also wouldn't have asked that, not in a hundred thousand years, because in another hundred thousand years, Gabriel would still be paying the price. Michael fought the chills curling through him.

Satan put on a charming smile. "Sometimes when someone says no, they only mean they require convincing."

Michael glanced off to the side. "For example, you're attempting to convince me to change my own refusal right now. It's an interesting tactic, but ultimately not one I can respect." He turned back to Camael. "If there's anyone else you'd like to talk to, we may be able to arrange that."

Camael spat, "Useless," and flashed away.

Michael turned to Satan. "Don't let me prevent you from leaving, too."

"In a moment of magnanimity, I'm going to show you what it's like to change one's mind." Satan addressed Raphael. "I would much enjoy a tour of the seventh layer of Heaven. Are there still those chained waterfalls in the mountains?"

As though he had been on his way there already, Raphael said, "Absolutely. Come with me," and they were gone.

Michael dropped onto one of the benches and closed his eyes, then stretched his wings and his legs. *They're insufferable.* No response from God. *Help me keep everyone safe this week. Please.*

Six and a half more days. And if Gabriel went along with Mary's plan, then there was no way Michael could keep him safe.

Gabriel appeared in Mary's garden, thoughts quiet, wings dark grey. Cold at his side, Israfel took his hand.

Mary sat on a bench beneath a rose-covered arch, eyes closed as she prayed, while Uriel shimmered in a dissociated form all around her.

Gabriel said, "You don't have to stay," and Israfel squeezed his hand before departing.

He'd prayed for so long he felt prayed-out. Instead, Gabriel made himself desolid in the silence of the garden, surrounded by the rhythm of Mary's prayers and the memories of so many souls who'd benefitted from Mary's yes that led to Jesus's yes that led to the Holy Spirit's enthusiastic yes and the final triumphant yes of the church.

What unknown good would spring from another yes?

He felt rather than saw Mary open her eyes and smile at his return. Her voice was soft. "I hope you aren't offended."

"Not at all." Gabriel solidified into his subtle body on the paving stones, knees up, wings tucked. "Your prayers lead you to believe we have a chance of success. I'm willing to try."

Emotion surged from Mary's heart, triumph mixed with concern. She'd likely reached for Uriel the same way Gabriel might reach for Raphael. Guardian angels and their human charges didn't have the same kind of bond as Cherubim and Seraphim, but it was close enough. Mary said, "I'm asking a lot of you, more than I've ever asked before."

This was true, so Gabriel didn't demur. The peace of her garden lingered, and he tried to settle the fear of what he was going to do and the questions about whether this operation would succeed.

Mary said, "Would you mind if I asked one additional question?"

They sometimes teased one another: *No, but that was in and of itself a question, so you're in the same position you were thirty seconds ago.* Today, Gabriel only inclined his head, and Mary brought him up the hill to her home. On a block table in the kitchen lay a page of sheet music.

Gabriel went cold. "Why do you have that?"

Israfel would have made her prior detonation look like a lightning bug.

Mary laid a hand on the paper. "I found this in the library, and I was astonished. This is the most beautiful hymn I've ever seen. The harmonies, the praises, the mysteries—it's a masterpiece. Yet I've never heard anyone play it."

"You wouldn't have." Gabriel sought out Uriel, currently discorporated. *You should have told her to put it back.*

Uriel hadn't been there when Mary came across it.

Maybe not then, but five minutes afterward? What about five minutes ago?

Uriel didn't respond.

Gabriel folded his arms. "Are you trying to break my heart? I've already agreed to put myself on the line for an impossible task. I want nothing to do with this."

Mary stepped back. "You always liked answering questions."

"Not this question. Not that music. You found it on a bottom shelf in a sub-basement that no one tends, in a stack of manuscripts no one ever catalogued." His feathers all stood apart. "Ask your Son why I might have left it there. Ask your guardian angel."

He was about to flash away when Mary apologized. Palms forward, she said, "I'm sorry. It was one page. It looked forgotten, and anyone I asked kept putting me off. No, they'd never sung that. No, they didn't have a copy of the full piece."

That should have been a hint. Gabriel glared out the window. "As far as I know, I'm the only one who ever sang that, and there's only one full copy remaining. They weren't lying, but they weren't entirely truthful."

Mary lowered her voice. "I haven't seen you this angry in centuries."

He leaned in the doorframe. "Why were you down there? If you required reading material, I'd have found you some."

"Elijah suggested that pagan poems might help convert the priests of Ba'al by reminding them they used to have a sense of God's goodness. I thought those might be uncatalogued." Her eyes watered. "Gabriel, forgive me. I'm sorry I violated your privacy."

He drew a deep breath. "No, I'm sorry for losing my temper. You didn't do anything wrong." He'd made his library public, after all. He could have burned this paper the same way he'd burned his journals. "Do not sing that hymn."

"I can't sing it." She chuckled. "The complexity is mind-boggling, not to mention the range."

"You're looking at part of the descant. While difficult, the entirety of the piece isn't a progression of musical stunts." He clenched his hands. "Since you found it, the answer is, the full piece is a hymn titled 'All Praise to My Creator.' It's a majesty of harmony and counterpoint, and the lyrics are poetry. No one's ever created its equal, and we can't sing it because it was written by Lucifer. Every word is a lie."

Mary backed away from the page. "Even when he wrote it?"

"Yes." Gabriel shuddered. "No. At the time he wrote it, we didn't — We didn't know what would happen. Life was God. God was love, and we were with God, and there wasn't anything else. The praises are real, but I don't know what sentiment prompted it, whether he resented God or if even then he had an exit plan."

Mary gestured to the paper. "No one can describe the total glory of God, but reading this, I thought it nearly did."

Gabriel kicked his heel back against the doorjamb. "If anything, that makes it worse."

Mary said, "Who has the full hymn?"

"Israfel."

Israfel would burn down the music library before giving that hymn to Mary, that was for sure.

Mary said, "I understand the tragedy. But why the anger?"

Because Gabriel had been used as a mouthpiece for something Lucifer didn't feel? Because by assigning Gabriel that descant, Lucifer had given his song credibility? Because with this hymn, Lucifer had changed the way the angels conceived of hymns at all, transforming their worship in a way that they could never go back to the way it was?

Back when all the morning stars sang together, Lucifer had declared to Gabriel, "You have nothing to offer me," except he'd felt entitled to take full advantage of Israfel and Gabriel's bond, giving them parts so difficult that only a bonded pair could have performed them. Then, centuries later, Lucifer had tried to snare Gabriel on a hilltop, gloating mid-seduction, "You made me sound better."

That was all Gabriel had been to Lucifer. Not a friend, just a beauty aid.

Gabriel glared out at the roses. "I've answered everything I feel comfortable answering. May I leave?"

Mary lowered her gaze. "Take the paper back to the library. I won't look down there again."

She wasn't going to find anything worse, but still he accepted the page and flashed away from her home.

Chapter Six

WHEN MEPHISTOPHELES SPOTTED ISRAFEL on the far side of Limbo, he alerted Beelzebub and then flashed over to her. "Are you available for transport off this level?"

She looked drab compared to the last time he'd seen her, but their last encounter had happened during the Second Coming when she'd heralded Jesus's return and been brilliant with flame. Drab—or perhaps unamused by his request. Mephistopheles continued, "I'm told you maintain a music library. I would very much like to visit it."

She flashed him into the depths of Heaven, and Mephistopheles craned back his neck to see all the way up to the vaulted ceiling.

He whistled. *These acoustics are fantastic,* he projected, not wanting his voice to carry as far and as long as the whistle had. *The building itself functions as a musical instrument. One assumes you designed this?*

Israfel projected an affirmation. "If you'll remind me what instruments you play, I'll show you the best places to stand for every one of them."

Mephistopheles laced his fingers behind his back. He hadn't played in thousands of years and would rather his squeaking forays back into music production occur in isolation. He projected that he'd rather peruse her catalogues.

She escorted him to an office with shelves packed as full as the ones in the main hallway. These, however, were ledgers lined with titles, composers, descriptions, and miscellaneous notes. She'd kept and catalogued music from every era of human history, back to the garden. If Adam hummed a tune while plowing, she'd transcribed it. Moreover, another cabinet contained three complete ledgers listing instruments preserved in a separate museum.

After she explained how the catalogs worked, Mephistopheles flipped through the list of instruments. "I'm surprised a Seraph did all this. And yet, this system of organization doesn't seem like Gabriel's."

She bristled. "Cherubim aren't the only ones who understand alphabetical order. Piles of disorganized sheet music wouldn't have been of use to anyone, least of all myself."

Mephistopheles replaced the list of instruments in its own cabinet and closed the case. Israfel didn't seem worried that he'd destroy her work, and momentarily he concluded that if he gave off any whiff of destructive tendencies, she would revoke his access before power could go from his hands to her shelves.

More to the point, he didn't want to destroy her work. He wanted to stay long enough to discern if she bore any discontentment with Heaven's reigning authority. Additionally, while Mephistopheles wasn't a musician himself, he appreciated the complexity of a well-written piece. He might as well take time to admire some melodic constructions.

To that end, he said, "Can you recommend a work with mathematical significance, but written either just before the Second Coming, or just after it?"

Israfel displayed a series of expressions Mephistopheles sometimes saw marching across Beelzebub's face, but then without any cutting remarks about his identity as a Cherub, she led him to an atonal symphony in five movements. As promised, it was intellectually compelling, and periodically Mephistopheles would re-create the vibrations of the notes to determine how it would have sounded in concert.

Israfel pointed to a passage. "Bear in mind that the way it's written isn't exactly how it would have been performed. Most conductors changed this section to remove the dissonance."

Mephistopheles' brow furrowed. "Eliminating the anharmonicity would undercut the movement's buildup toward the hopelessness of the finale."

"Exactly. Season ticket-holders wouldn't stop attending over one performance like that, but orchestra management never wanted to alienate occasional listeners." Israfel snickered. "Hopelessness doesn't sell tickets quite the same way as hope."

Mephistopheles said, "And yet, which is more realistic?"

Israfel murmured, "Hope is realistic."

Mephistopheles honed in on her tone. "Perhaps realistic isn't the right word. Hope is in many cases undeserved."

Israfel's spirit drew in on itself. Had he just identified her weakness? He tested the waters. "For example, do you think there's any hope for me?"

Israfel snorted. "Since we're talking about undeserved? No."

Weakness, confirmed. "And yet my kind are here." He met her eyes. "We've been allowed into Heaven on reasoning that's spurious at best, for a significant time period and for a significant event. Cherubim have skill at reading into the Divine Will, and I for one have reason to believe these festivities will culminate in an offer of amnesty."

Israfel's eyes glinted. "Our Cherubim have reached a different conclusion."

With his voice low, Mephistopheles murmured, "I can only assume each is interpreting the facts with an eye toward one's own desires. Confirmation bias is difficult to correct for." Again he reviewed the dissonant measures. Omitting these clever runs from performances was a shame, but monkeys were short-sighted, not to mention delusional. A composition pointing toward chaos was far more realistic than Bach's perfectly balanced cantatas. "When I probe the future, what I keep hearing is a chorus of saints begging, 'Lord, will You abandon to imperishable flames those who have broken bread at Your table?'"

Her anger prickled at the edges of his awareness. Good—but better not to irritate her enough to rescind his invitation.

Mephistopheles closed the book, then hesitated. "I have something specific I'd like to review, an early song. If I may revisit your catalogs...?"

Had she kept it? She'd have had no reason to. But then again, given all the music she'd retained, why would she not?

Oddly, the oldest of her old music was listed in the newest ledger. Mephistopheles ransacked his mind to remember if the piece he sought had a title. Back then, not all of them did—and none of them had composers. At least, not before a certain point. This piece would have predated that. Fortunately, she had catalogs of first and last lines.

He noted five catalog numbers that might be the work he sought, and on the fourth, in the middle of a shelf halfway up the silent great hall, between a pair of desks lit with slanting sunlight, he found it.

Found it, and didn't want to look at what he'd found.

Israfel rejoined him. "Is anything wrong?"

Had he been shedding emotions? His signature must have flickered, that was all. "I've identified the score I require." He laid the papers on a desk and stood over them with his wings spread, as though to shield the piece from Israfel's eyes. A useless urge. He should be ashamed of attempting that.

Israfel said, "Oh! I remember this."

It had no title and no author. Mephistopheles ventured, "Do you recall who wrote it?'

Israfel said, "No. It arrived five minutes before the liturgy began, which was a thrill, let me tell you, and I read through it just enough to lead us before we started." She leaned over Mephistopheles, and he shifted his wings to avoid her touch. "This section was tricky, and I wanted to smooth it down, but sometimes you just have to trust that the composer knows what he's doing."

Throat tight, Mephistopheles said, "Sometimes, the composer's zeal needs a little tempering."

She snickered. "Yeah, with nearly blowing the deadline, I assume the writer was a Seraph. Plus, it's too enthusiastic for any other choir."

As Mephistopheles trailed his finger over the notes, he reached for Beelzebub's heart to make sure he was still on the outer layer. If Beelzebub realized he'd tracked down these pages, he'd want Mephistopheles to destroy them.

But they were gorgeous. And Beelzebub had written them.

Angels hadn't signed their names to their music back then. Music was a gift to God, and stamping your identity on a gift was rude. He gave you talent, and you gave back a creation. Or He gave you intelligence, and you gave back a scholarly perspective. Signing your name to music or a monograph meant taking credit for a thing God had made.

Beelzebub would certainly want this immolated. Yet Mephistopheles had remembered this melody for thousands of years, and once more, he could see it. Except his eyes were burning. He should be analyzing it, and instead he was reveling in the memory.

He'd recalled this passage incorrectly. That must be why he felt so uneasy. A Cherub's memory ought to be perfect.

From across the layers, Beelzebub sent fire. That also left Mephistopheles uneasy. Detecting the disquiet, Beelzebub had attempted to steady him, but Cherubim were the steady ones. Everything was in reverse.

Behind him, Israfel strummed a guitar.

His feathers flared. "Don't."

"It's a well-written song." She focused on the pages. "I shouldn't have neglected this piece for so long. That's an injustice I can set to rights."

He didn't even take the opening to inflame her about injustice. Mephistopheles backed away from the desk, and with an unimpeded view, she played through from the top.

Longing swelled. Back then, Beelzebub—Belazael—had been so excited about this song, so impatient for it to be played. Mistofiel had offered suggestions about the lyrics, resting alongside his Seraph while Belazael had gotten ever more thrilled with using music to express love to his Father and Creator. There'd been other Seraphim with them, too: Mistofiel's two other primaries that he'd abandoned after election to the Maskim, when Beelzebub demanded Mephistopheles' full focus and bestowed his full attention in return.

Back then, Belazael had played snippets as he worked through the difficult parts. Closing his eyes, Mistofiel had contemplated what music meant as a part of creation. Why they could make it. What they ought to do with it. Why it had the effect of kindling even a Cherub's soul.

It seemed this hymn hadn't been played since. Not because the Heavenly Host were avoiding a song written by a demon, but because they'd composed better afterward. Israfel was merely mocking Mephistopheles and the to-her-unknown composer: it wasn't well-written. It was predictable, the transitions awkward and the progressions pedestrian. Back then, Mistofiel should have realized that one day he'd find it embarrassing even to listen to.

Destroying it was the right thing to do, only Mephistopheles stayed in place, eyes riveted to the page as he tracked Israfel's notes on their long march to the double bar.

With flames curling from her hair, she ended with a flourish. "Thank you for finding that. I should get it back into rotation. You don't know who wrote it?"

Mephistopheles tried to sound natural. "It was ignorant of us not to sign our names to those early pieces."

Israfel huffed. "Until Lucifer did it."

Mephistopheles said, "A work of that caliber was going to be recognized as his."

"Oh, he took no chances that we wouldn't recognize it." Israfel returned the music to its place on the shelf. "It wasn't enough to leave us to figure out his authorship. No, he had to give it a title, then sign his name on the first *and* on the last pages, just in case we forgot the beginning by the time we reached the end."

Mephistopheles said, "He absolutely wanted to hear us say he'd bested everyone else's compositional skills the one and only time he deigned to put a pen to paper."

Israfel turned to him, eyes blazing. "Wasn't that special of him? I'm the Angel of Music, but do I have the best hymn to my credit?

No. He showed everyone up, then dusted off his hands and moved on to the next thing."

Mephistopheles matched her glare. "How is that fair?"

"It's not."

He snickered. "One assumes it was with great pleasure you burned the manuscript."

"I did no such thing." Her wings vibrated. "After he named himself as the composer and gave it a title, everyone else did the same. The original sheet music is catalogued and filed along with every other piece because it stands at the fulcrum of musical history."

Mephistopheles shook his head. "Which, again, isn't fair. Moreover, once he's granted amnesty, he's going to breeze in here and demand your copy so he can stage a second performance."

Her wings spread. "It was always a performance for him. He handed Gabriel a descant that made Gabriel's feathers stand on end, then gave me a musical line that would take everything in my power to play, and he had a cadenza of his own. We did our best, though, because back then, he was the star, and we all wanted his approval."

Mephistopheles said, "Only we never got it, did we?"

He shouldn't have said that. If the faintest whisper of an echo of those words escaped this acoustically-perfect library, Lucifer would chain Mephistopheles in the ice fields and use his potential release as leverage against Beelzebub for the remainder of eternity.

Israfel snarled, "Even God didn't get Lucifer's approval, so you and I? We never stood a chance."

Her anger was brilliant, and it offered so many handholds for a Cherub seeking out discontentment. Mephistopheles said, "And for all that, he'll be getting welcomed back into Heaven anyhow."

Israfel glared at him. "God's presumed generosity is none of my business, and it neither requires nor would obtain my sanction. Is there anything else you want before I send you back?"

She was beautiful in the daylight, beautiful in her anger and beautiful in her unsettled resentment of a future that Mephistopheles had no delusion would come to fruition. The only thing that could make her more beautiful was the act of renouncing her allegiance, but Mephistopheles had no delusion he could make that come to fruition, either. He'd leave the rest to his master.

He said, "Since you preserved the manuscript of my master's hymn, I request to see 'All Praise to My Creator.'"

"No." Her soul was fire, but her smile was ice. "You can return now," and Mephistopheles found himself meeting his own eyes in a mirror at the Hilbert Hotel.

He reached for Beelzebub's heart first, then sent a message to Lucifer. *Sir, I have a target for you.*

Mephistopheles could keep his focus there: on Israfel, and not on what he'd looked up in her library, and certainly not the way his Seraph's hymn still echoed through the acoustic perfection of his thoughts.

In the first two minutes of Satan's "tour," a cheerful Raphael established himself as thoroughly useless for a direct access point. Satan would have to use him as a bridge to others.

Looking over a cliff at a waterfall, Satan said. "Where's Gabriel?"

"Last I heard, with Jesus's mother." Raphael gestured at one of the mountains. "We should visit that peak next. I love the view from this angle, but from above, you get a better vantage on the river."

Rivers and mountains meant exactly nothing in an angelic war, but Satan agreed that they should see something Raphael found so exciting. Shortly they were on another cliff.

"Perhaps Gabriel can join us. I'm sure he'd enjoy the view as well."

"He does." Raphael was frustratingly clueless. "He always finds something interesting about the action of water and stone on a geologic timeline."

As if a pretty rock mattered to angels. "Invite him so he can see it."

After a second's silence, Raphael said, "He's involved in something, but he'll join us when he's ready."

His tone piqued Satan's curiosity. Was that...unease? Concern?

Raphael continued showing Satan any number of kitschy landscapes. Satan said, "Let's visit the place where Gabriel fought the Leviathan. Have him come so we can reminisce about that."

Raphael grinned. "He's not going there, trust me."

Satan snickered. "He finds it that shameful?"

Raphael flexed his wings. "I don't know that he finds it shameful as much as he doesn't want to revisit it."

Satan murmured, "He did the same after Sodom, getting humiliated in a female form and never switching back to it. Although the whole business with being in a body for a year was the utmost indignity, and he returned to that site for hundreds of years."

Raphael smiled with the sun in his eyes, as non-offended as if Satan had admired the daisies. "Gabriel has many facets."

A similar jab about Mephistopheles would have had Beelzebub at the speaker's throat before the sentence finished. Would nothing get to him?

Raphael was saying, "I think that rock was where—" when abruptly his feathers burst into flame. "Sorry, we need to go," and flashed Satan to the gazebo outside the Hilbert Hotel.

Raphael raced to where Saraquael was on his knees on the grass, and he dived straight through a cluster of seekers. "Everyone, get back! And summon— Oh, you're here."

Michael flashed in. "Clear the area! I want this field as sterile as we can make it. Uriel, do we need to move him?"

Since Michael wanted a sterile field, Satan stepped closer to the action. There under a Guard was—well, an angel, but not an angel. A soul, but in no condition Satan had ever seen. Saraquael knelt, his clothing burnt, his feathers pitted. At his side was a colorless Uriel, shedding devastation. Raphael was already filling the Guarded area with healing light. Squatting, but with his back to

Satan, was—Ataf?

Shock spiked through Satan. Rahab.

Rage followed the shock because Rahab deserved whatever he'd done to himself. He'd failed to stop the Israelites from escaping Pharaoh. He'd failed to stop Moses from receiving the Law on Sinai. He'd failed to retain his place on the Maskim. He'd gone under the lake to escape his own inadequacy, and in doing so, burnt himself into nonexistence. Except he still existed, so he'd failed to do that, too.

Yet Ataf was here, scorched as much as Saraquael. Had they worked together to dredge the lake?

Ataf had lost his rank because of Rahab. He'd shrieked for weeks with the pain searing through their unbreakable bond as Rahab burned and dissolved.

It was possible Ataf wanted Rahab revived so he could do something worse. Satan wasn't sure what, but if he'd been that thoroughly disgraced, he would have spent the last three thousand years coming up with something worse.

Michael got down alongside Saraquael. "Is this all of him?"

Saraquael rasped, "All that's left," and coughed. "I couldn't. Couldn't seek him."

He coughed harder. Raphael said, "I'll help you in a minute."

Saraquael waved him down and switched to projecting. His team of seekers plus the demonic team (bipartisan seeking?) hadn't been able to pinpoint a location. Then a Special Ops officer had suggested recruiting a Throne for a reason that escaped Satan, but which made Michael sit up. Whatever they'd done, it involved Uriel using Ataf along with Rahab's other two bonded Seraphim to triangulate Rahab's position. Saraquael and Ataf had gone under the lake, and *this* was what they'd recovered.

Preternaturally still and lacking his normal color, Ataf sat on his heels. Raphael, by contrast, was movement itself, his golden light spinning within the Guard, his hands sliding over the outside, his feathers flexing, his facial expression altering as though he were having a conversation with what he was attempting to heal.

Gabriel appeared onsite, and Raphael's light intensified.

Satan snorted. "It's been three thousand years. You're going to fail."

Michael snapped, "Shut up. We're doing what we can."

With a sigh, Satan folded his arms. "Maybe if you scoop him into a basin and slosh him over the steps at the Throne of Glory, your owner will assist."

Gabriel's voice was low. "The first step is stabilizing him, and I assure you, everyone has been praying the entire time."

Satan huffed. "It doesn't surprise me that the Tyrant hasn't answered. I wouldn't answer for this one, either."

No one working on Rahab responded. Neither did Rahab respond. There were occasional suggestions to one another, and Raphael's other two primaries arrived to power him, but to no avail.

Mephistopheles' voice appeared in his head. *Sir? I have a target for you.*

Satan focused on the shapeless form of Rahab as Uriel trickled purple energy into the miasma. *Proceed.*

A moment after, Satan had a summary of Israfel's weakness and attitude: the demons' presence offended her sense of justice. Mephistopheles' bold assurance of redemption further offended it. Satan held in his mind the image of Israfel, rigid with outrage.

Noted. Identify a few more candidates.

Yes, sir.

Since Raphael would be of no leverage against Gabriel, perhaps Israfel would.

Saraquael cried out, and Raphael's feathers flared. Satan pushed closer just as the material inside the Guard quivered, and then with a shudder, it coalesced as the subtle body of an angel.

Gabriel blew off a long breath. Saraquael slumped, face in his hands.

Ataf's wings were shaking. "You...did it."

"We've forced him back into cohesion." Raphael's voice broke. "He's still in trouble, just not formless."

Satan couldn't detect Rahab's signature, but he had a frame again, yanked back from as close to nonexistence as he'd been able to force himself.

Ataf touched the Guard. "Is it safe to take this down? Do it."

Saraquael brought down the Guard, and Ataf extended a hand. He pressed his palm to the nearest wing, then shuddered with a sob.

Satan's feathers spread.

Ataf dropped onto Rahab, arms around him, face buried in his wings, shoulders jerking. Uriel draped over Ataf's back.

Annoyance burgeoned up within Satan, but Gabriel said, "Come with me," and tried to flash him away.

Satan whirled at him, shedding sparks.

Gabriel's eyes were a soft grey, his wings mottled. His tone of voice matched his color. "Ataf's tears don't reflect on you. Let them be restored to one another."

Satan glared at him. "What would you know about what he's going through?"

"I've never experienced anything of the like." Gabriel's attention flickered to the scene. "Yet even I can conclude the release of tension and grief would be overwhelming."

Satan looked over his shoulder. Raphael was clasping Ataf's hand.

Michael projected a question to Uriel, who responded in the affirmative. Then Michael looked at Gabriel, who replied, "The hotel should expand to accommodate."

"Not yet." Raphael looked up. "Right now, I'm bringing both of them to Ataf's quarters, and we'll continue working there." He met Gabriel's eyes, and again Satan caught the faintest glint of concern. "You know where to find me if you need me."

Satan glanced at Gabriel sidelong. "And you know where he'll be. He'll be with me."

Chapter Seven

ONCE AWAY FROM THE Hilbert Hotel, Lucifer said, "What did you expect us to do for a week?"

Since Gabriel had taken no notice of the itinerary, he flashed them to a crowded plaza. With an attention to detail Gabriel approved of, they'd established a Visitor's Center with brochures. Program in hand, Gabriel asked a nearby angel to give them a tour.

"The first problem we faced was how every human culture has its own style of celebration," the angel said, leading them in flight over the level. "A week-long feast seemed a good way to meet most expectations. We're setting up stations all around this layer of Heaven so the *viatores* can choose from a wide range of experiences." The angel's eyes were bright. "Everything from bronze age tribes roasting auroch meat to haute cuisine on square porcelain plates, we'll have it."

Gabriel said, "Pardon me, but *viatores*?"

Lucifer said in Latin, "Have you forgotten your languages?"

Gabriel replied, also in Latin, "I haven't forgotten a thing, but I didn't realize your people were considered *travelers*."

The angel's eyes shifted. "We chose a term that wasn't off-putting."

Lucifer snickered. "You needed a euphemism for 'damned'."

The angel flinched. Gabriel flew closer. "Never mind him. Please continue."

The welcome committee had compiled quite a program in a very short period of time, or maybe it had been a long period of time and Gabriel had been too engrossed in prayer to notice. Since the granting of Abraham's request, this entire level of Heaven had been turned into festival grounds.

Their guide flashed them to a stage. "Israfel was excited to expand our initial plan for a performance into a full-blown music festival, so now we'll host concerts and performances—thousands of them—covering all styles of music." Then, flashing them to a stadium, the guide said, "We're going to have competitions and tournaments—as if it's a World Series that covers not only the world, but all of time, in every sport. If the *viatores* want to compete or perform, they should sign up to do so."

Lucifer folded his arms and tossed his head so his platinum hair shifted around his face. "Our people are excellent competitors. I'm not sure your people will want that."

Gabriel furrowed his brow. "Why not?"

Lucifer regarded him with a mixture of surprise and...irritation? "We're going to win."

"As long as it's a fair competition, any experts should be glad of the chance to expand their skill set." Gabriel was supposed to be softening Lucifer up, but if anything, he was making Lucifer more jagged. "Also, some events will require a cooperative effort, which likewise would expand any competitors' overall skill."

Based on Lucifer's dubious gaze, Gabriel had not impressed him. "Why participate in a cooperative effort?"

Gabriel opened his hands. "For an activity like mountain-climbing, it's the squad against the shared challenge. Everyone wins or everyone loses."

The retrieval of Rahab had been a cooperative effort. A demon had alerted them to the need. The angels had created a response team. The demons had added seekers to the project. Special Ops had then brought in a Throne who leveraged a technique Gabriel had derived from a similar process used by the Maskim. Everyone won together, or everyone lost together.

He reached for Raphael. *Any improvement?*

Not yet, but one of Rahab's other Seraphim is a healer. She's taken over. He sounded spent. A moment after, he added, *Be careful.*

Gabriel sent, *I won't need to be careful. Recall Israfel's assessment of my ability to flirt.*

Although Raphael said nothing else, Gabriel detected stubborn relief: Raphael wanted him to fail.

Lucifer was saying, "How do you determine the best in a field when it's a cooperative effort?"

Gabriel tilted his head. "The best is the one who supports the needs of the team every time, even at cost of individual recognition."

Lucifer straightened his innermost feathers. "Pointless."

On the festival's first day, the place was still under construction: fairgrounds, stadiums, concert halls, playing fields, amusement parks, and so much more. Dotting the skylines were banners and rainbows and towering kinetic sculptures. On the ground were more hotels, habitats, and plazas of apartments. There were zoos and arboretums and museums and amusement parks. They had lecture halls and worship spaces. Some wiseacre had cordoned off a field and turned it into a "Renaissance Festival," run by individuals who'd lived in Renaissance Europe. Oh, and there were theaters. Theaters for performing stage plays, and also theaters for movies and other types of light shows.

Wherever they went, Lucifer attracted attention. Compared to everyone around them, his gestures were broader, his quips funnier, and his laughter louder. They came across a botanic garden with a hedge maze, where Lucifer observed that he could fly over it to give everyone directions, so Gabriel flashed him away to the flowers. There Lucifer pointed out which petals worked well for tea and which for poison, and which made sweet poison that tasted like tea.

There were angelic games, too, not just human ones—contests for spinning atoms, creating light shows, and an escape room designed by Special Ops. The officer at the door declared with enthusiasm, "No one's escaped it yet."

A demon approached Gabriel, saw Lucifer alongside, and fled. *Semifallen?* Perhaps Michael might be right that the fallen were seeking a means of return.

Gabriel dismissed their guide with, "Thank you. We'll take it from here," and the angel looked more than relieved to hear it.

Lucifer snorted. "What, no tip?"

Gabriel said to the angel, "Never accept criticism from someone you wouldn't seek out for advice."

Lucifer cocked his head. "As tips go, that's pretty handy, but I can't endorse. That would have undone too many of our snares."

They reached an outdoor kitchen where a dozen humans were cooking. Gabriel took on a human form, and momentarily he bowed to the woman in charge. Although she looked to be in young adulthood, Gabriel said, "Abuela, would you permit me to help?"

Lucifer projected nausea into Gabriel's mind, and Gabriel fought a grin. Abuela glared at the demon, her eyes narrow. "He doesn't touch a thing."

Lucifer sounded disgusted. "We are of one accord."

She made a furious noise. "We are nothing of the sort."

Abuela set Gabriel at a separate table, never taking her eyes off Lucifer. *Please tell her it's allowed,* Gabriel prayed, and God acknowledged.

The family was making tamales—a couple hundred dozen, according to one of Abuela's daughters, who was herself an abuela and who looked neither older nor younger than her mother. This aspect of Heaven had taken time to get used to: no elderly, no children, no babies, unless someone chose to be that age.

Meanwhile, the family chattered as they filled and wrapped tamales and loaded the steamer baskets. Gabriel manifested a chef's knife and started mincing garlic. "I love cooking."

Lucifer folded his arms. "And they call me arrogant?"

Gabriel paused. "Your implication being that I'm arrogant?"

"You spent less than one year in a body, yet you preen as though that makes you a world class chef." Lucifer gestured to the family. "Meanwhile creatures like your Abuela spent entire decades doing it."

Unnerved, Gabriel returned to the garlic. "Nothing I said implied mastery. Although I enjoy it, I'd be terrible at cooking. I used to study what Mary did so I could transcribe her recipes, but for her, it was all technique. A smidge of this, no, a bit more, cut this thing down, oh, and that needs something else."

Lucifer sat on the table's edge, earning another glare from Abuela. Gabriel might need to remove him sooner rather than later. "And after you recorded all her techniques...?"

Gabriel huffed. "I'd still be inadequate. If I were to try anything, it would be baking. Baking is scientific, with everything measured and proportioned. Cooking is more of a Seraph's realm. 'Hey, I have all these potatoes, a handful of cloves, a sea cucumber, and two cups of spelt. I wonder whether I can fry them up with some honey.'"

Raphael would have laughed. Instead, Lucifer lowered his voice. "I assure you, as a Seraph, I've never entertained any such thought."

Gabriel frowned. "I concede. Your thoughts were more like, 'I have two political parties at one another's throats, and a public crisis about to slide down the hill, so I'll heat things up with an earthquake.'"

Lucifer snickered. "You got dark. I thought we were talking about dinner."

Gabriel's mouth twitched. "You're never talking about the thing you're talking about."

Gabriel spread masa in corn husks, filled and rolled the tamales, then tied them up to stand in the steamer baskets.

Lucifer said, "Clarify for me, because you just contradicted yourself. You think you're terrible at cooking, yet you enjoy doing it?"

Gabriel frowned. "Clarify for me, too, because you created a contradiction where there was none. Do you only enjoy things you excel at?"

Lucifer didn't answer. Maybe he didn't enjoy anything anymore.

Regardless, Lucifer's presence was dampening the family's joy, so Gabriel thanked Abuela for the chance to cook with her. Then, to Lucifer, he said, "Let's fly over the layer. If we find anything you want to investigate, we can land," and he spread his wings.

With Lucifer at his side, Gabriel focused on the air, on the wind. He'd never been much for aerobatics, but Raphael loved it enough that Gabriel had learned a few tricks. They reached hill country with rougher skies, and Gabriel executed a barrel-roll the way Raphael had taught him. Then Lucifer shot ahead and pulled off a much more complicated version of the same, all twelve wings slicing open and shut as he corkscrewed through the sky.

At least Gabriel could fly fast, so he took off after Lucifer, who bent his head to look at Gabriel in his wake.

He can't fly in Hell. The caverns didn't offer this kind of freedom. Maybe the ice fields, but every time Gabriel had been there, it had been so stormy. Although for true aerobatics, perhaps the tumult increased the pleasure. It certainly did for Remiel, who used to gasp in excitement over every hurricane or typhoon. She'd ride the winds while they gathered strength over the ocean, then diminish them before they contacted human habitations.

Gabriel shot straight up, and Lucifer coiled around his path, wingtips trailing fire and light as he created a tunnel. Lucifer arched his neck and then curved his wings to tighten the helix.

Back before the Winnowing, Gabriel would have been shedding admiration and planning a course of colored light that darted in and out of Lucifer's projected pathway. They'd have painted the horizon with beauty and joy, warp and weft, and then, flush with exhaustion, they'd have landed on a hilltop to watch the colors bleed into one another.

With a burst of energy, Gabriel trailed light of his own, and now they were creating art. His straight strokes shimmered with silver and blue while Lucifer changed up his to gleam gold and orange. The colors moved through one another, and Gabriel tried to predict what pattern Lucifer was creating so he could juxtapose it with his own. It had been so long since Gabriel had done one of these. Usually the fliers combining their light were Raphael and Israfel, with Gabriel or Ophaniel on the ground giving feedback on who was designing what.

In days long past, Gabriel would have opened up his mind for Lucifer to spin out his flight plan. To do that, though, required trust. It required giving Lucifer access to his thoughts and Lucifer permitting access to his...which in a way meant Lucifer had to trust him, too.

Trust, or manipulate. Lucifer would let Gabriel into the anteroom of his thoughts and shield his real intentions. This was art, not spiritual formation. If Gabriel opened up, though, he didn't have the power to say what God had, "This far and no further."

For now, Gabriel worked into Lucifer's pattern with a predictable backdrop so Lucifer could perform the creative work. That was so boring, though. Gabriel expanded the canvas to frame it in three dimensions. What would it look like from this angle? What about from there? From overhead, it would give one impression, whereas from the sides, it might mean something else.

Lucifer realized what Gabriel was doing, and he expanded his light streamers in every direction. Oh, so much power. Now they were sparkling, shimmering. Lucifer inverted some of the light so it absorbed the other colors, and then he dove back through the light Gabriel had made, dragging it so it stretched. Gabriel exclaimed with surprise, and Lucifer faced him, eyes glowing green, radiance spreading in all directions.

Wide-eyed, Gabriel cast shining spheres from his hands, punctuating the sky.

Lucifer smiled—and was that real? Was he enjoying the development of art, the movement of air, the shedding of light? For the first time in centuries, had he flushed with the joy of creation instead of destruction?

Brilliant with movement, Lucifer seized Gabriel by the shoulders, then wrenched him into a spin.

In a panic, Gabriel pushed but couldn't get free. Lucifer's grip was tight—he was trapped—immobilized—until fire crashed into the pair of them and slammed Gabriel to the ground.

He rolled on his shoulder and flipped upright in time to see

Israfel facing Lucifer with her wings spread. Her fire rolled over the landscape while behind her blazed the kaleidoscope of the horizon.

Lucifer hovered, twelve wings unfurled, sword blazing. Flames encircled his head, and gone was that spark in his eyes. His face was hard, his body tight.

He blasted Israfel. Sword raised, she shielded Gabriel, but he felt the impact, and he braced her through their bond.

She was livid. She was protective. She was fire, and she was facing down a Seraph a dozen times stronger.

Michael!

Gabriel directed Israfel's defenses, but Lucifer attacked faster and harder than Gabriel could deflect. He felt her take a hit, then another—and then Michael was forcing them apart.

With Israfel still on her feet—somehow—Gabriel wrapped his wings around her. Saraquael arrived at Michael's side and looked from Lucifer to Israfel and back again.

Israfel snapped, "Secure him. I'm fine."

Her clothes and hair were smoldering, and her pain backwashed through Gabriel enough to make his vision blur. Even so, she was braced to keep fighting.

Michael was in full armor, sword drawn. "*This* is how you deal with hospitality?"

Lucifer snarled back, "And this is how you treat your guests? With an unprovoked attack while we were minding our own business?" He swung out a hand to take in the sky painting as shame churned in Gabriel's stomach. For miles, everyone would see how Gabriel and Lucifer had played with color and the wind—and with each other.

Israfel exclaimed, "You seized Gabriel and wouldn't let him go!"

Gabriel hadn't realized she was watching. Joy must have frothed up through their bond like the tangy spice of snake venom. When fear overwhelmed his joy, she'd blown in to protect him.

Lucifer squared his shoulders. "I didn't seize him."

Lucifer had been face to face with Gabriel, hands clamped on his shoulders. It was startling and terrifying, but had it been violent?

Or had it just been Lucifer taking whatever he wanted?

Because the moment before, on his face, that seemed like a soul uncurling, eyes to the sun and chains forgotten.

Israfel snorted. "It looked and felt just like restraint."

Michael raised a hand. "I don't care what it looked and felt like. Both of you, stand down." He turned to Lucifer. "Let me sort this out so I don't have to confine you to quarters." To Israfel: "Step back and let Gabriel talk to me." Then, to Gabriel: "Well?"

With a look at Lucifer, Gabriel swallowed. "I don't know."

Lucifer had grasped and immobilized him. Whether that was Lucifer in the act of harm or Lucifer in the act of forgetting himself...there was no evidence, no hypothesis, no means of testing.

Michael's eyes traveled over Gabriel, and Gabriel tried not to flinch. Israfel believed Gabriel couldn't identify a flirt unless the flirter wrote it across the sky. Here they stood canopied by a horizon wrapped in ribbons, visible to all of Hell and half of Heaven, and Gabriel still couldn't codify it.

Lucifer glared at Gabriel. "Don't prevaricate. Did I attack you? Or was it instead your Seraph who attacked us both?"

Michael had a level glare, and Israfel was burning both inside and outside Gabriel's heart. Gabriel averted his gaze from the colors. "I can't speak to your intentions. I didn't expect you to lay hands on me, and I didn't expect you not to let me go."

Israfel narrowed her eyes. "We don't need the scientific method."

Lucifer said, "And yet, doesn't this situation seem just a little unfair?"

His words cranked up the fire in Israfel. Gabriel interjected, "She felt my fear and responded to assist."

Lucifer held Israfel's gaze. "If I were really a threat to Gabriel, wouldn't your master intervene on his behalf? Wouldn't a servant as faithful as Gabriel deserve his owner's protection?"

With Israfel about to detonate, Gabriel said, "Given how I reacted, Israfel responded correctly. If you're angry, it should be with me for misjudging your intentions."

Michael said, "And yet, since you reacted to what sounds like a threat, no one's angry with you, either." Michael turned to Lucifer. "Whatever you wanted to achieve, it's over."

Lucifer gestured toward the sky. "I wanted to achieve artwork."

He hadn't. Or at least, artwork wasn't all he'd achieved. For a moment, Lucifer had achieved forgetfulness. He'd forgotten his vendetta against God, forgotten his pain, forgotten his jealousy. Forgotten himself.

It was a start, but Gabriel hadn't been able to entice him further than one selfless moment.

Michael leveled a glare on Lucifer that said everything his voice held back. "By all means, remain and enjoy your artwork." He turned to Israfel, who was still at a firm simmer. "Please come with me."

When Michael and Israfel flashed away, Gabriel went with them.

Chapter Eight

Michael brought Israfel to his office deep in the heart of Heaven, momentarily followed by Saraquael and, surprisingly, by Gabriel.

"I thought you'd remain with your target." That came out flatter than Michael intended. "You had him working pretty well with you, until he turned back into a jerk."

Saraquael approached Israfel, his hands glowing gold. "Let me help." She didn't push him off as he hovered his palms over her burns.

Eyes averted, Gabriel shifted his weight and tightened his wings around himself. "I have no idea what I accomplished, but it wasn't anything useful."

Looking up without stopping his healing work, Saraquael sparkled. "It was beautiful, though. A bit free-form for a sky painting, but he hadn't done one for a while."

Israfel muttered, "And naturally, the first time he does one in thousands of years, it's terrific."

Saraquael said, "I assume Gabriel had something to do with that."

Michael couldn't name the emotions ricocheting around Israfel, but she seemed to be fighting herself. He said, "Don't let him get you worked up. Protecting Gabriel was the right thing, and if you were mistaken about Satan's intentions, it's hardly without a cause."

From Gabriel came a soft, "I appreciate it, too. He did have me pinned. While I didn't pick up any negative intentions, I'm not an art tool, and he doesn't get to wield me like a paintbrush."

That drew Michael up short. Saraquael smirked. "Don't think you're anything special just because he tried to use you. He uses everyone."

Israfel said, "He tried to use God."

That also drew Michael up short, but Gabriel projected agreement. "I think that's when things capsized for him, when he tried to make God's gifts seem like that meant he deserved them, rather than a testament to God's generosity."

Israfel glared at Gabriel, who started, then corrected, "God can be as generous as He wants—it doesn't make us great."

Israfel snapped, "That's not what I meant."

Saraquael looked surprised, as if now he, too, wanted to know what she meant. "I think that patched you up okay."

Israfel flexed her wings, then raised one arm to reveal a burn Saraquael hadn't addressed, so he pressed his hand to her side. Gabriel said, "I'm sorry you got hurt, but thank you."

Folding his arms, Michael looked down. "I should have been closer."

"I should have had a better plan." Gabriel shook his head. "We've got six more days. I'll need to make efficient use of them."

Israfel stretched as Saraquael inspected her again. "Thanks. You got it all."

Michael said, "If everything's settled here, then, Saraquael, come with me. You two can stay and plan as long as you like."

Michael brought Saraquael directly to Ataf's quarters, where the room had enlarged around the crowd of angels and demons. Ataf crouched in the corner, knees against his chest, wings up. Raphael slumped in exhaustion while at his side, Uriel lay in a puddle of wings, knees to the wall, staring at the ceiling. A demonic Seraph and two other demons had assumed their healing work.

Saraquael approached Rahab, but the nearest Seraph stepped in between.

Ataf snapped, "Let him near. He was the first to touch Rahab in three thousand years, so keep your hands to yourself."

Saraquael inclined his head. "I won't disturb him. I wanted to compare to how he was when last I saw him."

Raphael said, "He's improving, but it's slow."

"He doesn't want to improve." Ataf's voice was bitter. "He went under the lake because he wanted everything to stop. Well, everything doesn't stop, but he's going to fight the only way he can, by dissolving back into nothing."

Uriel projected to Michael, *Ataf's correct. I've been trying to heal his spirit, but pinning himself in the lake was an act of despair. He's still despondent.*

Michael shuddered. Hastle had done the same. The living death trap, no matter what it would have done to him, had seemed superior to whatever future lay among the demons.

Michael said, "If he awakens, then Uriel, be on standby in case what he needs is a Throne. In the only other situation like this that I know about, the angel who broke through was someone who'd never been a soldier."

Without sitting up, Uriel indicated agreement.

Satan hadn't claimed any Thrones. All Uriel ever said was that Satan tried, but from other reports, it sounded as if Uriel had united the choir and kept them focused the way it mattered.

Michael flashed to the temple where Danel worshipped and Hastle huddled at the back, staring at nothing while making no response to the alternating invocations.

A Throne might be what it took to rouse Hastle, as well. But for now, Michael would let him listen.

For that matter, Michael would remain for a time, too. Listening.

Remiel sat with a notebook and watercolor pencils before the dissolving colors of Gabriel's sky.

She raced its dissolution in an attempt to make it permanent.

This wasn't artwork because it wasn't planned. It had no resonance, except for the peculiar way it resonated within her. Gabriel was staring down the gun barrel of grief and, instead of pleading, was waiting for the click of the safety and the cock of the hammer.

It took too long to select the correct color pencil, so Remiel started changing the color of the one in her hand, altering it whenever she found difference between her work and Gabriel's. She couldn't bring herself to say Satan's. If Mary's outrageous plan resulted in a bond, she'd wait fifty years and ask if a grieving Gabriel wanted a reminder of their brief oneness. He might hunger for it by then. If not, she'd destroy it. Her drawing wouldn't be the first beautiful thing incinerated because of Satan's recalcitrance.

In her heart, Camael tugged, and Remiel took down her resistance so he could join her.

She felt him arrive at her back. The sky was fading too fast for her to stop working, starting toward the center where their design had begun and then moving outward and upward. Her page was two-dimensional and the light show in three, so she expanded it into other layers and drew upward, downward, depthward.

Camael said, "Which part is Lucifer's?"

"I'm not trying to tease it apart."

"I agree. Some things are meant to be blended. I'm just surprised you're admiring his work."

Remiel kept her voice low. "I always acknowledge your side's work. That makes it easier to figure out what my side needs to do."

Camael peered over her shoulder, so close her heart tremored. "Aren't you tired of always playing defense?"

At the end, it hadn't been a defensive action. The Second Coming felt finally like an offensive. God had set Michael loose to do whatever he wanted in terms of flushing out their enemies from every pocket of Creation, and Michael in turn had given Remiel command of an army. And oh, the planning? The relief of not having to react to attacks when and where the enemy chose to hold them? The sheer pleasure of being able to choose battlegrounds advantageous to their side?

For aeons, they'd waged only a defensive war against Satan's incursions. At long last, they'd made an incursion of their own and driven him back. Back all the way to the border of Hell, then back beyond it, and in one glorious moment, Remiel had watched with stunned amazement as finally, finally, Michael had locked the doors.

Letting them out again put everyone in the same defensive position, and Remiel yearned for that moment when she'd been able to flex her wings and her authority to safeguard the human race the way she'd always craved.

Human souls hadn't been part of that army. Maybe that explained Abraham's bargaining and Mary's behind-the-scenes machinations. They wanted to go on the offensive, too. Except Mary's plan still required an angel.

Camael said, "I used to be able to feel when you were thinking this deeply."

Remiel said, "As you might have noticed, I'm working against the clock."

Weren't they all? Seven days together—now a little under six. After which, well, eternity was a long time.

Camael said, "I could bring up a wind and destroy it so you'll pay attention to me."

Remiel huffed. "Once that happens, I have no reason to stay, so it's up to you. You're the one who wanted to see me, and you're the one who can make me leave."

That was a lot more control than she ought to give him. Nivalis would call that "setting boundaries," but any ultimatum gave away your power.

Even so, Camael decided not to test her. He sat alongside to watch. "I didn't realize you still were drawing."

"I didn't realize you weren't."

Camael sounded testy. "I could."

Remiel gestured, and a sketchpad appeared on his lap.

Silence for several minutes. Camael's jab about being able to disperse the sky with wind had nudged Remiel to wonder what would happen if she removed all entropy from this area. Would nothing dispel? Forever, would this sky remain as a tribute of its own? Or would the very lack of vibration mean the light's immediate extinguishment?

A moment after, she realized Camael's silence meant he was drawing, too, only he was selecting colors and trying to force the image into a specific form. Gabriel should have planned it, of course. He hadn't. He'd accepted Satan's overture to paint, which again had put him in a position of responding rather than initiating.

Camael glanced at her work. "You're not de-emphasizing Lucifer's contribution. Why are you doing this at all?" He dissolved the notebook on his lap. "This is pointless, and you're using it to ignore me."

Long ago, it would have been enough to be together. If they'd been on this hill, watercoloring a sky that itself had been watercolored, there would have been a communion so intense that without realizing it, each would have created part of the same picture, and they'd have looked up at the end to discover they'd unconsciously replicated the entire thing.

Remiel at last made herself say, "What do you want from me?"

The image had faded out at the center, and now the edges were smearing away, too. She couldn't document an image she could no longer see, but she kept her hand poised, just in case.

Camael said, "I imagine the same thing you want from me."

"The thing we can't have." Her gaze stayed on the sky. "We've both had a lot of time to think this over. We're not identical anymore. I miss that, and since you're here, you miss that, too, but doesn't it hurt more when you see me and realize we're not the Irin? As in, never again. Nothing would be a good fit any longer."

Camael muttered, "I don't see why not."

He expected her to fit to him, which to be fair could work in that direction. Given free rein, he'd twist her until she existed as the same distortion of God's love that he did. She'd looked down that road and rejected it every time. Mary's hope, that Camael (and all the rest of them) could un-contort themselves into a reflection of

God's love the way they'd been at the start...well, Remiel rejected that, too. Not because she didn't want it, but because there was no way to achieve restoration without grace, and grace was the thing the demons denied. They didn't want it because it was a gift from God, and to make matters worse, the act of wanting grace was also a gift from God. To want to repent required the kind of grace that sanctified you. Telling the Holy Spirit, "No, keep your gift," meant confirming that you didn't want the gift that opened you to wanting more gifts.

Hence the adage among angels, you never refuse a gift from God. Accept it, and see what happens next. God was always a thoughtful gift-giver. He gave music and art and dance and questions and joy and the occasional long look in a mirror.

If the demons could somehow straighten out their souls, it would be like re-folding a bent paper clip. The spots of metal fatigue would remain. There would be lumps and unanticipated bends, and between Remiel and Camael, it still wouldn't be a perfect fit.

That was even before factoring in the ways Remiel had bent and unbent herself. Unfortunately, God wasn't the only one shaping her soul. Although God would have said, "Fortunately." God had given her free will so she could use it (another gift) and Remiel had responded by doing...this. Making herself what she was, all of which led to her sketching a vanishing sky alongside a vanishing twin.

Among the dissipating chunks of light, she found the final cluster Satan and Gabriel produced: a knot in the lower left quadrant where, when Remiel focused, she also felt Israfel's signature. That had been the place Satan had attacked Gabriel before Israfel had rocketed to his defense.

She set her pencil back to the work and hesitated, unwilling to document Gabriel's sparkling fear.

Except behind the fear lay something unexpected: joy.

She made a mark with her pencil, anticipating Gabriel's color, but it wasn't. It was one of Satan's.

For a heartbeat, Satan had touched light. Real light. Fun light.

His next act had been to seize and control, but right there in that moment had been purity. That was the last part of the image to dissolve from the sky.

She added it into the picture, then set down her pencil.

Camael said, "If you're done, now we can talk."

Pure joy.

For the first time, Remiel had hope. She hated it, but in her heart, that flicker was hope.

She flashed the picture into a locked vault in her home, then turned to meet Camael's eyes. Her own eyes. Her own capsized heart. "Now we can talk."

Still in Michael's conference room, Gabriel kept sensing Israfel strangely unbalanced. He tried several times pray with her, then when that didn't help, to mingle with her fire to empower himself enough to devise a strategy. Finally, she bridled with disgust. "If you're going to plan, you need Raphael to plot it."

Gabriel prompted, "Because I can't flirt?"

She huffed. "For someone who can't flirt, you attracted Satan's attention well enough."

That was a fair shot. Gabriel called to Raphael, *Whenever you can spare a few minutes away from Rahab, can you come plan with us?*, and he sent Raphael his confusion.

Shortly afterward, Raphael arrived. At his back was Uriel.

Eyes blazing, Gabriel snapped, "Why didn't you tell Mary to put back that hymn?"

Uriel went misty, projecting distress.

Israfel said, "Which hymn? The only—" She blazed. "Wait, *that* hymn?"

Sparkling with shock, Uriel discorporated.

Raphael said to Israfel, "How did Mary get it from your library?"

Gabriel said, "She took it from *my* library, looking for something she could use on the *viatores*. She didn't know what it was and wanted to know why I didn't sing it. And that question," he said, aiming his sharpened voice toward a dissociated Uriel, "was one you should have been able to answer. As in, 'Lucifer wrote that song, and nothing can compel Gabriel to sing it ever again.'"

Raphael's voice was low. "I'm surprised you didn't burn it."

Like the journals. It should have turned into ash.

"I stupidly preserved it as historical documentation, and one page got separated from the rest." Gabriel folded his arms. "However much you support Mary's plan, that was a step too far."

Shimmering with regret, hands wrung together, Uriel returned to view. "She requested you bare your soul to him. By comparison, the song didn't seem as much of an ask."

Israfel said, "You've destroyed it now, though?"

Gabriel's wings shivered. "I put it back in the library with the rest of the pages."

Raphael huffed. "You're too smart not to anticipate eight ways that can go wrong, but let's back up. You requested a planning meeting. What part of this is even *plan-able*?"

Gabriel flashed to the window so his back was to Uriel. It felt wrong. Everything felt wrong and had felt wrong since the moment Abraham asked an unreasonable question and God answered with an unreasonable yes. If Gabriel awakened to discover this was all a hallucination concocted by the demons, he'd just as soon believe that.

Except it was real. Every way he tested this, it was happening. So they had to move forward.

"To succeed, Gabriel needs Satan to find a bond entirely in his own interests." Israfel sounded bitter. "Just putting himself out there got Gabriel attacked. Or not—Gabriel thinks it wasn't an attack, only handsy nonsense by someone who thinks of himself as the great puppeteer."

Raphael fixed his attention on Gabriel. "For him to want you, the first step is a starvation diet. No fire for you."

Gabriel turned to him, eyebrows furrowed.

Raphael nodded. "A Cherub who's been isolated for a while tugs at a Seraph. There's an urge to protect you by firing you up and enlivening your spirit. Assuming Satan hasn't destroyed every part of his nature, you can fascinate Satan by getting cold inside and creating something of a vacuum that draws his fire to you."

Gabriel looked at Israfel, who pursed her lips. "Yeah, after one of you has had your face stuck in research for a week, when you're overstocked with ideas and shaking a bit, I want to rush in and breathe life into you."

Blinking, Gabriel said, "Why didn't I know that?"

Israfel huffed. "Because you never thought it worth paying attention to. The hardest part of that year you were away was knowing you needed help and being unable to give it."

Gabriel frowned. "Was that why Lucifer tried to bond me out by the bonfire?"

Raphael said, "I assume he wanted to bond you to help himself, not as a work of mercy."

"Granted." Gabriel rubbed his chin. "So you're saying, if I get fire-starved, he'll detect that?"

Israfel looked nauseated. "I don't want him to detect that. Everything about this plan leaves me wanting to get in between and defend you. What would he be doing to you right now if I hadn't freed you?"

Anything. The most rational answer was that Lucifer would have forced Gabriel to create more lightwork in exact lockstep with his own, but after the first minute, then what? Even if the initial impulse were artistic, Lucifer had never been one to let go of an advantage.

Leaning against the window, Gabriel said, "The problem with fire-starving me is that I don't have a week to get cold and then a few more days to soften Lucifer up."

Raphael shrugged. "We can prime you. I can prime you," he corrected when Israfel glared at him. "Israfel doesn't want to participate. While I don't like this, either, I want you set up for success. I've been thinking about when we first bonded, and the chief elements were newness, time, and familiarity."

Israfel said, "Trust."

"Trust," Raphael amended. "You were telling me all sorts of interesting things about the world, and every time I asked something else, you got more excited. It was making you so happy, I would have done anything to keep you talking."

Israfel caught Gabriel's eye. *Do you want to see this pretty rock I found?*

Gabriel looked aside, fighting a smile.

"I did trust you," Raphael said. "You were already half in my thoughts, so when I felt the impulse to let you all the way in, I went with it."

Israfel nodded. "It was similar with me, except because you and Raphael had already discovered bonding, I made the decision knowing what would happen."

Gabriel frowned. "I had all that with Lucifer, though. We spent a lot of time together, and when we debated a question or prayed together, he did access my thoughts. I had some access to his, too." Less as time went on. Maybe over time, he'd realized how cramped it was in a lesser angel's psyche. He'd needed to stretch.

Raphael said, "I'm betting the missing element was him prioritizing your well-being over his own. If he nurtured that feeling for even a minute, you'd have him—but if he never developed it before rebelling, then you don't have a chance of getting it now. The best you can hope for is that he might find it mutually beneficial."

The chance of that wasn't much better. Gabriel's "nothing to offer" was still in force.

Israfel shook her head. "My original objection stands. It can't even seem mutually beneficial because the moment Satan thinks you want a bond, that's the moment you'll never get it. You'd need to trick him, and you're not a trickster."

Uriel balanced on the edge of Michael's desk, knees and wings drawn up, chin resting on folded hands. "Except you mustn't trick him. If he doesn't consent to the bond, then there's no ground on which to build further consent."

Gabriel rubbed his temples as he considered the multiple contradictory conditions they'd just established. "His repentance would require full consent. He'd have to want God for the sake of God." He paced the room. "I'll need to get deep in his head."

Israfel sniffed. "On the contrary, make him pursue you. The flip side of a fire-starved Cherub is an over-fired Seraph who's desperate to spend that energy."

Eyes widening, Gabriel went still.

Tilting her head, Israfel raked a hand through her curls. "He's been on full burn since the dawn of time, and sure, he's learned to compensate—but once he's experienced what a Cherub can do? He'll flood you with his excess because it solves two problems simultaneously."

The first problem: too much fire. The second problem: Gabriel reading his soul. The solution: obvious and painful.

Raphael's voice was thin. "If you succeed in bonding him, run. Don't stay even a second."

That would be the hardest thing in the universe to do. The early minutes of a primary bond were intense, with the world on fire all around, and yourself as a Cherub hovering at the heart of the spinning flames, amazed and longing to grasp that energy and funnel it, temper it, reflect it back toward God. At the same time, to the Seraphim, everything had seemed new and delicious and curious, and they hungered to know—hungered to know everything. Everything, and Gabriel had yearned to tell them everything.

The term "playing with fire" had never meant anything to Gabriel before this moment. Gabriel played with fire on a daily basis, and the fire played back. Lucifer's fire, though, would burn. In Lucifer's mind, there were always winners and losers. No matter how it ended, Gabriel would get seared.

Uriel uncoiled off the desk and eased across the room. "We need a backup plan. Bilocate for me."

Gabriel doubled himself, watching Uriel with fourfold stereoscopic vision.

Raphael shook his head. "I should have thought of this."

Uriel took Gabriel's hands and then said to the other Gabriel, "Start diminishing this one and slowly draw your power, will, and thoughts back into the other."

Uriel was making a token, a spare Gabriel. If Satan trapped him or tortured him, the other angels could infuse this token with their energy and revive him so he could re-form in a secure location. The sensation was dizzying and a little ticklish. Uriel guided the process, keeping the second Gabriel from collapsing in on himself while the first grew stronger.

The fact that they needed to employ a technique developed only because Satan had attempted to annihilate Gabriel in the first place...? Following through was madness. If Gabriel had even an ounce of the intelligence he'd always credited himself, he'd throw the brakes on this runaway train. Instead, he studied the curious sensation of himself collapsing down into nothing, or rather, just being. Being still, being small. His awareness of Uriel dissolved even as his awareness remained. He was comfortably cold, and he was standing in the sunlight.

He looked at Raphael. "If the bond succeeds, you'll need to keep me separated from him for several hours until he's less angry and it's safe to return."

It would never be safe. Gabriel ought to admit it.

With the same gentleness as creating a garment of flower petals, Uriel gathered more of Gabriel together, condensing him bit by bit, closing the distance between parts that suddenly had gaps. Gabriel was drowsing to sleep, and Gabriel was wide awake.

Raphael avoided Gabriel's eyes while watching the token-making process. "You're going to want to go back to him."

Gabriel sighed. "I may get very logical and persuasive, but you'll need to hold fast."

Uriel projected happiness.

In Uriel's hands lay a silver sphere. Gabriel took it, anticipating a sensation of double-touch but instead feeling nothing. This was himself, but with no awareness, no willfulness, no independent thought.

He turned to Israfel. "Can you secure the token in the music library?"

"I've already had demons requesting access." Her mouth

twitched. "It needs someplace safer."

Gabriel teased, "It?"

She narrowed her gaze. "*He* needs someplace safer."

Raphael gestured around Michael's office. "Use a vault here. If anyone were to break in, they'd have the entire army on top of them before they could spread their wings."

"For that matter," Israfel said, "Special Ops would love protecting the token. The only trouble will be convincing them to give it back."

"Would you mind bringing it to them?" Then, when her heart still wasn't at ease, Gabriel folded it into her hands. "Can you protect this pretty rock I found?"

Chapter Nine

PACING HIS HOTEL ROOM, Satan glared at a mirror, shattered it, and shattered it again before it fully re-formed. Moments later, he was staring once more at himself, but this time he destroyed the image by walking away.

He'd gotten hooks in Israfel and would get more. Gabriel would be the key to that, so he needed Gabriel in play as much as possible.

For that matter, he'd very nearly gotten hooks in Gabriel, until the moment he'd grabbed him—an error in judgment Satan would never have tolerated from his underlings. Drawing out Gabriel meant doing things he didn't normally do, and he hadn't adequately compensated.

Satan found a location where none of the mirrors could see him. What he couldn't find was a place where the mirrors reflected one another back into themselves, creating several thousand of him. On the other hand, staggered mirrors meant he could find angles to shine beams of light so they ricocheted from one to the next for a reasonably long time before striking a wall. That was a fun game for toddlers. He'd rather stand in the single non-reflecting spot.

He ordered the Maskim to report. Asmodeus still hadn't found Hastle, which doubtless meant Michael was detaining the traitor on another level. Belior had located the main attachment points where this level sealed to the one beneath, and he had his officers openly examining those spots in front of the Archangel soldiers because it garnered a lot of attention—and meanwhile, he had a team of Cherubim in stealth studying the minor ones to achieve useful answers. Beelzebub was developing a strategy to defend and hold the level.

Mephistopheles was all over the place. He hadn't named any other angels who seemed discontent, but he also didn't seem to be trying. Granted, he was talking up his efforts (providing a long list of names, as though he'd invited each of those angels into an office to psychoanalyze them) because amongst his skills, Mephistopheles had a flair for padding his resume. Also amongst his skills, though, was a penchant for coming out of nowhere with brilliant ideas that transformed the way everyone framed a problem. The crowning glory of that had been annihilating an angel. It was hardly Mephistopheles' fault that God had tweaked the rules afterward.

Mephistopheles, report.

Mephistopheles sounded subdued. *No new developments.*

The lack of resume-padding intrigued Satan. *Where are you?*

A frisson of unease underlay his reply. *Rahab.*

Satan flashed to him.

There must have been conversation in the room until the moment of Satan's arrival because the sound hadn't quite dissipated, but his presence halted it all. That wasn't an unusual occurrence. "His condition?"

They'd brought in a bed as though Rahab were a sickly human. Not a hospital bed, which would have been a credible insult, but a bed large enough for an angel with six wings.

Ataf crouched at the bedside, glare level. He had one hand in Rahab's outermost wing, fist clenched on the flight feathers. Mephistopheles was sitting alongside Rahab's head, mid-study of the faux-annihilated Cherub. Also in the room were Rahab's other two Seraphim, and also Saraquael.

Weirdly, it was Saraquael who reported to Satan. "Most of our work now is firming him up. Uriel's devised a means of keeping him unconscious, on the grounds that the process would feel distressing. Once that's done, we'll fix him in an ecstatic state so

Uriel can access his mind without waking him fully, and we'll re-assess his progress."

So much work for such a useless creature. "How were you able to find him at all?"

Ataf said, "It turns out, all we needed was a Throne."

That was an insult, Ataf's thousands-years-late return fire for Satan once snapping at the Maskim that he'd trade all six of them for even the lowest member of the third order. Satan hadn't secured one at the Winnowing, and Thrones so rarely left Heaven that he'd had no chance to correct his gap.

Satan said, "I gleaned as much from prior updates, but they didn't specify what precisely a Throne could accomplish."

Ataf said, "I still have a bond to Rahab. Uriel was able to trace it back toward Rahab's location."

Ah, the technique Satrinah used with generational evil. Rahab's dissolution had taken place before she developed it, and with a terminal lack of ambition, Satrinah had never re-questioned a situation she considered resolved, whereas for Ataf, it never had been.

The other two Seraphim watched with hatred in their shadowed eyes. Why should they still care? Rahab had harmed them—harmed them immeasurably. If Rahab hadn't gotten rid of himself, the three disgraced Seraphim would have banded together and gotten it done. They should consider him as saving them the effort.

Satan kept coming up against these same ridiculous strictures every time he worked with his fellow Seraphim and their associated Cherubim: their bi-directional fealty, their codependency, their preference for one another, their mutual usefulness...whatever you'd call it, they persisted in it. In a similar situation, Raphael had stopped inches short of disowning Gabriel. Was it an addiction?

Satan asked Saraquael, "To what end do you want to access his consciousness?"

"Not to steal your military secrets." Saraquael kept his voice steady, a pathetic attempt at de-escalation. "Him feeling calm and safe will give us the best chance of keeping him stable once he's awake."

Ataf said, "They're clearing the way for me to get in."

Ataf looked as ready to fry Rahab as to console him, and Satan refused to guess which would be the outcome. "How long do you estimate until you can gain entry?"

Ataf said, "What do you want me to ask him? As Saraquael implied, any information he has will be three thousand years out of date."

Satan folded his arms. "Answer the question I asked rather than failing to predict my subsequent question."

Mephistopheles stood. "With regard to time, changes in state remain un-forecastable in both duration and quality. He's as likely to remain dormant for months as he is to awaken all at once in a panic. I can say for certain it's a fool's errand to attempt a plot of his recovery as though it were linear."

A lot of words to say Mephistopheles had no idea.

Ataf said, "We'll tell you if anything changes. Until then, let us handle it."

It made sense all of a sudden why Mephistopheles was here. Although he didn't have a primary bond with any of these, he did have lower-level bonds, and with them in this state, he could empower himself to do just about anything.

Satan huffed. "Let me know when you give up."

Ataf snapped, "Let us know when any of this concerns you."

Saraquael was on his feet between Satan and Ataf before Satan could react. "It's okay. We're all concerned."

Satan snarled at Saraquael, "Don't try lying to me. I invented it." Then to Ataf, "Would you care to convey what exactly you think are the limits of my concerns?"

Saraquael maintained an artificial calm. "He spoke without thinking. This is a unique situation, and everyone is tense right now." Ataf still had his hand in Rahab's feathers and didn't look like someone who'd misspoken due to tension. "Of course you should be concerned about one of your officers."

"These are all polite fictions." Satan pinned each of his Seraphim with a glare, one after the next after the next. "Rahab didn't go under the lake because of me." He looked directly at the other two Seraphim. "I heard the way you threatened him." Then to Ataf, he said, "When I stripped him off the Maskim, you ordered him to win back his position by doing the impossible, but then you offered no help whatsoever. If you're looking for the source of Rahab's pain, I suggest consulting any of the thousands of mirrors in this hotel. If that fails to suffice, then you can request further enlightenment from me." He turned to Mephistopheles. "I noted no objection from you to Rahab's demotion."

Mephistopheles inclined his head. "Sir, I offered none."

Satan turned back to Ataf. "You may have rewritten history after three thousand years, but I'm uninterested in fiction. Awaken your Cherub if you must, but don't attribute your actions to benevolence, nor my indifference to anything other than a commitment to reality."

Satan flashed back to his quarters and flared off heat and anger.

Bonds were idiocy. Being a Trinity all by Himself, God did so many things in the plural—things that didn't have to be. Thrones, for example, were solitary and settled. Everyone should have been made that way. Seraphim had emotions, yes, but why undercut them? With practice, any Seraph could harness those passions without relying on outside help.

It was unfathomable that Gabriel had muddied up that perfect soul with a bond. At the time it was understandable only because it was the first time it happened. Neither of them could have realized the snap-jawed trap into which they were stepping.

Why then would Gabriel willingly have entered a second with Israfel? The logical thing would have been devoting the rest of eternity to undoing the first.

Right after it happened, Lucifer had arrived to bounce a question off Gabriel. He'd found Gabriel asleep alongside Raphael —her body curled and her wings splayed—vulnerable and exposed, rings of relaxation sheeting out with a Cherub at the center. Angels only slept as a last resort after spiritual calamity, so Lucifer had rushed up to her, demanding Raphael tell him what had happened. An uncharacteristically clear-eyed Raphael had responded that he wasn't sure how to categorize it, but if Lucifer wanted to stay, they could discuss it and pray together when Gabriel awakened.

Fighting nausea, Lucifer had said, "I'll talk to Gabriel later," then fled to his place in the choirs and demanded God explain the reversal he'd encountered back there. Raphael, analytical and subdued. Gabriel—who had relinquished both consciousness and common sense—unguarded and weak.

To what end? To escape her mind?

Within days, madness swept the choirs. If any Seraph and Cherub met, they'd try to bond. Lucifer couldn't clamp down on the chaos, and inevitably, disgustingly, Gabriel had approached him. "You haven't bonded with anyone," she'd said, as though he required only a prompt to debase himself.

The best way to convince a Cherub was with logic. "I have no reason to." And he'd taken wing.

While they flew together, she explained at length (and at length, and at length,) the reasons behind sharing power and sharing perceptions, the functionality of the exchange, and how both of them would benefit if he did the one very, very small thing of granting permanent access to his entire soul.

After she finished, he re-centered the discussion on logic. "You have nothing to offer me."

She fell silent.

With their thoughts mingled, he felt her for the first time seeing herself through his eyes. He'd always considered her different. Less? Absolutely. That was a matter of metrics and measurements, something she would have been the first to point out. This time, though, she gauged the way God made her and concluded that she wasn't good enough. And so did he.

Lucifer's heart twanged because he'd hurt her. But no, think clearly. He was her superior, and this was as it should be. Her silence—her thoughts evaporating from his own—meant only that she was deep in her mind, probably charting a path toward improving herself so she could repeat the request when she did have something to offer. She might be preparing such an offer even now.

Instead, her brows furrowed. "You're right. You're complete on your own."

Gabriel never again brought up the matter.

This hotel room was an abomination. Satan stepped forward so the nearest mirror revealed his own face, unblinking. He discorporated, and his other self vanished. Fine, but he didn't want to remain insubstantial for six days, so he coalesced back into his subtle body and shattered the mirror.

Before it re-formed, he pressed his hand into the wall where the glass would have been, and the mirror couldn't re-form through him. As soon as he pulled back, it firmed up.

A dozen destructions in a row had no other effect. He destroyed it mid-reformation and it still came back in perfection. Shifting the wall so the mirror moved to a different location also didn't help. He manipulated the room to hang tapestries, but if anything, hiding them made their presence stronger.

Like souls. You could cinder them and break them, but they kept healing up. Except for Rahab, who was so badly burnt he likely would never heal, not even with simultaneous attention from his friends and his enemies.

Satan approached the nearest mirror and pressed his palm into it. What if, like Rahab, the mirror never broke?

Heat built on Satan's palm, but he didn't unleash it into the mirror. Instead, he allowed it to flow through himself into the air, and from the air into the wall. Glass melted at...was it fifteen hundred degrees celsius?

A thousand years ago, Mephistopheles had referred to glass as "meta-stable," and then had to clarify to Beelzebub, "Glass is kinetically stable enough that it seems solid, but because a first-order phase change crystallization reaction doesn't occur at the normal freezing point, it's an amorphous solid. Given time, it settles toward gravity."

Satan had filed that away (as with many things Mephistopheles said) as, "true, but unuseful." Except centuries later, perhaps it might be.

Mephistopheles was the number one argument against bonding. Alone, he was smart and effective. He kept to himself and carried out his orders and anticipated Satan's commands. But anchored to him was Beelzebub—who, while effective in his own way, served only to distract, distort, and dismay Mephistopheles. Yet for all that, Mephistopheles never said a thing against him. During the brief time Satan had access to a soul's inner workings, he'd offered to break their bond, but Mephistopheles had declined. Why? The only conclusion was that bonding made Cherubim less rational, whereas Satan needed his operatives more rational.

The room around Satan burst into flames. That was flashover, about six hundred degrees. With Guards sealing the room, the temperature should finish rising rapidly.

Back when Gabriel was separated from everyone and Satan stood a reasonable chance of swinging him to their side, Satan had held a long strategy meeting with the Maskim. They had weeks to plan and as long a trial period as they wanted, provided Gabriel didn't send him away. They observed and compared notes and plotted and tested—and finally Satan was ready to deploy.

The first two nights were a success, and then on the third, it had been Mephistopheles prepping him. Satan was going to lead off with an epic poem, so Mephistopheles coached him on literary analysis—but at the same time, Mephistopheles was doing something to the atmosphere. Satan hadn't picked up on it at first, but Mephistopheles had begun casting the same kind of rings as Gabriel had while asleep on that hill, only immediately breaking them apart. Mephistopheles would ask rhetorical questions, then smile and introduce new topics without providing any answers, leaving Satan's mind lingering over the unanswered questions. Mephistopheles would put forth more of that silvery-smooth energy, and when Satan was focused again on the poem, Mephistopheles would dissolve it as if he'd never been shedding it, changing the subject to vocal stress patterns and how they affected the poem's tone.

"Emphasize this mismatched parallel," he'd purred, running his finger across the manuscript, sinuous and cool in spirit, and then as fire surged in Satan's heart (*Over a poem? A human-written poem?*) Mephistopheles was once again rock solid and academic, leaving Satan wondering where his balance had gone.

Finally, Mephistopheles had hopped up on a stool and lowered his chin, gazing up at Satan through that waterfall of blond curls. He'd breathed, "Is there anything else I can give you?"

For a heartbeat, Satan craved his admiration. Satan wanted to display every bit of his glory so the Cherub would gaze...behold... be struck wordless with astonishment. What else could Mephistopheles give him? Mephistopheles could focus his intellect entirely on Satan and never pay attention to anyone else ever again —not their enemies and not himself and not Beelzebub, who not only didn't appreciate him but who outright abused him. A genius like Mephistopheles deserved something truly great to contemplate, and it could be Satan himself. Satan had only to open up and reveal all his inner workings. Mephistopheles' eternal devotion would be his.

As that feeling crescendoed, Satan snapped, "We're done," and forced Mephistopheles out of the room.

Five minutes later, with the Maskim hidden to feed him suggestions, Satan had appeared before a fire-starved Gabriel and all but driven him crazy.

He'd realized then—Mephistopheles had been priming him, stoking those flames so Gabriel would salivate for them. Satan would never have consented to that. For Gabriel to fall, Gabriel had to want it. He had to reject God, not just lose control.

Or had Mephistopheles been priming Satan in the hopes that the one who lost control would be Satan, and the one who benefitted would be himself?

Satan should have punished him. He never did. He wouldn't admit how unnerving it had been, and admonishing Mephistopheles would have emboldened him to try again—only sneakier.

The hotel room hit fourteen hundred degrees. The furnishings, drapes, and carpets were long past incinerated, the windows blackened with smoke. If the angels were paying attention, it wouldn't matter. The Hilbert had invited fire to prowl its halls, so what good would be fire extinguishers?

Just a little hotter—and then the mirrors began to sag. He backed off on raising the temperature, not wanting them fully liquid—only enough to ripple as they yielded to gravity.

He could make everything unfit for use. God had given them a pretty hotel, but for what end? To prove to Michael and the other sweetlings that He wasn't a tyrant after all? *See, My pets, the rebels had comfy quarters during their Heavenly imprisonment before I sent them back to fire and darkness.* No thanks. Not interested.

Satan focused on each mirror in turn, then called all the heat back into himself. He flashed power over himself to clear the ash from his wings, then waited for the reset.

One second. Two seconds. The carpet regenerated. The furniture returned. Paint reappeared on the walls. The mirrors stayed warped.

Test one, complete. Now for test two.

He shattered the nearest mirror, and after a breath, it reconstituted, rippled.

It still restores to base form, but I've warped the base coding.

For the same reason, Rahab wasn't going to recover. Raphael could put his body back together, and Uriel could probe his thoughts, but after all that time in conscious torment? After three millennia of forcing himself to stay beneath the Lake of Fire, ignoring the pleas of three different Seraphim he'd once proclaimed to love? Ataf could smolder all he liked, but recovery was self-referential, and that reference was corrupted.

Chapter Ten

HIS MASTER WAS CORRECT that Mephistopheles had offered no objection to casting Rahab and Ataf out of the Maskim. Mephistopheles had recognized the unfairness of the maneuver, but he'd also run down the possibilities and foreseen two ends to defending Rahab. First, that Lucifer might take the opportunity to disband his entire inner circle, and the more untenable second, that Lucifer would likewise eject Mephistopheles and Beelzebub, leaving only Asmodeus and Belior as his favorites.

If either happened, Mephistopheles could look forward to an eternity of being beaten to unconsciousness by Beelzebub, and then, immediately after awakening, getting beaten to unconsciousness again. At least, until Beelzebub forgot about him. Given the Seraph's tenacity with regard to things Mephistopheles would have preferred forgotten, that would never have happened. Mephistopheles therefore opted for silence. It wasn't an incorrect decision.

Even so, the instant Lucifer flashed away, Mephistopheles left Rahab's sickbed without even a perfunctory goodbye. Three angry Seraphim, all surrounding a Cherub whom Lucifer had branded useless, guaranteed a firefight. The sure result would be temporary confinement to quarters. Again, an untenable prospect.

Also untenable: his master's anger. To forestall that, Mephistopheles would have to find something both useful and interesting, and he needed to identify it now.

Mephistopheles checked in with Beelzebub, who'd chosen to unsettle Michael's forces by playing war games on one of the fields. That was clever: it would wear out the patience of Heaven's army long before any tactical strike. The best time to initiate a war would be days five or six, giving their forces at least forty-eight hours to isolate this level and dig in well enough to hold it.

Doubtless Michael knew this, too, but there was only so much secrecy to be had against an omniscient enemy. The key, as always, was to have a plan so good that the enemy couldn't do anything about it.

Another key was exploiting the unpredictable. Mephistopheles had experimented quite a bit with the travel issue. He could get back into Hell without restriction. The inner layers were far more problematic because of the one-to-one rule.

What they needed was a defector. A single convert would suffice to unlock the inner layers for thousands of demons because the angel could bilocate, trilocate, multi-locate into as many pieces as possible. The defector wouldn't have to do anything else, just make himself small and get carried along in a pocket. It was smuggling in reverse.

Regardless, without a tour guide, Mephistopheles would try to access the inner layers and get bounced back. He tried to follow angels who left the layer. He tried flashing directly from Hell. He tried asking for an escort and then flashing to a location different than the escort.

Then he flashed to a place he absolutely should not have been able to enter, and arrived in the Heavenly Temple.

Mephistopheles' wings flared, but here he stood—at the back, adjacent to two very startled soldiers.

A white-clad temple angel appeared before him. "As long as you remain, you are bound to silence."

Mephistopheles attempted to indicate understanding, but nothing happened. A total ban. He couldn't process his thoughts. He was in the moment. He was here.

Here also sat the traitor wanted by Asmodeus. The soldiers flanked him.

Mephistopheles had been bound to silence at other times. It wasn't uncomfortable. He'd think again, speak again, cipher out the world again—only, later. Now was time to listen to the liturgy, notice the incense rising and yet not gathering at the ceiling, and hear the music.

All was as he'd left it so many aeons ago. The lights. The angels moving on the peripheries. The side altars where souls prayed in solitude. The antiphonal prayers. The hymns. And him.

His thoughts kept getting cut off. Frustration built. He couldn't observe beyond the temple walls. Nothing was keeping him here. He should go.

Another white-robed angel approached and offered a hand. Mephistopheles didn't accept. He should never have been welcome here. He mustn't enter God's inner sanctum.

The angel offered again. Mephistopheles was curious. He took the hand.

Abruptly he stood in darkness, God's presence tangible all around and his thoughts fully present to himself once more. Wings spread, Mephistopheles cast out his senses only to encounter no limits, no walls, no other creatures. Just him and the Creator whom he'd rejected, to whom he owed both everything and nothing.

God said, *Here you are.*

Of course he was here, but why? What madness of the Almighty would permit Him to allow into His direct presence one of the highest demonic Cherubim, the same Cherub who had violated every moral and theological norm it was in his power to violate?

Was this the moment God snuffed him out like a candle?

Mephistopheles knew: No. He had entered the temple, and that was allowed. He'd been invited in further, and he had chosen to come. There was no danger in doing so, and there was no danger either in remaining or in departing.

With his feathers flared, Mephistopheles probed again. They weren't in a corner of the temple anymore. Technically speaking, this wasn't even part of Heaven. The inner dwelling was, using the strictest definition, "Eternity," completely outside time and outside location. This was opposed to the way the angels normally existed, which should most accurately be called "sempiternity."

Was he here now for God to take back everything He thought was His?

God replied, *Tell me why you're here.*

Mephistopheles had believed he was searching for a way to gain his master an access point into the deeper parts of Heaven. Once there, they could negotiate for what Mephistopheles considered the most reasonable outcome: the enemy conceding the outer layer to the Winnowed angels, unmooring it, and then leaving them to do what they wanted. Let Lucifer re-establish his kingdom in the expanded territory. Why did Hell have to be darkness and fire and cold when Hell could also be light and fields and breezes? As long as God wasn't there, any place was going to be Hell. Why should God claim it all just because He'd been the first to plant His flag?

God said, *Have you found what you sought?*

Bristling, Mephistopheles clenched his fists. Of course not. Either that or obviously yes—except Mephistopheles wasn't the one who could challenge God. Certainly not alone. And not unprepared.

You shouldn't have to prepare to face me, God said.

Nonsense. For thousands of years, walking into a meeting without preparation had meant humiliation and pain. If Mephistopheles had prepared for this, he could have debated clever questions or formulated a statement. Not knowing what to say left his heart contorted.

Finally he thought, *I know what I am, and I know who You are.* Mephistopheles squeezed his eyes shut. *If You wish to correct Your error in creating me, then do so.*

Except he'd never see Beelzebub again. In starting this investigation, Mephistopheles had committed a lapse of incalculable consequence. God claimed there would be no danger, but of course there wasn't any "danger" in being uncreated. You couldn't suffer after that point because you weren't. At least, that's what Mephistopheles had assumed from even the earliest days.

But Beelzebub would still *be*—and what would he do? Would he be broken, or would he chose a replacement from his other bonds? Would he wait three thousand years like Ataf and still long for Mephistopheles? Mephistopheles wouldn't know.

The horror of Rahab's situation was he'd tried to be nothing, but he'd continued being. That demon at the back of the temple had tried to stop being, too, but instead he'd stopped being able to do anything—and what had that done to his mind?

God said, *I have no such wish. Do you want a gift?*

Mephistopheles clapped his wings as though propelling himself backward in the air. *I never wanted anything from You!* He shook —with terror? With outrage? *Why won't You leave me alone? That's the only gift I'll ever accept from You—Your absence.*

His mind reeled with the presence of God, and it hurt—it hurt more than the pains of Hell, or maybe this was the real pain of Hell, that God was here where Mephistopheles didn't want Him to be. God could see into him, and he didn't want to be seen—but he couldn't see back into God. *Why won't You leave me alone?*

He was wearing armor, and he wished he could put armor around the armor. If God could see his thoughts, then God knew... everything. God knew those little moments, those doubts, those flashes of certitude. The disappointments. The grief. The despair. God knew it all, and for some reason Mephistopheles was still here before Him, suspended in Eternity rather than chucked onto the garbage heap to rot with everything else God didn't need.

I don't want Your gift. He wanted— He had everything he wanted. He had a function and a Seraph and a rank and respect. He knew who he was. He knew who he wasn't.

What if Beelzebub got in here and accepted the gift? And what if it changed him? What if Mephistopheles took the gift and changed in response—and then what if he just...never went back? This shouldn't be goodbye, not after all this. He and Beelzebub had to be together. God could offer gifts all day long, but from the start, only one thing had been necessary, and through every trial and setback and humiliation, Mephistopheles had clung to it. Anything that jeopardized it had to be wrong.

Jesus had said someone should sell everything to buy one special pearl. That's exactly what Mephistopheles had done. His decision couldn't be wrong if even Jesus agreed. Whatever gift was in God's hands, it couldn't be worth more than that singular pearl.

I didn't invite you here to make you afraid.

Mephistopheles clamped down on his mind. *I'm not afraid. I'm angry. The only worthwhile gift You gave me was free will, and when I used it, You took everything else.*

There was one more thing God could take. Mephistopheles tried to stuff it down so maybe God wouldn't see, but of course God could see—and the only hope left was that God would honor the free will He'd insisted was so important, and honor it by letting Mephistopheles keep the thing he'd chosen.

Keep it.

The thing he'd chosen.

The one he'd chosen.

Chosen.

Instead of God.

Please.

Please don't take him away from me.

Mephistopheles was standing in his hotel room.

He whipped toward the mirror, eyes to eyes. His heart snaked out for Beelzebub, and at the other end of the connection—fire. He suctioned those flames back into himself, and with his face in his hands, he dropped to his knees.

Satan flashed from place to place in Limbo, demanding updates from his underlings and occasionally stirring up problems for Michael's armored babysitters. It wasn't hard to stay just this side of the rules, leaving them no recourse but to watch in unease. In the meantime, he stopped Beelzebub mid-wargame to make tactical suggestions, then got reports from Belior on the number of hotels and their plasticity. From Asmodeus, he obtained further information about defensible positions as well as the timing of several events.

That left Mephistopheles, who hadn't reported since the clash in Rahab's room. Satan leashed him from across the level and dragged him into place on one of the fairgrounds.

Flickering with unease, Mephistopheles attempted to look composed. "Yes, sir?"

Satan said, "Have you done anything today other than spoon-feed a convalescent?"

Inclining his head, Mephistopheles indicated Satan should follow, and they reappeared in the dark, the moist air vibrating with power.

Extending his senses, Satan could feel nothing but the heavy charge coursing around them.

To see anything, Mephistopheles shed light, then stepped closer to the current. Projecting, but with his back to Satan, he made all his information available: that this was one of the smaller conduits between this level of Heaven and the next, and here he'd found the means of severing the connection.

Satan folded his arms and cocked his head.

Mephistopheles turned but didn't look him in the eyes. "My inclination would be to interrupt the energy here and divert this back onto itself." He created a latticework of light over the flow to diagram his plan. "That would interrupt the connection in this one spot, the difficulty being that, of these, there are thousands."

Satan said, "What's beneath?"

"It resembles a socket to which one could add more layers." Mephistopheles tilted his head. "By all appearances, after God detached the fallen Creation as Heaven's outer layer, He used similar sockets on an inner layer to affix the current one."

Satan said, "And the new layer was made of...?"

"I assume He created it *ex nihilo*. If we had a sufficiency of material, instead of interrupting the energy, we could continue this linkage to establish one further layer."

Satan's wings shot up. "Create a new layer of Heaven?"

Mephistopheles affirmed this as though it were a normal suggestion. "With our own layer, we would have a much improved chance of retaining it, on the grounds that it was never God's to begin with. Michael's forces might see fit to maintain their impervious barrier between the Limbo layer and the inner ones, and we could either yield our claim on Limbo as a concession or leave it available as common ground."

Satan rubbed his chin. "Other than the *ex nihilo* problem."

Mephistopheles inclined his head. "I haven't solved that, yet."

Beneath his methodical answers, Mephistopheles gave off an air of distraction. More than that, something had unnerved him, unnerved him deeply. Whatever it was—good. Since it kept Mephistopheles discovering things, let him remain unsettled. "I suggest you solve it."

Mephistopheles nodded. "We could in theory harvest some of this level's material in order to forge—"

Satan said, "What I meant was, solve it yourself," then terminated the interview by ejecting Mephistopheles.

The power coursing through this juncture was intense enough that Satan couldn't feel anything beyond the momentary relief that shimmered off his subordinate.

Satan reached into the energy to let it carry him toward an interior level, but he got blocked. Instead he probed downward. The structures Mephistopheles had described as "sockets" did, in fact, feel buildable. Building with no material wasn't going to be easy, but what if they detonated Hell and used that as the basis?

Or, come to think of it, what about Creation? That had been his kingdom, and God had originally peeled it off Heaven like the outer layer of an onion. There wasn't any reason Satan shouldn't put it back.

Energy like static walled him off from consulting Mephistopheles. Instead, Satan tried flashing directly to the Earth. And—

—arrived...?

Arrived in silence. Arrived in darkness.

Not a single molecule was in motion around him as Satan cast out his senses to absorb his surroundings. Where was this? He'd intended to go to New York City, not to whatever this was.

His heart went into the ground and forced it to yield its secrets. As if groggy, the planet turned back the largest land masses and the oceans. Definitely the plane of Creation. Certainly the Earth. This was New York. Specifically, Wall Street.

Satan craned his neck toward a sky darkened by particulate matter.

His enemies had done this. They'd yammered about how the world "proclaimed the glory of the Lord," but Satan had authority over it, so instead, they'd burnt it until it proclaimed nothing.

It should be noon. There should have been skyscrapers, even if only skeletons of dead structures. Mounds of twisted metal, perhaps. Decomposing automobiles. Instead, flatness. Darkness.

Oh, Babylon, my princess.

How was this right? "All of this has been given to me," Satan had said to Jesus, and Satan had never given it back. The world was fallen, but it was still a world. There should be activity, but instead, nothing. This chill was inimical to life. All around him lay a city chewed to dust and spread evenly across the surface.

Babylon, in just an hour, your judgment came.

He probed with his mind all over the planet: Jakarta, Tokyo, Moscow, São Paulo, Warsaw, Sydney, Kyiv, Johannesburg, London, Rome, Beijing, Montreal, Bogota. All desolate, all pulverized. *Babylon.* All its life and splendor—now, not one stone left on another. Not even an amino acid.

I won. Inside was as quiet as outside, so Satan forced the thought. *I left an imprint on the world so deep that God couldn't strip it off. Little surprises would remain for the enemy to find long into eternity. Their people would have remembered the ones who escaped, and then plotted a second escape from Eden. God's only choice was to destroy it and start over.*

By any reasonable definition of winning and losing, he'd won. God had sent His Son to the battlefield and set up encampments, yet still the demons had held this territory. They'd brought many to their side and kept the ones they claimed. Every time God had changed the rules, Satan had pivoted to work under the new rules until finally God had to flush them out of their strongholds. But even then, Satan must have retained pockets of it. As with the mirrors, warping the bones meant a thing never could grow straight again. God would leave this planet burnt out long enough to sterilize it from Satan's influence, then attempt to "renew the face of the Earth." Or maybe just make a new one. That meant He'd have to purge Heaven, too.

Satan bilocated back to the outer layer of Heaven and dissociated that part of himself. The arboretum. No, too fancy. Instead, the fields. He located a small shrub of heather, clamped his will on it, and pulled it across the divide onto the Earth.

Finally, the world had motion. Where the columns of the Stock Exchange should have been, Satan knelt with the plant, spreading his wings as he shifted the ground cover and settled the roots into the broken ash. He patted it in place, then sat back on his heels while the disturbed ash resettled.

In a thousand years when the Word came back, He'd find it overgrown with life, Satan's final mark on the world.

Except it was frigid, so Satan directed his heat toward the plant. Also, this breed of plant needed sunlight. Satan focused on the sky to sift the particles so light could penetrate, but there was so much. Therefore, while he continued forcing the sky to clear, he relaxed his shoulders, breathed deeply, and shone light onto its leaves.

You're a symbol, he told the plant. *Either you get your feet deep in this planet and survive, or else you die. If you survive, God has no choice but to kill you because you're mine. He's not going to let me re-contaminate what He sterilized. I, however, charge you to live. I charge you to prosper, and after you've prospered, I charge you to spread. If God moves you back to Heaven, then know forever that I've changed you.*

The rebellion could go on, even if in only a shrub. Someone in Heaven would know. Someone like Israfel would chafe at the injustice. Eternity was a long time, and any seed of discontentment could take root as the next rebellion.

The Earth was so silent. Hell had been full of noisy death, and the Earth had been full of noisy life: the movement of wind, the shifting of leaves, the breaths of animals, the churning of angelic signatures. Here, now, were only the cellular functions of one plant and the action of silt on silt in the air.

Also, Satan was alone. Almost alone. *You need me,* he thought to the plant. *You need my light.*

Was this what God had done at the beginning, spinning Creation like a top to explode out matter and energy, then gathering it into forms while watching and tending, waiting to see how it would congeal?

Separate the light from the darkness. Separate water from water. Sort and separate and arrange, and then at the end, God had looked at the souls with their free will and done one final sorting. God hadn't changed the rules this time. He'd just entered the next phase of gameplay.

Could Satan's forces re-take the planet? To leave it like this perhaps meant God had no further use for it. This should have been Satan's. It still was. If there were any justice at all, God could leave Satan's cohort to their former world and let them develop it however they wanted.

Satan spread his wings to sample the light from the sky. Impossibly weak, but the particulate matter had begun settling. He flashed the stuff off him, then flashed it off the heather. He'd need a water source, seemingly impossible when he considered the condition of the planet.

He could stay here, tending a garden and leaving the Maskim to fight out who took over. How many plants could he transfer down here during seven days? Could he get them to reproduce? What if he moved entire forests from Limbo and established himself as their light source, adjuring them to grow everywhere? With their roots laced together, those plants would hold the surface in place. They'd grow and die and make room for new ones, and the organic matter would turn back into dirt, and in time, the planet would thrive again and be green.

Terraforming the Earth had never been part of the plan, but

Satan could be the sun, shining on a planet teeming with life under God's figurative nose, locked away from the angels and the saints, enjoyed only by the ones deemed unfit for glory who instead enjoyed a lush glory of their own making.

Or, he could stop thinking stupid thoughts and devise a plan to take and hold the outer layer of Heaven.

His forces had three access points right now. Hell, the Earth, and Limbo. Asmodeus and Belior could contrive a means of holding the line here. A fight on Earth meant the plant would die, since material beings didn't fare well during spiritual warfare. With all the monkeys dead, the angels had no reason not to rip the atmosphere off the planet. It was a wonder they hadn't already.

That was the problem with being a realist: even daydreaming, Satan couldn't dream too much. Or rather, Satan had learned a long time ago that daydreaming led to places it made no sense to go. It led to Seraphim bonding with Cherubim. It led to the hope that God loved the things He'd made instead of finding them useful. It led to the conviction that having so much power and authority meant a destiny to use it.

In the end, it led to fire and darkness.

The plant kept stretching toward his light, and Satan intensified his glow. The thing would need water soon if it were to keep growing. In Heaven, some angel would have dutifully made it rain at prescribed intervals, but now the heather was going to have to toughen up. It would need those roots in good and deep for the dry spells when Satan couldn't get water to it.

God wouldn't provide for it, that was for sure. Like Satan, it would have to provide for itself.

Chapter Eleven

GABRIEL WAS GETTING FIRE-primed with Raphael when he felt Michael's tug on his heart: Satan wasn't on the outer level any longer, and Saraquael hadn't succeeded in finding him in Hell. He didn't have a one-to-one with anybody, so—did Gabriel have any clues?

He reflexively thought, "To Lucifer," and (of course) it didn't work. Instead, Gabriel thought, "To Michael," and he reappeared with Raphael at the Hilbert's gazebo.

Michael was armored. "His quarters are under a tight Guard, and amusingly, he's blackened the windows. Locked inside his room was my first guess, but he's really not in there."

Gabriel had been counting the seconds, and right on time, Raphael flared fire all around him, then snuffed it out.

It felt more uncomfortable every time Raphael did this. With insufficient time to fire-starve Gabriel, Raphael was priming him for a bond with timed energy surges. All it seemed to be doing was making Gabriel irritated. Israfel wanted nothing to do with the process, but Gabriel called her anyhow. *Lucifer's missing in action, and we're trying to track him down.*

Israfel sent, *I assume he was having too good a time and went back to Hell.*

Although that was sarcastic, Gabriel replied, *Already checked. Hell is a big place. But so is his ego.*

She appeared at the same time as Saraquael, who was

accompanied by, of all individuals, Ataf.

Ataf's bronze eyes glinted. "I will deny I ever said this, but since you did me a solid, I'd check the Earth." When Michael's brow furrowed, Ataf added, "It's his, and he hates when his playthings go missing."

Well, other than when Rahab had gone missing. Fortunately, before Gabriel could do anything with that thought, Ataf vanished.

Saraquael snickered. "I don't mind when Satan's house is divided against itself."

Michael folded his arms. "How could Satan get to the Earth? We can't get there."

Whenever they'd asked why the plane of Creation was locked up, all God would answer was that they'd have access again after the banquet, when He renewed the face of the Earth. So until then, they'd waited on the promised new Heaven and new Earth.

Israfel muttered, "I don't know why Satan would even want to try. Does he want to revisit all the places we trounced him?"

Gabriel rubbed his chin. "It might have strategic value, and Ataf has a point that it's his. Maybe we couldn't access the plane of Creation because Lucifer wouldn't have allowed it—but perhaps he could open it for himself? And having opened it for himself, might he have opened it for us?"

Saraquael disappeared.

Michael started. "Saraquael, did you make it there?"

I've arrived, and it's destroyed, Saraquael called. He followed that with, *His power is here.*

Gabriel folded his arms. "He's not forbidden to travel to the Earth, is he?"

"It's not forbidden because we didn't think it was possible." Michael's mouth twitched. "Even so, I'm not comfortable letting him wander unescorted. We did say anyone going off this level needed a one-to-one."

Gabriel smirked. "Here I thought I was the pedant."

Israfel muttered, "You thought you were the *only* pedant."

He fought laughter. "Corrections in the pursuit of accuracy are why I appreciate your conversation."

The harshness didn't leave her eyes, and that prickled. She should have given him a sarcastic arch of the brows and replied, "How do you know when a Cherub thinks you haven't been specific enough? He tells you." Uneasy, he looked away from her.

Michael said, "Gabriel, at the very least, you need to come with me to check up on what he's doing."

Israfel said, "Then I'm going, too," with a distinct projection that she still didn't want Mary's plan to happen.

Raphael projected his own assent.

Gabriel gestured to Michael, who flashed the group of them to Saraquael.

To devastation.

Gabriel dissociated immediately, allowing the particulate matter to pass through him rather than mix with his form. Michael remained semicorporeal.

The oceans had frozen over, and the ice was covered with ash. Thermodynamically, that allowed for the possibility of liquid water beneath: the ash-covered ice would serve as insulation, and since water was the only liquid that froze from the top down, that was how life had survived any of the ice ages. When Gabriel sensed as far down as he could, though, he felt no life had survived this one.

Israfel whispered, "This was a beautiful world. Satan did this."

Gabriel missed the green. He missed the blue. He missed the scent of this planet's air and the tang of its light when it passed through his form.

Raphael flared Gabriel again, this time with spiritual fire, and he wasn't prepared. His spirit flickered, and he caught Israfel's desperation.

That, followed by, *It isn't fair.*

He could access her emotions even though she was shielding her fire. Raphael had locked down even that, leaving Gabriel unsteady.

Michael sent to Saraquael, *Can you locate the source of his power?*

It's permeating the upper levels of the atmosphere. He's forcing the sky cover to settle.

A stronghold for his people? Hell formerly had connections to the plane of Creation through the Earth, and if Satan could re-create those, he might re-take the planet.

Saraquael sent, *It feels like it's coming from North America.*

The midwestern plains looked exactly the same as wherever they'd appeared at first: flat, covered in ash.

A sparkle pinged Gabriel's senses. *Something's alive.*

Michael's wings flared.

Gabriel focused eastward at the same time as Saraquael gestured the same way. They flashed in that direction, appearing and reappearing while Saraquael kept seeking. Then they were in New York and so close.

Finally, they arrived at a dome of light with Lucifer at its center.

Gabriel returned to his subtle body and approached Lucifer, who was sitting on his heels before a shrub of purple heather.

Michael called, "We were wondering where you'd gone."

Lucifer didn't bother to look. "You missed me? I'm touched."

Israfel bristled. "Are you finishing the work you started?"

Lucifer snorted. "This? I always left things alive."

Raphael chose this moment to flare Gabriel's heart, and Gabriel's hands clenched as he fought the dizziness. The aftermath did feel a lot like being fire-starved.

Israfel looked ready to fill Gabriel with fire and derail the plan. Glaring at Satan, she said, "Eternal death is more your style."

He waved her off. "Call it what you like, but deforestation held no interest for me. The two times the world has been destroyed—or nearly destroyed—I had no hand in the matter. Only a short-sighted prince would immolate his kingdom."

Israfel folded her arms. "Do you expect us to believe you're cleaning up the place?"

Lucifer still wasn't looking in her direction. "I don't expect you to believe anything at all. The fact that I could come here without an escort means it's still under my authority. What I choose to do in this spot is my own concern."

Gabriel edged toward the plant, a common heather. Lucifer had tailored his light wavelengths to exactly what the plant responded to, and he was heating the air around it. The roots had penetrated through the ash all the way to the soil, and some of the leaves looked like new growth.

Michael folded his arms. "The issue is, you were told to bring an escort if you left the level, and you didn't."

Lucifer said, "If you have a problem with the restrictions, the one to talk to is the one who crafted them. I doubt it was you." Gabriel sensed Michael bristling, and Lucifer must have as well, because he added, "If your Tyrant allowed it, either it's permitted, or else He can't bar me. Both are equivalent as far as I'm concerned, since I have no intention of complying."

Raphael flared again, and Gabriel closed his eyes. *I need you to stop. I can't think.*

I'll stop, but if you can't think, that means it's working. Raphael paused. *From the outside, it feels as if it worked.*

Bracing his heart, Gabriel squatted to touch one of the branches. Lucifer turned to him. "Does it meet your approval?"

Gabriel said, "*Calluna vulgaris* requires a water source. Also, given the density of atmospheric particulate matter, it's unclear whether there will be enough light to sustain it once you've left."

Lucifer smirked at him. "You're right. I should stay."

Israfel said, "Lying about yourself is one thing. Don't lie about Gabriel."

To Gabriel, Lucifer said, "You can speak for yourself, can't you?"

Gabriel raised his gaze. "When I choose."

Lucifer stood. "I was worried you'd lost your edge." He walked away from the plant, moving the center of the light dome with himself. The plant immediately ceased growing, and the air around it went brittle.

It's going to die if we leave it alone, Gabriel prayed.

God agreed.

This was a conundrum. The Earth should remain dead, so sustaining Lucifer's stolen plant ran counter to that. But letting an innocent plant freeze felt wrong.

I didn't realize he was fond of New York City. The finances, the communication industry—they'd made their center here, and that had been useful. But in addition, he must have found the city itself so alive.

Lucifer said to Michael, "Will you try to eject me? Bring in a thousand angels, and we'll see whether they suffice."

Michael shrugged. "I could handle the job myself, but I'm not entirely convinced it needs to happen."

Lucifer sparkled at the edge of Gabriel's consciousness with a crackle that left him hungry. Hunger? Yes, Raphael's manipulation had created hunger the same way filling a home with the scents of baking bread would trigger hunger.

Rather unfortunate. Now he had to act.

Looking into the plant, Gabriel vibrated the air molecules around it. This wasn't the same as Lucifer generating light and heat, but it would suffice to keep the plant unfrozen. Gabriel could shed light, too, but not with the same control over the wavelengths. Burning the plant wouldn't help, so he settled on a full spectrum. Then, reaching deeper into his angelic nature, he blessed the plant, encouraging it to grow faster and allowing it to access his energy.

Lucifer turned to Saraquael. "Have you made any progress with Rahab?"

Saraquael shook his head. "Nothing significant. Did Ataf really order him to intercept the Law before God could give it to Moses?"

Lucifer folded his arms. "It was all three Seraphim. They thought I'd change my mind if he pulled off the impossible, but the reason I demoted him wasn't his inability to do the impossible. It was his inability to do the *possible*. I wouldn't have reversed course. Ataf knows that. He's got excellent manipulation skills, as with throwing his sobbing self over Rahab's corpse, but this webbing has a lot more strands than the few he's tugging on."

Gabriel's light faltered. Ataf hadn't sobbed only to create pity. Afterward, Gabriel had kept picking up images from Raphael's thoughts: Ataf's angry eyes, his sullen stance, his fingers in Rahab's flight feathers. That initial outburst had to have been overwhelm. Ataf's Cherub, who'd been dead, was alive again. The one who was lost was found.

God—, Gabriel prayed.

Israfel flared power to blow off the gritty air, inadvertently triggering Gabriel's senses to higher alert. She said, "Why didn't you dive into the lake to find him?"

"Again, you assume I didn't. I do look after my own." He started, and Gabriel felt Lucifer's attention swivel toward him. "What are you doing?"

Gabriel said, "Feeding it."

Lucifer flashed back to him. "Leave it. It's mine."

"It's not yours to destroy." Should Gabriel cast a Guard around the plant, or would that provoke the offensive he wanted to avoid? "The Earth may be your kingdom, but you pulled this shrub from the outer level, so that makes it a citizen of Heaven."

Lucifer huffed. "A plant has a passport?"

Gabriel didn't raise his gaze higher than Lucifer's boots. "What wavelengths were you using to stimulate photosynthesis? My light keeps getting bounced back because of the particulate matter."

Lucifer huffed. "Not a surprise. Your heat is dispersing, too. You're trying to generate a self-sustaining field, but that won't work."

Gabriel said, "You were telling us about Ataf and caring for your officers. This is your littlest officer."

Lucifer's nose wrinkled. "You just claimed it wasn't my plant."

"I said it wasn't yours to destroy. It's Heaven's plant you've borrowed to tend."

The anger in Israfel's eyes prompted Gabriel to reach for her fire, but she locked him out just in time.

She could have let him sabotage the plan. He closed his eyes. *I'm sorry.*

That apology was directed at himself and Israfel and the plant and God Almighty. Gabriel tucked his wings. "If a self-sustaining field isn't possible, did you intend to remain on Earth for the rest of the banquet?"

Enough of Lucifer's thoughts were readable that Gabriel concluded Lucifer had begun with no intentions. He'd come here for some reason Gabriel couldn't fathom, then hand-over-handed himself into a situation where he'd found himself alone in a universe, tending a life.

Was Lucifer indirectly imitating God? Was that goodness? Or—and this was more likely—was Gabriel sifting for hope in a land where hope was long since reduced to grit and dispersed through the sky? When Lucifer imitated God, it was never imitation of the flattery kind.

Israfel folded her arms and lifted her wings. "It doesn't matter what he intended. He can't stay." She swept out her hands. "It doesn't take a military mastermind to predict what would happen if he starts encamping demons on the Earth."

Lucifer said, "God would have to send you down here again. Kind of unfair to let me wage a second war and then force you to repeat the burn off. We'd probably cause a lot of trouble."

Her eyes glittered. "Shut up."

Lucifer sharpened his voice. "Is it hard, being always on the defensive? Does it chafe to watch the enemy at work and itch for the order to stop being passive while always hearing your commander telling you no?"

Israfel strode toward him. "You need to leave. This may have been your world, but it isn't any longer."

Sweeping out a hand to encompass the entire planet, Lucifer said, "What has your tyrant done with it but left it fallow as a monument to the failure He refused to stop? If He had the power to crush us at the Second Coming, surely that power was His from the first moments of Eden. He gave us the Earth and then yanked it back, but He's still not using it. We can."

Israfel was vibrating with suppressed fire, and Gabriel knotted his hands in his outermost wings.

Lucifer tilted his head. "If the world's dead, that's not on us. God could have set His boot on the serpent's neck right from the start, and instead He let us strike at Adam's heel. I suggest you march into the temple and demand the reason behind that decision. You won't like the answer."

She blasted him. Gabriel threw himself over the plant, shielding it. Thrilled, Lucifer laughed, and she shot him again while Gabriel curled around himself like an egg, holding tight to his soul.

Raphael needn't have primed Gabriel at all. Israfel was inciting him just fine, her soul in an uncontrolled reaction, and Gabriel's heart screaming that his Seraph needed him.

Lucifer deflected her fire around himself so it scorched up the former Broad Street and rolled as far as Bowling Green. He advanced toward her, but Michael got between.

Lucifer projected, *Why do you still uphold the God who hobbled your defenses? For all your power, you're just as chained as I am.*

Raphael positioned himself between Gabriel and the fight. *Stay down.*

Gabriel prayed, *He's tempting her.* That unbalance he'd detected in Israfel's heart, Lucifer must have detected it, too, and he kept piling more weights on the wrong side of the scale.

How could bonding Lucifer be the right thing if it meant abandoning his responsibility to a Seraph he'd already bonded? The natural order should have had Gabriel infusing Israfel, leveling her out.

Her signature flickered. Michael had ordered her gone, but Gabriel felt her burning deep in Heaven, right at the head of the choir of Seraphim. All around her, they'd be singing, "Holy, Holy, Holy," and Israfel would be flaming out feelings of abandonment and betrayal toward God, who'd done neither.

Lucifer gaped at Michael. "You responded to my assertion that she had no authority by removing her authority?"

Michael ignored the bait. "I appreciate that when you're bored, you start fights, but we are not your entertainment. Consider this your eviction notice."

Lucifer gestured. "Kindly escort me home so you can lock the door behind me."

Gabriel said, "What about your plant?"

The irritation on Michael's face was apparent even to Gabriel, but Lucifer looked surprised. "You just finished detailing the limits of my authority and how the plant lay outside it."

Lucifer's emerald eyes were unusually bewitching. Gabriel folded his arms. "It's been a while since I brushed up on horticulture law, but one assumes we can obtain a temporary injunction to transplant it to Heaven while awaiting the preliminary hearing."

Lucifer smirked. "Do I have the right to competent counsel?"

Gabriel lifted his wings. "I'm not sure, but you do have the right to remain silent."

Lucifer laughed. Heaven help him, but Gabriel's heart illuminated with the sparks he shed. Lucifer said, "Do you remember that joke about God threatening a lawsuit and me asking where God would get an attorney?"

"Fortunately untrue, but you can represent yourself." Gabriel didn't dare look at Raphael. Seeing the Seraph's tension, he'd lose his nerve. "In the meantime, why don't you gather up your plant?"

Lucifer stepped closer. "You do it. I'd much rather see you get your hands dirty."

Gabriel knelt on the ash and worked his fingers around the roots, more than a little surprised when Lucifer got down on the opposite side. Gabriel said, "The roots went deep. I'm not sure I can free them all without tearing them."

Lucifer Guarded the whole thing in a sphere and yanked it out of the ground. Gabriel's feathers flared as the roots snapped.

"I'm not worried about leaving behind a couple of roots." Lucifer gestured so the sphere plunked down in Gabriel's arms. "If they die underground, they die. If you return in six thousand years and find the planet covered in purple heather, send me a thank-you letter."

Gabriel closed his wings around the sphere and pressed it against his chest. "Wax-sealed with a thumbprint?"

Lucifer met his eyes. "Only if it's yours."

Gabriel went warm. "For now, let's bring it home." And maybe bring a bond home as well. Maybe.

Chapter Twelve

Satan flashed Gabriel back to his hotel room, and Gabriel's wings flared when he saw the mirrors.

That made it worth the effort. Gabriel clutched the plant tighter. "You weren't supposed to be able to destroy them."

Satan made a sweeping gesture. "While I've done a lot of things I wasn't supposed to, your overly-technical mind should observe that I didn't *destroy* them."

Gabriel shifted his wings, as if keeping the plant from reflecting would somehow benefit it. Power was going out from him, and Satan waited for him to conclude that the glass couldn't be smoothed. Satan walked right up behind Gabriel and looked over his shoulder at the nearest mirror. In the rippled, dripping surface, they looked well-nigh identical.

Satan murmured, "I like the effect."

With him so close, Gabriel tensed. "I don't."

Satan flicked some ash off Gabriel's feathers. "Just like your tyrant, you love only the perfect things. The imperfect ones come to me, so I've grown to appreciate them."

Gabriel shifted to the side. "And if they shatter?"

Satan blasted over Gabriel's shoulder, smashing the three closest. Gabriel stepped toward the wall, and they reconstituted with the same warping.

Satan sighed. "It's a shame your owner couldn't put them back together."

Gabriel turned, grey eyes gleaming. "Fix them yourself."

Satan cocked his head. "I've already said I like it this way. You'll have to convince me why I should."

Gabriel leaned against the wall, wings raised, eyes bright. "I could, and yet, if you recall, I said we were here to find a pot for your plant, not conversation for your personal enjoyment."

Satan stepped closer. "Surely you're capable of delivering both."

Gabriel turned aside. "Nothing I say is of enjoyment to you, and I don't care to be your sport. Let's find a flower pot."

Satan felt Gabriel grasp him with his heart to flash them off the level, and he let himself go. He didn't care about the plant, but he might as well draw out Gabriel a little more. If nothing, his presence with Gabriel was sure to increase jealousy within Israfel.

At a plant nursery on a deeper layer of Heaven, Gabriel greeted the Angels and the humans in charge, all of whom momentarily swarmed him to get a look at the plant. "It's Lucifer's heather," he said, which caused them to back off.

Satan raised his hands. "I've no intention of incinerating anyone who touches it. Gabriel, deep in his rule-bound heart, believes the plant needs a pot to render it similarly bound."

The nearest gardener said, "We'll...make sure it's not root-bound."

Gabriel huffed as he walked inside. "Lucifer's trying to make you uneasy, so ignore him. I wanted to select a container."

Satan followed. "It's called *Calluna vulgaris*, so to honor its name, I want something vulgar."

Gabriel's eyes sparked. "From Latin for *common*. A common pot would serve, but I wanted something that made a statement."

Satan looked him up and down. "You're certainly making a statement."

Gabriel glanced over his shoulder. "Technically speaking, I've made several statements. Including this one."

Gabriel was zingy today. After the tumult with Israfel, Satan had anticipated another weighty cloud of thoughtfulness, but maybe Gabriel had topped himself up with enough outraged fire that he was spoiling to take on half of Hell by himself.

That would be fun to watch.

The gardeners kept avoiding Satan, so he embarked on a painstaking and thorough search of their entire inventory, making sure to comment on every single item and touch as many pieces as he could. Gabriel refused to let go of that plant, even when Satan wanted to figure out what size pot would be best. "Really, we should just stick its vulgar self in the ground somewhere," he said, while Gabriel demurred, "We need something you can transport, and it would be awkward to transport a lawn."

Satan said, "After I leave, you can tend it for me. Something to remember me by."

Gabriel narrowed his eyes. "As if I could forget."

Once they had a terra cotta pot adorned with mosaics, Gabriel brought Satan to a place he'd heard of but never seen: Gabriel's library.

The library, where they had—everything.

Monkeys had sayings about books being weapons and pens surpassing swords. A lovely aphorism for children, but even so, with the collected knowledge of men and angels in one place, surely Satan could find something of use. "You have no idea how disappointed Belior will be that you invited me here and not him."

Gabriel shrugged. "He's been disappointed before."

On the balcony, Gabriel proceeded to conjure soil and prepare it for the heather.

Sitting on the granite railing, Satan let the sun soak into his wings. "You're doing this entirely for yourself."

"I concluded as much thirty-six minutes ago. But as I said, you cared about the plant, so I'm caring about it, too."

Satan spread his feathers. "Caring is too strong a word."

"You invested it with typological significance." Gabriel quirked a smile, and Satan wondered just how much of that was teasing. "I chose to make it portable so you can continue exploring its symbolism. Do you find that language more fitting?"

Satan opened his hands. "I'm impressed."

Gabriel arched his eyebrows. "As well you should be."

If this were just the remnants of Israfel's fire, Gabriel would burn down shortly. For now, he called over a book and suspended it in midair while determining what a vulgar purple heather required in terms of soil pH, drainage, and nutrients. Satan said, "Did God consult a book?" to which Gabriel only replied, "I'm not God, and as proof of that, I offer that you're talking with me."

And then, as he proceeded to set in motion all the things he'd just learned, Gabriel summoned a different book and started reading aloud. This should have been annoying, except it was an oddly captivating investigation of whether the Earth's transit through the spiral arms of its galaxy had affected the formation of continents. Gabriel would stop every few sentences to add his own emphasis, saying, "So few planets have continents at all," or to create a light image of the Earth's passage through the Perseus spiral arm and muse on how the increase in stellar density would have likewise increased the early Earth's bombardment by comets.

About to take Gabriel down a peg by telling him there was no way this was useful information, Satan surprised himself with a thought. *I could bond him.*

Satan's hands clutched the railing. Bonding Gabriel would give Satan two things. First, access to Gabriel. Gabriel knew all Heaven's inner workings, and having that information at Satan's disposal would offer an undisputed advantage. It might even grant him transport off the outer level to any places Gabriel could enter. Secondly, it would allow Satan additional access to Israfel, whose frustration with God was a heartbeat away from the tipping point.

Every time Satan met Gabriel's gaze, his soul was the coolness of snow and the smoothness of steel. *I could bond him.* Gabriel had offered to do it long ago, but that had been a different Gabriel. She'd been prim and methodical about how he and she would benefit from such a transaction—more to the point, how she would benefit by fettering his soul with a spiritual anchor. The Gabriel in front of him, on the other hand, wore a wildness that must have blossomed in the last thousand years while Satan wasn't paying attention.

Gabriel's eyes were bright with science. "Due to the scale of the event and the timeframe, it never occurred to us to consider how continent formation might result from exogenous processes."

Satan replied with the one line that would always get Mephistopheles excited: "How can we test your theory?"

Gesturing as he spoke, Gabriel expounded on isotopes and sampling the crust and younger supracrustal sequences. They'd long since outstripped anything Satan felt comfortable discussing, so he defaulted to another question. "Should we go back to the Earth and obtain more samples?"

Gabriel sat back from the plant, eyes downcast. "That would be inadvisable."

Satan leaned forward. "Advise it! Wouldn't having you at my side satisfy Michael as to the presence of a suitable escort?"

Gabriel looked uncomfortable for the first time since they'd come to the library. Satan had better back off before Gabriel withdrew into the labyrinth of his thoughts. "Never mind that. Which isotopes did they eventually decide to sequence?"

Satan had no need to return to the planet. He did have need for Gabriel to loosen up, and asking questions was unknotting everything. Asking questions also meant admitting to having no working knowledge of geology, but without realizing that, Gabriel rushed like joyous seawater into the gap, filling it and splashing over the sides.

Abruptly, Gabriel tensed. "Are you teasing me?"

Play this carefully. "I never heard any of this before. I assure you, Belior didn't care one whit about why the Earth had continents, only which coastlines he could plunge into the sea."

Gabriel kept his eyes averted. "I don't have anyone to discuss all these theories with anymore. I feel as if I've worn out my welcome with a lot of topics, but they're fascinating."

Satan slipped off the railing to sit on the other side of the plant, eye to eye with Gabriel. "I always encouraged my Cherubim to study subjects that aren't practical. Sometimes a breakthrough in one field leads to a breakthrough in another."

Gabriel perked up. "For me, it reveals how God uses every force available to create the beauty He wants us to enjoy."

Satan would have to let that slide, otherwise Gabriel would shut down harder than the Earth during the Cryogenian ice age. "Is that what drives you to study?"

Gabriel crackled with curiosity. "I can see Him face to face, but I also love encountering His presence in the things He created. It's like finding an extra treasure." A smile twitched at his lips. "Israfel has a joke about sharing a pretty rock, but sometimes God does give me the equivalent of a pretty rock, and I want to look at it with Him. Then I want to show it to others."

Satan kept sensing tendrils of Gabriel's heart stretching for his and then getting pulled back. Was God getting involved? Or was Gabriel aware of how open he was?

Gabriel wouldn't be the first individual to want something he knew he shouldn't have. If Gabriel was an expert in geology, Satan was an expert in this. "Nowadays, you have no one left to show it to?"

Gabriel looked aside. "Some of the minutiae, no one cares about."

Satan pitched his voice lower. "Make them care. Show them why it interests you so much, and I know they'll care about it, too. I didn't care about plate tectonics until you convinced me to care."

Gabriel looked up, projecting questions.

Satan projected assent. "And horticulture, too. I grabbed a purple heather on impulse, but you researched how to nurture it. Although I still think it should be free and not caged in a jar."

"Like you." Gabriel cupped his wings. "It had an existence in Heaven, but you pulled it away to plant it in a harsh environment. It was nourished by pure light in Heaven but had to fight for light on the Earth. Now it's not like the other plants. It's tougher. In its absence, its spot has likely been overgrown. You may even have changed it to respond more to your specific light."

Satan fought irritation. "I'm not a plant."

Gabriel waved to swat away his objection. "The way I can see God's hand in plate tectonics, I can see your identity reflected in the smaller action of planting a shrub in a biome where it had no chance of survival, and then forcing it to survive."

Was this what it was like inside a Cherub's mind? If so, Satan had been smart never to bond. Was Mephistopheles always making these connections yet keeping silent out of terror that if he voiced any of this nonsense, Satan would give him the reaction he deserved?

Gabriel said, "You've survived."

Satan's mouth twitched. "I did more than survive."

Gabriel nodded. "You rebuilt your whole life. I only had to do it for a year."

Satan said, "On the contrary, you lost more than I did because God led you on further and then took back more."

Abruptly haunted, Gabriel stared at his hands. "That may be true. But I knew I'd be getting it back."

Satan prompted, "That wasn't fair."

Shivering, Gabriel projected agreement. "It was much lighter than I deserved."

Satan's innermost feathers flared. He wasn't going to get a hook in Gabriel this way. Instead he'd appeal to Gabriel's desire to answer questions as well as the universal urge to talk about oneself. "Help me understand something that's never made sense. Out in that field, back when you were shepherding, why didn't you order me to leave?"

Frozen, Gabriel leaked images of the moon and sheep and even the scent of bitten grass, but also deep discomfort and guilt. He'd never willingly talk about this. Satan got the impression that in three thousand years, Gabriel never had.

Pivot again. Satan remembered the poem they'd discussed that night, so he recited it. He voiced the words the way a dusky-voiced Mephistopheles had taught him, placing emphasis on the phrases he'd been told gave it added meaning.

Gabriel summoned a book to his hand, and a moment after, he was singing it. Human civilization had lost this poem a thousand years before Satan had resurrected it for the moon and the sheep and the semifallen Cherub, except Gabriel recalled the voice of the poem as the voice of beauty.

Satan joined the song, and Gabriel defaulted to what Satan had always thought Gabriel did best, harmonizing to him. Gabriel carried his line around and through Satan's, and together their voices blended.

Curling from Gabriel's mind was a stream of images—images from the poem, the image of Satan's own green eyes, images of a plant and a field full of sheep and the moon overhead. All of these were zested with a yearning that left Satan startled and delighted— but Gabriel kept holding back, so Satan started snaking out threads of fire.

He didn't have to bond Gabriel. He could torture Gabriel right to the brink and then exit, the same way he'd abandoned Mephistopheles on an emotional precipice. Let Gabriel fly back to Israfel, who'd doubtless consume herself with jealousy when she realized whom Gabriel truly wanted.

Gabriel's eyes glowed, and Satan hungered to tug that curiosity out of his heart and hold it in his hands. Gabriel, filled with wonder—but instead of wonder about literature, Gabriel could be gazing on Satan and wondering about him. All that awe didn't have to be focused on space dust and literary dust. Gabriel could love something that looked back at him instead.

One bond, and it could be Satan.

Once Gabriel saw and admired him, Gabriel would convince Israfel to do the same. Satan would see to it that he did.

Satan stopped mid-phrase, and Gabriel shivered. He tried to hide it, but Satan had been waiting for this signal: that reflexive reach and stop. He'd felt it so often in souls mid-temptation. Thrilled to be in this dance again long after he'd thought all chances gone forever, Satan reached for the book. "There are too many versions of the next stanza."

Gabriel swallowed hard, silver dancing in his eyes. "Pick one, and we'll keep singing. Every iteration deals with the best parts of the spirit: loyalty and perseverance and fidelity."

Satan ran his fingertips over the leather spine. "You believe loyalty is the greatest of virtues?"

Gabriel stared at Satan's hands on the book. "According to the poem, yes. In reality, no."

Satan breathed, "You're loyal."

Gabriel didn't answer. Images pulsed from him—images of Israfel's eyes. He got to his feet and walked to the balcony.

Absolutely not. Satan closed the distance, flashing right up behind Gabriel so their feathers were millimeters from touching. "What are you thinking? Don't tell me it's nothing. You're so deep inside yourself."

Before Gabriel lay a horizon marred by three cedar trees, cloudless and full of light. Gabriel's hands gripped the railing Satan had been sitting on. "I'm thinking about your plant."

He wasn't thinking about only the plant. Thoughts were flowing from Gabriel right now like steaming water from a colander, but at the base of it, Satan could feel a purple plant battling root shock, light-starved and parched.

Satan shouldn't have grabbed that plant in the first place if it was going to give Gabriel some kind of false entrance into his mind, but he'd done what he'd done. He tried to gather the thoughts Gabriel was emitting—and was fighting. The plant had been parched. Gabriel was parched. And like any parched thing, he could so easily ignite.

Satan said, "Why do you care about that plant?"

"Because you cared about it." Gabriel's heart yearned hard enough to make Satan's eyes sting. He'd never been this close to a Cherub who simultaneously did and didn't want a bond. A moment after, Gabriel calmed himself, cool and brilliant, and Satan's fire surged in response. Gabriel was reminding himself of Israfel and Raphael. He was remembering the plant, remembering reaching his hands into the soil—and in that moment he was reaching into Satan's soul, too. He yanked back, and Satan shivered.

Gabriel gathered himself. "I wanted to save it."

Satan lowered his voice. "Tell me why."

Gabriel should be facing him, admiring him, joining him.

Gabriel breathed, "I knew I could."

It wasn't the only thing he knew. Confusion sparkled around Gabriel, and caught up in the chaos, Satan slid even closer. "You, the plant messiah, redeeming the greenery?"

Satan would have done anything to keep him here. If Gabriel had fled, Satan would have followed—restrictions or not, he'd have followed Gabriel anywhere to feed on Gabriel's fascinated attention as fuel for his voracious heart.

Gabriel said, "Tell me..." and he was breathing deeply to steady himself, "...what do you think..." and really, it was taking all of Gabriel to resist a bond, "...of redemption?"

"Not now, I don't want it." He had to keep Gabriel on the hook. Gabriel would ask when he would want it, which would keep Gabriel in this conversation, on this balcony, on the very very very edge of everything he'd ever craved.

Instead, Gabriel said, "What *do* you want?"

He wanted Gabriel. He wanted to own him, bedazzle him, sate himself on Gabriel's admiration. He wanted to brag to God that the highest remaining angel couldn't resist him. He wanted that coolness of Gabriel's soul to extinguish the hot unrest in his own, to be the candle beneath his flame so he could fold his wings for the first time in thousands of years to settle in a place and a time and a heart.

Gabriel was smooth and silvery, so Satan said, "I want to want to repent."

Gabriel let off a ring of surprise. It expanded past Satan with the coolness of a spring breeze. Satan continued, "I've never experienced that craving to be forgiven. But I wish I could feel it. Just once."

Gabriel remained clear and focused, and Satan felt the clarity expanding in his own mind, as though for the first time he'd put on a pair of glasses and could see. "I don't want to return." His wings were relaxing, his eyes closing, his soul focusing on the fire within himself. For once, he could count and catalog every flamelet, every spark, every ember. There was so much of him, and it all burned so hot. "I want what I've lost. I want not to ask for it."

Gabriel's voice was soothing. "If you had a way back, would you take it?"

Gabriel wanted all of Satan's heart, and Satan knew it was in his power to give it. "There is no way back."

Gabriel's voice was a breath. "You didn't answer my question."

The internal focus was so intense now that Satan found himself opening up to questions he'd never asked. He'd always known the answer was no, but now, here, on this balcony—maybe yes, he might. But it would be humiliating, so he couldn't return that way. Not as a defeat. The only way back was and always had been unseating God, and every time Satan had succeeded in that, God had twisted the whole situation around so He was still on the throne.

Gabriel was marveling—although not marveling at Satan himself, rather marveling at the answers. Want to want to repent was a start! But then also Gabriel was questioning whether it was always humiliating to walk back a decision. After all, hadn't Lucifer walked back his early decision to love God?

Satan pulled away from him, burning—how dare the Cherub see that deeply into him? He'd been tricked by God in those early days when they were all impressionable and knew nothing—they knew nothing about how God would use them—

Except Gabriel was so cool that the anger settled at his touch. Satan remembered peace, the welcome of the early age, the community of the pre-Winnowed angels. And how much he wanted it again—or how much Gabriel wanted it. Satan couldn't tell anymore whose thoughts were whose, and when he reached for that previous focus—

His attention snapped onto Gabriel in his soul—found Gabriel feeding off his fire, forcing it into chambers that powered the pistons that made up all the compartments of Satan's mind.

Gabriel—triumphant that he'd scored a bond.

Bonded? And he'd wanted it all along?

Satan pivoted.

Gabriel's wings flared. He grabbed the plant and fled.

No!—and Satan clamped down on Gabriel's soul.

The fabric of existence screamed with two competing forces. Gabriel had recanted permission for Satan to be off the outer level —and Satan had seized Gabriel with the iron will that had kept him intent for thousands of years.

They crashed together into Satan's room, the only place that could accommodate both. Satan had to be here, and Gabriel couldn't leave.

Satan slammed together a Guard. For some reason, the idiot Cherub still clutched that plant in his arms. Satan flamed Gabriel, and Gabriel protected the plant even though that left himself exposed.

Intense and confusing, the feelings came from both directions. Pain. Betrayal and fear and disgust and confusion. Whose was whose? But did it matter? Because they were stuck this way, and Gabriel was invading his privacy and his thoughts, and apparently had been trying to do so all along? Had been baiting him into opening the door to waltz through? And for what?

Gabriel kept trying to flash out through the Guard, but Satan held it like steel. He ignited. He didn't care any longer about anything—just the flames in his heart that Gabriel wasn't taking down. Wasn't that the only thing Cherubim were good for? Except Satan was too much for Gabriel and always had been. The carpet was afire again. The mirrors were destroyed. Gabriel couldn't escape the room. Couldn't call out. Couldn't do anything.

Panicked, Gabriel backed into the burning wall, wings colorless.

Satan swatted the plant so the pot smashed against the opposite wall. Terror washed off Gabriel, but also—Gabriel was thinking faster than Satan considered possible. A thousand escapes followed by a thousand ways those wouldn't work, all those thoughts in multiple threads so actions and responses generated and regenerated continuously, but every instant, Satan felt Gabriel's growing conviction that there was no way out.

Satan could see through Gabriel's eyes: the people of Sodom, poised to sexually humiliate a stranger. Belior, chaining Gabriel over the Lake of Fire. Beelzebub, locking Gabriel in Hell to annihilate his soul. And worse than all those, Satan.

As he should be.

The flames were so high that no one could have taken them down, the room an oven with an unbreakable Guard. Two thousand years ago, above the Lake of Fire, Satan had held Gabriel in a Guard just as solid, then pierced his Guard with his hand to discharge an inferno. He'd brought Gabriel within one thermal unit of cindering and then dropped the remnants of him on the shore.

His thoughts flickered to that technique, but he didn't need it now. He erupted at Gabriel—who grasped Satan's power as it discharged. Satan felt it scorch through Gabriel, ripping through any blockages in Gabriel's heart. Gabriel couldn't withstand that power, so instead he channeled it and used exactly that technique to pierce Satan's Guard from the inside. The blast propelled Gabriel straight through the Guard and out of the room.

Satan snatched at him, but Gabriel vanished—vanished off the level and out of his grasp.

Satan swore every vow he could think of, his soul-energy slamming through the hotel like an earthquake.

That nasty, obnoxious, revolting, mind-gaming Cherub had been reading his thoughts. He'd stolen that technique. And now he was gone.

Satan could feel him, though. Could feel the pain and the horror and the second-guessing, and searing beneath it all, the unrelenting grief of failure.

Chapter Thirteen

GABRIEL SLAMMED INTO THE Ring of Seven like a comet, burning and crashing and then being caught mid-slide by cool hands, strong hands. Everything scorched and it hurt to think and it was too much power and too much anger and fire, so much fire, and escape had been possible only because Lucifer didn't have any experience using a bond, and he hadn't realized what Gabriel could do with it.

More hands. "I've got you," Raphael was crooning. "Let me help."

Gasping, Gabriel tried to push up and then collapsed in a heap. All that power. Everything had been re-aligned inside, like fleece through a comb back in the days when he'd worked for Tobias and there hadn't been any Seraphim.

Those eyes. Piercing green eyes that had gone black like a shark's, flat with predatory hate.

Humiliation burned, and Gabriel wasn't sure if it was Lucifer's. It might as well have been coming from Gabriel. Even so, all around were gentle touches and prayers and concern. Eyes screwed shut, Gabriel let them work.

They'd heal anything external. Whatever Lucifer had burned, they'd be fixing it now, but Gabriel couldn't feel anything over the emotional turmoil. That plant was gone. It didn't matter how much Gabriel had encouraged it to grow. Lucifer had set it afire along with everything else.

That hadn't been just hatred for Gabriel. There had been self-hatred, too. If Lucifer caused Gabriel months of agony and felt every minute of it, too, then it was no less than he was prepared to face.

Those eyes. Those eyes. Gabriel needed to go back.

Once again, everything felt wrong, and Raphael said, "I need you to stay down."

Raphael wasn't offering fire. Gabriel didn't want any. Maybe never again.

Gabriel should pray. Raphael was praying. Gabriel had nothing.

A presence encroached on Gabriel's mind, requesting permission to enter a burnt-out heart, and Gabriel flinched before recognizing Uriel.

Peace.

Gabriel couldn't have peace. Within Gabriel's heart was thrashing the least peaceful thing in creation, and it kept spreading, taking hold of more and more.

The worst was, Gabriel wanted it there. Every time it hooked itself in deeper, Gabriel recognized the rightness. This bond was a primary. They'd been made for each other. Gabriel had been made for this—and therefore, Gabriel could survive it.

Shark eyes. Hatred. Gabriel needed to explain.

"Stay down," Raphael snapped, only Gabriel hadn't even recognized an attempt to get up.

Saraquael's healing power joined Raphael's. "This looks awful." A pause. "Satan's trying to burn down the outer level. He's demanding Michael deliver Gabriel, but clearly Gabriel can't go."

Raphael's hands were firm. "Tell Michael if he wants to do Gabriel the biggest favor of his life, he'll confine Satan to quarters."

Israfel's voice: "We should chain him in Hell."

Raphael: "We need Satan where we can get to him. Confine him to quarters. It's the best thing Michael can— Gabriel, so help me, stay down."

Gabriel had felt it that time, the reflexive jolt of trying to leave one space and enter another, only Raphael had prevented it.

Gabriel rasped, "I'm supposed to be there."

"The Seraph isn't supposed to be trying to immolate you." That was Israfel, angry but with a subdued tone that meant another of her Cherubim was suctioning power out of her.

Gabriel curled like a comma. "All the connections. We're supposed to stay near. It makes everything stronger."

"Whatever happened was plenty strong." That was Raphael again. "I'm not joking. If you won't stay down, I'm going to have Uriel chain you up or knock you unconscious."

Gabriel tightened up harder. "I need to do this."

"Then quit trying to leave."

Leave. That was the impulse: to flash right back to the bondmate and stay there. Complete the bond.

That first bond with Raphael... Raphael's excitement had carried them through endless conversation because for the first time, facts had the most exciting applications, and ideas were linking to other ideas which then led to conjectures about the very nature of God. With all inhibitions evaporating, Gabriel had thrilled to the possibilities, and it had gone on for hours. Breathless, an exhausted Gabriel had rummaged in her mind for other information Raphael could connect to the emotional fabric of reality. She'd dropped onto her back to gaze at the sky. Raphael had asked, "Do you ever see pictures in the clouds?" and wonder of wonders, he'd reached into her mind and altered her imagination.

Imagination wasn't supposed to be used that way. Imagination was for Cherubim to derive potential answers to complicated questions, not to tell themselves lies. But there was Raphael, revealing shapes in the clouds, then stirring up the wind so they'd change form, so that Gabriel could revel in new images and new interpretations. Waiting for still more clouds to come, Gabriel had closed her eyes and slept.

Later, Gabriel would learn a lot of Cherubim reacted that way. Sleeping freed their minds to respond without self-consciousness to the Seraph's spontaneity, and during that sleep, thousands of little connections germinated alongside the big one. While the Cherub slept, invariably, the Seraph would reach for grounding in

God, planning and focusing. Gabriel hadn't fallen asleep after bonding Israfel, but she had after some of her secondaries. She'd felt safe. With her guard down, she'd felt no need to monitor everything around her.

Gabriel would never sleep again, would never feel safe. Those eyes...

Israfel sounded bitter. "Gabriel probably does need to be near him."

Concern suffused Raphael's voice. "Gabriel, we can move you, but you keep changing shape and emotional configuration. I want you at least a little more stable."

Gabriel focused on the Holy Trisagion, Heaven's ever-present background, but even the *holy-holy-holy* didn't provide support.

Another touch, this from human hands. "I'm so sorry. I never should have asked you to do this."

A projection came from Uriel, that this distress wouldn't be permanent. Gabriel tried to cling to that even though it had been aimed at Mary.

Mary's fingers rested so gently on Gabriel's wing. "How can I help you?"

Gabriel whispered, "I'm hollow."

It was all so fragile. If this had happened before the Winnowing, so much would have changed. Gabriel might have been able to stay alongside Lucifer, nurturing his heather, theorizing if plants could honor God, and if so, what form that honor would take. Would it look like flowers out of season? Would the roots burrow deep in the soil, holding together the Earth so the world itself could give glory to God?

Gabriel and Lucifer could have beheld the Earth and said to God, *Look at the pretty rock we found.*

Gabriel murmured, "I'd have fallen."

As Uriel touched Gabriel's hair, there came a series of projections: Gabriel hadn't fallen. Gabriel had done everything right. Gabriel would keep doing everything right.

Eyes, open. Raphael's hands came away, and Gabriel pushed to sitting. The world pitched like a kayak navigating the rapids.

Mary reached for Gabriel, and Gabriel sat rigid, without the confidence to reach back. Saraquael had been here, hadn't he? He wasn't any longer. Everything was confusion.

Drawn and frightened, Raphael said, "How many languages should I use to tell you how much I don't want to expose you to him?"

Israfel said, "You're in flux. Your form keeps changing."

Gabriel shivered. "His power—"

Those eyes.

Raphael said, "It's like unkinking a fire hose by opening the valve. I get it. But you're still whipping around."

Uriel projected long distance to Saraquael, something about the hotel and a secure room next to Lucifer's.

Could walls and a Guard be strong enough? Once Lucifer sensed Gabriel's presence, he'd pry open each room in the Hilbert like an infinite progression of sardine cans.

An alert from Saraquael: it was done.

Israfel said, "Register my objection."

Raphael said, "Right alongside my own, but we're too far into the process. Gabriel's got to go back."

With Gabriel's arms around his neck, Raphael transported them together.

Gabriel staggered across the room, then stopped and headed back toward the center before dropping to the carpet.

There were couches and a bed, but Gabriel wanted to stay exactly here.

Israfel glanced down. "We're directly over him?"

Sitting criss-cross, Uriel projected affirmation.

Gabriel took a moment to confirm what the subtle body had been saying for the last several minutes. This was now a female body. In realigning every part of Gabriel's soul to carve a passage through it, Lucifer's power had reprogrammed Gabriel into her first form. She tried to switch back into a masculine form, but her body wouldn't stay. She'd be able to do that later, but for now, she would have to go through the rest of this situation female.

Mary sat beside Uriel, eyebrows an inverted V. Uriel took her hand.

Israfel paced the room. "We're in danger. Satan's going to start feeling calmer, and he'll realize Gabriel's nearby."

Gabriel tucked up her knees. "He's not going to understand. I only escaped because he didn't realize how much access a bond gave me. He'll have no idea new partners want to be near each other. When he wants to be near me, he's going to assume he wants revenge." Which he probably did. Gabriel blinked hard. "He must be so confused. I should be there to explain it all."

Uriel projected reassurance.

"Of course I understand why I can't be! But this only unbalances the scales even further." Gabriel plucked at the rug. "We needed to be together from the start. I could have averted it then. If we'd done what we should have, we'd have been fine, and there wouldn't have been a fall, or at least it wouldn't have been Lucifer who initiated it."

Kneeling before Gabriel, Israfel wrapped arms and wings around her. "That's done. You're blameless."

Gabriel shook her head against Israfel's shoulder. "I only escaped being Winnowed because Raphael anchored me. In every iteration, if I'd bonded Lucifer because I convinced him to, I would have fallen. If I'd manipulated him to bond me, I'd have gone with him because I felt responsible. If he'd done it in exchange for my loyalty, I'd have fallen. But if he'd bonded me because he softened up to me, then he'd have stayed."

Raphael said, "You don't know that."

"We prayed about it!" No, wait, had that been Gabriel and Israfel, not Gabriel and Raphael? Gabriel and Lucifer hadn't ever prayed as a bonded pair, and wouldn't that have been amazing, all of Lucifer's zeal focused through the lens of Gabriel's knowledge? "We prayed about when he said I had nothing to offer, but I did have something to offer, and he could have held me to that when he left because the only thing I could have offered was my allegiance." Forehead to Israfel's shoulder, Gabriel worked her fingers into Israfel's feathers. "God made Raphael to safeguard me, and if ever there was a universe where both Raphael and Uriel fell, God would have destroyed it and started over."

Raphael rested a hand on Gabriel's. "Remember when you said we should hold fast no matter how logical you were? It turns out, we didn't have to worry about that."

Gabriel pulled back, but Uriel projected calm. Calm and an invitation: would Gabriel like silence?

Yes. Very much.

Her soul kept twisting inside her, writhing to find a way she could be stable in her subtle body and straining all the time toward her newly-forged bond. Prayer was a struggle, but Uriel prayed with her. A moment after, Mary joined.

Gutted and disoriented, Gabriel reached for God. *I don't know what to do.*

She'd barely escaped. The thing to do was stay right here.

But I don't know what to do.

Didn't know, or didn't like the things she did know?

I don't know.

Gabriel let Israfel's feathers enfold her. She was loved.

Lucifer was a wingspan away, a wounded starling fluttering on the ground. But at least Gabriel was close to him.

Could be closer.

Gabriel changed positions, agitated. Eventually, she rolled back the rug and flattened, cheek to the wood, fingers spread. With her eyes closed, she longed for peace.

Peace had come after Raphael exploded her understanding, laying down applications for all the facts Gabriel knew. Peace had come with Israfel, too. They'd been singing together when Israfel had united the mathematical perfection of music with the spiritual truths of Gabriel's very being. In an instant, everything harmonized. Gabriel had never loved music before, but after that moment, the love never left. Meaning and melody had blended, and Gabriel and Israfel had blended. Peace with Raphael, perception with Israfel...and with Lucifer, panic.

On the other side of a Guard was a Seraph. A Seraph who wouldn't understand why the exact center of the room felt like the best place to be, but who'd stay there nonetheless. The mirrors were distorted and the plant dead. He'd want to be with her. He'd be angry at her for that, too. He'd feel helpless, and that would intensify the rage. He'd miss her without understanding what that feeling even meant after thousands of years of missing God.

They could have been friends. They could have been bondmates.

Gabriel's smarting heart was surrounded by friends and filled with their love. They'd keep her safe. They were praying up protection and healing, and God was all around. Gabriel didn't have to be on guard, not for now.

None of this made sense. *I don't know what to do,* Gabriel prayed, and those were the last words she prayed before falling asleep.

Satan tried to follow Gabriel out of the hotel and got blocked, tried again, tried a third time.

He flashed into the sky, so far up he couldn't even feel the hotels, then tried again. When he stretched, he could make contact with Gabriel's panic and pain, but he still couldn't transport to him.

Satan blasted his anger into those fragments of Gabriel's emotions and attempted to follow, like a miner blowing open a cave. He could feel the pieces of Gabriel's soul shatter, and then he could re-shatter the slivers, but he couldn't get to him.

Well, then. Instead of trying to go to Gabriel, he sent his thoughts like hooks into the fragments of Gabriel's soul, and with a hard grip, he yanked.

He felt Gabriel nearly come to him. Almost. He tried again, and Gabriel's soul budged, but something blocked him from returning.

Blast it. Satan flashed to Michael with his wings in flames. "Gabriel." Satan's swords formed in his fists. "Now. Deliver him."

Satan didn't give Michael a chance to respond before rolling out fire for miles. They were in a field nowhere near the hotels, but he'd burn all of Limbo to the ground if he could.

That obnoxious Cherub needed to explain himself. Grovel. Die. It didn't matter what happened, as long as Satan could wrench that slithering maggot of Gabriel's thoughts out of his head and fling it like a corpse to the rocks.

There were soldiers everywhere, but Satan only strode past them through the flames toward Michael. "Now."

Michael clashed with him, but Satan blew him back. He could still feel Gabriel, Gabriel with all his attention fixated on what they'd just done and the terror of being trapped.

Asmodeus flashed to Satan's side, but Satan didn't need him right now and spun up a tornado of fire to wall in himself and Michael. "Michael, summon that Cherub."

Michael's gaze narrowed. Frustrated, Satan turned up the heat.

Gabriel's attention wavered off him. Deep in Heaven where Satan couldn't go, Raphael would be preening over Gabriel to assert his own importance, but Gabriel would forevermore be thinking about Satan.

Michael projected that Satan had one chance to tone it down.

Satan growled, "Gabriel owes me."

Michael's eyes narrowed. *Not my business.*

Arching his wings, Satan expanded the flames. "I will make it your business."

Gabriel's fear was calming—or else it was evaporating from Satan's awareness. Satan tried yanking Gabriel to himself again, and there came a response—except again, someone blocked him. Frustrated, Satan blasted out heat—and Michael pointed at him.

Satan was back in his room.

He tried to flash out, but he couldn't.

He blasted the windows, then hit the side walls and the doorway and the floor, then discharged all his power at the ceiling. It wouldn't give. He tried to shake the hotel off its foundation, tried to ignite the atmosphere, and finally detonated with the strength of a supernova.

It was futile. He could destroy everything in the room, and possibly everything around the room or even the ground beneath the hotel—he could do it for the full six hours if necessary—but he couldn't destroy the actual room.

Trapped. And Gabriel was hidden like a coward. But he was still thinking about Satan, so that much was worth it.

Satan tried again to crumble the hotel. He couldn't see out. Maybe the whole level was burning.

Except—stop.

If Satan knew Gabriel was thinking about him, did that mean Gabriel knew Satan was doing the same?

He focused on himself. His wings. His hands. His stance. Calm. Control. He went more solid, then less solid. Oriented himself. He pushed at the walls to reconfigure them, but they were at their limit.

Gabriel most assuredly did not have command of him. Gabriel would not indulge in even one second's worth of smugness that he'd dominated Satan's thoughts.

Satan paced the suite. He had to get out. The warped mirrors had horrified Gabriel, and he took refuge in that. If Gabriel found warped mirrors horrifying, then Gabriel would find Satan's mind just as horrifying, and now he was compelled to live partially inside it. Or at least, that's how the others made it sound. Satan would have to figure out the boundaries of this, but of course, he couldn't gather the intel he needed if he was stuck in a room until Michael ran out of authority.

Oh... That spotlight on his thoughts. Those enchanting moments when Satan was inverting and twisting the questions in his mind, when he was challenging his own opinions about everything he'd ever thought—no wonder the other Seraphim caved in to the temptation. That had to have been when Gabriel bonded him. At the very least, that was Gabriel's hand at work in his perception, and it had felt amazing.

Amazing, but also offensive. He didn't need help to think.

It was just as gratifying as he'd imagined to captivate Gabriel's attention. Unfortunately, Gabriel hadn't responded with awe. Fear was good enough for now, though. Gabriel had better be afraid because the moment Satan got to him, he'd demand repayment for this outrage. Repayment in the form of agony.

The excitement in Gabriel's eyes—had that been Satan's own excitement, reflected back at himself?

Although he'd never given it much thought, Satan had assumed bonding was like physical sex, something he also had no inclination to try. He'd figured there would be a long buildup of mutual attention followed by a conscious commitment to completing the action. For that matter, when he'd attempted to bond Gabriel toward the end of his year of disgrace, Beelzebub had prepped him matter-of-factly: just keep exuding fire until Gabriel can't resist any longer, and then he'll give you what you want. Which, again, sounded a lot like a physical seduction.

Satan had been waiting for Gabriel to yield like someone being seduced, after which there would be a clear-cut toggle between, "not bonded" and "bonded." That was why he'd misjudged everything.

Sharing thoughts and feelings was so much more disgusting than mingling body parts that Satan set fire to himself to scour it off, but he couldn't scrub the contents of his mind. Instead he moved to the center of the room for a better look at the plant Gabriel wanted so much to protect.

It was ashes. Satan left it in a heap, and whenever he craved that cool sensation of focus, he looked at it again to remind himself that was what Gabriel intended to do to him. Gabriel had carried that plant from the devastated Earth all the way into the heart of Heaven, picked out a pot, entertained him, and ultimately convinced Satan he was in control of the entire interaction, which was a high level of deception for a Cherub. Gabriel hated lies. So in addition to everything else, Gabriel must have felt a genuine urge to bond.

Had Gabriel really wanted him all along, and post Second Coming, did he feel safe to engage in something that while the war still went on would have put him in danger? Which—well, it was a thrill to be wanted, but that didn't explain everything. Gabriel had been intent on Satan caring for that plant. But from the plant, Gabriel had shifted the discussion to repentance, when Satan had indicated he wasn't entirely opposed to it if the conditions were correct.

That must have been when the bond went to completion. Gabriel had drawn a direct parallel between Satan and the plant, and Gabriel had been nurturing the plant, when all along, Gabriel had wanted to nurture him.

Satan closed his eyes and levitated to the exact center of the room. It felt better higher up, and enclosed as he was, there was no point fighting himself any longer. Maybe Gabriel was flying and Satan was picking up the residue, but who cared? No one was here to see except for God, and God hated him no matter what he was doing. If only one of them were to be satisfied, it might as well be Satan.

It annoyed him being unable to access that cold focus right now. Gabriel would have streamlined this jumble of thoughts. Think: Gabriel had nurtured the plant, but only after Satan himself had nurtured the plant. The plant had evoked light from Satan, and then he'd begun cleaning the air and urging the plant to grow. That's where the parallel broke down because Satan had been as a god to that plant...although Gabriel might say something about Satan making over the plant in his own image. Gabriel had in fact said the plant was changed because of his light, and it wasn't quite the same as the plants it came from. *Calluna vulgaris luciferis?* Sure, why not?

Gabriel wanted to save the plant. Therefore, Gabriel wanted to save Satan.

It was so ludicrous that Satan nearly dropped to the floor. Instead, he floated closer to the ceiling. *Gabriel* thought it possible for him to repent? Did that mean their conversation hadn't just been mental lock-picking, but Gabriel's ardent hope?

God would never let that happen. In another million years, God would keep crushing Satan to powder, and Satan would keep resisting because defiance was the only thing left. Satan had given up everything because he didn't want to be one of a trillion voices singing the same song. It would be a devaluation of the angel God had made him if he got on his knees now and said, "You were right. Let me worship."

And here's to the end of Gabriel's hopes. Satan extended a hand to ignite what was left of the plant, but nothing remained to burn. *Gabriel would have found something symbolic about that, too.*

Now he turned his attention to the mirrors, all of which distorted his own face and scattered his light. Wherever they'd been shattered, those fractures had attempted to knit but only created scars even more distorted than before. He'd created that, and good for him. He didn't want to look at himself anyhow.

That was Gabriel's fault. Gabriel had made him set fire to the room again.

Except, no, Gabriel didn't have power over him. Satan had wanted to frighten him, and he had. Gabriel had fled and wouldn't come back even though he was obsessing about the two of them.

How, then, to entice Gabriel to return? Gabriel wouldn't have formed a bond just to stay away. To contrive some kind of repentance in Satan's heart, Gabriel would need to interact with him. Both their goals required Gabriel to come back, so Satan should make returning an attractive prospect. Therefore, the first order would be restoring the room as a peace offering.

The flower pot was easy. Satan thought the broken pieces back together, forced them to join, and flashed all the dirt and ashes back inside. He'd find another purple heather for it later.

His wings bumped the ceiling. He'd levitated as far as he could, and the ceiling felt oppressive thanks to Michael's petty restrictions.

Next, he'd reverse his process with the mirrors. If he heated the room back to the melting point of glass, he could hold the panes in a flattened, smooth state while he drew the heat back out.

He noted when the room reached flashover, noted again when the walls burned—and then as the mirrors started melting, he held them taut in his thoughts. The ripples flattened out. Then, once he had all that smoothness affixed in his mind, he began the painstaking process of removing sixteen hundred degrees back into himself.

As the glass cooled, it stretched and pulled itself into warps worse than before.

He blew out a breath through clenched teeth, then started again. This time he kept the glass at a higher temperature for longer, and he prolonged the cooling process. And again, once the glass returned to a solid, the smoothness twisted until it was unrecognizable as mirrors.

He struggled to remember everything Mephistopheles had said about glass as thermodynamically unstable and the crystallization process and not having a stable melting point. Gabriel would have something to say about this—and again, Satan wished for that extraordinary focus. Oddly, remembering Gabriel's focus did help in a way. He'd shrink the test area and engage with one mirror at a time, beginning with the smallest. He'd pivot the axis of gravity around each mirror so the glass wouldn't sag. Finally, he'd control the evenness of the temperature as the glass heated and then as it cooled.

He had to set foot on the ground, since the smallest mirror was nearest the door. It felt wrong away from the ceiling, but he shook off the feeling. *Now...again.*

As he worked, he recreated how Gabriel's focus felt. It thrummed through him, oddly fulfilling, curiously powerful. The effort was a thrill as he brought up the temperature, held it, aligned all the molecules, and then worked it back down. Keep it slow, slow like Gabriel seeping into his soul. He was exhausted, but if this worked, he'd spend the rest of his confinement smoothing the mirrors one at a time. Finally, he'd send word that he'd taken up the challenge, and Gabriel could return.

The mirror hit a thousand degrees, and it started pulling in on itself. Satan forced it to stay in position but stopped lowering the temperature. *Hold.* He had good control over matter on a regular basis. Only a few hours ago, he'd been clearing Earth's atmosphere. The relative handful of molecules in a self-healing mirror couldn't possibly be harder than that. And as long as he focused, they stayed in place—

—Until they didn't, and the surface bubbled.

Satan backed off. The mirror cooled right down, distorting into ripples.

Congratulations. God had decreed that these oppressive mirrors couldn't be destroyed, and now they couldn't be redeemed, either. After this many attempts, Satan should have had more to show than this. Instead, it was permanent, and he'd ruined something beautiful.

He punched the mirror and shattered it. It came back together the same way.

From all around the room, his reflection leered back at him: an eye here, a feather there. On another wall he glimpsed a twisted bit of finger alongside something the color of his boot. There wasn't a place he could stand any longer that couldn't be reflected by one of the distorted facets. *All of us,* the images were saying. *You've ruined all of us.*

He turned his head, and just above the dead plant, he encountered his own eyes, piercing as knives.

Gabriel had looked at those eyes and wanted to redeem them.

The mirrors are what I made them, and I'm what I made myself. Making yourself was the entire point of free will. You had to leave your own mark on your soul, creating patterns with every decision, every intention, every action. The finished product was the thing you'd labored on every day of your existence, and at the end, you looked up at God to say, "My will be done." If God had wanted them to subjugate themselves, He shouldn't have given them agency in the first place.

Satan closed his eyes. Gabriel owed it to him to explain it all. Explain why the mirrors wouldn't come back together. Explain why Satan had said he was only one step back from wanting to return. Explain why he was proud of every single thing he'd ever done except for these mirrors, and why the mirrors hung so heavy in his mind.

Gabriel could explain it all, and what Gabriel could explain, Satan could fix.

Gabriel owed it to him to be here. It was an unfairness of the highest order that Gabriel had pried Satan open and then left him to himself. Satan needed him now, and Satan had never needed anybody.

I hate him. Hated those silvery grey eyes, the silvery grey wings, the silvery grey cool touch of Gabriel's mind. Hated getting himself into this position in the first place. Hated the feeling of incompletion. Hated himself.

He'd always been enough. Only now, he wasn't.

Gabriel was right. I am that plant. I am those mirrors. I'm all those things, and I destroyed myself.

Rahab had gone under the lake. Hastle had encased himself in ice. Now, in the center of the room, Satan stared at the ceiling trying to pull it down on himself. Down into the darkness, into the fire, into an eternity where nothing mattered any longer.

Chapter Fourteen

CAMAEL HADN'T LEFT REMIEL'S side.

When she had work to do, she brought him along with her. He also accompanied her (annoyed) to make onigiri in a stainless steel kitchen and eventually helped spoon up rice so she could be done faster. "I don't have a quota," she protested. "I just like making rice balls." He seemed irritated, but he stayed. He stayed when she broke up a fight between two factions of demons, and even more, he got in between and threatened to involve several higher powers.

"Thank you," she said.

He only huffed. "I didn't do it for you. Their behavior is an embarrassment."

Even so.

Camael's presence put an immediate end to Remiel's name-collecting scheme. Any demon who saw the pair of them together had immediate second thoughts about asking how she'd gotten on God's good side. They'd glare at the pair of twins, at which point Camael would demand to know their business, and suddenly they'd remember they had other business elsewhere.

The twins disagreed on so many things. That meant avoiding many topics, but it was mutually understood. He wouldn't tell her that God was a cruel tyrant, and she didn't tell him leaving God was idiocy.

This was going to hurt when he left. They weren't the same any longer, but they had so many similarities. It ached to think she could have been him. But now she realized, if he hadn't left, she wouldn't have become herself. A lot of the things she'd been doing because she was alone, she'd never have begun. They wouldn't both be on the Seven. Definitely not Remiel because Remiel wouldn't have done anything special. Not to mention, she wouldn't be "Remiel."

He asked to visit her home, so she showed him the studio. He looked for a long time and finally said, "Why?" The only answer was, "Why not?" so she had him bring her back to his room at the hotel...and instantly she backed into him.

Mirrors. Everywhere.

He'd hidden them behind curtains, but their presence loomed in her mind.

Camael exclaimed, "You, too?"

She tried to still her wings. "They're oppressive."

He shattered every mirror in the room with a surge of soul energy. "They'll reconstitute in three seconds. Where do you want to go?"

She closed her eyes. "Anywhere without mirrors."

That was directed more to God than to Camael, and immediately they were on the bottom floor. The air smelled of chlorine.

Her wings raised as she walked a tiled hall toward the source. "You have a pool?"

Camael frowned at her. "We didn't build the hotel. That means *you* have a pool."

The different buildings reflected accurate representations of different cultural spaces, and most resort hotels had pools. The implication was this hotel should also have a continental breakfast and an ice machine, and she giggled.

Camael caught the thought. "But look," he said. "Zero mirrors."

"The best number of mirrors." She stepped into the pool area to discover a handful of *viatores* had already found it. The chlorine smell also meant whoever planned this cared a lot more about verisimilitude than Remiel would have. She caught herself before asking if there was a sauna. At the end of the week, Camael would be back in a permanent sauna. She couldn't think about it.

She went to the water's edge and crouched. Cold. Chemicals. Probably not—

And Camael shoved her in.

Remiel blasted out of the water. "What was that for?"

Camael folded his arms. "Sometimes, someone needs a little encouragement."

That was when Camael received encouragement in the form of Remiel bilocating and her second self tackling him into the water. This was entirely too many Irin, but both Remiels were splashing and swimming, and then there were multiple Camaels, too.

One of Michael's soldiers approached. "Do you need any help?"

Camael said, "In armor? You'd hit the bottom like a stone."

Remiel pulled herself together in one location and changed her clothing to a swimsuit. "We're fine."

Camael sent a summons, and suddenly there were demons poolside—followed momentarily by dozens of human *viatores*.

It was strange. Actually, it was fun. Remiel had only ever swum in the ocean, so the pool felt tame—but on the grounds that you can't swim in the Lake of Fire, the human souls were enjoying themselves. Remiel prayed, *Okay, so whoever thought up the pool, this was a good idea.* Did every hotel have a pool? They should.

Also, whatever went on with the hotel's configuration to accommodate bigger and smaller rooms, it was also happening with the pool. The thing had gotten huge. The human souls were coming up with floating toys and other devices. Diving boards. Slides.

Best of all: still no mirrors.

She made her wings disappear so she could swim underwater, then changed her subtle body so there wouldn't be a need to breathe. It was good under here. Silent. Camael was nearby and playing.

When she broke the surface, she encountered a group that kept trying to splash the soldiers on the pool deck. "Break it up guys," she said, moving through the cluster. "You're here for the waves, not to irritate the lifeguards."

One of the demons called, "Poor ducklings, afraid to get your feathers wet!"

A human shouted, "Don't extinguish your halos!"

Someone else shoved past Remiel. "Will your harps warp in the water?"

In the next minute, it was raining soldiers. Remiel shrieked with laughter as Michael's forces dove into the pool. Their armor was gone, and they were right there, playing, too.

The *viatores* had— Well, they had no idea what to do. This wasn't supposed to have happened. Except now suddenly there were a lot of angels in the pool with the demons. Again, the pool expanded in size. That's when the splash war began.

Camael flashed alongside Remiel, looking confused. She splashed him. He dunked her under the water, and she pulled him with her.

That was pretty much the game—splash the being closest to you. Friend? Foe? (Sibling?) Or maybe recruit the nearest soul and gang up on the next-nearest. The ceiling oozed water. Humans started doing cannonballs that blew out the windows, which re-formed after a few seconds.

It wasn't war. They were having fun. There was laughter. And there shouldn't be.

Remiel formed up a beach ball and bounced it into the throng. Camael smacked it just before it hit the surface, and after that, the goal was not to let it touch down. Someone started a similar game across the pool.

It's cooperative, Remiel prayed. *We don't have teams.*

God agreed.

The ball bounced out of the pool, and Remiel was about to flash it back when someone poolside called, "I'll get it," and tossed it back. She bounced it, and the players started counting off bounces. The highest they'd reached so far was mid-twenties, but this time they only hit fifteen when another bad bounce sent it careening out onto the deck. "Ball-boy," one of the demons called, and again the ball came back.

Forty-five bounces this time before it hit the water. Start again. Someone missed bounce number eight, which earned a good mocking. Twenty-one, and back out toward the deck. "Ball-boy!" Again, it bounced back into the pool.

At thirty-six, the ball shot out over the concrete, but this time the ball-boy hit the ball back without breaking the streak. "Thirty-seven!" called Remiel, and they kept going.

The game had changed. Some players were aiming to scuttle the count by hitting the ball too hard or sending it off where there wasn't anyone, but others were trying to get the highest number possible. Fifty-eight—and down. Bummer, but that was a record. And then someone discovered that if you deliberately sent the ball to the ball-boy, the scuttlers couldn't interfere. He'd take the spin off the ball and bounce it back to someone who wanted to get the count higher.

Splashdown at eighty-eight. Remiel called, "Next stop, one hundred!" and they tried again. They got dusted at nine.

Camael muttered, "Really?"

Remiel had solidified all the way into a physical body. Her fingers were pruny, and she was cold, but she'd issued the challenge, so it would be ridiculous to back out before completing it. They started again, and Remiel slammed the ball toward the deck. "Right atcha, Ball-boy!"

He laughed, and that's when she recognized Jesus.

She nearly flashed out of the pool, but He looked to be having a good time. And the demons—there were *demons* playing a ridiculous game of keep-it-up with the Son of God? There was no way they realized. If they had, there would have been curses, and that ball would have gone right in the water because of who He was.

Camael said, "Did someone hurt you? You flinched."

Remiel said, "I'm getting cold," and jumped for the ball.

Fifty.

She made a bad play the next time the ball came to her. The obvious thing should have been to send it deck-side and get it bounced back, but what if the demons realized? Why was Jesus even here?

Camael came up to her again. "You're off your game. You should stop."

"After this." Remiel kept her eye on the ball, which was where most of the players were looking as well. "I need to see how this ends."

Seventy.

Someone sent the ball in low and fast, and the ball-boy dove off the pool deck to intercept it, bouncing it just before it would have splashed down. Remiel hit it high. That gave Him time to climb back out again, but now there were cheers and other players calling, "Ball-boy, come in again!"

Ninety.

Someone jostled Remiel, and Camael shoved him aside. "Leave her alone," he snarled, then leaped to intercept the ball over Remiel's head.

Ninety-five.

Ninety-seven.

Everyone in the pool was counting now. Even the scuttlers had stopped being disruptive. Ninety-nine. One hundred.

Someone threw the ball to the ball-boy, shouting, "Catch!" and Remiel braced herself for the next second because He did catch it —and someone shouted, "Jesus Christ!"

That wasn't a curse. That was, however, anger. *Viator* souls evacuated the pool. Fury. Irritation. Reaching a hundred didn't count because He'd been helping all along.

Camael's hands tightened on Remiel's shoulders. *Did you realize?,* and she put forward that she had.

He shuddered. *You should have warned me.*

Remiel flashed to Jesus and put herself back in angelic form, sitting on her heels and bowing her head. Camael towered behind her, saying, "Why are You here?"

Jesus said, "You seemed to be having a good time."

Camael swept out a hand toward the pool area. "We could have kept having a good time."

Jesus tilted his head. "Did I order you to stop?"

Remiel breathed, "He kept the game going."

"We didn't need his help." Camael towered over Remiel. "Come with me."

He hated Jesus. They'd spent the whole day together, and he still hated everything she loved.

He tried to tug her with his heart, but instead she said, "I need time," and flashed to the Ring of Seven. It wasn't until another five minutes passed that she realized her clothes were still wet, and her hair reeked of chlorine.

In the forty-seventh hour of "on call," Ataf paged Michael to Rahab's room.

The windows streamed with sunlight, and the bed was gone. All three of Rahab's Seraphim were in attendance—and Rahab was awake.

Awake, but his eyes were blank. Michael shivered.

Saraquael reported, "Rahab regained consciousness fifteen minutes ago. He's unresponsive, but otherwise fine."

Ataf scowled. "He's not fine, and Saraquael refuses to summon your other two healers."

Michael inclined his head. "I'm going to apologize for that, but Raphael and Uriel are dealing with an urgent situation that requires their full attention. Since Rahab is stable for now, the best we can promise is that one or both of them will come as soon as their circumstances permit."

Ataf's eyes narrowed. "This will take five minutes."

Michael didn't flinch. "Every one of us has a list of things that will take only five minutes, and as I said, you're their second priority. Once one of them is free, you can have a lot more than five minutes."

Ataf began vibrating, flames flickering from his eyelashes.

This was entirely too many Seraphim. Between Beelzebub

playing war games and Israfel growing increasingly intolerant of anything that looked like unfairness and Ataf pitching a tantrum over shoddy customer service and Satan trying to burn down the universe, Michael wanted every one of them to go take a nap.

Rahab huddled under the window, so instead of dealing with Ataf, Michael sat before him. Rahab remained unfocused, his eyes the palest blush of pink. Michael said, "Have they explained where you are and what happened?"

Ataf snapped, "Of course we have. He's not going to answer you."

Maybe not, but Michael wasn't about to treat Rahab like an interesting floor lamp. "Is there one specific thing we can do for you right now?"

No response, but that meant nothing with a Cherub. Gabriel non-responded this way, too, where Michael would ask, "Name one thing I can do to help," and Gabriel would appear to shut down instead of replying. If Rahab and Gabriel were at all similar, Rahab's flat affect meant he was working so hard to keep control that he'd never considered someone else's intervention might help. But always, long after Michael assumed Gabriel had written off the question, Gabriel would provide an answer.

Come to think of it, that was what had happened when Mary first suggested the bond, wasn't it?

Michael sent word to Raguel that for the moment, Raguel was to consider himself in charge and Michael unavailable. Forty-seven hours of nonstop emergency responses entitled Michael to remain with a thinking Cherub for half an hour.

Ataf didn't interrupt. His silence might mean Michael was right in his assessment.

Mephistopheles arrived, and after a brief exchange with Ataf, in which he did discuss Rahab like an interesting floor lamp, he subsided to observing.

Michael should have expected this. Demons hated indebtedness. The moment they were in a position where a normal creature would experience gratitude, they'd flip it around and make something your fault so they could blame you for it. Anyone could have predicted Ataf's bristling rage that on awakening after thirty centuries, Rahab was not immediately attended by Heaven's highest and best.

Even so, it stung.

Rahab focused on Michael, and Michael envisioned a book.

As with Gabriel, the answer was nothing Michael would have anticipated.

Ataf stood. "Which book?" and Rahab projected clarification. Music?, or maybe a book about music.

If he thought a book would help, Michael would check out half the library. "Can you be more specific?"

Rahab projected confusion.

Give him time. "Have they explained where you are?"

Rahab cocked his head, and disjointed information came to Michael. Heaven? And—defeat? Occupied territory?

Mephistopheles' wings rustled as he shifted his stance. "Is this disorientation a steady state? Do you think he's improving?"

Ataf said, "I can't tell. That's why we need the other two healers."

Mephistopheles shrugged. "I'll continue to monitor, and we're not without healers of our own."

Michael seethed. "Feel free to bring in as many as you like." To be fair, however, Hell didn't have any Thrones, and Rahab needed spiritual healing more than standard healing. Michael returned his attention to Rahab. "I'll escort you to Israfel's music library. Whatever you want, it should be there."

Ataf projected that Rahab would not be going alone.

The undertone of that projection was difficult to read. Anger, possibly. But also...pain? Loneliness? They'd been apart for so long. Michael said, "Saraquael, you accompany Ataf."

Mephistopheles said, "I'll come, too. Summon Israfel."

First off, you can't just invite yourself, and secondly, Israfel isn't your personal handmaiden. Because Mephistopheles would enjoy that kind of response, Michael instead replied, "I'll ask who's available." Momentarily, they were joined by an Angel musician who had a reasonable familiarity with Israfel's library. If

Mephistopheles thought it a subtle insult, he made no acknowledgement. But he also didn't say thank you.

Michael transported all six to the great hall and its perfect acoustics. For a long moment, Rahab stared without focus.

Supporting Rahab with his wings around him, Ataf said, "Tell us again what you want."

Once more: the thought of a book, and the concept of music. Ataf blew off a cloud of frustration.

Saraquael quipped, "On the bright side, if the only thing he wants is a music book, anything here will fit the bill."

That earned him a nasty glare from Ataf and no acknowledgement from Rahab.

Mephistopheles made straight for the index ledgers. "Anything he remembers has to have been written prior to the Exodus, so that sets an upper boundary on the search."

Saraquael said, "We don't even know if he wants a book about music or actual sheet music."

Mephistopheles thrust a ledger at the Angel musician. "Scan through here for anything written by Rahab or Ataf. I'll search this one."

Ataf's wings raised. "Why that?"

Mephistopheles didn't look away from the shelves. "He was separated from his Seraphim for three thousand years. Surely in that time, he wanted to make contact with something of you."

Deep inside himself again, Rahab wore a thousand-mile stare. Saraquael said, "With your permission, I'd like to try seeking whatever it is."

Michael anticipated that Ataf would hate what Saraquael did next, but at least Ataf didn't stop it: Saraquael stood behind Rahab, hands on his shoulders, wingtips touching, and started projecting directions. Think about the book you want. Consider any images around it. Hold the feeling.

After a minute, Ataf walked toward the center of the library, the most acoustically perfect spot in all of Heaven. He murmured, "Mephistopheles was here already?" He turned like a panther scenting prey, then stopped at a desk, hand on wood that tingled with Mephistopheles' energy. Finally he craned his neck and took flight.

Michael joined him. "Israfel did mention they'd visited."

"I assume that's why he knows her indexing system." Ataf frowned, tracing his hand over a desk among the stacks, and again Michael could detect the residue of Mephistopheles' presence. Not only his power, but also some other emotion had stained the materials. Ataf didn't pause long enough to identify it, just ran his fingers along the folders in their well-organized order, then paused and ran backward again. He narrowed it down to one.

Michael frowned. "These are ancient hymns."

Ataf huffed. "I'm glad Israfel's the one who saved them, and not Lucifer. Can you imagine? 'Ataf, here's the first song you wrote! I'm going to play it just the way you played it back then.' Talk about humiliating."

Michael didn't ask if the humiliation would come from the relative lack of skill, or the fact that demons had once written love songs to God.

"No titles, no attributions." Ataf flipped through the contents, then paused on one particular hymn. A moment later, Michael felt the Seraph projecting the notes as if they were sounds. A basic tune, but the paper crackled with emotion.

Nothing about this hymn made it stand out to Michael. He projected to Ataf, *Out of all Israfel's library, this is what Mephistopheles chose to read?*

Ataf smirked. *Based on what he asked his babysitter to search up, either he wrote this, or Beelzebub did.*

Michael smiled.

Ataf side-eyed him. *Keep that to yourself. It's excellent blackmail fodder, and you can't leverage it to maximum effect.*

Michael thought but didn't project, *Yes, how dare anyone feel fondness for the souls they care about?*

From the library floor, Saraquael projected to Michael and Ataf, *I'm not seeking up anything specific. All joking aside, maybe he just wants a book about music theory.*

Ataf shoved the folder back in its slot. "Rahab was a musician, pre-Winnowing. On the Maskim, as you can imagine, we didn't get a lot of time for our instruments, but he used to lurk in palaces and temples to listen to their songs."

Saraquael sent, *What were his favorites? If you put a book into a Cherub's hands, he'll automatically start to read. Maybe enough of his thoughts will click into gear that he can specify further.*

Ataf flashed to Saraquael, and Michael transported himself to the index room—where he found only the Angel musician. "Where's Mephistopheles?"

The Angel looked up. "He had a list of pieces to track down."

The whole point of an escort was to *escort* the individual. The one-to-one meant Mephistopheles couldn't leave the library, but the intention was to keep the demons from harming anything. Michael was already planning how to apologize to Israfel when he flashed to Mephistopheles and found him at a desk with sheet music spread before him.

The demon immediately stacked the pages together. "Oh, good, you're here. I thought one of these might be what Rahab wanted, but after further inspection, I think not." He handed Michael the top half of the stack. "You put these away, and I'll take care of the rest."

Michael flashed the remaining pages to himself. "I may put you away." He flipped through the assortment—all old, some of them Rahab's compositions—and then—

Israfel is going to detonate. That hymn.

Michael confirmed Lucifer's sigil on the front and back pages. "Let me guess—you had to pick several locks and undo a Guard to get this?"

"Guarding only one shelf in a library would be as good as a Dewey Decimal designation for Top Secret. It was hidden, but otherwise accessible." Mephistopheles frowned. "The Heavenly host never performed that again, have they?"

"You had not even the first intention of assisting Rahab." Michael dropped most of the music in the "to be re-shelved" basket. "Where was it? If Israfel realizes, she'll demand I confine you to quarters for the remaining days, and I'm going to honor her wishes, so it's in your best interest to be honest."

Mephistopheles flashed Michael to Israfel's inner office (which yes, had formerly been secured) and indicated a shelf behind a desk. "I've memorized it, so I no longer require the manuscript. Nevertheless, Israfel's behavior surprises me. As the Angel of Music, shouldn't she object to mummifying a truly beautiful piece rather than allowing it to breathe?"

Michael had witnessed the original performance. The angelic liturgy hadn't yet achieved its final form, so in the midst of its development, when Michael had seen "Lucifer" slotted in as leading a liturgy, he hadn't thought much of it. It was odd that he'd given his hymn a name, as though it were a living thing, but again, not Michael's business. Michael was merely an eighth-order angel. Every time, he'd show up and allow the angels who served as the glory of the orders to handle the details of their worship. Michael's job was to love God, and he did. That one time, he'd been taken aback by the majesty of the performance. The energy. The awe. The enthusiasm. The skill. Afterward, Hastiel had breathed, "I had no idea we could do that."

The next week, the liturgy had changed again. Lucifer wasn't leading it, but once more the centerpiece was a highly technical performance, with a named hymn by a named composer, played and sung by a few expertly-skilled angels and listened to by everyone else. In the middle of it, Michael had prayed, "But isn't this more about us than about You?"

Michael's discomfort with "All Praise to My Creator" wasn't about who Lucifer turned into afterward. It was about what Lucifer had temporarily turned worshipping God into: a performance. The angels' early songs had been them fumbling for the right words, thrilled and vulnerable and surprised and delighted. Their early hymns felt like questions, whereas Lucifer's felt like an answer—an answer with an exclamation point.

A hymn should be about the greatness of God, not about the greatness of the composer.

Michael had watched throughout human history as civilizations grappled with the question the angels had wrestled with first: what to do with the art of terrible people? When art was beautiful, even if its creator went to Hell, wasn't it worth preserving? Maybe it was the only beauty left from a soul initially forged in the image of God. King David had impregnated a woman under his authority, then ordered her husband murdered, and yet his psalms remained in the Bible. Solomon used his wisdom to commit idolatry, but his writings, too, were considered sacred.

Michael had brought this to God, and God had said, "I leave it up to you." Michael wasn't a musician, so he left the decision to the ones who were.

Saraquael flagged him, so with the music re-shelved, Michael flashed back with Mephistopheles. Rahab stood reading a book.

Saraquael beamed. "As it turned out, my joke was more right than I anticipated."

Ataf said, "It's a compendium of music history."

That text had to be five inches thick, the print minuscule. Michael said to Rahab, "You wanted to catch up on three thousand years of musical development?"

Ataf folded his arms. "You're not going to get his attention, but yes."

Fighting laughter, Saraquael said, "Let's set him up at a desk so he can read in peace," at which Ataf muttered, "And paper so he can take notes."

Mephistopheles stiffened, then disappeared as though torn away. Michael started.

Running a hand through his hair, Ataf grimaced. "I do not at all miss that part of being on the Maskim, when the master decides he requires you now, right now, and drags you inside." He started moving toward the desks, then turned back. "I understand you can't stay the entire time, but can you make it so Rahab and I have escorts and can?"

Michael nodded. "Absolutely. If Rahab ever raises his head, tell him we also curate a library of instruments."

Projecting darkness, Ataf folded his arms and stared at the floor. "Look. I know you don't have to do this. Any of this."

Michael blinked. "I didn't do anything."

"Your side. Your people." Ataf shuddered. "Saraquael had no choice but to find Rahab because God ordered everyone out of Hell. I asked because I know how to take advantage of inflexible orders. You could have justified leaving him there, but you assembled an all-star team who derived several new techniques to locate him. Once he was out, there was no further mandate. Instead, you've allowed us access to your healers, and even after he awoke, you're still helping."

Michael shifted his weight.

Ataf pursed his lips. "In five days, we're all getting flushed back to Hell, so you'll never see us again. Those actions shouldn't go unacknowledged."

Michael said, "We wanted to do right by you. Rahab needed help."

Ataf had needed help.

Ataf narrowed his eyes, but he didn't ask the thing Michael expected—maybe because he didn't want to hear the answer, or maybe he couldn't even formulate the question. But Michael could: *Why are you doing this for your enemies?*

Why, indeed? Michael himself wasn't sure, except that leaving Rahab in pain and abandoning Ataf to grief had felt wrong.

Reading about music they'd never hear wouldn't alleviate the pain of damnation over the course of eternity. Rahab and Ataf had today, though, and this was a kindness the angels could do today. Saraquael had sought out Rahab because he was a seeker. Raphael had healed him because he was a healer. Doing the work God made them to do was always the right way.

The words dried up in Michael's mouth. Ataf said, "Again, your unrequired efforts are noted."

Not thank you. "Thank you" was vulnerable. Passive voice meant Ataf himself didn't have to be the one experiencing the gratitude. The angels' kindness could simply...be noted.

Michael reached for God, and reassurance blossomed inside.

Also, Satan's time-out had ended, so Michael returned to the outer layer.

Chapter Fifteen

MEPHISTOPHELES STRUGGLED TO PREPARE himself as Lucifer dragged him away from the music library. Angels weren't used to this because God merely issued a summons, but Lucifer hauled you into his presence via subpoena. (It also came in handy when you didn't want to continue a conversation. If you vanished mid-sentence, no one assumed you'd tired of the company.)

He arrived in a room that tingled with the Asmodeus/Belior bond, but Satrinah and Moloch were also in attendance. Momentarily, their group was completed by Beelzebub.

Lucifer stood at the window, the glare of daylight at his back. His arms were folded and his gaze livid. After Lucifer had attempted to destroy the Hilbert and then spent the night locked up in his own room, whatever news they had for him, it had better be excellent indeed.

None of them knew what had gotten him angry enough to break every mirror in Limbo. Mephistopheles was sure it wasn't him, but there was always the risk of overflow. Even though you were innocent of this offense, you never were completely innocent, so once Lucifer was at a boil, you'd likely get punished for something.

Lucifer growled, "Report."

Every report was banal enough. Mephistopheles noted that Asmodeus made no mention of their missing Hastle, and then realized with surprise that Lucifer himself didn't catch the omission. He made comments but seemed otherwise disengaged.

Mephistopheles drew Beelzebub's attention to all these curiosities, and Beelzebub's wings lifted a fraction. Moloch, too, seemed very intent on the conversation.

Lucifer paced near the windows. "We need a breakthrough. Talk to me about Seraph-Cherub bonds."

Belior's feathers flared.

Satrinah seemed bored. "You mean forcing a bond across the divide? I wouldn't advise that as a means of accessing their side."

Lucifer said, "Many bonds were broken after the Winnowing. Can those be revived?"

Belior sounded strained. "Six primaries were broken. I can request meetings with the six on our side to determine if they've made any attempt to renew the bonds. It might give us a handhold into some of the enemy's operatives."

Lucifer said, "If one of them is carrying around part of the other, shouldn't that give them *carte blanche* to access the deeper levels of Heaven?"

Belior folded his arms. "Bonds don't work that way. We're not retaining pieces of the bondmate's soul as much as allowing them access to our own, and that access doesn't have to be in physical proximity."

Lucifer's eyebrows raised. "You would be able to access one another on different levels?"

Beelzebub said, "I was always able to reach Mephistopheles on Earth or in Heaven from anywhere in Hell, but that's not the same as him being accessible. I wouldn't be able to break through a Guard to join him, for example, and he could hide from me if he wanted."

Belior's voice grew tenser. "If you recall, Raphael and Israfel were unable to locate Gabriel in Hell for several days, so there are limits to locatability."

With his wings uncharacteristically tight, Lucifer folded his arms. "I'm not discussing Gabriel. If we get those six separated pairs to reconnect, say by dangling the promise that the fallen half of the bond might flip back, how can we use that?"

Belior shook his head. "Understand that weaponizing a bond

would mean a level of deception of which most of us would be incapable. The bondmate is accessing your soul. Anything one does that's intended to manipulate the other, it's detectable. The enemy's part of the pairing would sense our party's intention."

Lucifer scowled. "Surely the enemy's part of the pairing, as you put it, would have a similar intention. It might keep them engaged even though the enemy knows."

Mephistopheles said, "Don't underestimate the danger to our side. We've seen repeatedly that the enemy isn't eager to let go of His minions, but He'll absolutely claim ours. God will seize the opportunity if ours are so much as open to being open."

Lucifer's eyes widened. Beelzebub amended, "Although bear in mind, those were all un-judged monkey souls that were still alive."

Mephistopheles frowned. "For safety's sake, we have to assume every one of us is considered takable by the enemy. Why else would they call us *viatores* unless they're referencing the *status viatoris?*"

As opposed to the *status comprehensoris*, in which a soul comprehended God in completion. Or whatever they'd been in Hell. *Status infernalis*, perhaps?

Satrinah said, "A cross-bond could in theory be used to overpower the one on the other side. That works much better if the Seraph is ours and the Cherub theirs. Seraphim can overwhelm Cherubim with fire and leave them in a state near destruction."

Mephistopheles shivered. Beelzebub brushed a feather past his leg.

Belior's wings tightened around himself. "For a cross-bond to form, the enemy's part of the pairing would have to consent, and I can't theorize why they would."

Lucifer's eyes glinted. Asmodeus snapped, "Revive, not form."

Belior started. "I apologize for my imprecision. Yes, revive."

Lucifer paced again, rubbing his chin. After a long while, he said, "What about the Irin?"

It was Mephistopheles' turn. "I've studied them extensively, sir, and theirs is a different sort of attachment. They're one soul in two persons as opposed to two souls engaged in an exchange. Camael cannot burn out Remiel for the same reason fire cannot consume itself."

Asmodeus added, "They have, however, been spending time together almost exclusively. I'll isolate Camael and get his perspective on how pliable she is."

Belior said, "It would be ideal if Camael could get permission from Remiel to in effect be her, but the enemy isn't using the facial recognition technology for admittance to the inner levels."

Mephistopheles said, "If we could convince them to combine, even temporarily, Camael would have access to everything she does. In theory."

Belior muttered, "In theory, theory works."

Beelzebub bristled, but Lucifer had already turned to Mephistopheles. "Can you and Beelzebub *combine* that way? As one soul?"

If only. "We can get very deep, but we're still separate creations. The cross-bonded pairs would not be able to combine into a single unit and thereby gain us access to the inner rings."

Lucifer rubbed his chin. "I still feel like there's something to cross-bonding."

Belior offered, "I would be glad to remain and keep discussing it with you."

Mephistopheles didn't like that tone at all. Fortunately, Lucifer didn't sound as if he liked it, either. "If I find myself in need of additional knowledge, I'll be certain to consult you. On another subject," and that was a lovely shut-down from the Lord of Fire, "we have free access to the Earth."

Mephistopheles jolted to attention. "We didn't have access from Hell."

Lucifer cocked his head. "And yet, as befits traveling *viatores*, we do from Limbo. I was able to get there unescorted. Of course, the enemy sent someone to fetch me back, but I reconnoitered the planet. It's thoroughly destroyed, so I've begun the process of clearing the atmosphere. If we can create a linkage to Hell from there, that would be of untold strategic value."

Belior said, "Asmodeus and I can initiate that work."

Lucifer's eyes gleamed as he looked at Asmodeus. "Use the tunneling technique that Hastle hijacked for his little escape pod. I'm sure your guidance is how he developed it in the first place, and it may prove useful now."

To his credit, Asmodeus only inclined his head. "That was my intention. Are there any other locations to which we have free access?"

Mephistopheles said, "The Heavenly Temple."

The room went so quiet that Mephistopheles could hear a mirror un-shattering itself two floors away.

Lucifer sounded astonished. "We have unescorted access to the actual temple?"

Moloch blinked out and back. "He's right."

The angels hadn't corrected their oversight. Perhaps it hadn't been an oversight to begin with.

Belior glared at Mephistopheles. "Why were you in the temple? Brushing up on your psalms of praise?"

Beelzebub folded his arms. "He forgot to leave his offertory envelope the last time he was there, and he owed them a dollar. Or, perhaps—and you may want to sit yourself down—he was reconnoitering for penetration points exactly as our master instructed us to do."

Lucifer had flames around his head. "How long were you able to stay before they ejected you?"

Wings tight to his back, Mephistopheles said, "They made no attempt to eject me. In fact, I got invited in further."

It wasn't often you could surprise Lucifer. Mephistopheles mentally added one tally mark to the running total.

Belior said, "Did you go?"

"I was curious what would happen." Mephistopheles tilted his head. "Nothing of note did. I'd been bound to silence in the temple, but in the inner sanctum, I was free to move and speak."

Asmodeus drawled, "Did God give you a gift?"

Trembling, Mephistopheles said, "I refused anything He could possibly offer."

Lucifer grinned. "Now you're making me curious as to what it would have been."

A step backward brought Mephistopheles right against Beelzebub's wing. "With all due respect, sir, I'd prefer not to go back. I knew you'd want to be informed about the access point, and I was uncertain if any so-called gift would be my annihilation."

He'd never learn what that gift was. God never offered the same thing twice, so refusing a gift was a huge thing to do—a thing unthinkable to the other side.

Smirking, Belior narrowed his eyes. "Poor, scared Mephistopheles. Since this information was so important to tell our master, why did you wait, oh, twelve hours to inform him? What if the Almighty had used that time to seal off our access?"

Beelzebub said, "You sound upset that you didn't get offered the Heavenly Temple's party favor."

Lucifer waved them down. "I'm mind-boggled by this. Are you telling me we can walk into the heart of Heaven, and from there enter a one-on-one, face-to-face meeting with God Himself, unimpeded by anything?"

Since that was a thorough summary of what he'd reported, Mephistopheles said, "Yes, sir."

Lucifer began shedding light. "How can we use this? We can't flood the inner dwelling. Unless the rules have changed, souls always arrive in there alone." He turned to Beelzebub. "Analyze the strategic significance of both these access points." To Mephistopheles, "I still want an answer on the *ex nihilo* problem, but now factor in that we can use the materials from the plane of Creation." Back to Satrinah and Moloch. "I want a complete report from you on all the possible uses of a Seraph-Cherub bond across the divide, including a breakdown of the six broken primaries and all the secondaries." Then to Asmodeus and Belior, "You two are in charge of establishing stable passage between the Earth and Hell. Dismissed," and he vanished.

Mephistopheles was about to leave when Belior spurted enough power to shatter all the mirrors and disintegrate the furniture.

What? With his wings spread, Mephistopheles spun toward a

smirking Beelzebub.

Moloch said, "Gabriel?"

Asmodeus snorted. "Without a doubt."

Belior's eyes were bright enough to cast shadows. He stalked to the nearest window and punched, but the glass didn't shatter.

Satrinah folded her arms. "Which one would have initiated? Bonding is unlikely to have happened by accident, and based on his questions, Gabriel didn't explain anything."

Explain...? What? Bonding? Gabriel...*with Lucifer?*

Eyes black, Belior paced. "That boytoy. That conniving, manipulative boytoy."

Beelzebub snorted. "Gabriel was hardly in it for the fun. We just endured a boring analysis of bonding from a strategy perspective, and all of us admitted there were exploitable avenues. If Gabriel yielded to him, then we have to assume Gabriel had a tactical purpose."

Mephistopheles played back the meeting, reframing each of Lucifer's questions as a dive for information. Now he realized Satrinah had fed Lucifer that information in a way leading to one conclusion: if the Seraph were stronger, he could burn out the Cherub.

Mephistopheles murmured, "It has to have been Gabriel's doing. If Lucifer initiated the bond, he'd have bragged about it."

Satrinah snorted. "Oh, good, you've finally caught on." Belior was casting rings of rage, and to him, she added, "You'll get your turn. He's going to lose his mind in five days when they're separated."

Moloch added, "At least now you have a chance at the one you really want."

Beelzebub shrugged. "Maybe Belior should throw himself at Lucifer, just so Gabriel isn't the only game in town."

Of course, Beelzebub hadn't volunteered his own Cherub. But then again, Belior was radiating such jealousy that keeping a low profile had much to recommend itself. If Mephistopheles needed any encouragement in that train of thought, it was Satrinah's behavior—because at no point had she acknowledged that she herself stood a low but measurable chance of becoming Lucifer's primary.

Also, this tactic was provoking Asmodeus. Mephistopheles alerted Beelzebub, who said, "Gabriel did try to bond our master back before the Winnowing."

Asmodeus paused, then grinned. "And got shot down?"

Beelzebub smirked back at him. "According to Israfel, Lucifer issued a flat-out refusal and said that Gabriel didn't have anything to offer. Israfel was livid."

Asmodeus had a gleam in his eye. "Did Gabriel cry?"

Beelzebub folded his arms. "Gabriel agreed with him, which shows Gabriel's as smart as the press releases would have us believe. If Lucifer snared Gabriel now, then he has to think Gabriel does have something to offer."

It still sounded more like Lucifer finding a use for Gabriel retroactively, but since Asmodeus was calming down, Mephistopheles held that thought. These were strange times, so a Seraph calming a Seraph went right along with every other reversal.

Belior clenched his fists. "I suggest we contain Gabriel and figure out what that is."

Asmodeus spun on him, undoing all that de-escalation. "And I suggest you get yourself under control. You've always been shameless about wanting to bond him. You'll get your turn."

Mephistopheles leaned against the wall, rubbing his chin. "We do need to nail down Gabriel's intentions. Is he hunting for information?"

Satrinah narrowed her eyes. "Perhaps he's gone mad. There cannot be sufficient payoff. Consider the pain Lucifer could inflict from inside your soul. He's bad enough on the outside." Moloch blazed, and she put a hand on his arm. "Be logical for once. You can't protect me from him. The best protection is to keep him out of our heads."

Beelzebub squared his shoulders. "Except once we leave, he'll force every single Cherub to bond him so he can have exclusive use of them whenever he wants. Gabriel has to stay with him."

Mephistopheles raised his head, "Be careful. Gabriel's consent to a bond makes sense only if Gabriel intends to convert Lucifer. Among the monkeys, some of their theologians have posited that if God wanted to seduce Lucifer back to His side, God would make a hundred seventy-nine degrees of the turn, but Lucifer would have to make the last degree for himself. If he didn't, then the brainwashing wouldn't be complete."

Beelzebub flared, and Mephistopheles reflexively pulled in the fire. Satrinah was right about this: if Lucifer started relying on them to absorb his power, his primaries would be charcoal within a week, and then he'd start consuming his secondaries.

Mephistopheles continued, "The rules of free will say God can't do anything to us without our consent, so He makes subjugating one's intellect and will seem attractive. Lucifer can't be made to grovel on his own, but what if by leveraging this bond, our enemy could convince him to make that last little turn?"

Asmodeus glowered. "We can't resist if Lucifer attacks his own side."

Beelzebub said, "You realize that if he catches wind of this conversation, we're all six as good as cindered."

Belior snapped, "He'd still have to make that last degree on his own. He won't."

But maybe he should.

That voice popped up inside Mephistopheles—so faint, so soft that Beelzebub shouldn't hear it. Even Mephistopheles shouldn't be hearing it, but hear it he did. *Maybe he should.*

Maybe it was time to admit the things they'd done were wrong, and that they'd led one another astray, only to keep on scattering. It might be time to admit that when Mephistopheles looked at the friendships the other side's angels had with one another, he constantly noticed his side didn't have the same. He'd have to admit that even when Israfel was outright criticizing God's injustice, she wasn't the least bit afraid even though He could hear her. Mephistopheles might go so far as to admit that a God who would let His worst enemies into His most sacred spaces unescorted, with only a bond of silence so they didn't disturb anyone else, and then offer a gift...was maybe not someone they should have rebelled against in the first place.

Would it be possible to refuse a gift from Lucifer? No. You'd have to say thank you. By contrast, God had asked. Then, when Mephistopheles refused, God hadn't forced it on him.

Maybe Lucifer should look at what he'd created versus what the angels had created and ask what was the difference.

What if they were wrong?

Beelzebub said, a little too loudly, "All this speculation isn't helping. Right now, we have an operation to salvage."

Mephistopheles shivered. How much of his thoughts had Beelzebub overheard?

Satrinah started brightening, doubtless pulling power from Asmodeus. Calmer, Asmodeus said, "If we fail despite all the opportunities we've been handed, and then Lucifer gets fire-crazed because he's cut away from the only bond he ever formed, it's going to be the four of us who pay. Possibly all six," he added significantly. "Whatever he thinks Gabriel is going to give, he has to secure it. We've all got assignments, and those need to be cleared as well."

Why had God given them this chance to spit in His face? The Abraham story had made no sense from the start, and it still didn't unless whatever Gabriel was doing, God was in on it, too.

Minutes after the Resurrection, Lucifer had stormed in on Jesus, still in the tomb, and demanded an accounting. Jesus had conversed with him as though the Maskim had as much right to be there as the angels, only Lucifer had cut Him short. As the Maskim left, Gabriel had caught Mephistopheles' eye and whispered, "Mistofiel, stay."

Mephistopheles had not stayed. It was the right call because a few days later, he and Beelzebub got a promotion.

Gabriel might still want them back. Worse, he might have a chance of success.

Too many souls were hurting. If God offered them a way out, they might give in and worship, no matter how much it lowered them to do so—although right now, in this room with the specter of an over-fired, Cherub-deprived Lucifer towering in his mind, Mephistopheles couldn't remember why he'd thought worshipping the Second Person of the Trinity in a human form would have diminished him. Beelzebub had insisted it would, and Mephistopheles had gone with him.

Moloch said, "Also, just so you know, our enemies have transferred Hastle to the temple."

Moloch could have thrown Mephistopheles under the bus for not mentioning that earlier. Mephistopheles opted for confusion. "Holding Hastle in a place we can freely access?"

Beelzebub shrugged. "Sounds as if they're not holding him. Hastle must be there because it's the only place off level he can reach on his own."

Asmodeus balled his fists. "Thank you for that information. I'll make use of it."

Hastle had fled there for safe harbor, and God had allowed it without any benefit whatsoever to Himself.

Beelzebub said, "Everyone, report in if you encounter Gabriel," and then flashed back to his room with Mephistopheles, who let it happen.

Maybe he should make the turn. Maybe we all should.

Surrounded by mirrors, Beelzebub wheeled on Mephistopheles. "Don't blindside me like that. You should have told me you got into the temple so I could scout it for strategic value. Instead, Moloch and Asmodeus have the advantage."

Except God might offer another gift, and Mephistopheles didn't want Beelzebub to take it. "I hadn't considered that access point useful for war."

"What happened in the inner dwelling that upset you so much?" Beelzebub must have detected that urge to run because he stepped closer and trickled fire into Mephistopheles. "Did the enemy harm you?"

Mephistopheles looked aside. "He offered a gift. I told Him I didn't want anything from Him except to be left alone. But I believed He'd destroy me on the spot because existence itself is a gift."

Beelzebub frowned. "I'm glad He didn't."

It was something.

Mephistopheles braced himself. "If you're in there, no matter what He offers, don't take it."

Beelzebub grinned. "How can you not be curious about what it was? What if I were to open the gift and throw it back?"

God's gifts weren't like that. Opening the box meant accepting the present. "Please, don't."

For once, Beelzebub didn't force the issue. "At any rate, the next thing you need to do is talk to Gabriel, and that won't be hard." He opened his hands and laid out a miniature map of the hotel in lights. "Right after a bond, Gabriel would have wanted to be with him. Michael confined Lucifer to quarters, I'm guessing so he could do exactly that." A green dot lit on the map. "That means Gabriel is in one of these four rooms."

Four silver lights shone around the green. Mephistopheles blinked. "That's brilliant."

"I have my uses." Beelzebub chuckled. "Of us all, you have the best chance of drawing out Gabriel's motive, so I want you in negotiations with him now."

Chapter Sixteen

GABRIEL AWOKE WITH SUNLIGHT in her eyes and energy in her wings. The carpet under her fingers was pitted as if she'd been digging into it for hours, and her feathers were vibrating.

Music played, but the moment she reached out with her heart, the music stopped. Raphael's soul refused her entrance, and she frowned as she sat up. How long had she been unconscious, and what had happened in her absence?

Within herself, her new bond felt settled, its tendrils interlacing every part of her soul. Perfect. Everything she did next depended on the strength of that bond.

Mary stroked her feathers. "I'm so sorry. I didn't realize how hard this was going to be for you. All the bonds I've ever seen, they looked so natural."

"No apologies are required. I'm unharmed." Gabriel looked to Israfel on the other side of the room, sitting criss-cross with a lyre on her lap. "The early hours are crucial, and although we couldn't let things happen naturally, we compensated sufficiently."

Uriel had dotted the ceiling with dangling light sculptures, and every time one of the angels shifted, the ornaments all shivered with energy before dissipating it in multiple directions. These spiritual chimes kept lighting up Gabriel's mind, and she admired their beauty for half a second before realizing they also served to absorb the angels' signatures and prevent detection.

The air carried a faint scent of pine. Gabriel wanted to sing, but

Israfel wouldn't keep playing and instead stared as though this were a deathwatch. Raphael, too, was looking into Gabriel—but everything was wonderful. Better than wonderful. She had a handhold on Lucifer's heart, and although he'd opened only a little yesterday, (was it yesterday?), today she could engage him again and encourage him to talk with full freedom. Mary's plan had been right all along. They had five days remaining, and five days was enough time for Gabriel to carry out anything the plan required.

Everything was possible. She needed only to determine the best strategy and assemble a team to enact it all.

Her clothing didn't fit, so she adjusted it, then flexed her wings as she sent her mind into the world. She'd slept a little longer than six hours. Her heart still wanted proximity to Lucifer, but no longer with urgency. As a secondary note, though, that meant she had no idea whether Lucifer was near. He might still be in the room beneath—or he might have gone prowling about the world, seeking her.

Hunting her. Lucifer's eyes—the flames, the rage, the power discharged into her soul while she was trapped—

Gabriel shivered. *What have I done?* No, quit that. She had to follow through. Yesterday the plan had seemed like a series of steps to a specific end. She'd followed the steps and achieved the end, and now she had to follow a new series of steps to achieve a different, better end.

Uriel lay on the carpet, chin resting on folded hands, eyes penetrating. Breathing deeply, Gabriel allowed Uriel to stare all the way into her soul even though she'd likely been examined this way a dozen times. Still, Uriel checked over everything. No damage. None but the necessary.

Gabriel said, "My library?"

Israfel rolled her eyes, but Raphael said, "He scorched one outer wall and cratered the balcony, but your trees are still standing, and the Cherubim inside protected the books."

Except for one. That volume of poetry had been at ground zero. Gabriel would have to recreate it if she could, but at worst it was only one book lost, and repairing the balcony wouldn't be difficult.

It wouldn't have been possible to replace the cedars.

Someone banged on the door. Uriel bolted up, arms crossed. Gabriel raised her wings.

Israfel flashed on her armor. *That's Mephistopheles.*

Raphael was on his feet, too. *You're not ready. I'll have Michael remove him.*

Mary whispered, "Let him think the room is empty."

Lucifer dispatching his team to flush out Gabriel could mean any number of things. Should she open herself to them? Maybe she should invite Lucifer onto a deeper level of Heaven for privacy and an added layer of safety.

He's calling to me, Israfel sent. *He insists I must be in here.*

Raphael looked at Gabriel. *If he's about to summon Satan, you're coming with me.*

Wings raised, Gabriel replied, *The bond isn't any good if I don't use it,* but Raphael might have a point about her not being ready. Despite being able to detect every pip of energy in the room, Gabriel couldn't detect much in herself.

Israfel sent, *He says he's alone.* She hesitated. *He swears on his own bonds that Satan will not find out he was here.*

Mephistopheles swearing by his bond to Beelzebub was about as good a guarantee as they'd get. Gabriel got to her feet, and Israfel altered the guard so Mephistopheles could pass.

Mephistopheles started when he saw Gabriel. "It's true, then. We were full of speculation, but he's admitted to nothing." He moved closer, palms up. "You can stand down. I have no intention of starting a fight, and while your pretty wind-chimes will help, I would appreciate if none of you discharges energy that can be detected on me afterward."

Raphael folded his arms. "Aren't you demanding?"

Gabriel fought a grin.

"I've been called that." Mephistopheles stopped in front of Gabriel. "What are you trying to accomplish?"

Mary said, "We might ask the same of you."

Mephistopheles riveted his eyes to Gabriel. "Speaking to you as a peer, I have no interest in taking questions from humans."

Gabriel bristled, but Israfel had already flashed in front of him. "Speaking to you as the ones in possession of something you want, we have no interest in taking questions from demons. If you're not going to answer in a way that befits the mother of Christ the King, you can feel free to leave without whatever information you've arrived to collect."

Mephistopheles faced Mary. "My bonded Seraph suggested we examine the adjacent rooms to ascertain whether Gabriel was present, with the specific intention of verifying that a bond had taken place. His perspective was that a newly-bonded pair would have an innate urge to remain in close proximity in the immediate aftermath, and that Michael's confining our master to quarters was a thinly-disguised attempt to restrain him so Gabriel could safely remain in an adjacent location. In addition, I've a few agenda items of my own, and they may align with yours. Have I sufficiently answered your inquiry?"

He said that last with a glare at Israfel.

Mary said, "What of your agenda could possibly align with ours?"

Mephistopheles braced himself. "To answer that requires understanding your agenda. I do not. A frank assessment is that Gabriel's actions are madness."

Two days ago, Gabriel would have had nothing but agreement. Today, though, it would have been madness not to try.

Mephistopheles continued, "The most logical conclusion is that Gabriel may be exacting vengeance for Lucifer's initial snub."

Never, not once, had Gabriel considered that bonding Lucifer might look like revenge. Before she could object, Mephistopheles hand-waved her. "Regardless of everyone else's beliefs, I've ruled out that theory because it's at odds with Gabriel's overall comportment in the ages since. But that leads to the next conclusion, that Gabriel initiated a bond with the specific intention of causing our forces to self-destruct at the week's end after our deportation into Hell."

Gabriel recoiled. Mary's voice was thin. "Explain."

Mephistopheles said, "Gabriel and Lucifer will be separated. The intense grief this will cause Gabriel is justifiable if and only if the gains are proportionate to the suffering—which is, incidentally, one reason why your Son's consent to crucifixion makes no sense, but I digress." Yes, of course, get in a jab at God while soliciting His servants for help: it lessens the humiliation. "The agitation our lord experiences will result in an attempt to alleviate it by bonding with as many of us as he can. I'm going to be a target, as will Belior."

Gabriel went weak. From across the room, Raphael watched with shock.

"I predict he'll burn out each of his primaries within days, after which he'll move on to his secondaries. With a bunch of spent Cherubim in his wake, he'll have no further brakes on his energy, plus he'll be surrounded by any number of angry, jealous Seraphim." Mephistopheles faced Gabriel. "The carnage you've set in motion is impressive even for you, and I already stood in awe of your achievements."

Carnage? The anger of a jealous Seraph wasn't in Gabriel's repertoire, but their non-jealous anger was so incisive. Mephistopheles' prediction was too easy to envision.

The color had faded from Mary's cheeks. Uriel floated behind her, hands on her shoulders, saying, "Go on."

"There's no 'on' for me to 'go' to." Mephistopheles tilted his head. "Is that the end you envisioned for us? The final instability that would 'divide Satan against Satan,' and in the end reduce our house to rubble?"

Shifting her stance, Israfel said, "Do you remember a conversation we had about justice? No end is too harsh."

Raphael said, "What if the end we envisioned was every demon uniting to subdue Satan and chain him under the lake?"

Gabriel flinched. They hadn't envisioned anything of the sort. There had only ever been two ends in mind: either Gabriel succeeded, or Gabriel failed—but never a partial success followed by a complete meltdown.

Mephistopheles pffed, blowing a strand of hair from his forehead. "That works until some inconsequential peon thinks,

'What might I accomplish were I to have Lucifer's gratitude?' and frees him without realizing the first target Lucifer would immolate is the individual to whom Lucifer owes a debt. Which, given how quickly I thought of it, would occur within the first day, and certainly by the time any ascendent powers stood at odds with one another. If you believed we'd contain him for you, then your naïveté is too great for you to plan so much as a picnic."

Israfel folded her arms. "Our picnic is well-planned, so what other outcomes do you predict?"

Mephistopheles opened his hands. "I'm here to determine your goals so I can minimize the damage to myself."

Demons were so refreshing when they told the truth, but this might not be the entire truth.

Raphael said, "You're also hoping to minimize the damage to Beelzebub, who's not going to fare well against a jealous overlord who never excelled at sharing."

There. That was the entire truth, reflected in the fright Mephistopheles couldn't quite contain.

Israfel guided Gabriel to a couch. "Sit down before you fall down."

The chance of success felt suddenly small. The alternatives felt atrocious.

Deep in the details of the challenge, Gabriel hadn't once considered the further ramifications. Monofocus was a Cherub's tragic flaw—and one of the reasons they needed Seraphim. Raphael and Israfel had been intent on the potential damage to Gabriel, so they hadn't considered the collateral damage to all of Hell.

Except...Mary had come up with this, and Mary wasn't monofocused. Moreover, Mary had consulted with Uriel, who often saw to all ends. Mary had planned with other humans, with their personal experiences of possessiveness and revenge and jealousy. Someone would have foreseen the results of destabilizing the status quo.

Status quo. Status viatoris. Status comprehensoris.

Gabriel closed her eyes. "You're catastrophizing." She drew in

Raphael's fire and used it to steady her thoughts. No matter if it interfered with her bond with Lucifer, she needed to function. "You're elaborating an outcome that sounds shattering enough to have us walking back our intentions. You failed to factor in your master's legendary self-control. He's been prompted before to enter into bonds. He knows how to hold back. Consider how adept he is about temptations and telling half-truths." Gabriel looked up. "For that matter, consider yourself."

Head tilted, Mephistopheles wore a slight smile. "Always."

Stay steady. "Even if he accidentally burned out one of you, he would know better than to do it twice. He's quite intelligent." Gabriel knew it from the inside. "It's far more likely that he'd keep you away from Beelzebub because he'd want you on permanent retainer for his own needs, much as Beelzebub divided you from your other primary bonds. It will never come to relay seizures of power among a firestorm of widow and widower Seraphim. "

Raphael smirked. "It's a relief to know you really are just thinking of yourself."

Gabriel added, "Albeit dressing it up nicely."

Arms folded, Mephistopheles leaned against the wall. "You still can believe I'm highly motivated to mitigate the damage to myself, regardless of what you think of the other possibilities I've raised."

Israfel said, "So if we tell you our endgame, then you can trot back to your owner like a golden retriever with a message in your jaws, wagging your tail and hoping for a treat rather than a kick?"

"Why must you engage in outlandish imaginings? You've kindly established that this dalliance was of your initiation rather than his." Mephistopheles paced. "You've caused a great deal of inconvenience for me, so you owe me whatever assistance you can provide. I'm willing to advance your goals inasmuch as they advance my own. I want not to become a secondary victim, and as I recall, in the past you've gone so far as to strip knowledge out of my mind to 'save me the trouble of being beaten or seduced.' Both are a guarantee if this course of events continues unabated."

Raphael was in Gabriel's heart, a huge question mark. Israfel vibrated more like an exclamation point.

Mephistopheles looked directly at Gabriel. "Are you trying to convert Lucifer?"

Mary replied, "Would we have a chance if we tried?"

Mephistopheles strode in front of Gabriel. "To go so far as this, you've concluded you have. You've already agreed you would judge the pain to be justifiable if and only if the gains were proportionate to the suffering." No, that wasn't anything Gabriel had agreed to, nor what Mephistopheles had even said, but Gabriel didn't bother correcting him. "You've already won the war, so sowing further discord is an insult but stands you no further gain."

Gabriel frowned. "Would you push Lucifer to his knees before the throne of God just to benefit yourself?"

Mephistopheles' eyes flashed. "I'm not unfamiliar with the thought that his disappearance would benefit any number of us—and, yes, I just advocated treason to my master's bondmate—but surely you comprehend why I would never participate in anything of the sort."

Gabriel opened her hands. "Then we're at an impasse."

Mephistopheles squared his shoulders. "You and he have to stay together. The pain you'll cause in repayment for our supposed crimes is going to outstrip what God ordained, and God claims to be justice itself."

Israfel stalked across the room. "You attempted to murder Gabriel. Could any fallout on you be undeserved?"

Mephistopheles said, "At what point is justice satiated? When do continued payments on an infinite debt become unfair?"

The anger in Israfel's heart frightened Gabriel, so she tried to instill in her a sense of calm—and as Gabriel reached with her heart, her senses exploded into a question of where exactly she was.

Frozen, Gabriel closed her eyes and blanked her mind.

"Liar," Raphael hissed, striding toward Mephistopheles. "You told Satan we're here."

Israfel called two flaming swords to her hands, but Mephistopheles backed away, palms raised. "I did nothing. Satrinah informed our lord he'd be able to track Gabriel across different layers of Heaven. If he's attempting that now, he's experimenting."

The feeling vanished, leaving Gabriel's mouth burning as though she'd eaten a ghost pepper. No attack followed, so she must have squelched any answers before he got them. *He was prompting me to admit where I was, not detecting me. He has no idea how close I am.*

Raphael's eyes gleamed. *All the same, it's been long enough for all the connections to form. I want you out of here.*

Israfel projected agreement.

Uriel helped Gabriel to stand while watching Mephistopheles. "We're going to decamp. In the event that you truly want Gabriel and Satan's bond to continue, you're welcome to help us. Gabriel will be remaining in God's service, which leaves exactly one option."

Mephistopheles folded his arms. "That's not fair."

Israfel said, "We don't always get what is fair," and before Gabriel could object, she flashed them away.

Chapter Seventeen

AFTER REVIEWING THE STATUS of every ongoing project, Satan flashed back to his chamber's distorted mirrors. They couldn't even reflect colors properly, as if his light had gotten trapped in a permanent refraction.

Ironic. Now Gabriel was trapped in a permanent refraction in Satan's head.

Somewhere in creation, a Cherub must have compiled all their information about bonding, and that book would be in Gabriel's library. It would be invaluable for its detail, and yet it was useless because Satan couldn't access it. He'd tried, but numerous attempts had proven that Gabriel giving him permission to enter his head wasn't the same as Gabriel giving Satan permission to join him on the inner layers. That left Satan with whatever his team had been willing to disclose, and already that had helped.

First, that it was possible to block Gabriel out of his thoughts. He'd need to figure that out on his own, since it wasn't in Gabriel's best interests to drop comments like, "Oh, you didn't know this, but be advised—" Second, that it would be possible both to nail down Gabriel's location and to contact him at a very long distance. And third, that Satan could set Gabriel on fire from the inside out.

But not immediately. The fourth thing Satan had learned was that he would remain separate from Gabriel rather than the two of them existing as a revolting Cherub/Seraph puree, and that made the situation tolerable. No matter what happened, Gabriel wouldn't change him. Satan could put up with five days of discomfort as long as he wouldn't lose himself. He'd endured a lot worse.

The impetus to bond Gabriel had been the prize of snaring Israfel. He might as well leverage the opportunity.

All morning, he'd sent periodic feelers into that annex in his heart. After several hours, he'd achieved reasonable proficiency at accessing Gabriel, and he detected flashes of what Gabriel was doing or thinking. Satan tried to put energy into the system, and it felt as if Gabriel absorbed the energy. At times, he could evoke that cool clarity of thought—and that was a useful resource. But Gabriel wouldn't yield a location.

Beelzebub's declaration that he could pinpoint Mephistopheles even on other levels of creation had been breezy but with no indication how it happened. Given that lesser angels had figured it out, though, Satan could, too.

He settled himself in the center of his room, even though it no longer had the right-feeling of yesterday, and reached into its new annex. There was Gabriel's soul. There, that cool focus. Satan offered some of his fire, and as if from the other side of a tunnel, a steel hand received it from him.

Satan paid very close attention to the sensation, and momentarily he felt Gabriel paying attention back.

Keeping his anger under control, Satan waited. Gabriel waited, too, with that infuriating attitude of observation. Satan offered more fire, and Gabriel received it again, then offered back icy resolve.

Fragments of Gabriel's thoughts came to mind. Excitement. Curiosity. A little fear, which was a thrill. Anticipation.

This was irritating. Gabriel had started this, so why should Satan have to draw him out?

Because, Satan realized, Gabriel had more than sufficient concerns about the circumstances under which they'd parted.

Satan huffed. Those circumstances had been Gabriel's perfidy, followed by Gabriel picking through his thoughts. "Concern" was the least Gabriel should be feeling.

To be fair, though, if Gabriel hadn't done so, they would not be having this conversation.

Wait—conversation? Satan wasn't just thinking to himself? Was this mingling of their thoughts as they fed off one another's energy a function of the bond?

Affirmation.

Satan shut off the contact and flared flame all over his subtle body because—that's how it felt? Not knowing which thoughts were your own? How could this be anything his fellow Seraphim found appealing?

He had to rip these hooks out of his mind. Surely Gabriel was smart enough to disconnect them.

Even so: Israfel. Satan settled himself and accessed the bond again. Immediately he felt Gabriel apologize.

Satan sent a bristling anger into the bond. Cherubim were all about teaching, so Gabriel needed to spend some time enlightening him about this connection and the way it functioned. Instead, everything about it was being treated as a surprise. Gabriel had forged it under false pretenses and was making Satan extract every detail as if it were a secret.

Another apology.

Satan thought, *I want a user manual.*

His throat tightened: on the other side, Gabriel had laughed.

Not the reaction Satan had expected. *Where are you?*

Nowhere near him. Gabriel offered that a book could be procured, however, and if Satan wanted, they could meet somewhere to effect the book's transfer. In public. A quick tutorial sounded appealing. Exciting, even.

Satan tightened up. *Maybe Israfel should join us, so you can demonstrate how this bond works from the inside?*

Fear. Satan was abruptly back in his own self, with no other awareness in his mind.

He glared at the nearest mirror. If Gabriel had picked up that Israfel was his target, this would be the end of their interactions. Hadn't one of his team claimed that such a level of deception would be nearly impossible for a Seraph to pull off? Moreover, they meant experienced Seraphim, not a brand-new bond and someone who'd never wanted to participate in one.

He reached again for Gabriel. Israfel didn't have to come. No, Israfel wouldn't be coming. They should meet and talk, just the two of them. Gabriel would select a book. Satan would have to leave the hotel.

Beneath it all lay a trembling sadness. Satan glanced at the pot where the plant used to be.

Inside him, acceptance.

Satan flashed to a lake and watched the water ripple. Some *viatores* were sailing, and others were swimming. The lake had fish, and Satan nudged the water's edge with the toe of his boot so the creatures darted away. A moment after, he felt comfortable and clear-eyed. Gabriel was at his side.

Satan had changed Gabriel: that much was obvious. Not just the male-to-female switch, but also the angle of her wings, her tension as she appeared ready to run. Even so, brightness sparkled in her eyes. He offered his fire, and her grey intensified to silver.

She must be having a similar effect on him, but Satan didn't bother asking. She extended a book at arm's length, as though that extra distance would help were he to attack. He took it with a glance at the title.

Gabriel arched her brows and folded her arms. "I didn't trick you. You were making overtures to bond me, and given our current situation, be advised that I can detect when you're lying."

Satan waved a hand. "I didn't want *this*."

Gabriel tilted her head. "The fact that you didn't know exactly what 'this' would entail doesn't mean I tricked you. It means you signed a contract you hadn't read." Her wings flexed. "What do you want to know?"

Satan said, "How to break it."

Gabriel glanced away. "That's going to be a problem."

Satan said, "I felt the full breadth of your intelligence yesterday. If you turn your mind toward this one issue, you'll come up with a solution."

Ah, but first she'd have to want it, and she quite possibly didn't.

For one thing, she now had access to more power than she'd ever wielded with Israfel or Raphael. She also knew how to compartmentalize her thoughts. She and Israfel might even be plotting to leverage his power to unseat God.

Gabriel walked into the lake, letting the water lap against her boots. Interesting: today, she wore armor. Her hair remained short as it had been in her masculine form. Also, she tended to keep her arms folded, as though giving herself extra cover.

Satan fed her a little fire so he could sample her thoughts, and no, she didn't want to break the bond. In point of fact, she seemed entranced by it. She wanted something to happen, something that filled her with anticipation.

Her own anticipation mingled with his. If she could tell when he was lying, he'd need to learn how to compartmentalize his thoughts. Either that, or he'd have to use her and tempt her using only the truth—which simultaneously increased the degree of difficulty and also would increase the fun. He hadn't done anything like this in so long, and his first foray back was going to be his biggest challenge.

As the thrill spiked through him, it lit her up, and her hands clenched. She was reaching—reaching down into the waves where the fish clustered around her ankles, but then outward toward God, and simultaneously inward toward God.

Satan yanked away from her, and she spun toward him, startled. Prayer? He'd never wanted to feel that again, and she'd jammed it into his soul like a fistful of splinters. That tentative reach followed by—well, in his case, followed by nothing. In the hollowed-out parts of his heart, he hadn't felt whatever God did to her, only how she relaxed in response.

Gabriel's eyes widened. Prayer was reflexive. She hadn't considered he'd pick that up.

Finally, she said, "We have a little under five days left. Let's not spend them fighting. If our bond has to be broken, eternity is a long time, and I can break it then." She stepped onto the pebbles, dry the instant she left the lake. "We can look through the book later, and I'll answer your questions. We saw only a little yesterday, and today we need to see the rest of it." She flashed a list to her hand. A long list. "Let's have some fun."

Flashing the book back to his room, Satan braced himself for whatever a Cherub might consider fun. A lecture about neutrinos? This was Gabriel, so perhaps a hymn-singing competition? For that matter, why didn't Gabriel consider teaching him to be fun? But no, Gabriel transported Satan to a fairground where she tapped some of his fire before heading toward a musician playing steel drums.

The more demonstrations and booths they visited, the more Satan could detect that, unbelievably, instead of Cherub-fun, Gabriel was choosing activities she thought might be fun *for him*. For example, she'd picked steel drums because that might remind him of New York City. She brought them to a game of refracting light and another one that involved spinning electrons. Every time, she acted like it was a hit-and-run raid, letting the activity absorb and entice her, and then she'd look to Satan to see if he was similarly pleased. "Oh, a paradox puzzle!" she'd exclaim, then glance at him with joy in her eyes, waiting for him to be thrilled by the combination of a ridiculous question and a series of locks, and Satan would wonder what had happened to her.

Whenever they uprooted from one location and moved to the next, he felt her draw on her Cherub stolidity to stop thinking about one subject and begin thinking about the next. In the back of her mind, however, she was compiling a list of topics to revisit later, either without him in an hour, or long in the future, that way she could immerse herself in each until she'd learned everything there was to know about steel drums, or perhaps open new areas to explore.

It was transparently manipulative, not to mention offensive. He wasn't a child who required a variety of entertainment, and nothing for so long he got bored. Moreover, this over-the-top enthusiasm for every single thing she came across was not the Gabriel he knew. Case in point: the Gabriel he knew would never have said, "We can look at the book later."

They stopped by a game that mixed chance and skill—a vacuum

bottle containing a random assortment of molecules, where at the end of three minutes, the players would present a finished product, and whichever one spun the longest would win. Gabriel watched two consecutive competitions (while Satan watched her) before she turned to him with her eyes bright and already thinking of the next activity.

She kept acting as though he needed continuous distraction. Satan said, "You can stay longer."

Gabriel swirled with confusion. "But there's so much to do. We need to see everything."

Suddenly they were standing before a man who was softening hard pears in a syrup of wine, cinnamon, ginger, and saffron. The cook offered Gabriel a bowl of pear slices. Gabriel tasted one, then offered it to Satan. He refused. Gabriel ate the other two slices, then thanked the cook. They moved to the next booth.

Gabriel sent, *You've never eaten food?*

Satan shuddered.

It's a uniquely material experience. I didn't enjoy eating when I was depending on food to fuel a human body, but afterward, I experimented a bit.

This wasn't fun. No matter what Gabriel thought of this outing, it was of no strategic or intellectual value, and therefore a waste of time except inasmuch as it coaxed Gabriel to grant him access and answers. Every so often, Satan would inject sparkles of fire into Gabriel to determine what happened, and Gabriel responded by absorbing them and returning something that was either gratitude or focus, or both. If Satan offered nothing, Gabriel didn't draw the fire from him, but Satan had seen enough interactions to know she could. A more pertinent question was whether Satan could evoke that steel from Gabriel without her being able to stop him.

Periodically, an underling would flash to Satan, either to ask a question or to give a status update. Gabriel might be able to decode what they were projecting, but at this point, it hardly mattered. Oddly, three different times, low-order demons appeared before Gabriel, looked shocked to see Satan, and immediately flashed away with an aura of fear. When Belior arrived, by contrast, he awarded Gabriel a blistering stare and stayed, but said nothing.

Satan snapped, "Did you have a report?"

Belior's fists had tightened. "Yes, sir, but I'll save it for when you're alone."

As if he'd ever be alone again. But then Asmodeus appeared behind Belior, glowering. "Leave. Now."

For the first time, Satan considered the dynamic of their bond, and what Asmodeus was trying to prevent Belior from doing. It had never seemed important.

Instead, Asmodeus faced Satan, eyes smoldering. *I've gotten into the Temple. Hastle is unprotected, but I cannot get near. We are indeed bound to silence once we enter, but it's greater than silence. It's closer to paralysis.*

Satan folded his arms and huffed. *Surely you can figure out a way to leverage that.*

Asmodeus glinted. *After you finish touring the field with Gabriel, I would like to consult with you about how.*

Satan sent, *I suggest you solve this conundrum without my intervention, since Hastle is, in point of fact, your problem. Feel free to resume your work.*

Asmodeus bowed and vanished.

When Satan turned back to Gabriel, she was perplexed. "Why does everyone annoy you?"

Satan strode away, saying, "Everyone is annoying."

Pitching her voice lower, she said, "Raphael isn't annoying."

Satan huffed. "Good for Raphael."

He caught an impulse from Gabriel, half-formed and unthought as quickly as it appeared: that perhaps Satan's underlings were equally annoyed by him, only they didn't dare voice it.

He blinked, but she had already flashed him to a stadium where teams played a game involving curved baskets and flying balls. Gabriel gasped, then said, "Oh—"

Satan snickered. "It scared you that they weren't wearing helmets and knee pads? Those monkeys' bodies always did break so easily."

She shivered.

Gabriel's physical body had also broken pretty easily, come to think of it. Satan mused, "Compound oblique femoral shaft fractures were the worst. Seasoned gladiators who'd tear the heads off live rabbits would be sobbing for their mothers."

Gabriel shot a lance of anger through him, and Satan laughed.

He probably did annoy the demons around him. It was better that way.

What they'd been watching had been a warm-up, as Satan discovered when the teams began playing their national anthems. First for different human countries, and then, to his disgust, "Dedication of the Stars."

As far as Satan could piece together, "Dedication of the Stars" was Israfel's, composed days after the Winnowing. With God still outraged by Satan's bid for freedom, Israfel had scored a melody to placate Him. It wasn't intended for liturgical use, only something for the enslaved angels to sing before ordinary activities as a means of convincing themselves they'd been right to lock their chains. Mercifully, they sang the short form. Unmercifully, Gabriel sang it, too, and Satan could feel the resonance through her soul as it backed up into his.

Disgusting. He'd feel that every time she sang, wouldn't he?

The question was, would they also play Hell's anthem? That was Beelzebub's composition, although Rahab had tossed one of his own in the ring. Amazingly, they did. Gabriel didn't sing this one, but she sampled Satan's thoughts to see if he approved. Satan shut that down.

When the game started, the field was shielded against outside interference, otherwise Satan would have changed the spin on the ball to find out what did happen to resurrected bodies that got pegged with solid rubber at ninety-seven miles per hour. May the best team win—meaning, his team. In the next moment, though, he realized it wasn't "Hell versus Heaven." The teams were remixes of rosters from Earth, and that made each a combination of *viatores* and saints.

He leaned forward, changing focus to identify each player. Why were they commingling? Or had the human saints created a fantasy league after debating for hundreds of years about whether such-and-such a team could have defeated that other team even though chronologically they never could have played one another, and the rules had changed in the interim?

Satan mused, "Will we sacrifice the losers?"

Gabriel's mouth twitched as she sent a correction: since God deserved only the best, it would be more fitting to sacrifice the *winners*.

He couldn't help it: he laughed.

Once it seemed obvious who would take the match, Satan felt Gabriel reaching out to other angels, and momentarily she'd transported him to a musical performance. The field was crowded with monkeys. Shuddering, she pulled her wings tight around her. Satan grabbed her hand and flashed her to the top of the fence ringing the arena. It took three seconds to place the style of music, and a few moments after that to realize the stage was set up for dancing. In addition to the human dancers were angels.

The stage itself backed up on the water. Dozens of boats had arranged themselves behind the stage. The sound must be carrying for miles, and anyone who couldn't fit in the audience was listening from behind. The whole construction was ingenious. He'd have to figure out a way to mock up something like this in Hell.

Gabriel's gaze focused across the field on Israfel, onstage, who stared daggers at them both as she played guitar. Satan couldn't feel if they were exchanging energy. He brushed Gabriel with his outermost wing.

Turning to him, Gabriel didn't thrum with the same current she did after Satan fired her up, so at least she hadn't sullied herself with Israfel's power.

Israfel played lead guitar with a band comprised of humans and angels. Whatever song it was, they must have been near the end because she started jamming. Facing each other, she and the bass guitarist traded cues as they filled the arena with sound—loud sound. The energy was high and brilliant, and behind them, the drummer pounded out the beat while a singer encouraged the audience to join in.

The song ended, and the audience erupted in applause, whistles, and cheers. Gabriel beamed at Israfel, who ignored her and instead summoned Remiel. The band changed, and Israfel was no longer holding a guitar.

With her soul vibrating to the music, Gabriel called a program to her hand and scanned it. She lit up anything she thought Satan would find enjoyable among the potluck of musical styles and performances. According to Gabriel, gatherings like this were taking place all over the level. "It's a wedding feast. At a wedding, music and dancing are frequent occurrences, as well as food. If you don't like this one, we can try another festival area, or see a performance, or we can watch more of the sports." Gabriel hesitated. "Or participate?"

Satan recoiled. "Excuse me?"

Opening her hands, Gabriel produced a flute. "You can play, and I'll sing. Or we both can play. You played for me before."

Through Gabriel's eyes, he saw himself among the sheep, his glow muting the stars, the rain pattering like the applause of ten thousand listeners. He heard his own music and felt his own subtle weaving of flame and fugue, and behind it all, he felt Gabriel's awe.

He'd have done anything for that, back then. He should want it now, too, but Gabriel wanted it, and he needed to keep her hungry.

He turned away. "You'll have to be content with the memory."

She ran her fingers over the instrument, a momentary emptiness arcing through her. Then, as if it nauseated her to speak, she said, "You wrote a song."

His feathers flared. "Feel free to sing it as much as you want after I'm gone."

She said, "Well, at least we're in agreement on one thing," and flashed the flute away.

He snapped, "Meaning?"

Her eyes narrowed. "My meaning was clear."

They'd never sung it again, had they? But how could they? No one else could have managed his part, and their failure would have resulted in nothing but humiliation.

Gabriel leaned forward on the fence to listen to the next song, extending her wings behind for balance even though she could have gone desolid. Again she was singing, but instead of any established lyrics, she spun out her own free-form words. The song vibrated back through Satan as before, and he dampened himself so his heart wouldn't ring like a bell.

Remiel and Israfel were both dancing. The musicians played a style of music popular within their own culture, and as with most popular music, it had an engaging rhythm. Israfel and Remiel danced together, neither using a style particular to this music, and not the same style as each other. In addition to movement, Israfel employed light and fire.

As it appeared they'd remain here for the time being, Satan could attempt Beelzebub's suggestion again, and "find" Gabriel. Knowing Gabriel's location would make it easier to figure out how to track Gabriel at a distance.

Satan released his mind into dancers' motion. Once that captivated his external focus, he concentrated on the vibrations of Gabriel's song until he could feel her at his side. Nothing special about this—he could have done as much without a bond. But now Satan pushed to detach himself from reality, focusing on the concept of Gabriel rather than the presence of Gabriel.

The song ended, yanking away those tonal vibrations. Remiel, laughing, backed away from Israfel, who teased her. Gabriel was picking up Israfel's side of the argument: *Are you saying the Angel of Dance can't keep up with the Angel of Music?* Grinning, Gabriel narrowed her eyes. Although Satan couldn't feel a summons, shortly Raphael joined the pair onstage, and Remiel was pulling him toward Israfel. Gabriel sent a burst of encouragement, and when yet another band started a new song in a new style, Raphael and Israfel danced together.

Remiel flashed to Gabriel, staying on her opposite side. Since the most disconcerting thing Satan could do to Remiel was leave her wondering, he ignored her. The music was in full swing, with Gabriel once again singing nonsense, and Satan resumed tracking her.

It took a minute, but he felt Gabriel at his side as a concept, not just as a presence. Progress.

Except—it also felt as though Gabriel were somewhere else, somewhere deeper inside Heaven.

Satan relaxed further, and as he did, he detected Gabriel engaging in her own curious dance. As she watched Israfel's movement, she allowed that information to flow to Raphael so he could coordinate his motion with hers. Likewise, Gabriel was making Raphael's actions available to Israfel.

This was a battle tactic. Satan's bonded pairs had done this during every fight, the Cherub hidden in a defensible position to funnel tactical information to the Seraph. With no battle before her, Gabriel was doing it anyhow, and to great effect. Raphael and Israfel coordinated their light and fire displays through Gabriel's mind, and although Gabriel wasn't a participant in the dance, in a way she inhabited it all.

Still, that second signature nagged at him. Was Gabriel bilocating? Perhaps once again in the library—or maybe even in the Ring?

This was offensive. He should have all of her, not half.

Gabriel was Satan's one-to-one escort and had given him permission to be with her, so with her attention absorbed in the music, he bilocated to the other Gabriel.

He remained on the fence at Gabriel's side, but now he was also in darkness, discorporated. Small. Secure. He probed outward but couldn't sense anything. Wherever he and Gabriel were, they were under a snug Guard.

He tried to draw a response from Gabriel, but instead of the small Gabriel in the dark, it was Gabriel on the fence who turned to him, curiosity in her eyes.

The other remained inert. Satan needed an excuse. "You're guiding the dance?"

Gabriel shook her head. "They're guiding the dance. I'm providing information."

Abruptly, he could perceive what Gabriel perceived. Breathless, he flexed his wings, and he saw himself flexing his wings. He also detected the movement of air behind himself and the way bystanders turned their heads. His spirit flared as he saw his own green eyes and cornsilk hair.

The mirrors in his room had been nothing. Gabriel was a living mirror.

This was incomprehensibly useful. Satan could have used someone on the outside reporting to him at all moments how he looked and how best to act for maximum effect.

And Raphael...used it to dance?

As quickly as the perception began, Gabriel turned it off, and Satan struggled not to look as stunned as he felt—although of course, now he couldn't double check to make sure he looked impassive. Gabriel glanced away, but that small smile meant she'd picked up his astonishment.

He'd have to deal with her later. For now, he returned his attention to the duplicate. Which, in a way, meant he was still dealing with her.

In the darkness, Satan made a flicker of fire here, and only here. Gabriel on the fence smiled as she watched the performance, and in the dark, the fire winked out.

This was a very diminished Gabriel, a Gabriel so powerless that it was barely Gabriel at all—except it was fully Gabriel.

A copy? The angels must have done this after the attempted annihilation, duplicating themselves and leaving those duplicates secure in Heaven so if it were to happen again, their alternate selves could be reconstituted.

This was brilliant. Gabriel must have forgotten her duplicate, not realizing it gave Satan an entry point into the deeper layers of Heaven. Moreover, it might be true that every escorting angel's duplicate could provide similar access. Satan couldn't leave this locked location yet, but surely at some point he would find a way, and he'd carry this small, senseless Gabriel with him. After which, for as long as Gabriel maintained permission for them to be "together," Satan had access to any place Gabriel did. Meaning—everywhere.

Smiling on the fence, Gabriel sent a message to Remiel. Unable to decipher it, Satan still could guess based on the laughter and the flash of Remiel's eyes.

How to extract this sphere from its lockbox? It felt very far into Heaven, maybe the second or third layer.

This was an unusual Guard, too. It tightened whenever it detected movement. It also felt like a basket-weave of several angels' energy, and when he tried to perceive through it, the thing was mounted into another Guard. He shone light, revealing the copy to be a silver sphere. They were in a case less than a handspan wide.

Satan grinned. It had been a while since he'd done any sneaking around. What if he got caught? But who was going to capture him? And what could they do if they did, considering he *had* followed all the rules? Even a nitpicker like Gabriel would have to admit this clandestine rendezvous followed every stipulation God had established.

Raphael and Israfel were shedding light, blending it and then separating it. Gabriel's wings curved as she watched. Her heart was in the music, and her heart was in this safe. Satan curled around the sphere, but it wouldn't budge. He tried to reach her heart on the fence, but similarly, he couldn't. The music absorbed her. The motion. The joy of the dance and her love of the dancers.

He smoldered in her heart to get her attention, but with an annoying monofocus, she remained engaged in the loop with her other two.

Earlier, he'd asked to view her bond with Israfel from the inside. Although she'd refused, here he had exactly what he'd requested: the brilliant interplay of Gabriel's heart and Israfel's, Gabriel's and Raphael's. The breathy exchange between Cherub and Seraph, as balanced as systolic and diastolic, as in motion as the sea and as rhythmic as its waves. Open. Vulnerable.

Would Gabriel make herself vulnerable like this to him? No wonder a Seraph could burn out a Cherub. If Satan were to course all his power through her, she'd incinerate.

He prodded the Gabriel in the safe, but there was no openness here, no vulnerability.

Raphael and Israfel's lights shimmered. Remiel breathed, "They're amazing," and Gabriel didn't hear because she was riveted.

She was warm, and she was smiling. Rapt.

Wrapped around her in the safe, Satan tightened up.

On the fence, she leaned forward, bubbling with a thrill he'd never felt from her, and it wasn't directed at him.

Thrumming with love, she'd forgotten all else. He was at her side, but she was absorbed in someone else's beauty.

Flying with her, he'd been absorbed in beauty.

In the safe, his sparks crackled around her. During that moment in the sky, he'd forgotten everything. For a singular moment, they'd been as one, and he'd seized her.

Gabriel had denied him then, was denying him now. Instead she was reaching for God and for Raphael and for Israfel, but not for him.

Love—and not for him.

He clamped down on her in the safe.

Not for him.

He shattered that sphere.

Both parts of Satan crashed together even as Gabriel collapsed onto herself with a cry, hands pressed to her head, wings flared. Remiel grabbed her, and then Raphael was around them both. Israfel flashed between Satan and Gabriel.

Gabriel swept up her head to stare at him, betrayed and startled and hurting—and yes, focused on him the way she should have been all along. Betrayed? No, he was the one betrayed. She'd allured and enticed him, promised him everything, and then traipsed back to her original lovers.

I'm your Seraph. He blazed light into her heart, but not fire. *I'm your Seraph now.*

Sword in hand, Israfel glowered. "Leave her alone."

Gabriel wasn't letting either of the other Seraphim into her head. Satan felt her locking down, sparkling with fear that Satan would attack them.

Let her be afraid.

Raphael still had his wings around her, but he must know he was useless to defend her. Even better, Israfel bristled before Satan, his true target.

Satan met Israfel's eyes. "How does it feel, knowing the one you chose has chosen someone else?"

Israfel glowered. "It feels like if I wait four and a half days, you'll be eating your heart out in Hell."

He leaned toward her and lowered his voice. "It feels to me like if I wait four and a half days, you'll both be stuck with me for eternity."

Gabriel flashed to a stand, gaze level, expressionless.

Mephistopheles did that all the time. Now Satan could feel what was going on behind the flat affect: thought so rapid no facial expressions could keep up with it.

Jealousy?

Gabriel had just pinned a name tag on Satan's emotions. He bristled, but there in Gabriel's heart the pieces clicked together, and the picture formed. Possessiveness. Impulsiveness.

Satan glared at her. *Don't you judge me.*

How was this judgment when it was fact? Gabriel's surprise left Satan abruptly unsteady because Gabriel had never encountered this. She didn't own Raphael or Israfel. They didn't own her. She'd never try to unseat Ophaniel, nor shove Zophiel out of the way. And then, before Satan could even protest, she concluded that her heart was enough for everyone.

Gabriel was not enough for everyone. Gabriel couldn't pay one hundred percent attention to three different individuals—or four, considering that God always demanded His slice of the cake be plated first.

Gabriel's wings lifted, and he felt her smallness in the face of something tremendous. He was about to agree, except then he realized the tremendous thing wasn't himself. Instead, the tremendous thing was something she wanted, adjacent to satisfying him but not itself satisfying him. She didn't want to please him or provide a service for him or complete him. She wanted...him?

He yanked back. "Your mind-games are pointless."

He flashed to his room.

Her book lay on the carpet, and he very nearly ignited it. How dare she?

Except—

She wanted him. Not his power, nor his authority, nor any benefit he could provide for her. Gabriel wanted to spend time with him. She wanted to hear his thoughts and contribute her own. She wanted to connect.

That joy she felt with Raphael and Israfel, she thought it possible to experience with him, too. It was the same as when they'd flown together, and Satan had forgotten everything other than Gabriel.

No one wanted that with him. As she said, he annoyed them—or rather, they feared him. All of the Maskim reported to him when they had to. They accessed him to further their goals or put down their enemies. They wanted what he represented or what he could give. In thousands of years, Satan hadn't heard any one of them say they liked being with him.

Gabriel had sat on that fence and enjoyed nothing more than the act of sharing time. She wanted him, but not to own him.

Had the Second Coming destroyed her mind? Even God wanted to own him.

Instead of burning her book, he flashed it to his hand, and he opened to the table of contents.

Chapter Eighteen

ON HER KNEES BEFORE God, radiating rings of frenzy, Gabriel hadn't blinked for two hours. At her side, Raphael was engulfed in flame. Uncertain what to do, Michael joined them.

The only way out is through. That was the only answer Michael got from Gabriel.

A bit more informative, Raphael reported that Satan had destroyed her token. Which, given that Satan had been able to access it at all, Michael now realized had been a ridiculous error on their part. Saraquael's eyes had flared, and he'd exclaimed, "Satan would have been able to carry that all over Heaven!" and they were fortunate both that Satan had insufficient impulse control and that Special Ops had an uncrackable safe.

Within seconds, any angels who still had tokens were ordered off escort duty, or ordered to re-absorb their tokens.

Raphael reassured Michael that there'd been shock and pain when Satan crushed the token, but it was over in a second, leaving Gabriel unhurt but very startled.

"Crushed the token" was a euphemism for "killing Gabriel." There had been two Gabriels, and now there was one.

Oh, but that wasn't what had sent Gabriel to her knees and hadn't allowed her back up again. The bigger problem, as far as Gabriel was concerned, was the way Satan viewed...well, everything. Relationships. Friendship. Ownership. Gabriel would need to teach him the basics of how to relate to everyone, including himself, before there was even the wisp of a hope Satan could relate to God.

Raphael sounded overwhelmed, so Michael prayed with him some more and then flashed to the Heavenly Temple. Hastle remained at the back, but this time Danel was beside him emitting a mist of faint projections.

Tell me again why you permitted demons free access to the temple, Michael prayed, which was a bit of a misstatement because God hadn't told him a first time. *What if they try to breach the inner dwelling?*

God wouldn't be worried about that. It just didn't seem fitting.

Speaking of not fitting, though, Michael flashed to the music library and found it full of demons.

Demons...and angelic escorts...and Israfel, who was profoundly unamused.

Michael had arrived during a break between performances, although music still played in another part of the library, plus several soundproof practice rooms were occupied.

Michael approached her. "Other than your perfect pitch, is everything all right?"

She tilted her head. "Once Rahab's other Seraphim joined him, their Cherubim came, and word got out. Add in all the escorts, and the crowd is impressive."

Michael prompted, "And they're behaving?"

"For the most part, yes, although after some of these songs," and here she shuddered, "I'll need a purification ritual." She walked toward the front, and Michael followed. "I want to knock Gabriel unconscious and bind her in that safe over in Special Ops, but she's driven."

Michael said, "Is her energy an effect of the new bond?"

Israfel huffed so hard she shed sparks. "What do you think? Her soul is drawing fire from Satan like crazy because the bond's so new, plus he's so much stronger. It's making her zealous on a level that's going to horrify her once everything calms down."

Michael frowned. "Is the flip side also true? Has Gabriel made Satan smarter?"

Facing him, Israfel's eyes glittered. "That's exactly what we wanted: for Satan to get smarter."

Michael shifted his weight. "And yet, Gabriel decided this was a clever thing to do."

"I was there during the discernment, and 'a clever thing to do' was never once a consideration." Israfel ran a hand through her curls. "None of this is right, and I pushed so hard for Gabriel to refuse. I said..."

She trailed off, gazing back at the crowd.

What was she paying attention to? She hadn't gotten distracted. It was as if she couldn't bear to say whatever she needed to, but on the other hand, it scorched in her throat.

Michael prompted, "You think Gabriel's going to get hurt for no reason?"

Israfel folded her arms. "I have no idea what God's doing. Why are we celebrating with souls who would rather burn than acknowledge Him? He gave them their choice. They took it. They keep reaffirming it."

She was looking at Rahab, wasn't she? Rahab, sitting with that textbook on the desk, sometimes reading, but other times watching the musicians. He seemed alert. Saraquael's instinct had been on target: with words in front of his eyes, he'd pulled himself together to read them.

Michael murmured, "Kindness is never wasted."

"I disagree in the extreme. None of these are going to back to Hell to share their newfound love of song. Listen to what they're singing!" This piece was, Michael would have to admit, a bit rough around the edges. "For thousands of years, they hurt people, and they enjoyed hurting people. They indulged every whim and looked for ways to take their urges even further." She was shedding heat. "They don't deserve kindness now, and when they're locked away again, they won't deserve kindness then."

Michael breathed, "That's not to mention the implications of Mary's prayer."

Israfel folded her arms. "I'm not mentioning that."

Except that was the goal. For Mary, at least. For Abraham. For

Gabriel.

Rahab focused directly on them. Michael's shoulders tensed as Rahab flashed to him and bowed. He still held the book.

Wings spread, Israfel stepped backward. Michael said, "I'm glad you're doing better."

Rahab focused on Michael and left him with a series of impressions: he hadn't wanted to be freed, but since his freedom had been secured, acknowledgment was required.

He chased that with the very strong impression that he was only doing this because Ataf insisted, but Ataf was generally insightful about such matters.

There was no possible response. At least, nothing that wouldn't sound flippant or heartless.

Israfel said, "The credit goes to Ataf for interceding on your behalf."

Michael stood corrected: Israfel sounded neither flippant nor heartless.

Rahab tilted his head, then flashed back to the desk with his book.

Michael tried to speak four different sentences before deciding none of them were worth saying.

Israfel hissed, "I hate that."

Michael turned, questioned.

"I hate that after all they've done, they're still under there." She pivoted away. "Their personalities. Their attachments. Their values."

Michael considered Hastle, silent in God's Temple.

Israfel folded her arms. "It makes everything five times more tragic, and every time I see glimmers of who they used to be, Satan's rebellion feels even more unforgivable."

When the de-facto Angel of Grief starts to ask how you're doing and collapses before she can finish her sentence, you know it's bad. Basically.

Remiel sat with her arms around Nivalis. It wasn't just Nivalis's tears on her right now, either, so she let it happen.

Three days of the festival were spent. Four remained. Four impossibly long, far-too-short days, followed by a separation both inevitable and eternal.

There hadn't been a night over the outer layer, only a different caliber of daylight, more golden, harder to move through. Remiel had abandoned it for her studio, even though home still tingled of Camael. Here, at least, it got dark. When she'd chosen her own spot in Heaven, she'd wanted the cycles they had on Earth. There were other places she could go for endless day. Her home would also experience darkness and wind and rain and the occasional snowfall.

Tonight, she hadn't lit the interior, so Nivalis had arrived in the dark, and as Remiel held her, she likewise held her in the dark.

Nivalis finally entered Remiel's prayer. It wasn't much of a prayer, but once Nivalis joined it, they prayed together. They prayed for the bereaved guardians and the angels who'd lost friends, the angels with broken bonds, and one specific angel who'd lost her brother.

Remiel told God, *Not so much for me. I knew what I was getting into.*

Nivalis negated that and prayed for her anyhow.

Knowing what you were getting into didn't mean that you fully predicted the outcome. Mary had said once that while she knew having a baby meant she'd be tired, it wasn't until Jesus was waking up every two hours, inconsolable, for weeks, that she comprehended what "being tired" truly meant. Physically exhausted, emotionally spent, leaking milk, and consumed by grief over the murder of Bethlehem's every baby boy—then she'd known about being tired. Yes, she'd agreed to it, but no, she hadn't entirely understood what she'd consented to.

Remiel had likewise agreed to jump into the meat grinder that was talking to her brother, but maybe she hadn't predicted exactly how those teeth would crunch up her heart.

For that matter, Camael had agreed to jump into the meat grinder that was deserting God. Had he known what separation from the light would mean? Had he known it meant subjugation to a god entirely without light, or had he assumed a fallen Satan would be just like the unfallen Lucifer, clever and admirable and brilliant?

On the other hand, Remiel assumed Satan had to have known what he was doing when he severed allegiance to God. He'd had insight into God's plans and been privy to God's will in a way that would have made Remiel jealous if she'd allowed herself to really think about it. Why create one being so much higher than the rest? Gabriel was next in line after Lucifer, and Gabriel demurred that they weren't on the same scale. Why set the angels up that way?

Israfel had raged about the unfairness of forgiving the fallen, but Remiel thought it a greater unfairness that they'd been made in so many different power levels to begin with. If they'd all been equal, someone could have talked Satan off the ledge. Satan might not have looked up at God and thought, "One step more, and I'm there." He wouldn't have been surrounded by angels who said, "One step more—and we can propel you the rest of the way."

Now here in her arms was Nivalis, who'd grieved a lost soul and then guided countless others through the pain of grieving a lost soul, who above all had known the pain it would cause to see her little lost one, and then it turned out she hadn't known at all.

Either that, or knowing didn't make it hurt any less.

Nivalis whispered, "He didn't recognize me. A demon lured him to me and told him who I was. He hid."

Remiel pressed Nivalis's head to her shoulder and buried her eyes in Nivalis's hair.

Nivalis projected that he hadn't wanted to see her. She hadn't had a chance to say even a word.

Remiel whispered, "Shame?"

Nivalis shivered.

"I was naked, so I hid myself" manifested in so many ways, none of them good. Remiel could work with guilt. Guilt was useful when it got people to examine their actions and change their trajectory. By contrast, shame caused them to hide or to run or to recommit to doing things the wrong way because any change meant admitting to failure—and failure re-triggered the shame.

Half of hell, of course, was well-versed in converting guilt into shame. Guilt would be, "I shouldn't have betrayed my God." If they salted it up, though, it served much better to corrode a soul in the form of, "Of course someone as broken as I am betrayed my God, and now everyone sees."

Nivalis had done so much good after losing Judas. She'd trained other angels to do the same, and she'd kept leaving her comfort zone to help more. She'd helped Remiel. She'd helped the Cherubim and Seraphim with broken bonds, all of whom had been approached in the last several hours. But here, in this moment, it was for nothing because the one she couldn't help was the one she'd yearned to help most of all.

Praying for her, Remiel flinched because on the other side of the spectrum was Camael, who felt neither guilt nor shame.

Four days more, and it was all over.

Remiel whispered, "Are you going to try again?"

Nivalis tightened up in her arms. "I have to."

The same thought kept presenting itself to Remiel, too. Even though it was going to hurt, they had to.

Four days remained. In the midst of an update from Raguel, Michael felt a summons from Danel. *Michael, it's Hastle.*

He didn't find them in the Heavenly Temple. Instead they were in the dry land Danel had claimed as his own. It was still dark here on this plane of Heaven, but it felt to Michael as though dawn would strike soon. Danel and Hastle were kneeling on the desert scrub, forming spheres of tiny Guards and arranging them on the ground.

Michael's heart pinged. How many times had they done this pre-Winnowing?

This wasn't an emergency, though. Michael alerted Danel to his arrival, but Danel didn't pause in making spheres and handing them off to Hastle to fill.

Raguel appeared. Michael sent, *I'm not sure why we were summoned.* But after another moment's consideration, he paged Miriael.

Miriael, who'd never stood on ceremony, strode up to Danel and Hastle and started producing glinting spheres. Michael focused on the twinkle in Danel's hand, picked up its faint signature, and traced the linkage of spheres backward. Hastle had already ringed most of the field.

Michael put into Raguel's head, *Before the Winnowing, we used to pack these spheres with all sorts of things and then set them off in a chain reaction to create light shows and other effects.*

Raguel replied, *He's doing something, at least. Gabriel got Satan to play with light, so maybe light play is something demons do in Hell.*

Hastle was loading the spheres and flashing them out into the field as quickly as Miriael and Danel could create them. Michael flipped the image around in his mind to get a better sense of where everything was. This area was flat, and Hastle's configuration was nothing more complicated than a circle.

No, not staying here. Hastle's last known project had been a deathtrap that would have encased its target in living darkness. Having all five of them contained in a mystical circle when Hastle set it off wasn't a smart move.

Michael flashed outside the circle. Raguel joined him. *You should get out of there,* Michael sent to Danel and Miriael.

Miriael replied, *I want to see what's going to happen. It's been a while since I've had to fight my way out of Hell.*

Michael projected shock, and Miriael grinned at him from a quarter-mile away.

Raguel murmured, "You never can tell with Special Ops."

"Half of Special Ops would run *into* the mystical circle. I'm surprised they weren't the ones to lobby for a heavenly banquet, just for the challenge." Michael folded his arms. "As long as Miriael can yank Danel out of there when this thing swallows them, it should be okay."

Michael prodded Danel. Showing no concern, Danel replied, *He asked me to take him somewhere quiet, with no other demons.*

Michael replied, *How very convenient that you would then be all alone. I'm glad you called me.*

Danel sent back confusion.

Michael replied, *Ambush.*

Danel projected sadness. But he didn't disengage.

Neither was Gabriel disengaging. Neither was Remiel. Neither was Nivalis. Meanwhile Michael had witnessed demons threatening other demons and demons in firefights and demons savaging one another, and they weren't disengaging, either.

Energy stopped sparkling in the field, and Miriael flagged Michael: Hastle had ceased accepting new spheres. Everything was in place.

Michael breathed, "Show's about to start."

Between him and Raguel, not to mention Miriael, they could subdue Hastle if they had to.

With sunrise threatening over them, Hastle sat with his hands clenched and his face screwed up in pain. Miriael looked relaxed, which meant he was coiled like a spring inside. As for Danel, Michael could feel him praying, so Michael prayed, too.

Whatever is happening, God, please help.

God teased Michael, *Do you think I should bless it?*

Jaw tight, Michael replied, *I'm not in charge of what You bless.*

God replied, *Wait and see.*

Michael clenched his sword. *I've seen too many things.*

God replied, *Now you get to see one more.*

The first rays of sunrise appeared. Hastle removed his hand from Danel's, and squaring his shoulders, he pointed at the first sphere.

It glowed, expanded, and played a note.

Its expansion touched off the next sphere, which played another note, and then more cascaded around the field: lights and music, and—

"That's a hymn," breathed Michael.

Specifically, the spheres were playing Danel's morning offering from the liturgy. Five angels were on a hilltop with the sky engoldening above them and the light spheres spreading color along the ground, and all the while, Hastle's creation echoed Danel's hymn.

Michael flashed inside the circle. On his feet, Danel was singing. Hastle knelt with his eyes closed. Two thousand years under the ice. Two thousand years in silence, and this was the way he'd broken it.

Miriael kept pivoting to watch each new pop of light, and Michael spread his wings to let the sound ripple through them. *Endless is your compassion. Great is your faithfulness.*

Hastle crossed his hands over his chest. Danel crouched at his side and wrapped Hastle in his wings while Michael took over the song, joined momentarily by Raguel.

Blessed are you, Lord High God, King of the Universe.

The spheres closed the circle of light, and the last few popped together in a fanfare of color and chimes.

Michael finally answered God's question. *Yes, please, bless this. We have no right to ask You to accept this prayer, but if You will —if You can be merciful to him—please, bless this.*

Hastle drew up his wings suddenly, and Danel held him tighter, praying just as urgently as Michael. Miriael fell to his knees.

Hastle covered his face in his hands and sobbed, and then a moment later, he prostrated himself on the ground while light shone about him, light that wasn't his own.

Peace. Acceptance. Love.

Forgiveness.

Shaking, Michael closed his eyes, gushing with gratitude even though he couldn't find the words.

Miriael rushed toward them, helping up Hastle (Hastiel?) and encasing him in his wings. He looked at Michael. *Should we move him?*

Back into the Temple? Maybe? But for now this space was sacred because it was the space of mercy, the plain of repentance. A field of penitence, and a song of redemption.

Michael crossed his hands over his chest and bowed his head.

He reached for Raguel, who likewise radiated awe. Then Michael flashed them both to the Ring, summoning Remiel and Saraquael as he went.

In the Ring, Raguel raised his hands. Raphael was still in flames as he prayed, but now at his side, Gabriel was staring unblinking into the heart of God, pulsing with silver rings. Uriel knelt, hands crossed, wings up, exuding peace. Remiel appeared, vibrating with urgency as she prayed—prayed for mercy and for the ability to accept mercy. Saraquael flashed in with joy, his soul poised on the tip of a song. Michael closed his eyes and offered his sword and his heart and his entire being.

All seven of the Seven faced inward, trained fully on God. This song. This prayer. This need.

Thankfulness for the one. Joy in the return of the first. And now, a request.

So many souls. So much mercy. God's mercy would have to be fathomless to absorb and forgive it all, but they prayed. They were seven, and they were one in intention, and they all focused simultaneously on the desperate way creation groaned with need.

The need for love.

The need for a return.

The need for redemption, which had arrived through a song.

Chapter Nineteen

ANOTHER SUMMONING OF THE Maskim. Another yank through space and across levels of Heaven to report to a debriefing that Lucifer himself felt no immediate compulsion to begin. This time, they met in Beelzebub's quarters.

Now that Mephistopheles knew to observe, he compiled the differences in Lucifer's behavior. It should have been obvious yesterday, except that Lucifer bonding anyone was so preposterous as not to be possible. Given how many other impossible things had happened, however, questioning everything seemed a better tactic. To whit: demons welcomed into Heaven, the damned freely able to access the Temple, a demon invited into the inner dwelling and offered a gift, Rahab reeled out from the Lake of Fire, and free access to the Earth.

Mephistopheles shifted closer to Beelzebub. Why were they avoiding Lucifer's quarters? In Hell, meetings always took place in Lucifer's chambers, but here, after the first day, it was someone else's. Averting the detection of Gabriel's signature? How much time had Gabriel been spending with him? And what was this cross-bonded couple doing during their time alone?

With a sidelong glance at Beelzebub, Mephistopheles struggled to repress any feelings at all.

Lucifer finally said, "Let's get started." He hadn't summoned Moloch and Satrinah.

Asmodeus said, "We've established nine stable pathways

between the Earth and Hell."

Lucifer's wings raised. "Impressive. I would have thought it would take a couple of days."

Belior stood a little taller. "Once we had individuals tunneling from both sides, we were able to use the reinforcement technique to establish a passage. Each channel is narrow and takes a significant amount of time to transit, but it's stable. There's no reason to assume we can't create as many as we need."

Mephistopheles said, "Once we're sent back to Hell, will access through those tunnels be cut off?"

Belior scowled. "That remains to be seen, but I have reason to believe they'll persist."

Lucifer glanced out the window.

Beelzebub said, "We believe it is possible to disengage Limbo from the rest of Heaven, but it will require a full-scale military offensive. It wouldn't be only a matter of sneaking a few demons into key pressure points."

Lucifer rubbed his chin. "Detaching Limbo was always a reach goal. Being able to expand back out into Creation would improve our situation substantially over where we were five days ago." He folded his arms and frowned. "I'd really like to dig in and hold this layer, though. Do you have an outline for what a detachment might require?"

Beelzebub handled this part of the meeting. Mephistopheles had examined all the connection points between the layers, comparing them to what God must have done to detach Creation from Heaven after the fall of humanity. It was within their power to achieve it, given sufficient time and resources. It wasn't clear they had either.

Lucifer said, "And your analysis of the strategic significance of the temple?"

Belior said, "None whatsoever. Despite the delay, we've repeatedly confirmed the initial flag, but nothing else."

That was an unveiled slur at Mephistopheles, who chose to ignore it.

Beelzebub didn't. "Hastle is no longer sequestered in the temple.

Did you remove him?"

That was directed right at Asmodeus, whose wings flared. "I did not. He was there the last time I checked."

"And he was not, as of my last surveillance." Beelzebub titled his head. "Although I'm not sure our master needs him anymore, since you've already employed Hastle's technique to re-create the tunnels between Hell and Earth."

If anyone ever wanted to know why Mephistopheles loved him, this was why: in one sentence, Beelzebub had exacted revenge for Belior's spite. He'd reminded Lucifer that Asmodeus had allowed his target to escape, reinforced that the long-hidden technique was valuable and quite possibly had been taught by Asmodeus in the first place, and then informed Lucifer that there had been illegal tunnels connecting Earth and Hell for a substantial time period.

Projecting nothing at all, Lucifer faced Asmodeus. That was as dangerous as it got, when Lucifer was stockpiling rage, and it was all directed at yourself.

Belior chose a diversionary tactic. "Also, Satrinah has looked into the matter of the six broken primary bonds, with interesting results, particularly when the Seraph is on our side and the Cherub on theirs."

That attempt was doomed to failure, but Belior had positioned it to be as tempting to Lucifer as possible.

Lucifer's voice was scalpel-sharp. "*Re-create* the tunnels?"

To his credit, Asmodeus didn't look terrified. "Hastle had created one tunnel between Hell and the Earth, with a branch into the edge of the Void. He collapsed it at the time of his disappearance."

Lucifer sounded even more dangerous now. "I assume you used it to collect the Sheol fragments for your weapon." Tendrils of fear began emanating from Belior as Lucifer faced him. "Don't give him the credit. It was Belior's technique—or possibly Satrinah's? Am I to believe that incident was the one and only time you utilized that kind of tunnel?"

No response. Lucifer pinned Asmodeus again with his glare. Perhaps this was why they needed Gabriel. A Cherub to draw off

Lucifer's fire would have been much handier than secret tunnels. Except why would Gabriel enter a room to prevent Asmodeus and Belior's immolation? The better move would be to stay out of the fray and enter later, when she could make herself more useful without any competition.

Beelzebub said, "Regardless of why he came up with them, they're certainly handy now. Getting out to the edge of the Void would also be a bonus."

Why was Beelzebub speaking up? In a situation such as this, the best strategy was silence—silence, and the hope that Lucifer would forget you were in the room. That was easier in total darkness. This could so easily play out with Belior tortured and Asmodeus cindered, followed by Lucifer turning toward Mephistopheles and Beelzebub with a brittle request (taken as a demand) that they fix the situation.

Lucifer faced them, and now Mephistopheles nearly did call Gabriel. The only thing stopping him was that Gabriel wanted Lucifer brainwashed into compliance with the Almighty. If she witnessed Lucifer's true nature, would she have the slightest interest in remaining with him? Over the longer term, it made more sense to let Lucifer have his way with the other two Maskim and hope Gabriel remained ignorant.

Lucifer said to Beelzebub, "Were these tunnels of use to you?"

"As rumors? None whatsoever." Beelzebub shrugged, letting his wings fluff as he did so. "As reality? They should be of immeasurable use in a few days' time. The Earth is clearing up after the processes you initiated. I had Mephistopheles monitor light filtration, and it's increasing. We're investigating ways to smuggle some low-light plant life back onto the planet so we can simulate something of an ecosystem to stabilize it."

Mephistopheles said, "Sir, I would like to establish a plant nursery—"

Snapping, "I've heard enough about plants," Lucifer turned back to Belior. "I'm done with you. Let's have Satrinah's update."

He pulled her into the room. Asmodeus must have warned her about the emotional climate because, with her wine-dark eyes focused right on Lucifer, she wore an unusual obsequiousness. "I've interviewed those with broken primary bonds, and on your authority, I ordered them to resume contact with their separated bondmates. Results have been mixed. In two cases, the enemy's part of the bond has refused all communication. Of the remaining four, while they're willing to spend time together, none have rebonded. I've been able to observe two secondary pairs in action and determined the bonds are completely broken, not just suspended."

Mephistopheles said, "Is there any way to gauge whether a rekindled bond would occur at the same intensity?"

Satrinah said, "That's a logical question, and the answer is, it's impossible to predict. While we've always assumed we bond at a specific level because we were created for it, it's possible the level of bonding depends on the compatibility of the partners at the time the bond is formed, as well as the amount of time the bondmates remain together afterward."

Lucifer's brow furrowed. "What happens if they bond and immediately separate?"

Satrinah opened her hands. "I've never seen fit to conduct a survey, but I'd hypothesize that a pair who should have been primaries but immediately separated would form a stunted tertiary."

Lucifer seemed puzzled. "How long and how close would they have to remain to ensure they formed a primary?"

Mephistopheles said, "Sir, under the current circumstances, I cannot believe we'd be allowed to imprison the enemy's member of the bond and then position our agent on the opposite side of the wall."

Mephistopheles saw the moment Lucifer put together that Michael had done exactly that. Beelzebub sent encouraging fire through the bond, and Mephistopheles indulged in a little smugness.

Beelzebub added, "We shouldn't need to enforce it, though. New bondmates have an intense urge to be near one another for the first few hours."

Lucifer paced. "Have them keep working on it. All six, even the ones whose former partners refused contact."

Having just been useful, Mephistopheles could edge his toe into dangerous water. "Sir, I have no reason to believe this is possible, but what if our party to the bond is more in danger of conversion than theirs?"

Lucifer's gaze darkened, so Beelzebub added, "To consent to a bond, their side would have to believe such a defection were possible."

If Lucifer was surprised by this, he hid it well.

Mephistopheles pushed. "Our efforts would be devastated if we lost key players."

Satrinah said, "None of the six primaries are key players, but I agree they should all be monitored to ensure they're not tempted to switch allegiance."

Asmodeus said, "For that matter, we should be maintaining a very close watch on Camael."

Lucifer ignored that attempt to change the subject. "We'd spoken about a Seraph burning out a Cherub, but is there an opposite danger, that a Cherub can freeze out a Seraph?"

Mephistopheles detected a curious fear from Beelzebub.

Satrinah said, "Because the enemy set things up so every authority has a counter-authority, and every power has a counter-power, we can. Cherubim have been observed to pull all the fire from their associated Seraphim, leaving them listless and despondent. Recall how Rahab did that to all three of his Seraphim before going under the lake."

Mephistopheles swallowed hard.

Lucifer snickered. "And despite that, Ataf was still sobbing over him like a baby?"

Mocking that connection was possible only because Lucifer hadn't felt it. Not really. He'd never gazed all the way into his bondmate's heart and been overcome by the beauty. Before the Winnowing, Gabriel had reportedly accepted Lucifer's refusal by saying, "You're complete as you are," which indicated Lucifer had never needed to look to someone else to find fulfillment.

The completion between bondmates was never perfect. It couldn't be. Even so, the act of reaching for someone else to fill the gaps meant acknowledging your "spiritual other." At its best moments, a bond meant that when you found yourself lacking, you could meet another heart and understand that your shortfall wasn't shameful. It was merely how you were made, without all the pieces, because God wanted to be the only perfect one. Everyone else had to mock up perfection for themselves, and you always had to keep looking because other than God, where would you find someone who completed you in every way?

Naturally Ataf wanted Rahab back. Being with Rahab had likely been one of the few times Ataf had experienced love and acceptance. It had likely been one of the few times Ataf had been able to give those, as well.

Lucifer had never seen the need for a "spiritual other." Whenever he'd needed what a Cherub would offer, he'd dug deeper to find the resolve or the discipline within himself. Mephistopheles had seen Gabriel do the same during his year in human form, learning to simulate emotional fire.

A curious Mephistopheles had tried it, too. It worked, just not very well. He'd never disclosed these experiments to Beelzebub.

In the next moment, Mephistopheles realized—none of them had answered Lucifer's derision. Worse, Lucifer realized it, too. He sounded shocked. "If Ataf would feel that way about Rahab, then is there truly a danger that someone from our side would swing to theirs, just to preserve the bond?"

Belior muttered, "If they were weak."

Good tactic.

Satrinah added, "Note that leaving our side for theirs would mean breaking other bonds in order to secure the one. Since the mixed bonds would be one among several, the party with the higher number of bonds would be the more secure."

No, no, no, no! Why was she encouraging Lucifer to make more bonds when that would result in disaster? Except Belior wanted it, and among her other faults, Satrinah was ridiculously loyal.

Lucifer's eyes glowed. "Could we set off a chain reaction? Would a Cherub with two rebel partners abandon one enslaved partner to join them?"

Blast it, Lucifer did want to keep Gabriel. He wanted it so much it was going to muddy his judgment.

Beelzebub said, "And then what? Have any of our Cherubim mapped out all the bonds? I'm not willing to risk the key players we're sure to lose. If it's only a numbers game, that chain reaction will end up putting many of our Seraphim and Cherubim into slavery."

Belior sniffed. "Or springing millions of theirs into freedom, which I think more likely."

In Mephistopheles' heart, Beelzebub was blazing—an urgent, brisk burn tinged with anxiety. Mephistopheles drew it down, but that left him holding the anxiety. Belior wanted a bond with their master. He'd craved it for thousands of years, and teetering on the cusp of obtaining it, he wasn't going to let a little matter like the destruction of his soul stand in the way. Not after he'd defied God rather than submit. They'd all risked destruction back then, except for some reason, God hadn't done it.

Why not? From a logical perspective, God had no reason to keep them around other than to serve as handy testing agents— and He hardly needed demons for that. Raphael had been sent to test Tobit, and had done it in a way that not only revealed Tobit's flaws but also encouraged him to correct them. In theory, God had created all the angels as free creatures because of love, but after some had rejected that love, there was no requirement for their existence to continue.

Mephistopheles tensed.

Unless that "first good" of His love had perseverated.

Was there still love for all those prodigal angels who'd vanished into a far-off country to gnaw on garbage with the swine, slaughtering the kid goats and stealing the occasional fatted calf? Jesus had asked Gabriel if God ever loved the Winnowed angels, something Gabriel had affirmed without hesitation. Then Jesus had asked if God changed.

That...was unexpected. It supported the conclusion that when

Jesus said to love their enemies, He Himself had been doing it first. Giving Gabriel permission to pray for those who mistreated him meant God would likewise be doing good to those who hated Him and blessing those who cursed Him.

Mephistopheles had never disclosed that conversation. It was preposterous and perplexing that Gabriel wanted to know if he should be praying for demons, and yet Mephistopheles had known it was too vulnerable a question to mock it. Laughing at Gabriel for crying? He'd do that all day. Insulting Gabriel for getting rejected by his Seraph? A treasured memory. But that moment when Gabriel had asked if he should pray for the fallen—and Jesus had, in effect, said yes?

Logic said otherwise, but what if admitting to the permissibility of the prayers meant the possibility of actual graces waiting on the other side?

Mephistopheles had rationalized his silence as avoiding his master's extracting the entire conversation. Lucifer would have immolated him for what Christ said about Lucifer trying to return without capitulating—even though Mephistopheles would have framed it as Lucifer trying to win. Mephistopheles having that information would have been deemed an insult too great to be borne. Silence was the right decision.

Even so, silence had meant letting Gabriel continue praying for them, stockpiling little lights and graces in a bank account from which no withdrawal would be possible. For whatever reason, Gabriel had wanted them there, compounding interest at a rate known only by the Almighty.

Mistofiel, stay.

Gabriel had said those words after Mephistopheles had pulled off the biggest act of his life—except it wasn't an act. He'd tugged every loose thread in Gabriel's heart in an attempt to create a run in the fabric binding him to Raphael. Raphael was already opposed to Gabriel, so it was a matter of reducing Gabriel to frayed ends before Raphael's inevitable apology. And, oh, Seraph apologies were ravishing. They meant everything when delivered—the devotion and the grief and the promise to try again. It was worth getting burnt just for that cool salve. Gabriel would succumb and love every second of it. Mephistopheles had intervened to ensure he wouldn't.

Except, Gabriel had. Ataf had. Mephistopheles had.

And God...?

What would it take?

What would they lose?

Could it be worth it?

Would God kneel like Ataf before the ruined corpse of His beloved, sobbing with relief when it revived, because after thousands of years and millions of insults and incalculable offenses, they were once more together?

Beelzebub flared fire in his head, and Mephistopheles jerked back to the present. Lucifer was asking Satrinah and Belior very technical questions about Cherub-Seraph bonds, these focused on how a Seraph could influence the interactions of a Cherub with that Cherub's other Seraphim. He knew more than he was letting on. He must have raided a library or interrogated Gabriel for hours.

The upshot was, he wanted those dead bonds reinstated. He judged the risk of losing their members to be worth it. And somehow, no matter what he asked, every question kept getting back to, *What would it take to seduce a Cherub over to our side?*

Mephistopheles brushed a wing past Beelzebub, who warmed his heart.

We're going to get through this, Beelzebub sent. *I'll see to it we do.*

Promises meant nothing. Promises were so easily abandoned.

Still, Mephistopheles couldn't hope for better. Trust didn't exist. Hope didn't exist. Only three things were supposed to remain after the Second Coming, so with those two gone, only one thing remained, except Mephistopheles was no longer certain what it was.

Chapter Twenty

THE ANSWER TO THE Cherubim's unanswered question, "Can't or won't?", turned out to have been, all along, "won't."

"Won't" could become "will." They had proof of concept.

When Gabriel told Mary in her rose garden, she closed her eyes and whispered, "Thank you, O God, my Savior."

Hope. They had hope. And three days.

Three days wasn't enough time—except it needed to be enough because that was all they had.

Gabriel summoned Nivalis to a private room in the library to tell her the good news, only Nivalis sat with her hands between her knees, shaking.

"I don't think I can do it," she whispered. They were the same words she'd whispered into Gabriel's shoulder after Judas hanged himself, only back then she'd meant, "I don't think I can face the next minute, the next hour, the next day, the next eternity."

Then, by grace alone, she had. She'd monkey-branched one minute to the next to the next, and here they stood at the opposite end of time, facing one final leap from branch to branch—and it was a long one.

Outside the room, the stacks were full of demons. Demons, reading. Demons, arguing.

Gabriel said, "If it makes you feel any better, you aren't the one doing it. God's the one offering the grace. Judas is the one who has to accept it. You and I—we're just nudging the pieces into the right positions on the board."

Nivalis huffed. "Here, I've got only pawns."

Gabriel said, "I'm not even sure what I have, but if that's all we've got, God can make it enough."

Not enough to override someone's free will. But enough to clear the obstacles.

Danel had presented Hastle...actually, Hastiel...at the temple, and Hastiel had been invited into the inner dwelling. Gabriel hadn't heard what happened after—what form that interview took, what Hastiel might have asked, how long Hastiel thought it had taken. Michael would want answers, too, except Michael hadn't gone with them because Michael had the same number of days they did, and just as much work to do.

Prayer with the Seven had soothed Gabriel's soul, and now she reached across the layers to find Lucifer. He was... He was hiding himself, which gave her a startled smile. He must have read the book, which should have been called, *Seraph-Cherub Bonds: An Owner's Manual.* Her head was still reeling, but instead of dwelling among her own books, she flashed to Israfel.

The Seraph stood at the fountain before the front of the music library, eyes boring into the churning water. Joining her, Gabriel reached for her heart.

Israfel's wings tightened. "Don't."

Gabriel withdrew.

Israfel lowered her voice. "I have a library full of demons who just concluded an hour-long jam session using instruments from every era of angelic and human history. Half of them watched their escorts or me every time they sang something blasphemous, daring us to shut them down."

Gabriel projected understanding.

Israfel's hands tightened, and Gabriel felt her heart crackling: she could deny them permission to use the building, and they'd have to leave. Except—

Gabriel closed her eyes.

—except Gabriel wanted this, and Israfel had come to accept Gabriel's judgment even when she disagreed with it.

Gabriel sent, *I trust you, too.*

Israfel said, "I'm not sure you should. I want the opposite of what you want, but I don't want to undermine you."

Gabriel frowned. "Technically speaking, you do want to undermine me."

Israfel whirled on her. "You're impossible. I want you to fail. I want an honest and thorough failure, though, not because I played you dirty."

"I understood." Gabriel was still armored, but that might be making Israfel more tense. Every change to Gabriel's bearings had to be striking Israfel as wrong. In a soft voice, Gabriel said, "I appreciate everything you've done so far. If you decide to eject everyone from the music library, I understand that, too."

"Why is God doing this?" With sharpness in her voice, Israfel stepped closer. "And before you deflect, a Cherub's job is to explain the Divine Will. Not to nitpick the imprecision of my word choices. Cherub. *Fullness of knowledge.*"

"I'm aware of the meaning." Gabriel closed her eyes. "I can't plumb the full depths of the Divine Will. But God is merciful."

Israfel folded her arms. "This will be chaos. It will be injustice."

An image of Gabriel's human form appeared between them. "With one action, He was merciful and just to me at the same time. You trusted Him back then. We need to do the same now."

Israfel said, "He wants them back."

Gabriel cocked her head. "We all do."

Israfel whispered, "I don't."

Gabriel didn't reach for Israfel's fire. She wasn't offering it. Instead Israfel sent, *They deserve Hell. They demanded separation. We should honor that.*

Honor the dishonorable? Gabriel made the image disappear. *We're not forcing their free will.*

Israfel swept out a hand. *The throng of human viatores that just got their week out of Hell are a testament to how much damage our enemies have done. Every single one of them had a name and was a soul mowed down by our fallen siblings. God accepted Hastle, but what of the humans Hastle harmed? Hastle worked on a weapon to destroy Michael. How does Michael feel about him parading back to shouts of joy?*

Gabriel sent, *How easy is it going to be for the ones who return? They can't stay as they are. I dealt with Hastle when he was working on the weapon. He was nasty, rude, and self-absorbed. When God brought Hastiel into the inner dwelling, he was grieving and subdued.*

Israfel's eyes flashed. *I know what he did.*

So does he.

Her hands clenched. *I can't fight God. But the same way I disagree with you, I can disagree with Him.*

Gabriel inclined her head.

Israfel turned away. "I don't want to talk to you anymore."

Gabriel said, "Call me when you do," and flashed to Raphael on the outer layer.

It wasn't any easier to locate Lucifer on this level. Gabriel could ask around instead of probing, since Lucifer tended to make his presence known, but instead she sat on the grass at a bandshell where Raphael was playing the piano. Although she quieted her soul, the slightest change in pressure of fingers on keys alerted her that he'd recognized her presence.

Gabriel prayed with her eyes closed. *God, please. Israfel's so angry.*

God acknowledged.

Everyone needed prayer right now. Maybe not Raphael. Raphael burned steady.

Gabriel stroked the blades of grass and tried not to notice how many people were around her. *I feel vulnerable,* she prayed, but the inevitable attack would come from inside. Tense, she let Raphael's playing absorb her. This piece was one Gabriel had heard so often while reading before Raphael's hearth—waxing and waning in volume, a clear through-line, and strategic alterations in the theme with every repetition. Now, Raphael was innovating away from the melody Gabriel knew, and she repressed her instinctual criticism that the song was just fine the way the composer had laid it out. Raphael understood music. Whatever he was doing, he had it under control.

Even so, Gabriel prayed, *improvising in front of an audience wouldn't be my first choice for a performance.*

God replied, *He finds the risk more exciting.*

Predictability had its uses. Gabriel let her heart feel the notes as Raphael played them, holding back from his mind so she couldn't influence his changes.

She was about to start improvising her own lyrics when she realized another presence had fixated on the song.

Gabriel opened her eyes, but her question was the equivalent of Jesus asking a churning crowd, "Who touched me?" Everyone was paying attention to Raphael, so who was the one paying special attention? Human. It felt human. It was—

Her. A shade of a human lurking near the stage, trembling like a slender stem supporting an oversized flower. She shivered.

Gabriel shivered, too. She reached for God. *Please.*

Please. The prayer God always heard.

Raphael became conscious of the shade. She slipped alongside the piano, enthralled. And then she sang.

This song didn't have words, or at least, no words Gabriel had ever heard. But the soul sang softly about snowflakes and frozen ponds and glistening spears growing down from frozen roofs.

Melt. Please, melt.

Her voice vibrated, and Raphael modulated the song so it worked better with what she sang, disappearing from the music so she could make it her own. She stumbled over the words, but Raphael's playing supported her so she could try again. Notes slipped out of time, not quite forgotten but also unremembered.

Where was her guardian? But a word would drive this soul away, so Gabriel locked down tight and shielded every thought from Raphael.

Probably thinking the same thing, Raphael vented a surge of emotion and power into Gabriel so his eagerness didn't startle the soul.

More attention, this time from outside. Lucifer was probing Gabriel's thoughts to uncover what had her so engaged and

Raphael so energized. Gabriel hadn't realized Lucifer would detect that.

The shadow sang about roads and danger, but now Raphael was singing too—singing about movement and change. She sang danger and fear while he sang about mercy, about acceptance.

Pushing into Gabriel's mind, Lucifer tried to pin down her location. He was experimenting! Gabriel fought a thrill, and Lucifer caught her embattled emotions with a snicker.

The song continued. Gabriel stared at the harness on her boot because the obvious next thing to experiment with was—

Lucifer tried to see through her eyes. She guarded her emotions, but still she could hear how the call and response between Raphael and the shade created an antiphonal effect.

A question arose in Gabriel's heart, and she suppressed her instinct to answer. Lucifer pushed the question as the singer moved closer to Raphael.

Gabriel trembled with anticipation. Lucifer detected it and again tried to see through her eyes.

When the shadow sat on the piano bench, Raphael enfolded her in his wing. The soul cupped her face in her hands, and she gave her prayer to Raphael to present before God.

From across the field, Raphael's joy surged into Gabriel's heart, and he flourished the song to a close.

Lucifer appeared as Raphael flashed the soul away.

Raphael's overflow joy pulsed from Gabriel in rings. Applause. So much applause. How many realized what had just happened? And, oh, *Thank you, God.* Did anyone else know what God had just won? *Thank you for one more soul.*

Rage overwhelmed her. Rage from Lucifer.

Gabriel braced herself for the burn, but that didn't protect her when it came. With white-hot fury, Lucifer stared into her eyes, and she refused to flinch.

He wasn't projecting his thoughts, no more than Vesuvius blasting Pompeii could be called a projection. Satan had worked for these souls according to God's rules and claimed them— justifiably—claimed each one of them—and God was the sorest of sore losers if He'd invited Satan's prizes here so He could cherry-pick a few extras out of his hand.

Lucifer leaned closer, and now he was seeing himself through her eyes in order to make himself look even more threatening. She *should* be afraid. That thought had come from him, but instead of quavering, Gabriel detached and calculated where she was, where everyone else was, who could help when he seared her, and if she could taper his wrath.

Finally able to form words, Lucifer sent, *This was the plan all along?*

Gabriel projected that she'd felt surprise equal to his.

Ablaze in her heart, Lucifer dwarfed anything Gabriel could sense. In among everything else came a demand—an offended demand. Was Gabriel trying to lure him back, too?

Gabriel tensed.

The swirl of thoughts roiled up from him. If such a thing were to be attempted, Lucifer had no qualms about dragging Gabriel into Hell by her hair as the gates closed. She could rule as his co-regent, manacled to his side wearing a crown of razor wire, Queen of the Maskim until the day she exceeded her usefulness, at which moment he'd burn out her heart, annex her mind, and cement the rest of her under the Lake of Fire.

Gabriel let the facts register while keeping the emotions elsewhere.

Lucifer wanted Israfel. If Gabriel didn't order the angels to stop this soul-stealing, then by using Gabriel as a snare, Lucifer would lasso Israfel, and he'd chain her up as handmaiden to his Cherub queen. Let this be a warning.

Israfel. Oh, Israfel.

Gabriel wouldn't submit. Lucifer knew this, and the flames roared in her heart. It hurt. She focused so hard to keep on top of it.

Lucifer flared her again, then vanished.

Gabriel couldn't feel him any longer, only the burn. She fled back to the Ring. She craved the safety of her books, but her library was a reminder of Lucifer, and anyhow, the building was full of demons. She needed her Father. Her Father. Her Father.

After an hour, she looked up from her prayer with Remiel wrapped around her, also praying. Urgent. Desperate. Determined.

I can't do this, Gabriel prayed.

In her heart, God replied, No. She could not.

In his room, Satan called an emergency meeting of the Maskim, then pulled in Satrinah and Moloch as well. All six arrived, the Cherubim wearing their typical flat expressions that meant they were thinking faster than their subtle bodies could keep up with, and the Seraphim off-balance as they beheld the warping of the mirrors.

The six of them coupled off immediately. Satan shone with enough light to make up for the blackened windows, and he let the ruined mirrors reflect whatever they would. This further unsettled the Maskim, but right now, he wanted everyone uneasy. The room reeked of smoke, just like Hell. His team should miss it by now. Air ought to make itself known. So should the full spectrum of light, and it didn't when the wavelengths traveled as a unit. If they ricocheted in the mirror-equivalent of stained glass, that was better.

Satan said, "The enemy just stole a human soul from our side and welcomed it back to theirs."

Beelzebub crackled with light. "That's not supposed to happen."

"We're dealing with a petulant sore loser in the Almighty, so it doesn't matter what's supposed to happen." Satan glared at him. "The point is, our forces are trapped in Heaven for the next three days, during which our enemies are going to engage in a full-on evangelization of even our lowliest members. We anticipated vindictive behavior, but I didn't realize they'd reverse every one of their values in order to spite us."

Asmodeus said, "We need to circle the wagons."

Beelzebub said, "At the very least, we should protect our strongest key players. If the enemy wants to burn off our dead wood, let them. The monkeys aren't good for anything in the first place, and most of the eighth and ninth order demons are useless."

Satan turned to Satrinah. "The cross-bonded pairs: where do they stand?"

Light flashed through her eyes as she attempted to figure out how not to tell Satan she'd warned him that reopening those bonds would risk losing their members. "Every one of them has rebonded."

Satan huffed. "I'll save you the trouble of saying you told me so. We concluded the benefits worth the risk. Given our new information, I'm interested in risk management."

Mephistopheles tilted his head. "Sir, the biggest risk is not in cross-bonded pairs who resumed contact because you ordered them to do so. The biggest flight risk would be someone to whom the other side made overtures, and who may have responded positively."

What? Satan swung his head toward him, but Mephistopheles looked blank.

Satrinah added. "We need to shore up anyone who was solicited in that way, preferably by increasing their number of bonds within our side."

Ah. Yes.

Belior muttered, "Or by cindering the one who did the soliciting."

Wheeling on Belior, Satan flexed his wings so Belior jerked back into Asmodeus. "If anyone has the pleasure of ripping off Gabriel's wings, it's going to be me."

Belior stammered, "My lord—I meant no offense."

Even before Gabriel had lit up every corner of his mind, Satan hadn't by any means been easily deceived. Post-Gabriel, however, Satan had a much better understanding of the inner-bond dynamics. All six had conspired. They knew about his bond. They just didn't want to admit they knew.

One at a time, Satan turned his stare on the rest of them. "The six of you are implying I'm in danger from Gabriel. I'm more than a little offended by the presumption."

Satrinah sighed as though his anger didn't rattle her. "We're not implying a thing. I will state for the record that Gabriel is neither weak-willed nor stupid, and if he entertained your advances, then he had an ulterior motive. Given today's defection, and given your rightful concern over the other six cross-bonded pairs, we have every reason to believe he has designs on you."

Belior muttered, "It's *she* again."

Satrinah rolled her eyes. "I don't care. What I do care about is, if we lose you, Master, then we've lost everything. Gabriel is positioning the enemy for a checkmate in one move."

Beelzebub said, "Whenever I bonded, in the frenzy beforehand, it was impossible to tell whose thoughts were whose. If you thought you could swing Gabriel, then Gabriel may have been thinking the same."

Satan folded his arms. "To the contrary, I was thinking I could use Gabriel to snare Israfel. And, for the record, Gabriel attested she was as surprised as I to learn the plan to steal souls from us."

Asmodeus said, "Then we need to start canvassing and see how many of their side are spoiling to come to ours. But not you."

Beelzebub said, "Satrinah's right that Gabriel may be looking to checkmate us. You need to avoid her."

Satan caught the moment Beelzebub drew energy—or maybe information—from Mephistopheles. Mephistopheles seemed blanked-out, but using Gabriel as a model, that meant he was serving as an information bank.

Nevertheless, "I'm not staying locked in my room for fear of psalms and a persuasive argument."

Satrinah said, "In that case, I recommend you bond Belior, that way you have an advisor who can reveal all of Gabriel's tricks."

In his peripheral vision, Satan caught the flare of power around Beelzebub.

Mephistopheles snapped to. "On the contrary, sir, I recommend you not bond anyone else. You don't want to get accustomed to that kind of infiltration. As Gabriel already pointed out, you're complete on your own."

Satan turned to him. "I'm surprised to hear you say that."

"Sir," Mephistopheles said, looking as honest as he'd ever been, "this is not in your best interests. I don't know what witchery Gabriel is attempting, but even in this conversation, your reactions are off. I've known you since our very first days, and you're—

Satan exclaimed, "What?"

"—less decisive. You're soliciting a lot more input from us. You admitted we'd made a mistake in judgment." Mephistopheles stepped forward, eyes huge. "If Beelzebub had suggested you stay away from the action two days ago, would you have debated, or would you have cremated him? Bonds are insidious. They change us, but as you're already close to perfection, it can only harm you."

Belior's wings flared. "Why don't you shut up?"

Mephistopheles' voice ticked up, his words jumbling in an attempt to get out all at once. "If I'd bonded Israfel, and you noticed my behavior changing, you'd chain me to the wall. You wouldn't risk the damage if they were to get their hooks in me. Sir, you can direct us well enough from behind a Guarded door."

Satan stepped before Mephistopheles, looking him dead in the eye. Mephistopheles backed into Beelzebub, but Satan followed him. In thousands of years, he'd have staked everything on having seen Mephistopheles in every possible iteration, and yet here he was entangled in a crazed chain of ideas.

Rahab had been disordered like this when begging for another chance, but that had made sense—and Ataf hadn't been backing him up.

Satan lowered his voice and spoke slowly. "Before you follow this insulting chain of ideas any further, am I to understand you would prefer me to have 'cremated' Beelzebub?" When Mephistopheles shook his head, Satan said, "Are you insinuating I've changed?"

Mephistopheles swallowed hard but didn't respond.

In fact, none of them responded.

That was an accusatory silence.

Satan kept his voice steady. "I assure you, this process has in no way altered me. I have an additional tool at my disposal, one I plan to employ to its full extent. If the circumstances were flipped, I would indeed chain you to the wall, Mephistopheles, because you're irrational. I may do it anyway." He turned to the others. "Are there any further suggestions that don't involve Belior's jealousy, Mephistopheles' paranoia, or my indefinite seclusion?"

Asmodeus said, "I recommend advising our people not to be alone with the enemy. They should travel in groups."

Moloch added, "That will mean no solo trips off the level, since the one-to-one escort by definition requires being alone with them."

Satrinah said, "I will notify all our cross-bonded pairs of the scope of the situation."

Mephistopheles said nothing, which was just as well.

Gabriel's book mentioned that bonds could effect change in the bondmates (a disgusting term). Because the majority of angels had bonded while everyone was still malleable, however, it was difficult to tease out which changes happened because of the bond versus which would have occurred due to maturity and experience. Late bonds were a rarity, and of course they'd been studied (relentlessly—Gabriel would have enjoyed that) but the data was inconclusive.

Even so, late bonders were still Cherubim and Seraphim with prior bonds, so it wasn't a matter of going from zero to one. They'd already cleared space in their souls for a roommate.

The text implied that Satan had a few other potential primaries. Belior was a given. Judging from how Mephistopheles had prepped him to bond Gabriel, he seemed a likely candidate. Satan hadn't settled on the rest. Given his overall strength, he'd probably have needed seven.

His Cherubim should change to suit him, the stronger partner. Him changing to suit them? Never. A harder substance should chip away at a softer substance. That was how reality worked.

On the other hand, chemistry didn't work that way. Atoms changed when they bonded into molecules, irrespective of their initial strength. The book had been very clear, though: a Seraph didn't give away his soul in a bond. Bonding was limited to access. Whenever Satan chose, he was strong enough to take whatever he needed.

What nonsense: *whatever he needed.* He didn't need Gabriel. He was using Gabriel as a lens to boost his focus and sharpen his perceptions. He'd been reaching for Gabriel more often as he got used to the benefits of doing so, but she'd admitted he was complete on his own. Mephistopheles had reiterated the same.

He very nearly reached for Gabriel's steel so he could clarify what "complete" meant, but he caught himself in time. How ridiculous would that be? Annexing Gabriel to prove that Satan didn't need Gabriel was tantamount to Satan asking the Maskim if he should disband the Maskim. It was in their best interest to answer a certain way.

Satan said, "I will not cower in terror of Gabriel. I want every operative working every angle we can. We've identified several targets as possibilities for culling away from the herd, and you may now consider Gabriel on that list."

Mephistopheles shifted, scared. Belior carried a faint charge of Asmodeus's energy, and his ulterior motive was easy to guess. Mephistopheles', less so. It didn't matter.

Satan said, "If they can take ours, then the field is open for us to take theirs. Dismissed."

Chapter Twenty-One

MICHAEL ARRIVED IN THE music library, his sword still hot from the last fight he'd broken up. Acoustically-perfect arguing rang through the main hall, and it didn't take the entire second order of angels to anticipate Ataf would be at the center.

Of course, Israfel was also involved, but it looked as though she had Ataf on her side rather than as her opponent. The tumult had even gotten loud enough for Rahab to look up from his book.

Michael flashed into the middle. "Everyone, back down. What's going on?"

Hot like magma, Ataf glared at three demons across from him—Rahab's other two bonded Seraphim, plus one additional Cherub. Israfel seemed like she'd sear the paint off the walls as well, so Michael focused on the opposition because Israfel probably had it right.

The opponents said, "No more liturgical music," and, "No hymns and praise songs."

Israfel gestured toward the doors. "If you don't like the music here, I cordially invite you to exit the library."

Michael said to the opponents, "It's her library, and on the outer layer, any number of musical performances are taking place. Several are hymn-free."

Ataf folded his arms and leaned back on one leg. "Allow me to spell out their objection. Rahab has requested Israfel perform a piece described in his book. Leaving won't solve their problem because they want the work not played at all."

Michael turned back to the opponents. "To be clear, you want to police the music Rahab hears?"

The healer Seraph said to Michael, "Rahab isn't well. You're poaching our members, and playing these songs is taking advantage of Rahab when he doesn't have full rational capacity."

Ataf huffed. "Therefore, out of concern for his ability to consent, they're taking away his ability to consent."

The healer snapped, "That is not what I said."

Israfel opened her hands. "Music wants to be free. Rahab should listen to whatever he wants. Before I retract their permission to remain in my library, Michael, I thought you might want to hear them out and give us a neutral opinion."

As if Michael would give a neutral opinion about matters of faith?

Sneering, the healer swept her wings toward Michael. "As if he'd give a neutral opinion?"

Michael fought a laugh. "Well, I can give a very neutral opinion about music, since it's not an area of expertise."

Ataf rolled his eyes. "We have only a few days. What's the harm in Rahab experiencing music he'll never hear again?"

Michael raised his hands and turned toward Rahab's other bonded Seraphim. "If you're worrying he'll hear music so beautiful that he'll want to betray your side, then consider how if he leaves here, he's going to be moving freely through the outer level's concert performances, and absorbing music from every era of history—much of which will contain hymns anyway. If we're attempting to poach him, then you should ask yourselves whom he's more likely to favor: the side willing to give him what he wants, or the ones trying to deny him what he wants."

The healer Seraph's eyes smoldered, but Michael turned his back on her. If she were to attack him, her escort would revoke permission before her blast struck. Instead he faced Rahab, who seemed a lot steadier than before. Michael said, "What did you want to hear?"

Rahab showed him the book, open to an analysis of Mozart's

Requiem.

Michael glanced at Israfel, who pointed downward, toward the concert hall beneath the library. She was ready to go.

Michael said, "Israfel can do that. We could even introduce you to Mozart, if you'd like."

Behind Michael, the healer Seraph snarled, "You're trying to seduce him."

Michael said to Rahab, "Do you feel seduced? Or did you come up with this on your own?"

A shadow passed over Rahab's eyes, and from him came three projections: the book called Mozart 'pivotal;' this was his last piece; therefore, it must be his best.

Michael turned to the angry Seraphim. "His logic sounds solid. If you're arguing that Mozart died young in an attempt to trick a demon into listening to the *Requiem* at a banquet after the Second Coming, I'm not willing to entertain that level of delusion. You can simmer down, or you can leave."

In the concert hall, Israfel had Rahab and Michael stand in the best area of the hall for sound quality. Ataf hovered near while the concert hall filled.

Turning to Rahab, Michael said, "On one of my last assignments on Earth, I was assisting a human who had to travel a hundred miles to another city. She wanted to listen to this, too, so she put the sound onto a box this big," Michael held his fingers a couple of inches apart, "in the form of electronic coding. Then she used a vehicle not much larger than a bed and drove a hundred miles in an hour, using sound-projecting devices the size of her hand to hear the memory of a seventy-five piece orchestra and a chorus of forty voices."

Rahab breathed in an oddly wispy voice, "Isn't that something? I never thought the monkeys' technology would achieve wonders like that. The last I saw, they barely managed to forge iron."

That was the most response he'd gotten from Rahab.

The other two Seraphim stuck close, along with the spare Cherub. Michael remained, just in case. Shortly the hall was packed with other listeners, though, so he could have left.

Except—well, he liked Mozart, too. He hadn't at all minded a hundred-mile drive streaming the *Requiem* to the automobile. Plus, Michael got mentioned in it by name, and that was fun.

The music began in D-minor. Rahab's wings flared as after three thousand years, he experienced what a human orchestra could achieve. It was the same feeling as Michael listening to Lucifer's hymn before the Winnowing: *We can do this?* Rahab's attention was a rigid force, his focus attuned to the sounds while at the same time cataloging the ways the players handled the instruments. He'd just read a textbook that discussed all these instruments and likely encoded the sounds on the pages, but without ever having heard an orchestra in action. Now he could experience a glissando or a suspended chord, and he'd be pairing the written commentary to the music he was experiencing. Every measure would be a matter of, "Oh!" and "Is that how they do it?"

Michael closed his eyes. There was anger from the Seraphim, but from Rahab, only awe rippling off in rings. At his side stood Israfel—patient.

Michael shivered. *She's waiting for the* Dies irae, *isn't she?*

God reassured him.

Rahab would never have experienced a Christian liturgy. He didn't know the format other than by reading the book, but would a music text have explained the progression?

The third piece began: the sequence, *"Dies irae,"* the Day of Wrath. It was a prediction of the Final Judgment, the summons of the trumpet, and finally the general resurrection followed by the sorting of souls into Heaven or Hell. The piece opened strong, and it didn't let up.

Rahab trembled until Ataf cupped a wing around him. Israfel was glaring at them, but although Rahab began to shake, neither he nor Ataf fled the hall.

There were no interruptions and no protests. Although Michael would have loved to just listen, he kept his attention on all the participants, both the saints and the *viatores*. Every few moments, his attention returned to a rapt Rahab. Rapt, but also shedding rings of desolation. Though potent, they didn't travel.

At the end, everyone applauded. It was masterful, and it was amazing—and it was also a complete version because the angels could answer the manuscript questions of an unfinished work. Amidst all the applause, though, Ataf sought out Michael's gaze. *Can we go somewhere alone?*

Michael tapped a second escort, then flashed Rahab and Ataf into an empty practice room.

Rahab slumped against the wall and covered his face in his hands before cocooning himself with his wings. Ataf folded his arms and faced away.

Michael approached Rahab. "It's a lot to take in the first time."

Rahab whispered, *"When the judge takes his place, what is hidden will be revealed. Nothing will remain unavenged. What shall a wretch like me say? Who shall intercede for me, when the just ones need mercy?"*

Michael extended his wingtips to Rahab's. "Keep reciting."

With perfect recall of the words he'd just heard and his voice soft like a breeze, Rahab worked his way through the *Recordare*, but then he stopped.

Michael whispered, "Ask God for mercy."

Rahab shuddered. "I'm unforgivable."

Ataf turned toward him.

Rahab wouldn't raise his face from his hands. "I failed everyone. I harmed my Seraphim. I destroyed Ataf and can never restore him. There's nothing worthwhile about me. Not even God can forgive me."

With his feathers spread, Michael put his hands on the Cherub's shoulders. "Rahab—"

Ataf edged Michael aside. "I hold nothing against you. You don't owe me a debt."

Rahab was only shaking his head.

Michael swallowed hard. "Ataf just forgave you. Therefore, you're not unforgivable."

Ataf twined his fingers into Rahab's. "I don't want to lose you again. But if you can ask God for forgiveness, do it. If He grants it, then that's good for you, and I want what's good for you. It's better than leaving you under the lake."

Rahab kept shivering. "They'll blame you. I'll have harmed you again." When Ataf looked aside, Rahab added, "You ask, too. Ask together with me."

When Ataf stiffened, Michael said, "You aren't unforgivable, either. Whatever you did to Rahab, it's clear he's forgiven you."

Ataf released Rahab's hands and stepped back. "I wouldn't know how to begin."

Rahab followed him forward, raising his wings. "Recite all the *Requiem* with me. We'll say all the words, and by the end, God will have decided."

They didn't need music. Ataf knew the Latin prayers from the liturgy. Rahab knew them from the piece they'd just heard.

My prayers are unworthy, but, good Lord, have mercy, and rescue me from eternal fire.

They didn't get far before Rahab stopped reciting, eyes fixed a thousand miles away and heart engaged with a conversation the others couldn't hear. He crossed his hands over his chest. Ataf kept breathing out the words, but his voice had broken, so Michael recited with him. *Grant them eternal rest, Lord, and let perpetual light shine on them, as with Your saints in eternity, because You are merciful.*

Warmth filled the room. Beneath the recited words, Michael counter-prayed, *Please, Father, bless this.* What a joy for two more souls to fly back to God. From despair, God could coax hope. From the sticky splinters of hatred, God could spin love. The tarry morass of harm could become crystalized redemption.

The room felt bigger, brighter. Facing Ataf was Jesus, and Ataf hit the floor, prostrate with his wings spread over his head. Rahab dropped to his knees. Jesus rested a hand on his hair, then looked back to the Seraph.

Pulsing with confusion, Ataf drew in on himself, knees and arms up under his chest. Rahab, though, extended a hand and clutched Jesus's cloak.

Jesus crouched before Ataf. "Arise."

Ataf knelt up, covering his face with his hands and all six wings.

The room vibrated with his awareness of his spiritual nakedness.

Jesus said, "What do you want me to do for you?"

Ataf choked out, "Lord—" and Michael's heart stuttered because that alone was more than he ever thought he'd hear from a demon. "Lord, I want—"

Heart trilling, Michael thought, *You want to be forgiven. You want to come home. Say it. Even if you only add 'my' to Lord, that may be enough.*

The Holy Spirit filled Michael with calm and a caution to wait.

Ataf had spent thousands of years lying. Between him and Rahab, they'd have realized whatever he said now must be the truth, only here knelt Ataf in paralysis, without any idea what was true.

Rahab was glowing. Whatever had transacted between him and God, it had gone to completion. He shimmered with tiny, intense rings as he had during the *Requiem*, but tinged with more than a little panic.

Ataf whispered, "I want to make it right."

Jesus said, "Do you think you can?"

Hands and wings muffled his voice. "I can't."

Michael nearly urged him to ask more, but the Father steadied him.

Ataf shivered at the core of his heart's flame. "I have no right to ask anything of you. But—"

Jesus reached past Ataf's wings and put a hand on his hands, then gentled them away from his face.

Colorless, Ataf looked at Him, eye-to-eye. "Make me clean. Make me understand. Make me sorry enough. I can't fix everything I've ruined."

In the next instant, there was Ataf grasping Christ's hand in both his own, tears streaming down the Seraph's face as he spilled out his desperation and his faults and every pivotal moment where he'd turned away from God. Michael dismissed the second escort (Rahab no longer needed one) and was about to leave as well, except God told him to stay. Ataf's crimes had been public, so his confession could likewise have this little audience, and Michael knew better than to repeat any of what he was hearing.

Jesus guided Ataf to a stand while Ataf's words tumbled out with urgency, and the longer Jesus listened, the steadier Ataf became. He wasn't looking anywhere but at Jesus. Then, when he faltered, he tried again to cover his face, but Jesus kept holding his hands.

Turning his face aside, Ataf whispered, "I haven't loved anyone for thousands of years, but if You'll tolerate me, I think I can love You."

Jesus pulled Ataf into a hug. "Tolerating you was never my goal." Jesus pressed Ataf's head to His shoulder. "Loving you was."

Ataf collapsed in Jesus's arms. Rahab rushed to him, and Jesus wrapped him into the embrace as well.

Spent, Michael dropped his head against the wall. One angel dragged from the lake, and one more pried from the jaws of death. *Thank you.* Michael couldn't manage more right then. Only, *Thank you.*

Chapter Twenty-Two

IF I DON'T GO back, then there wasn't any reason for the bond.

That had run like a litany through Gabriel's head every minute she stayed away from Lucifer. Huddled in a corner of Raphael's home, she repeated it to herself each time she felt afraid to go back. She'd resolve that she had to return only to find her resolution had resulted in no change of location.

Raphael joined her now, his fire low like a banked hearth. Gabriel tucked her knees to her chest, hugged her legs, and pressed her forehead into her crossed arms.

With her eyes closed, she probed her heart. It was tired. Lucifer burned at a rate she'd never anticipated. Mephistopheles had claimed Lucifer would consume one Cherub and move onto the next, and at the time, Gabriel had deflected: one, perhaps, but Lucifer was smart enough not to burn out multiple Cherubim. Now, however, Gabriel wondered whether there would be any choice in the matter.

It kept happening: from across the layers of Heaven, Lucifer would connect the energy between Gabriel and himself so he could refine his thoughts, and his power would flow into her because she had so much less of it.

When Gabriel retreated from focusing on herself, she could feel Raphael praying for her.

Lucifer had threatened to do worse than burn her out. He'd threatened her vivisection. He'd keep the parts he wanted—her intelligence, her steadiness—and immolate the rest. Given how much he was already doing, she had no doubt he'd accomplish exactly that.

Finally she sent to Raphael, *If I don't go back, then there wasn't any reason for the bond.*

Raphael replied, *If you don't go back, it makes perfect sense.*

Gabriel tried and failed to force a smile, but it didn't matter because she had her head down. *Are you saying, if I do go back, I'm being senseless?*

Raphael couldn't even laugh. *I'm yours to do whatever helps you most. If you choose not to go back, I'll hide you here. I'll gather a thousand Cherubim and do nothing but keep them energized until they figure out how to break your bond. But if you want to go back, I'll be with you, wherever you need me to be, however helps you best, in whatever capacity I can.*

Except that would make Raphael a target.

I don't care about that. Raphael had gotten urgent. *You're already a target. If I can take some of the burden for you, I will.*

Jesus had stepped into danger to save humanity. Raphael was his guardian angel. They were so alike.

Raphael murmured, "I'm honored you feel that way, but He's so much more."

Gabriel raised her head. "If I don't make it through this, you should know how much I admire you."

Raphael huffed. "I refuse to hear what you just said, so you have no choice but to survive. You're not destined to become the barbed-wire queen of the Maskim, ruling Hell from a trench beneath the Lake of Fire."

If Gabriel could have made a wisecrack about whether a burning cloak paired well with a razor-wire crown, she would have made herself smile. She couldn't. She and Israfel had sat on the temple steps, giggling about flirting, and that togetherness had given them the strength to face God in prayer and accept His answer. Here now with Raphael, Gabriel couldn't connect with the joy.

Instead she said, "Lucifer threatened he'd use me to take Israfel. I can't endanger her."

Cold swept through Raphael and up into Gabriel, swirling with that constant burn from Lucifer. "She's not in any more danger with you out there than with you hidden. She's still in the open."

Gabriel got to her feet. "Then I have to be available to her."

Raphael flashed them to one of the crowded music festivals where Israfel was at work, and Gabriel stepped closer to him. Still, the music was amazing, and Raphael projected a low-level caution that kept anyone from coming up close.

Raphael sent, *Do you want to sing together? I'll pull a few strings and get us a slot.*

Gabriel sent him an image of a ten-string lyre.

That's plucking, not pulling.

She glared at him side-long, and he grinned. Finally, she smiled, too.

Lucifer tugged on her soul in response, and she experienced momentary vertigo.

Raphael said, "I'm calling Israfel. Let's do this together."

Shortly they had a stage and an audience and a group of backing musicians. Raphael bantered with Israfel about what Gabriel should sing (with the audience calling out requests). Finally, Israfel won the argument by tucking a violin under her chin and starting the song she wanted—a sweet, dramatic ballad—and Gabriel laughed when Raphael had to change the instrument in his hands.

Israfel's musical presence got the crowd standing. Gabriel sang while Raphael encouraged the audience to join in on the refrain.

Israfel's music was more than sound. She encapsulated the emotions into the melody, and in that release, Gabriel was able to open her heart, too. The song embodied joy, and Gabriel let it carry her upward, outward, forward. She could feel the audience participating, and that floated her heart even higher.

Raphael had asked Gabriel if she wanted to sing with him and Israfel, and there could only ever be one answer. Euphoria flowed from her, and it mingled with the fulfillment from Israfel.

How often could she cut loose like this? Using her full vocal range, she went for a grand performance, with dramatic notes held as long as she could, crescendos, and hope. Always hope.

God, who'd given her this voice, could receive love in the form of this same voice.

Gabriel hadn't always been able to sing this way. She'd always been able to sing notes, of course, but until her year away, she'd never emoted. She'd had the range and the technique and the ability, sure. When she'd come back, though—the feelings, the emotions? She'd been able to instill what she was feeling into the songs. Her song had always had been her worship, but only afterward had her voice become her prayer. She hadn't been able to sing the things she couldn't feel—and after having felt them, she couldn't not sing them.

Now, as then, she felt the urge to open the gates to her heart, and when she gave in, the love burst out.

The audience was growing, calling for their friends, summoning still others. *"You've got to hear this!"* Their buoyancy carried Gabriel out further, and she reached for God, reached for every ability she had. Raphael and Israfel backed her melody in a way that brought her even deeper into the song.

Abruptly, among the audience was Lucifer.

Gabriel's heart slammed shut, but she forced it back open. With him staring—such a vulnerable feeling—Gabriel reached for Israfel's soul, only Israfel had put a mute on herself.

Gabriel's joy must have vibrated back through the bond.

Except...when had Lucifer last felt joy? Only that glimmer while they'd been flying together. When it had reminded him of what he'd been missing, he'd tried to keep it.

Therefore, why not now? Why not five minutes of joy?

Gabriel let it thrill through her, unleashing everything. Was she vulnerable? All the better. Let him feel by proxy the emotions he'd shut away. Gabriel could draw from Raphael and Israfel to focus those feelings through her heart and project them out her voice.

They were together. Her. Her three Seraphim. God. And a song.

Israfel went to the front of the stage and got the entire crowd singing along. Well, not Lucifer, but the rest of the crowd, and Gabriel rode the crest of that wave. Feel it. Feel it all.

Israfel gave the song back to Gabriel, who modulated and went right for the broadest part of her vocal range. When the song came to a magnificent, huge ending, the crowd was screaming. Gabriel glanced toward Raphael, who was smirking because he'd been right—and then toward Israfel, who'd loved every second of that performance. *We haven't done that in a long time.*

Gabriel scanned the crowd in case she could see Lucifer.

Israfel called out the next song, then added, "We need a bass. What do you say, guys?" The crowd cheered. "A really good bass?" More cheers. "I don't know—you don't sound like you really want me to call a bass."

Lucifer was a bass. His heat rose in Gabriel's heart.

Instead, Israfel called out, "Michael? We need you!"

Michael appeared as if responding to a crisis, and when the crowd cheered, he looked with annoyance at Israfel.

Gabriel clasped her hands as she faced Michael. *Please. This is the first time she's released her anger,* and with that, Michael relented.

Israfel had chosen a fun song, and after a shuffle of background instruments, she counted down with Raphael to start.

Again there was joy in the song, but this time, part of the joy was the confusion. Raphael loved the fact that their musical roles were all jumbled up. For one thing, Israfel had never met an instrument she couldn't play or a role she couldn't voice, and it had never occurred to her that any specific line *shouldn't* be the lead. For another, this song made the most of human language's ability to create an infinitely long sentence by stringing together prepositional phrases, one added on every go-around. *There's a dog near a house under a tree in a woods near a river by a mountain...* The goal was to get each verse as long as you possibly could until someone eventually forgot a word...or was laughing too hard to continue.

The chorus was the only section of the song that broke into parts. Gabriel had figured she'd take the alto line because Israfel would sing soprano, except Israfel left that for her (and the entire audience). Michael, for all that he could sing, wasn't actually a very good singer, so his bass line was more like the melody line, and Raphael was doing the variations the bass should have done. In fact, this wasn't even the most common arrangement, and when Gabriel reached into Israfel's thoughts to figure out what she should actually be singing, she slammed into jealousy—from Lucifer.

He was livid. Had Israfel picked Michael to make Lucifer territorial?

Gabriel almost faltered on the endless sentence in the verse, then got back on track. Jealousy had erupted from Lucifer when he'd destroyed the token. Now it was jealousy plus...humiliation?

Israfel sent a flare of thought at Gabriel, who returned her attention to the song. She opened up again to joy, but this time, that vulnerability didn't mean Lucifer was experiencing forgotten emotions. Instead, she felt his.

Not humiliation, but...self-consciousness? No, that didn't make sense. Lucifer didn't care about their judgment. He loved being watched.

Again, an acid possessiveness consumed the edges of Gabriel's heart.

Lucifer shouldn't resent her other Seraphim. Bonding wasn't marriage. There weren't vows, and bonds weren't monogamous. Had that been why Lucifer resisted from the start?

The weight increased inside: hatred of Gabriel for cavorting with these others, hatred of Michael for taking a place that should have been his. Michael had done that in so many ways. Michael's title, "Prince of the Heavenly Host," could have been Lucifer's. Gabriel's title, too, for that matter: "Prince of Heaven." How many other titles would Lucifer have claimed had God not inverted the order? That wasn't even to mention the angels being "sons of God," which Lucifer had overtly rejected when God presented them with His only begotten Son.

Also—the longer Gabriel felt him continuing down this path of thought, the more Lucifer picked up the secondhand smoke of her discomfort, and the harder it got to sing. She was pushing him past the point of self-restraint, and that was the opposite of a

Cherub's role.

Gabriel's attention turned to Israfel—and that was likewise secondhand smoke. Lucifer wanted to inflame Israfel's hyper-awareness of injustice.

It was Raphael who forgot whether a rock was by a cavern or under a leaf, and everyone was laughing. All but one. The crowd called for another song, but Gabriel flashed away because Israfel might be orchestrating more than music. Provoking Lucifer into a public attack against Michael or Gabriel would get Lucifer locked down again—might even trigger his ejection from the banquet.

I can't let her do that. Gabriel's heart hurt, and not only from Lucifer's fire. *It would be bad for him—and it would be bad for her, too.*

Satan followed Gabriel. She'd flashed to the Hilbert Hotel's gazebo and had her eyes trained on Satan's smoke-blackened windows. He stepped into her line of sight.

Gabriel started, but her expression was flat.

"Quit that." Waving a hand, Satan gestured to all of her. "I hate the blank look while you're figuring out how to manipulate me. Be honest."

Gabriel offered her steadiness. "Looking blank is honest."

"You hide everything you're thinking, only now I can feel what you're doing." His voice was a growl, but he drew her energy because it was focusing him.

A moment after, Satan (or was it Gabriel) noticed a crowd on the opposite side of the lake. Satan fixed his attention across only to hear...Ataf?

Ataf, rallying a crowd, ranting about God?

And then Satan realized what he was hearing from his former minion.

Gabriel blew out a ring of joy—wonderment and thrill and then hope for Rahab, too.

In flames, Satan flashed right up in front of Ataf, but Gabriel intercepted him the moment he struck. Ataf didn't even flinch as he shouted, "We can come home! God is willing to take us back!"

Gabriel flung up a shield between them, deflecting as much of Satan's power as she could while Ataf preached louder and faster over the *viatores'* jeers. Satan scanned the area because doubtless Rahab was tucked away to feed suggestions to the Seraph.

Michael and Israfel flashed into position, but not before Satan blasted Ataf off his feet, then pivoted and aimed toward a far-off niche to knock out Rahab.

Ataf took to the air, his voice echoing over the expanse of the lake. "They can't silence us! Forgiveness is real!"

Gabriel was simulating a thousand scenarios in her mind—planning to move Ataf, except Ataf wasn't going to be moved—and that was just fine because Satan could pick out the most likely outcomes as well as she could. Also from Gabriel, he felt horror because a brand-new convert shouldn't be putting himself out there, not with everything so raw.

None of that was news to Satan. Engage an overzealous new convert, and half the time you had a re-converted convert. Double that chance for a celebrity convert. Even better, Israfel would be present to witness the turnaround, and maybe he could swing her at the same time.

Satan flew at Ataf again, but Michael entangled Satan in the air before he could get a hand on the traitor.

For a distance weapon, Satan still had his voice. "You were useless back when I demoted you. Now you're going to be useless for the other side."

Ataf spread his wings, grinning. "I don't have to be useful. I'm forgiven and loved. When was the last time anyone loved you?"

Ataf had just proven he'd respond to whatever cues Satan offered. That meant Satan could get him re-hooked.

Again, Gabriel moved faster than thought to shield Ataf before Satan struck, but able to feel her intentions, he got around her shielding. Abruptly there were soldiers surrounding them:

Michael's soldiers, followed momentarily by Satan's. War hadn't broken out in Heaven since the first one, and here might be the opening strike of the second.

Stand down! Gabriel sounded desperate, but he could feel Israfel agitating on the other side. Gabriel might be urging either of them. *It doesn't have to be this way!*

Stand down and let Ataf go? Keeping him was a matter of pride. Satan called, "You're talking a good line, Ataf, but once everyone knows what you've done, they'll never accept you."

Taking the bait, Israfel glared at Ataf.

Ataf spread his hands. "I'm Ataf, and I convinced Cain to kill Abel. I'm Ataf, who urged Joseph's brothers to sell him into slavery. God knows exactly who I am and what I've done. I'm Ataf, a demon who plotted God's downfall and denied Him and spit at Him, and—"

"—and made no attempt at amends." Satan snorted. "Anybody can say words. How much have you changed if you're using your fallen name?"

Ataf's eyes glowed. "This is the name I was using when God forgave me, and that makes it the most precious name I could possibly have."

Gabriel tried to draw down Satan's fire, but he shut her out. Even so, she stood in his flames as though she belonged there.

Which—she did. So he put his hands on her shoulders, and Israfel's feathers spread.

Satan focused past Gabriel at Ataf. "If God loves the mockery you've made of yourself, then that doesn't say much for His taste and discernment."

Ataf smirked. "Considering how I've spent the last several thousand years, I can't say much for mine, either."

Gabriel managed to tap Satan's energy. *Please back down. Michael might lock you away again, and we don't have much time.*

Satan glared at her. *What makes you think I want to spend time with you?*

Well, don't spend it with Ataf. Gabriel's will was steel. *You followed me here. Stay with me.*

There was enough jeering every time Ataf spoke that he wouldn't get heard. A throng of Michael's angels, including Raphael, had gathered where Rahab had fallen, so Ataf wasn't getting help from that quarter, either.

Meanwhile, Israfel seemed as if she'd isolate every participant in solitary confinement for the remainder of the banquet, including her comrades. She needed one more push.

Satan sent, *Asmodeus, I want every Seraph or Cherub bonded to Ataf or Rahab under surveillance, if not locked in their rooms. Then, put the entire army on standby.*

That done, Satan needed to reel in both Ataf and Israfel. He snapped at Ataf, "Stay out of my way."

Ataf taunted, "I'll pray for you," and Satan barked out a laugh. Victory.

"Whoa!" Michael was, unfortunately, smarter than Ataf, at least this once. "Absolutely not. You are not using prayer as a weapon, and God is not your hired gun."

When Ataf's wings flared, Michael added, "We get it. You're new to this. But you need to get up to speed because the same tactics don't apply."

Israfel looked horrified and disgusted. That made her as good as his. Satan looked her dead in the eye and said, "God set the bar an inch off the ground for your new friend, but he limboed right under it."

Ataf squared his shoulders to engage again, but Michael flashed him away.

Satan turned to the crowd, but he was watching himself with Gabriel's vision. He looked and sounded amazing. "Behold! They love and accept you until the moment you're unlovable and unacceptable. Don't trust their words. Trust their actions."

Even while speaking to Satan, Gabriel was staring at Israfel, eyes wide. "Ataf wasn't ready. He shouldn't have been doing that at all."

"Free angels shouldn't need Heaven's written permission to talk." Satan swept out a hand toward the laughing onlookers. It

Dedication of the Stars

looked dramatic. He should be wearing a cloak, but too late to change that now. Instead he just fine-tuned the sparks encircling his head. "You can disperse. Our friend will rejoin our ranks within the hour, after God tries to crush him into a little cubby hole." He glanced back at Israfel, and said in a lower voice, "Or maybe He'll keep that manipulative beggar because it's enough to check the boxes with a few perfunctory words."

Satan flashed himself and Gabriel back into his hotel room. At least, he tried to flash her into his room, but she blocked him. Instead, they landed in the hallway.

He'd swing Ataf back. Like so many shiny converts, Ataf loved the idea of God and would recoil once he realized God's unconditional love was conditional on changing every last thing about himself. Now, for the next problem.

Satan faced Gabriel. "Won't go in with me? Afraid I'm going to lock you inside?"

Gabriel folded her arms. "Afraid? I'm certain." Even so, he could feel her trying to mentally reconfigure his room so it wouldn't be able to take a Guard. On the fly like this, she couldn't. "I'm not getting repeatedly cindered, and therefore I'm not going in. Also, therefore, why I want you not confined to quarters."

Satan tilted his head. "You had no qualms confining me to quarters when it meant completing our bond."

Delight pulsed from her. It was obnoxious how proud she was of him for figuring things out, as though he were a kindergartener reciting his first letters.

He cupped his wings. "What can I give you to entice you in there?"

"Nothing you can't give me out here." She opened her hands, and again that flute appeared. "Is there something I can give you, something to remember me after the end of the week?"

Satan said, "You'll sing my song for me?"

She clicked the flute's keys. "I'll sing the descant, but you have to sing the melody."

"Except singing together wouldn't be a new memory, would it?" He'd never repeat that performance—for several reasons, the first

277

being that you don't sully perfection. "If you really want to give me something to remember you, give me something you never gave Raphael or Israfel."

Frowning, Gabriel made the flute disappear. "That would be my journals from my year as a human, and I can't. I burned them."

Satan's heart surged. Gabriel could pretend she was all-in to keep him engaged, but she wasn't, the same way he'd gotten her on the hook by pretending his return was possible.

She caught that thought from him, too, and there was disgust that she'd been tricked, followed immediately by the wisp of frustration: Gabriel should have shut down this plan the moment Mary suggested it.

Satan flared his wings. *That woman? Really?*

Gabriel jerked backward.

Satan followed her. "Of course this lunacy was her idea. You've always been her puppy."

He stirred up Gabriel's memories. Mary's puppy—how would that have been different? *Gabriel, fetch this. Sit at my feet. Guard the house.* Gabriel loved that human who'd spent her days raising the Son of God as though He needed her. Then that woman had spent the rest of eternity with her heart bleeding for all the people God had decided should replace every angel who'd exited His stage play. God had put enmity between the snake and the woman, so now the woman had sent her plaything to infiltrate the snake's heart.

Gabriel closed her eyes. That was pain, and Gabriel deserved pain. With his spiritual fingers in Gabriel's mind, Satan evoked all her interactions with Mary. Satan laughed at that so-called friendship because Mary had made advances to Gabriel in a way that benefitted herself but not at all Gabriel. Gabriel had never been smart enough to recognize manipulation. Satan, at least, had declared outright that Gabriel had nothing to offer him. Mary had nothing to offer Gabriel, but this setup proved Mary considered Gabriel disposable—just her trained puppy.

Gabriel had her back to the wall, but Satan pushed closer. Their wings were touching, their foreheads millimeters apart. Satan whispered, "God used her, and now she's using you."

Gabriel turned her face away. "I was there. She consented."

"Consent after brainwashing isn't consent," Satan breathed. "Do you know how many souls God stole from me using that loophole? But don't think you're special. He used me, too. He needed an enemy. It makes no sense to give creatures free will but then nothing to choose. You're useful, but I was useful first. An accuser. An alternative."

"He loved you," Gabriel choked out. "He loved us so much that—
"

"No one loves their tools." Satan's voice thrummed like a heartbeat. "He went one step too far by giving His tools a face and a name. He wanted me as a role instead of an individual, and then He tried to crush the individual. Except He hasn't succeeded, so He sent that woman to send you to pry me open. When He's done, He'll toss you and me and her and all His other tools back in the box."

With Satan's door at her back, Gabriel clenched her hands. "You use everyone as a tool, your allies and your enemies."

He surged his flames through her. She absorbed as much as she could and let the rest flare out as heat. She couldn't keep doing that, but for now, it appeared to energize her.

Satan vibrated, a purr. "The apple landed right on the roots of the tree. The Second Person of the Trinity told His allies to pray for their enemies and do good to their persecutors. But where are the prayers for their first enemy? What good have I received from the hand of my persecutor?"

It flashed through Gabriel so hard and so quickly that Satan recoiled, denying he'd felt it at all—except—

Prayers?

For him?

He almost laughed, except this wasn't Ataf's sniper-fired, "I'll pray for you." This was real.

Tentative, Gabriel raised her head.

They shone in the grey of her eyes: the prayers and the wishes and the words—sometimes *pro forma*, but sometimes because

Gabriel had hungered for something no longer to be grasped, a longing so keen that the request erupted from her in prayer to the only Other who could understand.

Longing. For him. For who he'd been. For their friendship. For a friend who'd used and rejected her. For an enemy who'd set lures and sprung traps and planned her homicide. Longing—and for what?

"How dare you?" Satan wanted to shout but couldn't notch his voice above a whisper. He wasn't the soul Gabriel remembered. He'd done everything to burn God's image out of himself, so why would this Cherub freeze him in her mind as Lucifer, her friend from the past? It was nauseating and horrifying and sad—sad. He snarled, "What made you think I'd ever want such a thing?"

She cocked her head. "I don't understand. Five seconds ago, you were offended it didn't happen." Surely she was tapping his energy, otherwise how could she be upright in the face of his rage? "Your wants weren't my concern. I did what *I* wanted, a choice you should find very familiar."

She'd gone for what she wanted, and Gabriel wanted for her enemy—her former friend who existed only as memory—to have good things. No, not even a memory. A nightmare.

Satan became aware—actually, no, Gabriel became aware—that the walls were blistering with Satan's heat.

He wouldn't have permitted his people to come to Heaven. He'd have dug in his forces and held the line in Hell. It would have taken Michael longer than seven days to flush them out, and Satan would have staged raids to retrieve any souls Michael kidnapped. Long before Michael could have extracted them in significant numbers, the banquet would have ended.

Except it didn't matter what would have happened. That logic came from Gabriel. It only mattered what happened now.

Praying for him? For two thousand years?

Satan tried to focus Gabriel's clarity on the question without Gabriel sensing what he was asking, but he couldn't turn up what Gabriel actually wanted.

His silence had to be burning her more than even his power. He saw all the way into her, and still she kept her motive hidden so deep he couldn't wrench it from the ground, a weed secured by its taproot. Belior had said it was impossible to manipulate a bondmate because they'd detect it, but every time he dug deeper, Satan found only that Gabriel wanted good things for him. For her enemy. Blessings for the one who'd persecuted her. Good for the one who hated her. She'd missed him. Long ago, she'd loved him.

Satan's fists clenched. "You're wasting your time. You've wasted thousands of years of your time."

With that frustrating, icy calm, Gabriel didn't avert her gaze. *It's never a waste.*

She hadn't projected it. She was merely certain.

Love was the worst waste of energy. Love meant spinning wheels and diverting thoughts and spending your energy on things of no benefit. Love crimped the reasoning of Cherubim and bled off the ambition of Seraphim. Love reforged as despair had put Rahab under the lake, and love that fermented into jealousy had manacled Belior. Gabriel was wrong. Love was weakness.

And God was love.

Satan snarled, "You have nothing to offer me."

Wings vibrating, face glowing, Gabriel raised her chin. "On the contrary, I have everything."

Before him, she stood with her heart and wings wide open, the logic and the facts and the memories of a Cherub, all tinted with thousands of years' yearning. Her eyes gleamed silver as her fingers in his soul evoked those moments he hadn't anticipated— their joy in flying together, the spice of bantering over the heather plant, the unexpected admission that he might want to want to repent. *"Not now, I don't want it."* Her cool thoughts lit up the labyrinth of his mind: *Not now, but when?*

For all that Ataf was obnoxious, there'd been joy overspilling his street-corner preaching. That joy could be Lucifer's, too. Not just for a moment painting the sky, but joy in meeting, joy in being, joy in—

Satan shoved her aside. "Get out of my head!"

Gabriel caught herself before slipping. "You have so much, but

I'm holding the rest."

Her adoration? Her devotion? Her loyalty?

Except that wasn't her offer. She was offering her companionship. Her thoughts. Her reflections. Her self.

And what she wanted from him—his self.

To yield everything. To relinquish his self-contained wholeness. To be a knot in the mesh she could envision in her mind. In that weaving, she held a place where he could be secure and treasured and wanted, a part of the framework rather than broken off and dangling.

As a pair, they'd make beauty. They'd create completion.

Satan backed away, and Gabriel stepped nearer.

He flashed to his room. She wouldn't follow him here, but still he felt her in the hallway. He slid down the door, the ripples of its ruined mirror against his back, his knees tucked and his head down.

On the other side, she was doing the same.

He slammed shut the doors of his mind. She'd begun by wondering if he annoyed everyone he interacted with, but now she'd moved on to wondering if anyone followed Satan because they loved him—if he considered anyone his friend. That wasn't something he'd ever asked. If they were afraid, all the better. Fear ensured obedience. If they hated him, they'd focus on him even more.

He should tell Gabriel to prove she loved him by bringing him Israfel, except proving herself wasn't on her agenda. The only proof she held out was hope. Mary may have offered up Gabriel as a sacrifice, but Gabriel had stretched out on that altar, saying, "Will this help him? Then he can have it."

Satan didn't want it. Hadn't wanted it. These parts of his soul had slept since the Winnowing. Why awaken them now?

All the mirrors were warped, and Gabriel had wanted them clear. The plant was dead, and Gabriel had wanted it to thrive. The windows were dark, and Gabriel had wanted light.

Gabriel could enter and be the only undamaged one in the rippled darkness. Gabriel would have carried beauty into the room. She was a lamp illuminating his perceptions, a trowel straightening the path for ideas he'd never thought.

Satan was a sieve for straining away the things God didn't want. The net. The winnowing fan. God didn't love His tools, but if somehow Gabriel loved Satan, that meant Gabriel hadn't been trying to use him.

Gabriel was being used, though. By Mary. By God.

Back before the Winnowing, Satan had used God. It was easy. He'd used God often enough since then, employing religious regulations to trap the monkeys in snares of self-righteousness, or wielding doctrinal certitude to pivot hearts toward spiritual pride. But before all that, Lucifer had used God as a vault to launch himself even higher than he'd been made. If Lucifer could prove he loved God more than the rest of these, then all the angels would emulate him. If Lucifer could prove he worshipped God better, loved Him harder, served Him more completely...then every other angel would admire him twice as much. They'd want to be like him. They'd remake themselves in Lucifer's image and likeness.

He'd been succeeding, too.

Then God had presented the test, the Second Person of the Trinity in human form, and in doing so had handed Lucifer the perfect opportunity: Lucifer could protect God from Himself by showing the other angels what real worship looked like. Adoration meant elevating God, not putting Him down. They'd hold fast, with no choice but to unite under Lucifer's guidance. Lucifer's light would challenge God and change God, control God, and in doing so, Lucifer would control everything.

God couldn't have made an angel so strong and so perfect and so endowed without intending him to reforge creation around himself. Lucifer had been on a quest for a way to use all these skills, the one angel worthy of ruling them all.

Gabriel had nothing to offer Lucifer in that quest. He was so far above her.

Except now Gabriel could crawl into his heart and curl up in that empty space where long ago he used to encounter God. She'd broken into an abandoned cathedral, lit not by sunlight but by one guttering candle, then crunched over shards of stained glass toward an altar covered with fallen plaster. That space longed to be inhabited, and beneath it, she'd taken shelter.

Gabriel remained on the other side of the door. If she came inside, he'd hurt her. But if he went out to her, he'd hurt her more. That door had to stay.

"Want to want to repent." Mephistopheles had warned him that was enough. Satan should have realized.

He sent a message to the Maskim: he was not to be disturbed. They'd obey. They might realize why. He'd take care of that later. With his head down and his wings a cocoon, he blasted his anger at Gabriel. *Leave me.* She had to leave because she wanted more good for him than he wanted for himself. If she stayed, he'd hurt her again, so she had to go. He sprayed fire not meant to energize but only to scorch, drawing back nothing. *Leave!*

His soul echoed. She was gone.

The room was silent, a ruined cathedral with no altar for its idol and no pawns left in the pews.

He was losing souls. Ataf would return, but Satan had likely lost Rahab. He'd lost that one mewling human, and he'd possibly lost Hastle as well. If everyone left, what then?

Being alone had sufficed for millennia, but now his newly-awakened soul stung with loneliness worse than hellfire. He could blame God for the fire, but for the isolation, he couldn't blame anyone.

"You have nothing to offer me," he'd said. First he'd said it to Gabriel, but then he'd said it to God.

Can You fix it? The thoughts welled up, unstoppable. *I can't fix the mirrors, and You can't fix me. I've created a stone so big You can't lift it. You created an immutable force and became the immovable object. I am the sifter and the wedge. I'm the tool You never loved. You claimed You could do anything, and I've proven You can't. Or, if You're really who You say You are—then do it.*

This wasn't another game change by God. Satan couldn't fix the mirrors or the plant or the emptiness. He didn't want to repent, but he wanted something. Gabriel had clutched a dead candle for thousands of years. Satan should be able to give her something better to hold, maybe the repair she wanted, or the light, or even the plant. Instead, there was only ash.

I have nothing to offer.

Chapter Twenty-Three

MICHAEL TRANSPORTED ATAF DIRECTLY to his office, already braced for the barrage of anger, so he just spoke over him. "I understand you're thrilled to be back, and I'm thrilled to have you back, but you aren't ready for preaching."

Ataf was ranting, "—a duty to make up for all the crimes I've committed, and—"

"—and you aren't ready to be in front of a crowd using yourself as an example. Give it at least another hour, okay? Hey, Raphael," he called as Ataf continued his tirade, "as soon as Rahab's well enough to be moved, I want him in my office."

Raphael sent an acknowledgement.

Ataf snarled, "If I'm that useless to you, maybe I should just leave again."

Michael turned back to Ataf. "Will you please pray with me?"

Ataf's eyes sparked. "You were mid-lecture about how we shouldn't use prayer as a weapon."

"The fact that you can't tell the difference is reason number one not to start preaching just yet." Michael stepped forward. "Humor me."

As Michael took Ataf's hands and touched his outermost wingtips with his own, Ataf's eyes sparked with bronzy rage. *God, please...*

God rested on Michael's heart, and Michael reached for Ataf's heart as well.

Ataf was angry—but angry with himself. He was so aware of the ground he needed to make up and the impossibility of setting things right. Most of his anger toward Michael was frustration at not getting started.

Momentarily, Michael felt another presence coiling around Ataf: Rahab, radiating intense rings of confusion and terror. Ataf tried to settle him, and after that, they were confused together. That's when God slipped into the mix to guide their coils into straighter lines.

Michael withdrew, and when he did, he was facing Israfel.

She was in flames. *Is* this *what you want on our side?*

Michael responded, *I was there when Ataf flipped, and yes, it was the best thing that ever happened. He only needs redirection and spiritual formation.*

Israfel snorted.

Ataf had gone misty, but Rahab was still semicorporeal. Michael sent, *He had a good impulse, but a Seraph's good impulse is the equivalent of a comet strike.*

Her eyes flared. *He bragged about hurting people! He was self-aggrandizing by saying it's a marvel that even God could forgive a sinner as amazing as himself.*

Michael sighed. *Like Paul writing to the early Christians, listing his own crimes over and over again? Ataf's overjoyed that he got forgiven. I'm not seeing the problem.*

Then you're blind. When Gabriel flips Satan and Mephistopheles, they'll oust you from the Seven. You're fine with that?

Michael narrowed his eyes. *Perfectly fine. I shouldn't have had this position in the first place.*

God squelched Michael's thought before he could finish. No one was getting demoted.

Really? Not what he'd figured, but also not the point of the conversation.

Israfel turned toward Ataf, and Michael felt an unspeakable emotion like a lance in her heart as her flames winked out as if snuffed. Gabriel should be here, or Ophaniel. They could stabilize her so she'd get on top of the anger, and instead it was him.

Or I could have you here for a reason, God told him.

Struggling to figure out what emotion had knifed through Israfel, Michael braced himself as Ataf became solid again. Ataf was radiating grief, but Rahab was shedding fear.

Clutching Rahab's hand, Ataf faced Michael. "Apparently, you're right."

Israfel let off a hard breath.

A bloodless Rahab's wings were shaking. "It's my fault. Don't punish him. I agreed that evangelizing was the right thing. Please don't throw us out again. I'm so sorry."

That was someone used to Hell's way of doing things. Raising his hands, Michael softened his tone. "No one's throwing you out. You both had good inclinations, and I do think you can help. Just, not yet in public. Did God put any strictures on you?" When Ataf shook his head, it was with curiosity in his eyes. Good. A curious Seraph was the best kind of Seraph, especially with a Cherub alongside to funnel his energy. Moreover, his curiosity was settling Rahab. "Getting attacked in front of a crowd isn't in your best interests, but how about meeting one-on-one?"

Ten seconds later, Michael had Tabris in the office, bearing a list as long as his arm of demons demanding to know how he'd rebounded from being semifallen. Tabris said, "They won't listen to me, but you...?"

Israfel intercepted the list. "These?" Her mouth hardened. "Do you know what they've done?"

Ataf's eyes narrowed. "It can't be worse than what I've done."

"Oh, of *course* you did worse than they did." She flung open her arms and wings. "You were the worst and the most heinous, and even God broke a sweat trying to forgive you. We've got it. But I'm talking about the *actual* harm these *actual* demons have *actually* done." She snapped the paper to punctuate her words. "They're not just names. These are angels who destroyed families and doused people's faith and damaged their bodies. They condemned human souls to hell, and now they want to leave that behind because living with the consequences got too uncomfortable."

Ataf looked horrified, and Rahab stared at the floor. Michael said, "Maybe they've learned better."

"What good does their learning do all the people they've harmed?"

"I want to do good to the ones I've harmed." Ataf took the paper from her hand. "Let me start with these." He turned to Tabris. "Will you come with us? I'm going to need help."

Tabris said to Israfel, "I harmed a family, too, but God was merciful. I never would have been able to make that right on my own."

Israfel's hands clenched.

Michael said, "Are you angry because God is generous?"

Israfel spat, "Absolutely."

Michael's heart stuttered.

"We gave Him everything." She stepped closer, but not on fire. "You think we've got pitiful lost souls on the brink of conversion, but you're wrong. They're not attracted to God. They're attracted to being powerful, and as the balance of power is shifting, they're aligning with the winning side. That's not conversion." Not only was she not on fire, but her voice had gone cold. "Satan said after the Resurrection that if God gave His love to everything He made just because He made it, then it wasn't worth having. For the first time, I wonder if he was right."

On the one hand, it was good she was laying it all out there. It benefitted no one to have a relationship with God and withhold your feelings from Him. But on the other hand, the things she was saying—? Why had God wanted Michael doing this?

Ataf stepped forward. "If my return harms you, then I'll go back." He held out the list. "I'll make that much right, at least."

Israfel recoiled. "If you can even make that offer, then God means nothing to you."

To Ataf, Michael said, "Stop. I don't want you to go." Michael turned to Israfel. "Ataf is changing. Rahab is changing. Hastle is changing. Converts start with repentance, but it takes time to realign old ways of thinking and to make reparations, or even to know how to do that." He met her eyes and didn't back down.

"They're responding to grace, but they can't do it all at once."

Israfel tossed her head. "You saw evil at its worst. How can you be happy with this?"

Michael gestured to the two ex-demons. "How can you not be happy? They're home!"

Israfel flung her hand at them as well. "And they just walk in the front door? All of them?"

"Yes! They walk in the front door. They track mud on the carpet and drop their wet coats on the couch and dump their backpacks on the kitchen floor—and it doesn't matter because they're home." Michael stepped forward, hands clenched. "The mess can be cleaned up. If all of them come home, we'll clean it all."

Israfel's eyes were wide. "Where's the justice in that?"

Michael said, "God's mercy and God's justice are so often the same thing."

She said, "And God's love?"

Michael swallowed. "He never stopped loving them."

Her breath caught, and she blinked hard.

She still wasn't in flames. If anything, that scared him more than her anger. Michael lowered his voice. "If God stopped loving them, they wouldn't exist. Their existence is, in and of itself, the first good."

Israfel looked away, emanating hopelessness.

Michael edged closer. "He didn't change when they did. And He loves us the same way, too."

Israfel whispered, "How is that fair?"

Michael took her hands. They were icy. Why wasn't Gabriel here? Michael needed words, and God wasn't giving any.

Ataf's voice was barely audible. "God isn't unfair. You have the Beatific Vision. We don't."

Staring at the floor, Israfel murmured, "Eternity is a long time. Whether you grow into it a day from now or a month from now, it's all the same."

Ataf extended a wingtip to hers. Michael braced for her to pull back, but she didn't. Ataf said, "Please pray with me. I'll leave if it means you can stay. But I do want to stay."

That was martyrdom. Michael was watching the making of a martyr. *Don't take his offer.*

God filled him with reassurance.

Israfel didn't raise her head, and finally she slipped her hands from Michael's. "I can't do it." To Ataf she said, "It's not *you*. It's the list. It's the unfairness."

Israfel vanished.

Michael closed his eyes. *Oh, God, please.*

Whatever God had intended Michael to do, surely this couldn't have been it.

After a momentary silence, Tabris spoke. "If you want to approach the list, I'm willing."

Rahab brushed his wings against Ataf. In a voice still oddly wispy, he said, "I won't return to the music library because it's Israfel's home, and she should have that spot. I'll find another place to pray for your work. But, please...approach all our bondmates."

Demons, praying. Reuniting was everything the angels should ever have wanted, only now Michael wondered whether finding the lost meant they'd lose some of the found.

From stage to stage to stage, Remiel attended the music festival— sometimes multiple performances at once. From rhythmic drumming to prayer chants to rock music and every iteration in between, she listened and admired and applauded the human performers. Then she'd attend angelic performances featuring every style of angelic music, and there she'd cheer as well, sometimes for her friends. She avoided the all-demon ensembles.

Sometimes Camael listened at her side. Sometimes not. She didn't always tell him when she was bilocating to hear simultaneous singers, although at times she'd find herself standing beside him in three places at once. While it shouldn't surprise her that they enjoyed similar music, it did keep surprising her that out of so many choices, they kept selecting the same ones. Identical tastes meant identical decisions—other than the most important decision.

Except now there was hope. If Ataf could return—if Hastle could return—then why not Camael?

During a string quartet performance, Nivalis called, and Remiel flashed all of herselves there because Nivalis needed her entire presence.

Atop a hill, Nivalis sat with her knees drawn up, concentrating on a figure at the base, sitting beneath a fruit tree. Remiel crouched alongside Nivalis. Who else would it be but Judas?

Shaking, Nivalis emitted tendrils of fear. More than fear—desperation. At this point, her team would have notified every guardian angel who'd lost a charge that human souls could return. She'd been encouraging them to reach out—again—and try—again—and maybe get their hearts broken. Again.

Nivalis reached for Remiel's soul with her own, and they sat in silence.

Judas wasn't attending the festival activities. Whenever they'd identified his location, it was somewhere alone. He'd wrapped himself in silence rather than music, in solitude rather than camaraderie. He'd avoided his fellow Apostles. He'd avoided his former friends. Rather than watching stories acted out on stage, he'd stayed mired in history.

Shame had driven Judas to die, and now, shame kept him pinned. The betrayal stung even though he was the betrayer.

To approach Judas again meant exposing him once more to the betrayal he kept running from.

Remiel turned her attention to Nivalis. Of course Nivalis would go to him, but until then, she was praying.

How could they convince a soul that shame was, first and foremost, a liar, when the first thing shame did was claim to be the sole possessor of truth?

Satan hadn't set this trap for Judas. Satan had leveraged a zealot's impatience with an un-militaristic messiah to spark the engine, but once Satan had set that in motion, he'd operated the rest of the machinery and forgotten the igniter. It benefitted Satan when humans thought themselves so defective that even God couldn't love them, but he hadn't paid enough attention to Judas even to plant that seed. Judas was just a tool.

Nivalis shivered.

Remiel sent, *Remind him that he cast out demons. Remind him that he cured the sick. Remind him that he preached the good news, and people listened. Souls converted because of him.*

Nivalis frowned. *Won't that make it worse, that even with all that blessing, he still failed?*

Remiel sighed. *If God blessed his efforts then, that means God can bless his efforts now. He's afraid he's unlovable, but he'll admit God loved him then. And God doesn't change.*

Nivalis flashed away.

A moment later, Remiel felt Camael.

Having him at her back felt like a shade tree in the desert. She kept her focus on Nivalis.

Camael said, "That one can't return."

Remiel's hands clenched. "What did you do to him down there? You must have been horrible. You laughed at him. You mocked what he became, or maybe mocked what he was before."

Camael said, "All that."

Remiel's eyes narrowed.

"Don't ask questions you don't want answered." Camael's voice was subtle, a wind rustling the trees. "You already knew."

Judas didn't run from Nivalis. She raised her wings and sat near him. He was doing something with his hands, but from this vantage, Remiel couldn't see what. Maybe weaving grass stems into tiny baskets.

Camael said, "When you were in Hell pretending to be me, what did you see?"

Her feathers flared.

He huffed. "I figured out a while ago what you did. My memories got redacted, but there were enough inconsistencies to piece together that I wasn't the main player. What did you see?"

She couldn't relax her wings. "I saw no reason for you to stay with them."

Camael said, "You became me, and then you went back to Heaven."

Her nerves lit up. Far down the hill, Nivalis and Judas weren't talking. They merely sat side by side.

Camael went on, "You weren't only pretending to be me. Lucifer passed his power through you. If you'd held back, you'd be dead, so you became me."

Michael wouldn't have gotten to her in time. The first two annihilations would have taken place within minutes of one another.

Camael said, "How did you do it?"

Nivalis moved closer to Judas, but still he wouldn't look up.

Remiel closed her eyes. "I picked the lock of your heart by hating the thing you hated most. Once I had that, it was easy." Too easy. "From there, I hated anything that reminded you of the thing you hated. I hated the things you used to love. And then—"

To complete the change, Remiel as Camael had filled to the brim with self-hatred because Camael reminded himself of Remiel.

Camael's voice thinned. "The thing I hated the most being you?"

Remiel rested her chin on her arms and refrained from saying that Camael shouldn't ask questions he didn't want answered. For thousands of years, all Remiel's best days had been apart from him, and she assumed he would say the same, inasmuch as anything made him happy.

She closed her eyes, but at all moments she could feel Nivalis below her. She should send Camael away. She should be paying full attention to Nivalis so she'd be able to comfort her if Judas fled, or flash her a warning if it looked like everything was about to go sideways. Stronger angels should protect weaker ones. Except was she strong?

Judas got to his feet. Remiel tensed, but he didn't leave. Nivalis stood as well, and he handed her whatever he'd been making with the grass blades.

Nivalis would keep it. It might be all she ever had of him again.

Remiel said, "I'm not sure why you keep coming back to me. I'm the worst thing that ever happened to you. I'm the reminder. I'm the thing you hate most."

With his thoughts sparking through Remiel like pins and needles, Camael went tense. "But you came back? From all that?"

Remiel blinked like Nebuchadnezzar seeing four men in the fire because the scene at the base of the hill had resolved from two figures into three. The third person was Jesus.

Please don't let Judas leave. The prayer seeped from her, and she drew up her wings. *Please.* Except God would always let you leave if leaving was your choice.

Judas didn't leave. Nivalis stepped back and bowed her head, arms crossed over her chest. Jesus put a hand on her shoulder while still talking to Judas.

The last time they'd have spoken was when Judas kissed Jesus in the garden. Here, in a different garden, Jesus kissed Judas.

Camael bristled. Rather than have him draw attention, Remiel flashed away, tugging him with her.

They arrived in the first place she'd thought to escape to: her studio.

As though they hadn't changed places, Camael spoke in a voice that echoed. "How did you come back?"

"I wasn't about to let a little thing like hating myself keep me away from God." She tightened her wings to her back. "It never stopped Him from loving me. Every way I was despicable and useless, He didn't find it a problem. He didn't care that I failed or that I was wild and weird. He didn't mind that not all of me was here. He didn't look at me and see you. Eventually, I stopped fighting and let Him love me."

That brought her back. It always brought her back. She could fail a hundred times to love God the way He deserved, but at no point had He failed to love her.

Camael said, "Even though you still hated yourself?"

He hated himself. Of course he did. If they both liked the same music and enjoyed the same scenery, then they both felt the same way when they looked in a mirror.

She closed her eyes until she could hear the Holy Trisagion, and momentarily the eternal repetition flowed through the studio. *Holy, Holy, Holy.*

Keeping her eyes closed, she began to dance.

Hating Remiel had been the first step of becoming Camael, but it hadn't been the last step of reverting to Remiel. Jesus hadn't hated her. Jesus had come for her special. He'd held her hand and told her He loved her.

Since God knew everything, presumably God would have known if she were something hateful.

As she moved, she felt motion at her side: Camael, dancing with her.

Her body dissociated as she moved, dancing in the form of light and sound and thought, and through it all, he paralleled her in the rise and fall, the sway, the spin, the glide, the curve of her motion as the music crescendoed. Together, their movement formed a rhythm and an offbeat. He wasn't synchronizing his action to hers as much as they were existing as point and counterpoint. They'd begun this dance ages ago as one note, but now they'd split into two notes of a chord in search of their third.

A two-note dyad could be anything, but a chord required three to complete what it was: major, minor, suspended. Remiel and God were two notes. Remiel and Camael were also two notes. But for a chord—for accord—

Her dance became an offering. Herself. Her motion. The beauty she could create. The unsettling power of music, a voice given to longings unvoiceable—all of these could be offered to God, and God could accept what pleased Him. Among the things that pleased Him was Remiel, so she gave Him everything, and then gave Him more. All along, God had done the same with her.

She raised her hands and wings into the light, and at her side, Camael did the same. Two Irin, identical but no longer indistinguishable, united and parted, two voices, two offerings.

Two prayers.

One request.

A third note in the chord.

A resolution.

Remiel collapsed to her knees, but Camael spun with energy—with joy and comprehension and acceptance. In his heart he held a union he'd rejected and had thought he'd never want again until the moment he did want it, and the moment he apologized because his sister had believed all along that asking meant receiving, and seeking meant finding.

The song persisted. Remiel rejoined the dance at Camael's side, and together they offered up their motion in thanksgiving.

Chapter Twenty-Four

DARK IN THE ROOM.

Silence. Stale smoke.

Reports came from Satan's underlings, but Satan didn't reply. Let them solve problems on their own. For once. He'd go back. For now, he was here. Here with his knees and wings drawn up, his head down, and his grip tight. Even God rested on the seventh day, whereas Satan had worked that day as well as every day before and since.

He needed to do something. React. Shore up his forces. They were losing souls. It was hard to get a full accounting, but souls were going off level and not coming back. Unlike Ataf, they weren't announcing their treason.

In the hollow of his heart was nothing. Wherever Gabriel had hidden, she'd shuttered her soul tight enough that nothing leaked through. He'd detox from her poison, and he wouldn't let another Cherub inside. Belior was rabid to bond him, but the thought left Satan nauseated.

Ataf had cried over Rahab after three thousand years. In two days, Satan would be over Gabriel. That was the difference. To remain devoted to something useless was weakness—hampering and humiliating. If he bonded another Cherub, his own underlings would assume he was weak. They'd judge him as incomplete—or they'd judge him as judging himself incomplete. They'd snicker when they thought they wouldn't get caught. They'd think they knew him.

Best for a clean cut. Gabriel would be gone in two days. Belior could spend eternity eaten alive with the shame of not being worth a second glance.

It was only fair. God had done as much to Lucifer.

Sure, Lucifer had been useful to God at first, but when it came time to shake things up, had He turned to the powerful angel He'd positioned to do exactly that? No, He'd made a mockery of the natural order and expected the highest angel to plunge to the bottom.

More reports came in of who they'd lost and who they suspected they might lose. Enough of the past. The present required him.

As for the monkeys, who cared? Cutting them all loose to swim upstream would alleviate the overcrowding, and Satan never valued them anyhow. They'd been useful as hostages and as collateral damage, territory to stake and claim and then burn. In some ways the monkeys were entertaining, and it made sense to collect as many as he could, but if sacrificing them meant he could secure all the angels, that was the way to go.

He needed to do something. Take action. Move.

Except, he was tired. So tired. His team had warned that the opposite of a Seraph burning out a Cherub was the Cherub smothering the Seraph's zeal. Gabriel's absence created a vacuum, and fire couldn't burn in a vacuum.

Satan had slammed the door on love, but back then, he'd filled the space with rage. Offense stood in place of isolation. Plus, there'd been so much to do, a new order to forge, and a war to plan.

The room grew lighter. Fine. Once the sun rose, he'd get back to work.

Except...the sun didn't rise on this level. Six days, and there'd been no darkness.

As the room brightened, Satan opened his wings and raised his head.

Soot was fading off the windows with the same effect as a sunrise: reddish light followed by yellows, followed by the full spectrum. On the mirrors, the ripples were stretching out, flattening, no longer distorted but instead reflecting all the light at once, everywhere.

His feathers stood out from one another as motion caught his eye. From the pot, a green blade rose.

Heather could grow back after a burn-off. He remembered that now, how mere days after fire had blazed through a forest at twelve hundred degrees, shoots began pushing through the carbon.

The room kept lightening. The plant absorbed it. The mirrors grew flat and straight.

Heart roiling, Satan got to his feet. With a glance in a mirror, he altered his clothing. Cape. Boots. Armor. Helmet? Not that. Sword. Dagger. Gauntlets.

He wouldn't be able to speak once he started this, so he thought, *I demand access.*

He flexed his fingers and flashed right into the Heavenly Temple.

In the time it took for anyone to register his presence—and Satan made note of every single demon or ex-demon in the building—he got summoned to the inner dwelling.

The shackles came off his voice in that dark space, eternal and unchanging. He'd been here before, here so many times, and for thousands of years afterwards, he'd combed his memories in case he'd missed a way God was vulnerable. Satan's admittance meant God wasn't. Or rather, God knew Satan wouldn't find that vulnerability. It didn't matter.

"What are You playing at?" Satan clenched his fists. "The whole point of our choosing was we could keep the thing we chose. This blatant manipulation is a mockery of Your own orders. You deployed Gabriel to infiltrate my soul, and now You're trying to make me question my resolve by feigning attention."

He couldn't see God face to face. He hadn't expected to, but momentarily he could see Jesus in His human body. Satan shone to reveal it was just the pair of them in the void. He dialed up his light enough that it would be painful to the human eye.

Jesus didn't squint. "Did you, or did you not, ask me to fix it?"

Satan's wings flared. "That's the prayer You chose to answer? Not the millions of humans who suffered and died from easily-preventable—"

Jesus waved it aside. "Our discussion is not about how I choose to answer prayers."

Satan said, "The entire discussion is about how You change the rules of the contest whenever You please."

Jesus said, "While I understand that you view relationships as a contest, you did something close enough to prayer that I opted to answer. If you didn't want it, you shouldn't have asked." Satan started to object, but Jesus talked over him. "We both know that at the moment, you did."

God was a hundred times more infuriating than Gabriel. Satan could shut out Gabriel.

Of course, if Satan couldn't shut out God, neither could God shut out Satan. Immediately after the Winnowing, Satan had challenged himself to envision the worst possible things he could, and in doing so, affront the Almighty enough that God would regret having made him. If Satan couldn't be ruling Heaven, Satan could still violate God's omnibenevolence with his thoughts and desires. God knew his heart? Good, let God know blasphemy and sacrilege. Even if it was only a spoonful of sewage in the ocean, there was forever defilement in the mind of the One that wanted to set up Itself as pure. For all eternity, every vile concoction Satan imagined or did was likewise something God knew or had permitted, and God would have to keep it all.

Now Jesus stood here, smug because He'd capitalized on a weakness that lasted no longer than a tenth of a second.

One drop of weakness in the ocean: a flaw forever suspended in a thing that wanted to set itself up as impervious.

Satan's eyes narrowed. "Don't talk to me that way."

Jesus shrugged. "You came to me."

"I came to tell You this." Satan swept out a hand. "Let my people go back to Hell. They made their decision. You're beguiling them with music and food and a party so they'll change their minds, and once the door slams behind them, You'll have them trapped again."

Jesus shrugged. "I'm giving them a second chance."

Satan flared his wings. "And afterwards? Do they get a third chance when everything they objected to the first time is still in force?" He stepped forward, but that was an idiotic reflex. Any of the Maskim would have backed down, only of course Jesus didn't. Satan was off his game. "Every thousand years, will You declare an open enrollment period when everyone on both sides can choose a different eternity provider?"

Jesus tilted his head. "You would find that unfair?"

Satan said, "It's unfair that You're holding the keys to my kingdom."

Jesus folded his arms. "Your kingdom?"

Squaring his shoulders, Satan lowered his voice. "I'm not playing word games. Everything I've said is fully comprehensible. I don't want You cherry-picking souls from my subjects. I don't want You manipulating my feelings or my perceptions. I don't want Your spies pretending they care in order to soften us up."

Jesus matched Satan's tone. "You have much to say about what you don't want. How about what you do?"

Satan didn't look away. He wanted to cull Israfel, and he wanted Gabriel's admiration, and he wanted more space for his side... But those were small wants, temporal wants. "Want" encompassed so much more. "Want" meant lacking, and lacking meant vulnerability.

Want to want to repent.

He was two steps back. He could make it one step back.

Stop. He'd said that to allure Gabriel, except it had come from somewhere deep enough that it might even have been true.

Satan wanted God destroyed, except that also was inaccurate. He wanted God to concede. He wanted God to admit creation had been folly from the start, prodigal and wasteful, always with the deck stacked. God was a player standing over the board, manipulating the pawns, and here in the endgame, was maneuvering for checkmate.

Satan couldn't checkmate God, but he could stalemate Him. Against an omniscient, omnipotent player, even that much was victory. You move here, I move there to avoid, and then you move back. But I can move again to the original position. For all eternity, no one wins, but in never conceding, Satan won.

He could do it. Just keep sliding the pieces, over and over and over.

Was that what he wanted? Endless repositioning with no winning?

Satan snarled, "I told You not to talk to me that way."

Jesus shook His head. "That thought didn't come from me."

"Then leave me alone. You know everything I want." Flames curled through his soul, but Satan shut them down. "Quit seducing my people with false promises and glamour."

Jesus opened His hands, as if to say, "As you did to mine?"

The nail marks were still visible on His wrists. A moment after, Satan could pick out the imprint of the thorns on Jesus's forehead. He'd wear those tiny injuries forever, a crown of painful love jammed onto a mind that would remember each wound without ceasing.

Satan's stomach lurched. God, displaying weakness—forever. Cloaking Himself in defeat. Strutting around in the tatters of death —

Satan snapped, "Don't answer me again."

He was back in his room.

So was Gabriel. At the room's heart, she hovered with sunlight streaming around her as she paid attention to the resurrected heather. Before she could react to his presence, Satan tried to snap on a Guard, but the room wouldn't take it. She'd twisted the walls and windows, and although the effort was burning significant power, she was holding the hotel in that position. He could ensphere her, but she'd likely be able to break it. It wasn't worth the attempt.

Satan set his jaw. "Why are you here? Did He tell you to come?"

The grey of her eyes had softened from yesterday's silver. He could get inside her mind. He could dump power into her and make her excited, or he could draw strength from her to think clearly—except that meant examining what had just happened, and he wasn't going to let her see it.

She'd twist it the same way she was twisting the walls. She'd try to convince him God meant something He didn't.

"You were seen entering the temple." Gabriel looked back at the plant. "You fixed the mirrors and windows. I'm glad you're letting in the light. The heather will need it."

Satan's teeth clenched, followed by his fingers. "Take it with you."

Her wings shivered, and her hair fluttered in the ripples of her power.

He shifted his stance. "When we go, the hotels will vanish. If you care about that plant, you'll take it before it disintegrates."

Energy flowed hard from her to keep the room in this shape. She shouldn't even be here, a fact of which she was aware. "Come with me."

"I ordered you to leave." He'd flame her to drive her away, but he'd learned enough about bonds to suspect she'd use that as an entry to his thoughts. "I have other work."

"What could be more important than me?" Her eyes tightened as her strength shuddered. The hotel by its nature struggled to clamp around her like a bear trap. "After another day, we'll never be together again."

Satan said, "Then you really ought to take that plant to have something to remember me by."

Her energy dipped but then returned. An urge to power her burgeoned up, followed by a simultaneous refusal to do any such thing. She was weak, and he hated her for it. He said, "As long as it keeps growing, you'll have something of me. That should suffice for you, unless Cherubim are far more sentimental than you've indicated."

"Perhaps it's Seraphim who are far colder." She opened her hand. "If you likewise want to remember me, you can have this."

Something flew to him. He smacked it from the air, and like a wasp, it stung where it made contact. Power.

Was she so stupid as to give him her sigil? Surely unrequited desire didn't have that effect on a Cherub, otherwise Belior would have devolved into uselessness five thousand years ago. Granting Satan access to her energy reserves outside the bond must mean it gave her another wedge to jam into his soul. He wasn't sure how, but he didn't need to know the exact mechanism in order to avoid it.

Satan folded his arms. "I already told you the only thing I want, but you wouldn't unveil the chronicle of your weakness."

"You don't want my weakness. You want my humiliation." Gabriel flashed the potted plant into her arms. "My weakness is your weakness. Everyone's weakness is your weakness. For all your power, weakness is the one thing you never were able to handle."

Satan snorted. "I shouldn't have to, and neither should you. With a name like 'God's strength,' weakness opposes your nature."

"Or else making peace with weakness is the fulfillment of our strength. Perhaps you can dwell on that during eternity while you're missing me." Gabriel's flat voice and blank expression belied the grief frothing inside. "If it does come to that, I'm sorry. I gave the only thing I could offer, but as always, the choice to accept a gift is with the recipient. I choose to accept your heather."

She vanished. The room crashed back together, shattering the mirrors for a heartbeat before they all re-formed, flawless. Her sigil remained on the floor.

And there it could remain for the rest of eternity because Satan had no interest in giving her deeper passage to his mind.

On the other hand, a sigil meant access to Gabriel's not-insignificant abilities. Which, he would add, had been deepening since they'd bonded. Gabriel had always demonstrated an inexplicable reluctance to tap into the full reservoir of her strength, but to twist the shape of the hotel, she'd been using more than he'd ever believed possible—and that was despite diverting some into this tiny package.

It took a second to dissociate and surround the object. She'd formed it as a sigil, but then enclosed it in a Guard of the kind that had hidden Hastle for two thousand years. Humming with energy, it resembled a silk cocoon with one tendril dangling, a clear invitation to pull it and uncoil the whole.

If he tugged it apart, would it unspool into a thousand yards of emotional webbing, trapping him in an egg of living death just like Hastle's?

Was it another duplicate Gabriel? How many did she have?

Unfortunately, the object made him as curious as being in her presence. He left it where it had fallen. If it was a duplicate, the last thing he wanted was to carry that thing into Hell only to give Gabriel the means to pester him eternally.

For the time being, Satan had work to do. He had minions to shore up. And the first thing he did was to send an order: all civilians, back to their quarters. Alone. With his people secure, he'd figure out how to seize back the traitors who'd switched sides.

Chapter Twenty-Five

IT WASN'T OFTEN THAT Mephistopheles had no idea what to do.

He stood at one of the junctures affixing the outer level to the rest of Heaven. Prying it loose was possible. Anything was possible, Mephistopheles had come to realize. Anything, as long as God gripped the handle of the pot and maintained it at a rolling boil. As Lucifer kept saying, God changed the rules whenever He wanted.

He clearly wanted to do so now.

Lucifer had locked down the damned in their hotel rooms—one individual in one room at one time. Easily understood, except their apostates had learned the hotels allowed room service. No, really. It was possible for a *viator* guest to request one non-*viator* visitor.

Then, if the room service delivery agent was persuasive enough, it was possible to check out.

The soldiers were allowed freedom of movement because (of course) a commander couldn't issue an order like that not to enforce it. As social animals that wanted to live in a troop, the monkeys weren't going to self-isolate and meditate on the unfairness of God, not when there were carnivals and the promise of cotton candy followed by freedom if only they groveled at just the right frequency. In point of fact, as one would expect of rebel souls, most *viatores* were ignoring the order. Someone needed to put them back. That meant "everyone into their rooms" was only a subset of "everyone," and it being a subset meant there were breaks in the wall.

They were losing their subjects. When Lucifer re-emerged into the fray, he was going to vent his rage on his highest ranking officers. The punishment would be mind-blowing, unless Gabriel had softened him to the point that it wasn't.

Which, in a way, was worse.

The way Lucifer had made himself unavailable for this long—? He didn't do that. Gabriel had changed the unchanging. Lucifer had by all accounts been in top form confronting Ataf by the pavilion and had roasted Rahab from a quarter mile away. He'd mobilized the army for what was certain to be the initial battle of a new war. Then, ten minutes later, it was, "Hey, Maskim? You're on your own."

Mephistopheles wanted to believe Lucifer had ensconced himself with Gabriel to cement their union. But what if it were the opposite, and Gabriel were cementing her union with him?

In Lucifer's absence, Beelzebub had organized patrols to keep the *viatores* away from the enemy, and Mephistopheles had disappeared into the level's foundation, fighting nausea whenever he thought about the past.

Wait, not the past. The future. Whenever he thought about the future.

Not the past, when he'd made the right decision.

It was hard keeping everyone else convinced it was the right decision when they had an unhinged Ataf screaming that God loved him, and when the angels treated them as honored guests and even let Mephistopheles stand here at the juncture between two levels of Heaven where he could be planning exactly the thing he was planning. Mephistopheles had picked up whispers that perhaps God deserved more than a passing recognition for waiting with His hand on the doorknob just in case any of them set foot on the front porch. It caused second looks when angels submerged themselves in the Lake of Fire to dredge up the carcass of a demon who'd wanted never to be found, and then not only healed his body but also attempted to heal his spirit.

When God's highest ranking angel was willing to subject herself to a Seraph who had spurned her in her entirety, all with the hope of bringing him home—that threw the narrative into question.

Yes, it was hard to convince their forces that those angels were not in earnest. It was hard to keep them convinced that God didn't love them after all. It was hard to convince himself.

Because Rahab... Michael didn't have to be so obscenely kind to a demon who'd never been worth all that much to his own side, let alone to theirs. Michael's actions hadn't been performative, nor had they even been calculated. Ataf believed the angels genuine, and Ataf had never been easy to deceive.

Moreover, Ataf wasn't flighty. A Seraph who'd remained committed to a bond three thousand years after the Cherub had removed himself—who'd remained committed to his master for three thousand years after being demoted and humiliated—had switched loyalty.

The silence of Ataf's other Cherubim indicated Rahab might not be the only one taken. And what of Rahab's other Seraphim?

Beelzebub.

With eyes closed, Mephistopheles leaned into the energy coursing through this layer of Heaven from the next. Beelzebub. Always there. Always the reason. Always.

Back at the Winnowing, Mistofiel had caught his breath wondering how God could pull off the reversal of being worship-able while becoming lower than the angels. Belazael had grabbed Mistofiel's hand and said, "Come with me." Come. Don't stay and see how it'll be done. Don't give God a chance to explain the mystery. Object, and fight, and leave—and Mistofiel had gone with him even though—

He'd made a choice.

"It was the right choice," he'd said so often when he saw the atrocities God permitted on Earth because of His brazen commitment to free will. Mephistopheles said it about so many choices, but it always came back to that one moment where Belazael had grabbed Mistofiel's hand and looked over his shoulder, his eyes sunrise-bright. On the cusp of doing a new thing, he'd wanted his bondmate at his side, and as always,

Mistofiel wanted to make him happy.

Staying in Heaven would have meant—

Leaving now would mean the same.

So much energy connected this level to the next. Mephistopheles could interrupt the current and peel it off. It would take time and a number of their forces, but it could be done.

He had to make a choice. For the first time in centuries, he faced a choice that mattered.

A warm concern spread through him, but he didn't open his eyes.

The concern grew. Mephistopheles swallowed hard, and then the fire arrived. It was tinged with irritation but also with fear— unless the fear was his own.

Beelzebub's voice. "It looks bad now, but we'll get through this."

Mephistopheles swallowed. "We shouldn't."

We. God wouldn't let anything be more important than Himself. If Beelzebub turned back first, and Mephistopheles followed to stay with him, God wouldn't accept that. Likewise, if Mephistopheles got on his knees and confessed every way he'd spat in the face of God—if Beelzebub then said, "Yeah, me too," God wasn't going to accept that. How could He? There was no off-label use of grace. If you went into Heaven, you did it for God, not for the side effects.

Mephistopheles tightened his wings. Beelzebub pulled away, but not with anger. He said, "How are they tempting you?"

Mephistopheles' voice was thready. "They've left me completely alone to think about it."

Beelzebub tried to laugh. "Well, there's your problem."

This might be the end, and if it was, Mephistopheles couldn't ask for something to keep afterward, only the memories...unless God took those, too.

In a lower voice, Beelzebub said, "I've felt what you're thinking. You're not wrong."

Mephistopheles shifted so his back and wings pressed against the wall, and Beelzebub stood before him, hands to the wall over his shoulders. Then he bowed so they were forehead to forehead.

This searing pain was too much to contemplate. What happened when God held out His hand and demanded the pearl of great price? What remained after it fell from your fingertips?

Beelzebub said, "I won't leave you alone."

He could read every fear and pain inside Mephistopheles. Maybe some of it was his, too. It was the corollary: if Mephistopheles lost him, he was likewise losing Mephistopheles.

Maybe that was the price they paid for everything they'd done. They were in hell now, but they were anticipating the greater hell, the hell they really deserved.

Mephistopheles said, "What if we try, and we get rejected?"

Beelzebub snorted. "Hell isn't half as hot as what Lucifer would do to us. It's worst if one of us gets scraped off. The one who remains will get it all."

He felt a flicker in Beelzebub's mind, that if only one of them made it, he should make sure it was himself. Go first because the second one had more to prove. The thought was only a flash, but Mephistopheles would be lying if he claimed he didn't recognize it. He'd had the same idea already.

God would accept Beelzebub. Beelzebub always delivered apologies with full feeling, able to craft exactly the right words to wring your heart because they were the words you hungered to hear. He'd give God all the best phrases and all the key emotions with a passion Mephistopheles would never be able to deliver.

This was the worst kind of prisoner's dilemma. Souls didn't go in front of God in pairs.

Beelzebub said, "Not true. Rahab and Ataf repented together."

Mephistopheles' eyes opened. "How did you find that out?"

"Angels talk." He huffed. "The two of them locked themselves in a practice room in the music library, and Michael made them recite the same thing."

Reciting was enough? Mephistopheles exhaled so hard that his breath fogged back from Beelzebub's shoulder. "So—right here? Right now?" That would help if one of them failed. The other could deny they'd participated at all. "We'd need to get it right the first time. What did they recite?"

Beelzebub muttered, "They'd just heard the *Requiem*. Maybe they sang their way back."

Mephistopheles forced a laugh. "How about the hymn you wrote?" When Beelzebub recoiled, Mephistopheles crinkled his eyes. "Would you believe Israfel played it for me?"

Beelzebub shed sparks. "It was terrible!"

"It wasn't that bad." Oh, no—Israfel. If they did get on their knees and convince God to switch their allegiance, Mephistopheles would have to undo the snares he'd set for Israfel.

Beelzebub rested his hands on Mephistopheles' shoulders. "We should ask what to do."

Ask whom? Because on the list of individuals who knew the answer, Mephistopheles could mark each name with a neat little x. His former friend whom he'd watched demoted from the Maskim without a word of objection? No. How about the Seraph whom he'd failed to help when his Cherub was being humiliated? Likewise, no. They could approach the Archangel who'd thrown them into Hell in the first place, against whom they'd pitched battles and plotted numerous assaults. Another no. Crowning the list was the Cherub whose murder Mephistopheles had orchestrated.

Mistofiel, stay.

His wings shook. Gabriel might actually be their best chance, but because of her bond, Gabriel was also the greatest risk. If Gabriel reacted at all, Lucifer would pick it up. For that matter, if Gabriel had ulterior motives, her first move would be reporting their attempted defection to Lucifer. Mephistopheles would understand if she did it anyway.

"Mistofiel, stay."

Beelzebub sent sparkles of encouragement.

Mephistopheles closed his fists. *We've never established Gabriel's intentions, nor under whose orders she's working. We've too many variables to manipulate, and nothing is certain.*

No. One thing was certain, and it grew more certain the longer Mephistopheles sat with the thought: they were wrong. He'd chosen the wrong pearl. Or rather, his pearl was valuable, but he shouldn't have sold everything else to keep it.

He sorted and re-stacked everything he knew, back-flowing into Beelzebub's mind as he re-analyzed an eternity's worth of data. Over and over, God had offered the humans covenants and the promise of salvation, offered chances and guidance and protection. Offered them gifts. Offered them love. He'd offered all that despite the obnoxious evils humanity had devised, some of which were things even the demons wouldn't have contrived, and once contrived, the humans had leaped aboard those distortions like so many wild stallions and whipped them into a frenzy. Still God had waited, dismantling kingdoms and drawing souls toward Him, one by one gentling them back and soothing their quivering spirits.

Jesus had indicated a swift return and then delayed and delayed and delayed. Maybe He'd done that so He could prove to the demons that for them, too, He'd be waiting.

The information had been there all along. Mephistopheles had ignored it every time because admitting this meant revisiting his initial conclusion and conceding it had been the wrong decision.

With no way back.

Unless there was.

Beelzebub nudged him. Mephistopheles took his hand.

They were about to lose each other. God wouldn't accept second place.

Mephistopheles sent a projection to Gabriel.

She arrived in the dark alongside the thrumming of two levels of Heaven, crackling with the residue of Lucifer's signature.

Lucifer. She was flush with his power. With fear spiking his heart, Mephistopheles tried to flee.

Beelzebub pinned him in place. *Don't.*

She's going to betray us.

Beelzebub sent, *It's in her best interests to win.*

Gabriel lowered her voice. "There's a lot of interference, so I assume you don't want anyone to overhear. Do you need to get off level?"

Mephistopheles couldn't find his voice. It was Beelzebub who spoke. "Can you help?"

"Of course." As Gabriel relaxed, fear forked like lightning through Mephistopheles. She was reaching for Lucifer, fair exchange for all the times Mephistopheles had betrayed her. She had more power now than she'd ever possessed, with additional access to Lucifer's strength and Lucifer's ability to avenge himself.

Beelzebub grabbed his shoulders, but Mephistopheles twisted away. "We've got to get out of here!"

Instead of Lucifer, Raphael arrived. "Does it matter where?"

Gabriel urged, "Just go," and Raphael flashed Beelzebub away.

Instead of letting Gabriel take him, Mephistopheles anchored himself.

Gabriel backed up a step. "Don't you want our help?"

Mephistopheles vibrated hard. From across the levels, Beelzebub reached into his heart with a question and reassurance. He was in Raphael's home with no one other than Raphael. Gabriel, though, reeked of Lucifer's energy.

Mephistopheles said, "Let him get in first."

Calm spread like an oil slick over the surface of the sea. That was a plan. The one left behind would suffer, and on the off-chance that it was Mephistopheles who got in and Beelzebub didn't, Mephistopheles couldn't stay in Heaven knowing Lucifer was endlessly tearing his Seraph apart. He'd have to leave again, and there was no guarantee God would let him.

If Beelzebub made it, and it seemed like Mephistopheles hadn't tried, then at least Lucifer wouldn't view Mephistopheles as a traitor in his own right.

It wouldn't matter. Lucifer could hardly do worse to him than God could.

Gabriel took his hand. "I'm not going to betray you."

Pulling back, Mephistopheles clenched his fists. "Why not?"

In Gabriel's position, Mephistopheles would have betrayed her five times by now. He'd have ensured he got repaid double for every pain he'd been dealt.

Gabriel's eyes softened. "I want you home."

Mephistopheles' voice pitched up. "I've harmed you, and for all the harm I've achieved, you know I intended far worse." He wasn't in control. He should stop talking. "I'd have stripped Raphael off you and left you leery of all Seraphim. I'd have torn you from Raphael and left him gutted. There's no benefit to you from helping me and everything to gain by abandoning me to what I deserve."

Gabriel's brows formed an inverted V. "Is that who I am?"

"Mistofiel, stay."

Two thousand years after that, Gabriel had asked, "Can't, or won't?"

That had been after Mephistopheles nearly murdered Gabriel, and Gabriel had not only left the door cracked, but when Mephistopheles refused, had treated him with consideration anyhow.

Mephistopheles closed his eyes. "Let Beelzebub go first. If he makes it, then I'll try."

Flashing with energy, Gabriel shivered. "You can't hold onto him."

"If he doesn't make it, he'll be tortured."

Gabriel's light dimmed. "Wouldn't you get tortured, too?"

Mephistopheles swallowed hard. "Perhaps it's not possible to hurt more than one hundred percent."

"Lucifer's going to try." Gabriel moved nearer. "We're going to get discovered. You need to ask."

Mephistopheles shivered. "Lucifer's going to retaliate on you."

Gabriel grimaced. "Well...you did just theorize that it's not possible to hurt more than one hundred percent." She took his hands. "I'll guide you."

Why was she behaving as if he'd never seen a conversion happen, and as if he'd never been instrumental in stopping one, twisting all the words around so the soul converted from worshipping himself to worshipping his own urges in a different form?

Mephistopheles whispered, "Why would you forgive me?"

Shedding power, Gabriel felt more like Lucifer than Mephistopheles would have thought possible. It reassured him. He could take orders from this. In the grasp of a being tinted with this particular signature, Mephistopheles could pirouette on a tightrope of danger over oceans of pain because he always had.

Gabriel squeezed his fingers. "I know who you were, and I trust what you can become."

Waves of prayer emanated from her like an outgoing tide. They tugged him forward, and his soul slipped. Mephistopheles sensed God all around.

A second later, panic. Had Beelzebub made it? Had Gabriel lured him in before he could make sure Beelzebub had made it, too? Because—

Around him, God grew warmer. Pause. Consider. Consider.

I can't leave him to face whatever happens if You reject him. He's counting on me. I rejected You for him, and if I have to do it again to protect him, then that's what I have to do.

God didn't withdraw. Mephistopheles clenched his hands. This energy at the nexus between levels was baffling detection, but it wasn't foolproof. Gabriel was praying hard, and Mephistopheles hoped Lucifer couldn't feel it.

Until—suddenly, he hoped Lucifer could.

He wished with every jot of his being that Lucifer could experience this same warmth, the flow of grace, the sweet motion of God's actions in the universe. This was everything, and it was more than everything.

Gabriel's prayer grew urgent, but then God cut them off from one another so Mephistopheles could feel Gabriel's hands but not her prayers. They brought their wings forward, tip to tip.

I was wrong. Mephistopheles tried to reach for God but couldn't because God was already grasping him. *I was wrong, and I kept doing wrong after I knew I was wrong. I confirmed every wrong decision with another wrong decision. But I shouldn't seal all my mistakes with the ultimate selfish decision. If You won't take him back but would take me back, then take him and leave me.*

God said, *I deal with souls, not proxies. You each decide for yourself.*

And what about Gabriel? If she helps me only to get hurt afterward—

God said, *Stop looking to everyone else to excuse your decisions. This is a choice you should have made for yourself all along.*

Are you telling me to be selfish? Mephistopheles set his brow. *You didn't do that. Besides, didn't Jesus approach humanity to stand as a proxy for them?*

God hadn't made His own existence contingent on their acceptance. When God brought that to mind, Mephistopheles pushed back. *You didn't abandon the humans to us. That territory was ours, and they pledged themselves to our service, so it would have been fitting for You to leave them to our hands. The same way You didn't abandon them, I won't abandon him.*

God said, *You mustn't hold yourself hostage to someone else's decisions.*

Mephistopheles' heart hurt. Talking again to God felt right. He'd refused so many times to hear God's replies, even when he'd talked to Him.

God said, *Do you trust me?*

Mephistopheles deserved to be double-crossed by God far more than he'd ever deserved it from Gabriel. Yet here stood Gabriel, praying with their hands and wings together. If Gabriel could do that, could forgive that, could even love that...then, yes.

I trust You.

God said, *Do you want to come home?*

Frustration shot through Mephistopheles. Why was God basing His acceptance on what Mephistopheles wanted when everything Mephistopheles had ever wanted was wrong? He'd sacrificed his relationship with God in order to have a relationship with his Seraph. He'd twisted himself and then twisted others, and then those others had harmed even more—and all those were things he'd wanted.

He was responsible for all that, as well as for the times he'd encouraged Beelzebub to do worse than he'd already planned. Mephistopheles had sharpened the blade and showed Beelzebub just where to insert it and with how much force to push. Human souls had perished because of situations Mephistopheles had concocted and techniques he'd perfected. He itemized his crimes in a list too long to forgive.

For little sins like a human could do, Jesus's sacrifice could cover that, sure. For this catalogue of evil, Mephistopheles needed eloquent words and a heartbreaking speech, only those weren't things he had at the ready. How had Beelzebub always apologized to him? Where were those words now, and why couldn't he even remember them? He needed a soliloquy passionate enough to thaw God's heart, but he had no warmth. Mephistopheles had only himself, and after everything he'd done, he wasn't sufficient to earn God's love. He never could have been.

Ataf had been listing his crimes when Lucifer shot him down. God had molted away all of that like an outgrown shell. Even Ataf hadn't done what Mephistopheles had, though, and Ataf probably knew beautiful apologies the way Beelzebub did.

Mephistopheles shuddered. He couldn't apologize like a Seraph.

God said, *I don't want a Seraph's apology.*

I'm sorry. It was pathetic, but those were the only words Mephistopheles had. *It in no way benefits You, and there's no reason You should accept, but please, forgive me.*

It was the right decision.

Warmth flooded him, and then he felt Gabriel's arms around him, too. Mephistopheles buried his face in Gabriel's shoulder, and a shudder wracked through him. *I'm sorry.* The lost time, the abandoned ways of knowing God, of learning about everything—of seeing God in all the specialness of the Earth and the world He'd created, all the little losses. All those moments were gone, just gone, when they could have been together. Then he remembered again not just what he'd failed to do, but what he'd actually done. There was the horror of the things he and Beelzebub (Belazael?) had done to one another. Memories. All those memories. God hadn't taken those from him. He and God would have time to go over all that together, and Mephistopheles would have to carry that weight for a while.

But for now, Gabriel's wings smelled like cedar, and God soothed him in his heart. They'd make it right. *I'm so sorry.* It would take time, but they'd make it right. *I'm so, so sorry.* Everything he'd done would be passed through fire and burnt to ashes, but he could be with his Father. God loved him, loved him despite all the things he'd done and all the things done to him, and that was what he needed.

On another layer of Heaven, Mephistopheles could feel Beelzebub was having a similar conversation, and Beelzebub longed for his bondmate. For now, though, here at the juncture of a connection he'd wanted to break, Mephistopheles clung to a fellow Cherub so he could learn the most important things. Now he could learn how to love God, and he could learn how to be himself.

Chapter Twenty-Six

MISTOFIEL WAS SPENT, SOBBING. Raphael had prodded Gabriel twenty-two times in eight minutes because Beelzebub was ecstatic, to the point that Gabriel eventually cut him off. An eternity's worth of grief needed to spill out of the Cherub. The least the Seraphim could do was give him a quarter-hour.

That assumed Gabriel could freeze her emotions enough to go undetected for a quarter-hour. Lucifer's presence in her head—something she'd taken to calling her brainchild—was heavy and watchful. If she yielded to the joy of her former friend walking back, Lucifer would feel it.

Holding Mistofiel, Gabriel turned to math instead of joy. Math was its own kind of euphoria. It had been a while since she'd explored topological morphology. Mathematical knots could occupy most of her brain. How about cataloging all the prime knots with eleven crossings? Start with k11n34, the Conway Knot. From there, mutate it to k11n42, the Kinoshita–Terasaka knot.

If the brainchild pried open the toy box of her mind and found a lineup of five hundred fifty-two knots, he could teethe on them a bit and assume Gabriel had yet another useless hobby. Either that, or maybe he'd discover he really liked math.

Mistofiel had grown still, and Gabriel rested a hand on his hair. She had a possible candidate for k11n56, but it felt suspiciously like an unknot. For one thing, they shared an Alexander polynomial.

Lucifer probed her thoughts, and she showed him the knot. He withdrew in disgust. They needed to leave.

In the whirring darkness, Gabriel whispered, "Are you ready?"

Mistofiel swallowed. How could he be? He had to face the one he'd hurt and the one who'd hurt him—and not only that, but the God he'd tried to hurt. And on and on and on. But they had to leave. It wasn't safe. He yielded.

When they flashed into Raphael's home, Beelzebub grabbed Mistofiel out of Gabriel's arms, hugged him, and thanked God they were together while Mistofiel went stiff as a pine tree. Gabriel stepped back to the wall, eyes downcast.

Her attempt at k11n56 had unfolded into an unknot. She'd have to mutate one of the crossings.

Raphael studied Gabriel, confused, but then he shed sparks when he realized why she had to remain only intellectually satisfied for now.

Joy could come later. Much later. Assuming Gabriel could ever feel joy over the grief of getting Lucifer stripped away.

Stepping closer to Gabriel, Raphael lowered his voice. "Belazael wants to use his given name, and also, he's chafing to go back to the outer layer and confront Satan head-on."

Gabriel frowned. "That is such a terrible idea—"

Raphael raised his hands. "He knows what happened to Ataf, and he accepts—grudgingly—that he needs to stay out of the fray for the time being."

Trouble was, the "time being" was just about twenty-four hours. Gabriel turned her thoughts away from mathematical knots and toward God. *I'm going to propose an argument that since a day is as a thousand years, and there aren't sunrises and sunsets on the outer layer, that there's no reason to hold fast to the banquet as consisting of seven twenty-four hour days. When we hit the hundred-sixty-seventh hour, I'm going to stand before You to request a stay and a continuance.*

God didn't need to laugh in reply. Raphael was already laughing. Gabriel narrowed her eyes. *You correct me when I get overly literal.*

Belazael sounded unnerved. "Is she arguing with God?"

Raphael snickered. "Who better to do it?"

Mistofiel murmured, "Israfel."

Gabriel spun toward him. He ducked his head so his curls covered his eyes, and he wrung his hands. "It's my fault. I flagged her to Lucifer, and I initiated overtures to flip her. Let me go to her and explain."

"Speaking to you as a peer," Raphael said, actively suppressing anger as he mimicked Mephistopheles' earlier words, "she'll have no interest in hearing apologies from you."

Mistofiel's shoulders shuddered. "I'm so sorry."

Gabriel struggled to relax her wings. "Then pray for her. If you hadn't flagged her, someone else would have." Even so, because Gabriel was also on the brink of anger, she turned to Raphael. "We do need to help her, but in this state," and Gabriel gestured to herself, thrumming with Lucifer's overflow energy, "it's not me, either."

Raphael forced a smile. "You've got one Seraph to work on. Leave some work for the rest of us."

Belazael rested a hand on Mistofiel's shoulder, and Mistofiel started.

Raphael didn't act as though he'd seen that interaction, but Gabriel felt him flinch. Instead, Raphael said, "Both of you need to spend at least the next hour in prayer."

Gabriel turned to Mistofiel. "Belazael may want to be with others right now, but you need solitude. If you don't mind, I have a suggestion."

That jump—that momentary fear in Mistofiel's eyes—? This pair had too much history. It was repairable, but not all at once.

Gabriel transported Mistofiel to Mary's rose garden. A skittish Mistofiel kept his wings tight. "Not a reading room in your library?"

"The place is packed. Every one of your Cherubim—your former Cherubim—wants to read as much as possible before leaving." Gabriel tried to pass by the verbal slip, but Mistofiel's feathers were standing out. "They won't come here."

Mary arrived with Uriel. Although shocked when she saw Gabriel, she redirected her attention to Mistofiel and accepted his apology.

Uriel said, "Pray with me," and led Mistofiel down the path.

Under the flower arch, Mary took Gabriel's hands. "You keep changing. I shouldn't have asked you to do this. I didn't realize it would hurt this much."

"He's the light-bearer, so consider it more as a sunburn than pain." Which, Gabriel would have to admit if pressed, was pain. Mary didn't press.

Mary took a deep breath. "I'm going back to the outer layer. We've had so many people returning. It's wonderful, but they need guidance, and sometimes they need assistance."

Gabriel gestured toward Mistofiel, seated on a bench with Uriel but still ramrod straight. "I'm aware. Let's go together."

The final banquet had begun, the reason for the invitation of all Hell in the first place. There were tables set with food. There were dance floors and music. The humans wore beautiful clothing and adornments of light. Everywhere were people—saints and *viatores* alike—talking and laughing and feasting and carrying tall glasses of colorful drinks.

Mary clasped her hands. "This is just what Abraham envisioned."

Gabriel introduced Mary to Abuela where she was delivering ten thousand tamales. Mary gushed with thanks, then to Abuela's delight, sampled a tamal and agreed it was amazing.

Abuela dragged a man over to Mary by the elbow and forced him to introduce himself. He was Abuela's son, and a *viator*. Mary hugged the man and then walked with him as they talked.

Abuela looked from them to Gabriel, worry ghosting her eyes.

Mary was saying to the man, "You don't understand. If you had been the only one in need of salvation, He would still have done it all for you."

Gabriel said to Abuela, "He's in good hands," and Abuela hugged her. "I'm sorry to leave, but there are so many more."

Abuela handed Gabriel a tamal, then shooed her off. "Go! Take care of your work."

She wouldn't have said that if she knew which soul Gabriel wanted to convert.

Gabriel flashed to the arena where Israfel was performing, to eat while listening. Delicious. The moist masa outside and the spicy filling were just as complex in flavor as the time Gabriel had sat with Abuela in a rainy San Jose parking lot, listening as she cried about her son.

Israfel must have been spoiling for a fight because she'd positioned a stage to face the Hilbert Hotel, and she was manipulating the acoustics so the sound would penetrate the walls. Her angry music played with an energy that had the audience dancing and must be captivating the guests watching from the windows.

The demons would view that as an attempt at proselytizing—or else they'd be enjoying the show.

And maybe, God willing, some would request "room service."

Lucifer's officers wouldn't stand for this. The demonic army was conducting patrols already, but they'd engage before much longer. Israfel would be right in the fray. Except—on whose side?

Gabriel sang along with the musicians, keeping her voice low but not worrying that her brainchild might pick up the vibrations. If it bothered him, he should stop listening.

Most of the civilian demons and all the humans were enjoying the festivities now, risking the wrath of their superiors because, as Mistofiel had said, what were the higher-order demons going to do? It wasn't possible to hurt more than one hundred percent. If this were their last chance to get out under the sunlight, to hear music and to fly, then why spend eternity regretting having missed it?

Mistofiel acted as though it were possible to hurt more than one hundred percent, though. With every reason to believe he was right, Gabriel would have to brace for the inevitable. She'd known from the moment Mary asked her to begin that this story would have no end. Either Lucifer would return, and their bond would be eternal, or Lucifer would lock himself in position—and their bond would still be eternal.

The charge Gabriel carried right now could have illuminated twenty-first century Los Angeles, and she kept taking on more. Lucifer wasn't even pushing it. She had so much less power than him that her soul functioned as a basin of negative pressure, drawing off his strength because that much power wanted to equalize. Raphael had skimmed whatever he could, but that only created more empty space inside Gabriel—which Lucifer refilled.

This couldn't keep continuing. Fortunately, it wouldn't have to for much longer.

Unfortunately. Lucifer was nowhere near backing down.

Israfel finished her song. The crowd was screaming so that souls would hear it all over Limbo, and watching Israfel urging them even louder, Gabriel smiled at her.

Israfel glanced right through the crowd at Gabriel, eyes glinting.

A demon approached Gabriel, unnerved by her energy signature. Gabriel kept her voice low. "Do you need help?"

Glancing around, the demon projected an affirmative.

Gabriel raised her hands. "Don't project to me. We'll be overheard." She did, however, call for Saraquael—who immediately escorted the demon off the level.

She ought to be overjoyed. Instead she started reciting the names of the prime knots. *Unknot. Trefoil. Figure eight.* She mustn't let her emotions awaken the brainchild. *Cinquefoil. Three twist. Stevedore.*

Michael joined her. A new group of musicians had begun, something Gabriel didn't envy. Who could follow Israfel? At least they were playing a different musical style, and Gabriel's head swam as she struggled to place it. Celtic, but she couldn't remember which century, not while thinking about mathematical knots and knots of the heart. She should be able to do this. She was exhausted.

Shoulder to shoulder with her, Michael murmured, "I hear you claimed Mephistopheles. That beats Ataf."

Gabriel tightened her wings as if she were cold. Maybe she was. Lucifer's heat was a fever that kept rising. "I claim nothing. God's doing the work."

Fourteenth century. That was it.

"Oh, sure, give God the credit." Michael chuckled. "When you get a chance, take a look at the hotels from above."

Brow furrowed, Gabriel glanced over her shoulder. "What have they done to the hotels?"

"Figure it out." Michael shot her a smile and vanished.

She nearly called across the distance to ask if anyone were in charge around here, but that would have made her wonder which side she was on. Curiosity nagged her until the song finished, and she spread her wings.

High above the hotels, Gabriel took note of the buildings dotting the landscape. Same locations, same number, same shapes... further apart? No, they were all in the same spots, so what—

Were they smaller?

She flashed directly over the Hilbert Hotel and sent her mind into the building's structure. It was contracting.

Wings spread, Gabriel cast her vision as far as she could, to every hotel one after the next, because everywhere, it was the same. Smaller hotels. Notably smaller, not by one or two rooms.

It burst out of her in rings, the realization, the relief. *Oh, God! What You've done—my God, my Lord, my God—!*

Mary had been right. Abraham had been right. Everyone had been right. The lost ones were returning, not just drifting home but rushing home. One at a time, and then two at a time—and what would it take for entire families to unite? For a whole order of demons? *O Lord, my God, my savior!*

Pain scored her like lightning, and Gabriel arched her neck. *Blast.* Lucifer had felt that. "*More joy in heaven over the return of one prodigal,*" and she'd been beholding the return of millions.

His iron grip clamped her arms. Face to face, Lucifer's green gaze bored into her.

Gabriel tried to flash him off the level so they could fight in isolation, but he wouldn't go. He wanted Israfel involved, the same way Gabriel wanted Israfel to stay away. They were near the festival's main stage, and like their sky painting, any altercation between the two most powerful angels would be visible over half the level. Therefore, Gabriel mustn't fight back.

Lucifer said, "You're doused in Mephistopheles' power." Then, with a dangerous growl, "You took him."

His eyes—so hard. So shallow. With Raphael or Israfel, she'd have sensed depth in their gazes, but from him, it was all blocked off. He annexed her thoughts, and she didn't bother shielding herself. Of course she'd taken Mephistopheles. It didn't matter what Lucifer had demanded. The good to be done—

He drew energy off her with a force that left Gabriel seeing stars in place of his eyes. "I told you to stay out of this."

Gabriel clenched her hands. "I don't take your orders."

"That was a threat. Not an order." This time when he drained her power, it came like cool relief. All his energy left her soul, except now he was supercharged. Had he just used her to overclock himself? "You've penetrated enemy lines in the most dangerous way possible."

His hands tightened on her, and Gabriel didn't turn her face from his even though she couldn't see through the glare of his rage. "I'm aware there's no extrication."

He'd drag her into Hell when he left.

Below their feet was music. Weddings were the start of a family —and at the Wedding Feast of the Lamb, families were reuniting. Without any further reason to suppress anything, Gabriel allowed the joy and the relief to pulse out of her heart. Love had burgeoned up like a fountain in the desert. Love had cracked the gates of Hell, and those souls could feel love for the first time in ages. Finally, they could give it, too. They could give their love to God and could accept God's love in return.

Lucifer shook her. "Stop that! It's not going to last! They chose me and mine!"

Now they'd chosen something else, though, and God would honor that because God had wanted nothing more. The unapproachable one was approaching them.

Her ears buzzed. Lucifer was using her intelligence, calculating situations and strategies with a rapidity he'd never been able to without her. Every time, it was the same question: how to get out of Heaven with all his forces, even the ones who'd attempted to leave, and how to keep the new ones who ought to be his. He would keep Gabriel. He wanted Israfel.

Gabriel shut down any connection to Israfel. Israfel mustn't feel that. Lucifer shouldn't reach through one bond to interfere in the next.

He had workable solutions, was the problem. He had an army. He could badger and threaten Mephistopheles. He could bait Ataf. He could do all these things at once because with so much power, he could be at all the key points simultaneously. Even so, every plan had to factor in God's interference.

Lucifer hissed into Gabriel's face, "So? Do you love me?"

There wasn't an answer. Or rather, there were too many questions that splintered off the first. Love him the way he was now? Love his potential? Love his origin? Jesus had said perfect love casts out fear, so did that mean fear casts out love? Did it suffice that even if fear cast out perfect love, Gabriel's love didn't have to be perfect?

Lucifer smirked at her non-answer. "I thought as much."

Gabriel clutched his arms. "Come home."

He shoved her away, breaking her grasp. "Home is what I've made for myself. If you have the slightest sense, you'll grab Israfel and hide deep in Heaven until I'm gone."

"I don't want you to go." Gabriel's vision still hadn't cleared. "I've been praying for you to stay—" Lucifer fired soul energy through her, but she absorbed it. "—and I'm not the only one. Are you going to terrorize Michael and Saraquael and Abraham and Mary? Ataf and Rahab, Beelzebub and Mephistopheles—"

Lucifer flared even brighter. "I'm not here to get preached at. I'm preaching to you: back off."

He vanished.

Gabriel plummeted to the ground, landing on her knees with her fingers pressed to her temples. Her skin was hot. That might be his anger, but maybe she'd been so steeped in his power for so long that her soul was oozing it.

A presence enfolded her. Uriel helped her stand, but then everything felt like futility because Gabriel rang with the sense of Lucifer doing exactly as he'd said: he was blanketing the layer with his presence, exhorting the *viatores* to stay true. He ordered the army to gather together the humans. Worse, with all that energy he'd banked in Gabriel and pulled back out, he'd managed to strengthen himself beyond anything he'd ever achieved.

Gabriel whispered into her cupped hands, "What have we done?"

Uriel held her close. "The best we've ever done. Come with me off level so I can help you."

Gabriel shook her head. "There's no help for me. We need to be here. Everyone needs to come home."

Chapter Twenty-Seven

As THE BANQUET WENT on, Michael couldn't keep up with the number of conversions, but accounting was for the Cherubim. Instead, emboldened, he dispatched Angels and Archangels into the hotels to penetrate rooms one at a time, the same way they had in Hell. Coax souls out of there. Get them into the throng and get them talking. Give everyone access to someone familiar, someone they respected, or someone they longed to be with.

As Michael deployed a team into another hotel, Uriel's voice sounded in his heart from miles away. *You need eyes on Gabriel.*

Gabriel looked wretched. Michael came up close, and Gabriel raised her hands. "Before you suggest anything, I refuse."

Michael took in the pallor of Gabriel's wings, accompanied by the the flush of her cheeks. "What if I suggest you stay here and keep putting yourself in jeopardy? Will you refuse that, too?"

"No word games." She glared with an iciness that reminded Michael of Satan. "I'm not under your authority."

Michael tilted his head. "I'm not your commanding officer, but I thought I was your friend." Gabriel didn't soften. "You're struggling."

"You adding to my struggles isn't to anyone's benefit." Gabriel stood straighter. "I can feel Lucifer tightening his ranks against us. If anything, the current landslide is making him more determined. I should have told Mephistopheles to wait until the last minutes. We might have had a chance."

"On the contrary, you'd have lost Mephistopheles if you'd given him any reason to think you didn't want him." Michael took a deep breath. "It's not just you versus Satan. Every angel is helping. Every saint is helping. God is pouring out opportunities."

Gabriel set her jaw.

Uriel stroked her arm. "Don't make the same mistake Lucifer did."

Gabriel's brows furrowed. "Thinking I can unseat God?"

"Thinking it all depends on you as the chosen one."

Gabriel straightened in surprise.

Uriel raised a hand. "Mary asked this of you because, as she said, you were the only one who could bond Lucifer. But that doesn't mean you have to cross the finish line alone. You're overestimating your strength in a way that's a danger to you and the entire gambit."

Gabriel's eyes widened. "It's not a game."

"All the more reason to assess your resources."

She shook her head. "The only way out is through."

Michael sighed. "The other way out is down, where you get spent badly enough that you can't act when it's most important." How would a Cherub say this? "Analyze your energy expenditure versus your current reserves. Will you make it to the end of the banquet?"

Other than a frown of concentration, Gabriel went blank. Finally her fists clenched. "Why would God call me to this and not let me finish it?"

That was an answer: on her current trajectory, she couldn't last.

Uriel said, "Because the finish isn't up to you. Lucifer's destination was always up to God and Lucifer."

Gabriel blew out energy strong enough that Michael's eyes watered. "What would you order me to do? Yes, I'm in pain, but I assure you, if he goes back to Hell, with or without me, that pain will have only begun."

Michael had no idea what he'd have ordered. Fortunately, as Gabriel had already observed, he wasn't the one giving her orders. "I would tell you to take five minutes to pray."

Wings rising, Gabriel glared. "Is it your opinion that I haven't prayed enough—or at all?"

"Prayed enough to coerce God to override Satan's free will? Come on." Michael sighed. Every part of her was strain and tension. "The fact that you'd think such a thing means you're at least one step back from your rational self. Pray so you can touch base with God and get yourself ordered, and maybe restore your strength."

Gabriel blanked out. Then, just before Michael was about to settle in for ten minutes of Gabriel thinking, her eyes snapped back to focus. "I want to sing."

Cherubim. Never, never what you expected.

Uriel said, "We'll sing as a prayer." Then, with a hug, "We've even got a stage and an orchestra."

Gabriel shuddered with a laugh. As she turned her eyes to Michael, he raised his hands. "Sorry, but you saw what happened the last time I joined you."

Uriel called, "Israfel, we need a musician."

Israfel blew into place before them, and if Michael thought Gabriel looked awful, then Israfel looked "terrific" in the archaic sense: inspiring terror. She burned like an icicle, glittering and scorching. Pure black, her eyes were an abyss, and the universe distorted around the gravity of her heart.

Despite which, Uriel reached for her hand. "Gabriel needs us to sing with her."

Israfel took it. "Then we should sing."

She had no warmth in her voice. Gabriel extended a wingtip to hers. "Thank you."

At least Gabriel didn't seem horrified, and Gabriel had insight into Israfel's soul—or else Gabriel's poker face was in full force. Israfel transported them to the wings of the main stage and projected something to the conductor, who immediately cut all the repeats of the current performance.

Michael projected to Gabriel, *Singing doesn't replace prayer.*

Without looking at him, Gabriel projected back, *This I acknowledge. But singing strengthens us to pray afterward.*

With a wing around Gabriel, Uriel projected calm, followed by hope.

Hope. So many good things were happening. Michael had to focus on that and trust God to straighten the highway for more good things.

Glowing enough to cast shadows, Israfel turned to Gabriel. "Dedication of the Stars?"

With a glance at Uriel, Gabriel agreed, and the three of them took the stage.

Michael called Raphael as they started. *You may want to get over here.*

Raphael appeared behind him. "That sounds concerning." Followed by, "Oh. Now I'm concerned, too."

Michael sighed. "How can I help?"

"Gabriel just told me to inform you she will, indeed, pray after this is done." Raphael snickered. "Thank you for insisting on that. Oh, but this song—?"

These words and this melody had restored the purpose of a tattered and stunned angelic population. The host had yearned for an offering in response to Satan's degradation, and Israfel had given them a voice to rededicate themselves to God, to purify themselves and voice their resolve to start again. For all that everyone claimed "All Praise to My Creator" was the best song ever written, Michael privately felt that honor belonged to "Dedication of the Stars." Israfel had written just the right song at just the right time, crafted to meet a common need and to be sung with a common voice. Perhaps because of its unassuming nature, "Dedication of the Stars" had become so normal to begin activities with that Michael hadn't thought twice when Israfel suggested it.

Only now, as she played, she brought to bear a different tone. This song should thrum with hope. Instead she'd changed the instrumentation, leaving no fanfares and no trills. She played the long form, played it slower, pitched it deeper, and rendered her voice duskier.

Perhaps not conscious of the effect, Gabriel altered her tone to match. And, oh, the result— This was no triumphant regathering of angels, resolute to prove themselves to their Creator. Instead, even with all the words the same, Israfel transitioned it into a theme of devastation and betrayal. Between her spare tones and Gabriel's bronzy voice, Michael felt himself balancing on an emotional precipice the same way he had on the far edge of the war, looking out over angels shattered with grief, his heart surging with God's grace but at the same time broken because so many were lost.

This wasn't an anthem. This was a dirge.

When the piece ended, Gabriel's eyes were dull as gunmetal.

Michael flashed to her. "Five minutes. Now. Then come back, and—"

—and Michael drew his sword to block a demon before he could finish the sentence.

Gabriel turned right into the attack, not drawing her own weapon but shimmering with defensive power that stank like Satan's.

"You whore!" It was Belior, vibrating and shedding light. "You slut! You had everything, and you took him!"

Israfel blasted him back, but more shocking than Belior's attack was Gabriel's lack of response, as though the worst that could happen to her already had. Belior blasted her again, but with a curt gesture, she deflected it skyward.

Michael seized Belior mid-charge. Pinned in place, Belior screamed, "You bonded him too late! You were too cowardly to seduce him at the start, and he took everyone down!"

Michael dragged Belior backward, prepared to isolate him.

From Gabriel: *Don't confine him to quarters! With so few hours remaining, that's a death sentence.*

Belior screamed, "You destroyed everything! We got Winnowed because you were weak!"

Before Michael could flash Belior away, a blast shook the stage, wrenching Belior from Michael's arms. Satan?

Instead, before them stood Asmodeus, armored in black, hair in flames, grasping Belior in a headlock.

"Gabriel is not responsible." Asmodeus' bass shook the stage like a volcano. "You made it clear I've never been enough for you. I should have listened from the start." Belior choked out an objection, but Asmodeus barked, "Enough! The Winnowing wasn't Gabriel's fault. It's our fault. Your fault. My fault."

He chucked Belior at Michael's feet.

A half million souls watched from the audience as the demonic army assembled around the stage, taking positions on the ground and in the air—and finally on the stage as well. Moloch and Satrinah flanked Asmodeus. Keeping his wrists crossed over his chest and his wings drawn up, Belior shook in a position almost like an angelic worship posture.

At Gabriel's side, Uriel was overshadowed by a cloud of prayer.

Belior rasped, "Why Gabriel? Why did he have to choose her?"

Asmodeus swept out a hand. "And why did he have to humiliate you in the process? Why did he act like you and Mephistopheles were nothing but an annoyance? Why did we tolerate that and sacrifice ourselves for that?"

Gabriel was fully blanked out, as though not even here. Oh—she didn't want to respond in a way that would alert Satan. Not that Asmodeus seemed to care.

Of course, with the demonic army assembled, Satan was bound to come. Gabriel was buying seconds, not minutes. Michael summoned any and all available soldiers to the main platform, now.

Belior covered his face with his hands.

Asmodeus towered over him. "We've wasted too much time on a lie and a leader who never thought twice about any of us. If he let Gabriel into his head, it only proves how little we mattered. I refuse to sacrifice anything else. I don't want to be parted even one more minute from my God and my King."

Belior tightened all the way up, head tucked, wings closing around himself.

Asmodeus crouched before Belior. "Do you love me? Then love my Creator."

Michael stepped forward, but before he could speak, Asmodeus stood. "My Cherub may have lost command of his senses, but I still have command of the army. Say the word, and I'll order them to disarm and seek their peace with the Almighty. They will then identify and deliver every remaining *viator* to the temple for reintroduction."

Oh, no, it didn't work that way. Maybe coerced alliances sufficed in Hell, but God wouldn't accept conversions under duress. Still, Michael alerted his soldiers to pick targets from among the demons to pull off the level if they wanted to flip.

At that moment, attention swept over them. Malevolent attention.

Michael's forces had Moloch and Satrinah off the level a moment before Satan arrived, but Belior refused to move, and Asmodeus wouldn't leave him.

Satan blasted them. Michael threw himself in between, but the blast never hit home. Instead, Gabriel stood before all three, wings spread to absorb the energy. "Michael, get them out of here!"

Belior screamed, "I still have a chance!"

Gabriel met his eyes. "I'm giving you the only chance you'll get. Run!"

Satan shoved Gabriel at Israfel and strode toward his minions. *"Asmodeus!"*

Michael said to Asmodeus, "You didn't want to wait another minute. So help me, that minute is up."

Satan raised Belior by the neck. Asmodeus shouted, "You could have given him everything he wanted! Why did you make a joke of him?"

Michael could feel Saraquael attempting to flash Belior off the level, but Belior wouldn't consent. *A thousand times a second,* Saraquael sent. *If he wavers, I'll get him.*

Satan glared into Belior's eyes. "Is that what you want? Eternal union?"

Belior's back arched as Satan sent fire through him, but Asmodeus tackled Belior out of Satan's grasp, then pivoted so when Satan fired again, the blast nailed Asmodeus.

The human crowd was flashing away, and then an order went forth from Asmodeus—amplified momentarily by Moloch, and then from Beelzebub. When had they gotten back? Michael pivoted toward them, but demon soldiers were streaming out of the area—to the temple?

Satan emitted a concussion blast, and the exodus halted. Belior was frozen in place. Still in flames from Satan's blast, so was Asmodeus. Satan was pinning every one of his forces with his will. Demons and damned humans alike—he'd reached for what was his, and he was holding them all in position, binding them to silence.

He could do that? He was powerful enough to hold—millions?

Flashing in, Mephistopheles was on the ground in front of Belior, hands on his shoulders. "Please, believe me," Mephistopheles urged. "You're hungering for completion, but no Seraph can give that. Only union with God can complete you."

Then alongside Mephistopheles was Rahab, followed by Satrinah, all of them urging, urging—

Michael prayed, *Please, just a second, even a heartbeat—*

Satan detonated, hurling Gabriel into Michael and crashing everyone, angel and demon alike, to the ground. In the chaos, Raphael swooped to Asmodeus and extinguished the flames. Ataf flashed over Michael, projecting a midair Guard. Satan turned toward Belior, fire in his eyes.

Belior looked at Mephistopheles—and vanished.

Asmodeus popped out, too.

Gabriel collapsed in Michael's arms, shaking. Michael prayed, *Thank you.*

Then Satan tore Gabriel from Michael's grasp. Eyes blazing, he loomed over Michael. "A Cherub for a Cherub. Does that sound fair?"

Chapter Twenty-Eight

HOVERING ABOVE MICHAEL, SATAN tightened his grasp on Gabriel even though she wasn't struggling. Her soul had forked like lightning, branching for Israfel and Raphael. It would do no good. Satan had stockpiled power inside her, and it was his for the taking.

Every remaining member of his forces was in thrall. He hadn't realized until now that a smaller cohort meant complete control. He should have culled them from the start, employing the strongest and chaining the rest until he required replacements. With a truncated army of automata, none of them seeking their own will, he could have overrun the world.

Satan flooded Gabriel with so much fire so quickly that she screamed, wings scissoring, spine arching.

Her pain scorched back through him as though he were burning himself, but he'd dealt with pain for centuries. She was brand new to it. The distress of a concussion-addled human with a broken arm was nothing compared to a regular day in Hell, and he could triple that with less than a thought.

Michael was fighting panic. "What will that get you?"

"Everything. No more approaches to my people, or I will know about it." He could feel the thoughts of every one of those in thrall. "I want your forces out of the hotels. I will give you my terms at cost of Gabriel's soul."

With head down and eyes closed, Gabriel was focusing deep to get control. Satan forced power into her again, and she seized up.

Mary appeared, but Uriel blocked her before she could rush into the fray.

Satan said to Michael, "It's your decision how much Gabriel suffers."

He flooded Gabriel again, only this time, someone acted from the other side to suction the fire from her.

He glared at Raphael, but instead it was Israfel, eyes burning. Perfect. Let her feel Gabriel's agony and beg him to stop by offering the only thing she could: herself.

Except then more power went out from Gabriel and into Raphael.

Were they trying to prevent him from turning Gabriel into a husk? Satan opened the floodgates. He could overpower all three.

Head down, Gabriel didn't fight. Instead, she let the power flow. The other two Seraphim were glowing brighter than Satan had ever seen. They flared as they reached maximum capacity, exactly as he knew would happen—except once more the pressure released.

Dotting the crowd were three Cherubim glowing with overflow power.

Gabriel gasped, raising her head, but not from pain. Because in the next moment, she was flushing all that power from herself into the two Seraphim, who then pumped it into their bonds. Those Cherubim likewise had other bonds, so they shunted Satan's power out toward their Seraphim.

Were they actually going to try this? Satan had more power than any few dozen of them combined.

Gabriel's eyes blazed like twin suns, and her feathers shone too brightly for even angelic eyes to behold. Energy leeched out her fingertips, and with every heaving breath, light puffed like vapor on a cold day. White-hot, she made straight her soul to let his power pass without resistance, and from there, light spread through the Seraphim and Cherubim, one to the next to the next.

Were they all connected?

Satan saw suddenly what Gabriel perceived: a cat's cradle,

paired pyramids point to point, herself blazing at the center. She was rapt with delight as the image in her mind became an image in reality. As if each angel were passing a candle from one to the next, igniting lanterns of their own, the light spread, and Gabriel beheld with joy as light crossed from one inverted pyramid to the other.

Before him, Mephistopheles was glowing, and Beelzebub. Ataf and Rahab. Satrinah. Moloch. His own demons had begun passing the light after it had jumped the divide through six bonds once broken but now re-forged.

It didn't matter. His natural abilities were enough to flood every last one, and Gabriel couldn't serve a conduit for it all.

That was when the Thrones started drawing light off the Seraphim and Cherubim.

Gabriel was beyond pain, dazzling and dazzled. *God!* Her euphoria rippled out in rings, and the lower order angels drew off her energy that way. *Oh, God, so beautiful. This is how it should have been all along.*

By now every angel was filtering his excess light, and a horrified Satan realized he wouldn't be able to overpower the entire host. He tried to clamp it off, but like a siphon, Gabriel kept drawing it out. He shook her, hit her, but the high pressure in him automatically flowed into the lower pressure in her, and from her, all his power diffused into every other angel. Light was even dispersing through the humans as their guardians spread it around.

Stop it! He flared fire over her, but she unfurled her arms and wings and focused on God. He couldn't break their connection, and she wasn't trying to. If anything, she was suctioning it out even faster.

Gabriel exulted in the wonder of light the way it should have been. From the start, Lucifer should have been the one closest to God, knowing the most, loving the best, and then receiving God's life to shine it through them all. Through her, but also through others. If this was the only time it could happen, the only way— this truncated and tortured distortion of God's light—then this was the way it had to happen.

Satan was running out of power. Gabriel urged him that if he asked, God would open the taps, and he could keep going. Then it would be God's light filling all creation.

Satan could think of nothing more disgusting. Plus, if he bided his time, in a moment he'd be able to reverse the siphon.

Michael grabbed Gabriel away from him, brilliant with overflow light even though he was eight choirs down. Raphael tugged Gabriel into his arms, but her eyes never wavered from Satan. His soul vibrated with her prayers.

That voice, inhabiting a part of his soul silent ever since he'd severed himself from God.

Her joy, thrumming in a heart that hadn't rejoiced in equal time.

Her yearning, longing for a friend in someone who'd sacrificed all companionship.

Her peace, when he'd always been restless.

Only now—

Now.

The instant his power drew level with Gabriel's, Satan threw the flow into reverse, to back everything out through her and possibly more. Prepared for this, Gabriel snapped tight around herself, but Satan focused harder. That meant releasing the host he'd possessed—and they fled. Slavery to him was the ultimate end of leaving God, and if they'd abandoned God for freedom, domination by Satan wasn't the better option.

Every hotel vanished except for the Hilbert. Gabriel cut contact with Raphael and Israfel so Satan could access only her. Fear overwhelmed her joy, like a wave rushing up on rocks, but her eyes were on God.

Behind her, Israfel projected music.

Gabriel's head snapped up, and Raphael pivoted. A moment later, Satan realized she was playing—*that* song?

His song.

Anger flared, but it was Gabriel's. Was Israfel trying to get Satan angry enough that he'd leave and never reconnect? But Satan couldn't even approve of Israfel's betrayal because if she was trying to anger and offend him, this was the way to do it.

Wearing the cloak Gabriel had worn into Hell to save her, Israfel rose into the air and played a violin formed from her soul material. As the instrument pealed over the crowd, she smirked right at Satan.

He tried again to call back his power and drop her like a rock, but Gabriel kept blocking.

As that hateful cloak rippled around her, Israfel projected her voice. "If you don't want to hear your song again, you'll have to stop me."

Gabriel was shaking. Satan said, "I know for a fact it's you who don't want to hear that song."

Light glinted off Gabriel's silver seal at her neck. "Maybe I want to remind you of the only good act you ever committed. The most amazing hymn, the most beautiful gift of love that transformed our concept of worship—"

He blasted her, but she deflected it. Curse this weakness. He drew harder on Gabriel, and as he did, Gabriel's clarity rearranged his thoughts. At the same time, Gabriel was drawing from Satan's understanding of psychology to cipher out Israfel's motives and tactics. That cloak was a provocation, an attempt to humiliate him. The song—

Israfel called, "You were so on fire with love back then," and Satan shot her again.

Michael tried getting in between, but Israfel flashed to the stage, and there she sang.

Before Satan could flash to her, Michael had a Guard around the stage. A moment after, so did Ataf.

Satan was the last one standing. Every one of his followers had yielded to God's bribery.

Gabriel flashed to the stage, where she stumbled into Uriel's arms. A moment after, that woman was there with them both, and Gabriel leaned hard on her. Leaned on a human. Weak. Ridiculous.

Even so, Gabriel focused Satan's thoughts on the song, on everything it expressed. *How could you write that and not feel love?*

In her mind, he saw himself pre-Winnowing, but he rejected that image. He'd been deluded. Naïve. He hadn't realized yet that God wanted only to use and discard him.

Gabriel refocused his attention on his own song. That wasn't naïveté. It was love. And why couldn't he recapture that love now?

After all this? Was she out of her mind?

No, not out of her mind.

Gabriel started singing, and Raphael joined them. Israfel was not only playing the violin but also singing the part he'd written for himself.

Satan cringed to feel Gabriel's song vibrating through her soul—his song—but this was an opportunity. With Gabriel linked with the other two Seraphim, Satan had the opening to draw back his power. She was weak. He'd wear her down. It took energy to close off a bond, and once he ran her out of energy, he'd access Israfel and Raphael.

In fact, he could probably do that now.

Israfel was easy to reach. She was angry. She was engaging with his song and linked tight with Gabriel while they coordinated the most difficult parts. Her anger sparkled in a way that thrilled him as much as their past joys. God may have taken all Satan's forces, but Satan could still take Israfel. She bridled at the unfairness of demons being forgiven, and he could use that. He always had. Moreover, she couldn't disengage when the music was consuming all her attention. He'd pulled every musical trick when writing that thing, inventing new techniques when the ones at his disposal didn't suffice. In fact, the biggest musical trick he'd pulled off was figuring out exactly how complex he could make it before he outstripped Gabriel's ability to sing and Israfel's ability to play. Making it unplayable, while a thrill, would have left him looking incompetent. Instead, by holding back just a little, he'd written a masterpiece.

Gabriel's mind was racing to keep up with her part while simultaneously separating him and her, him and Israfel. It was too much. She'd crumble before she reached the descant.

Israfel hesitated in the song, and then—

Wonder.

Answering wonder from Gabriel.

Their combined realization rushed through Satan. They'd never sung this piece since the Winnowing. All this time, his hymn had remained frozen in their minds in the way they'd experienced it back then, as the pinnacle of music and the moment everything changed. At the peak of perfection it had remained, and yet in that time, creation had developed all around it.

They'd learned and grown and deepened—this was Gabriel's thinking. Now that she could emote her music, she was trying but couldn't find anything here to emote. Stronger than that, Israfel's realization slammed into Gabriel like a clapper striking a cathedral bell: since the Winnowing, the angels had experienced God in a myriad of ways they never could have before. They'd participated in God's mercy and God's healing and God's benevolence. Until there had been a need to forgive, they'd never experienced God as forgiving. Before a need to return, they hadn't known God as welcoming. In every way, their understanding of the Divine had erupted, and as divine light penetrated new depths, it gave them more ways to emulate God to others.

Now the song felt flat. It was technically perfect, but music wasn't just about perfect execution. To Israfel, the song felt joyless. To Gabriel, it was a string of pointless virtuosity. It wasn't the pinnacle of musical creation. It was only a historical curiosity.

The thought blossomed within Israfel that she had experienced God and loved God and built a relationship with God, and if God opened His arms right now to embrace all the fallen, they still didn't have *her* relationship with Him. She'd labored in His fields beneath the heat of His sun for the same reward, sure, but she'd gotten her hands in His soil and learned to love His vines as tenderly as He did.

From Gabriel came a breathless wonder because God was too complex for any one of them to fully comprehend, but all these experiences had so many angels knowing Him and reflecting Him in different ways. With all their internal refractions combined, they knew so much more than they could have back when they all related to God one way, the same way, as their creator and provider but not as their protector or their redeemer.

Satan's wings spread. How dare these two *O Fortunate Fall* him? He wasn't a learning opportunity, and he wasn't the reason Israfel should fall back in love with God right when she'd been on the brink of spitting at Him.

Satan scorched an unguarded Gabriel from the inside out. She dropped to all fours, shaking. Israfel abandoned the song and wrapped around her.

Satan felt his fire consuming Gabriel's soul as if it were consuming his own. Trying to stay in control, Gabriel clenched her fists like a petulant child. *How can love become hate? How can a star bend its rays inward?*

Satan replied, *A more pertinent question is, how much fire can you take before you crumble to ash?*

Gabriel was frantic. *Think about your time with me. You kept losing yourself to something greater and then didn't know why. Each time, you came back together as a little less of yourself. I know what's missing. It's in me. Didn't you want to want to repent?*

He hadn't. What he'd wanted was Gabriel, and to get to Gabriel, he'd needed to want to repent. Therefore, he'd wanted to want it. But that wasn't the same as wanting a desire for repentance. If anything, he'd been three steps back: he'd wanted to be in a state where Gabriel would find him attractive, and then Gabriel would be his.

Gabriel raised her head. *What loved once can love again.*

Satan replied, *I never loved you.*

It was a lie. Lucifer had loved Gabriel whenever she sang for him and every time she illuminated the world for him. He'd loved her when they'd prayed together and she'd opened up new possibilities before him. He'd loved spending time with her and creating art with her and listening to her lecture the lower-order angels. He'd loved when she'd stop mid-discussion and defer to him because she wanted to hear his verdict.

There had been others, too. He'd loved being with Israfel and

Raphael, with Mistofiel and Belazael. They'd talk or play or relax or pray together. They designed a temple and they staked out territory in Heaven and told stories and invented games. Uriel would sit with them for an entire afternoon, saying nothing but creating a sculpture in light with a streak of color for every conversation topic. Lucifer and Gabriel had stood in the tall grass and gazed at the sky as she murmured, "The light is beautiful, and God made you out of light."

He'd loved God, too. Back then. Loved him with all he was, at least until the moment he'd realized God loved all the others the same as himself. He wanted to be more, recognized more, giving more, doing more. Which he did, only then God accepted his gifts just the same as everyone else's gifts. Over time, standard acceptance began to feel like rejection because it should have been greater. Jealous of the love God showed the other angels, Lucifer had needed to outshine them all, except it was never enough for God. Lucifer should have been the only one.

Now he was the only one, but in the opposite direction. He'd been alone for so long, and henceforth, he'd be alone forever.

Struggling to hold herself together, Gabriel pleaded, *You don't have to be alone. Ask to stay.*

Satan replied, *Do you think I have the grace to ask?*

Let me ask for you.

The idea was repulsive, letting her ask as though he were a child. He should ask for himself. God would refuse, and then Gabriel would recognize all this prattle about benevolence for the nonsense it was.

God won't refuse. Gabriel leaned on Mary to get to her feet, but her wings were limp. *He wants you home.*

Heaven hadn't been Satan's home for thousands of years.

Gabriel replied, *Then let my heart be your home.*

She had nothing to offer. Nothing except for everything.

Hell had never been a home. It had been a base, a bulwark, a fortress. It had been a refuge against God, and then the Second Person of the Trinity had established a Church that smashed its gates anyway.

Gabriel sent, *If I can't give you anything else, at least let me ask for you to have the grace to ask. Want to want to repent. That's close enough.*

Israfel resumed singing his song, but it must have been too complex even for the Angel of Music because she'd smoothed it out and made it easier to follow. But then something else was happening, other voices joining where they shouldn't. His was a showpiece, not a choral arrangement. It wasn't designed for congregational singing, only for him and a few others in a liturgical setting to display what real music could achieve. By streamlining it, Israfel had made it accessible to everyone, even the humans.

She'd also changed the tempo, and in the spaces between his words came another set of words—her words. She'd set "The Dedication of the Stars" in counterpoint with his song. "Dedication" was being sung by, of all creatures, Rahab.

With her fingers digging into Mary's shoulder, Gabriel fought to stay upright. *We belong together.*

The tunes melded so well. As if they'd always meant to be together.

Except—

He didn't want to be saved. He most certainly didn't want to be saved by Jesus.

He ought to slam the door on all this, lock himself in his lightless office, and then walk out again after the banquet had ended and the gates been re-sealed. Then, and only then, could he figure out what remained. Himself. His kingdom. Maybe he'd have retained access to the Earth. Maybe the living roots of his heather were insulated in the ash at Wall Street, and maybe with that, he could start again. Start something.

Or maybe Gabriel could ask and get him one step closer. Her eyes shimmered as she stared at him. "Want to want to repent" was very close to repenting. Maybe it didn't have to have been a lie.

If he turned back, though—the humiliation. The admission that he'd not only made a mistake but persisted in it for so long, was a task too heavy even for him to bear.

Gabriel's voice had gone urgent. *It doesn't matter what anyone thinks about you. It never mattered.*

By now her soul was hot not only from his power but also from the equivalent of metal fatigue, a thousand twisted pressure points stretching and getting pushed back into place. For all that she was weak, she was holding on with a determination that showed the truth behind her name.

Holding on for him.

Love was keeping her upright long after she should have fallen. Love had called her to him and kept her with him.

She was sacrificing herself because she wanted good things for him. After everything he'd done, Satan couldn't love God, but maybe he could love her. Given that everyone else had flipped, performative worship should be enough. If he said the right things, he could slip in the door. Once inside, he could figure out how to make it tolerable to stay. If not, he could leave again.

He'd use her strength and clarity to get it done. She'd know the right words. She could show him his performance through her eyes and help him fine-tune it. If she collaborated with him in tricking God, he would even get hooks in her to bring her out during a second rebellion.

He suctioned energy and focus from her, which she opened herself to give.

And as her power came, he knew what she knew: he'd pushed and pulled too much energy through her. *The other way out is down.*

Gabriel looked him dead in the eye as she channeled her last energy toward him, the cold focus, that beautiful spark that was her—and he couldn't stop her. *"Strength of God,"* but she was offering the last.

No!

Gabriel dropped like a sack of rocks.

Chapter Twenty-Nine

MARY CAUGHT GABRIEL FROM behind, and then Raphael scooped her into his arms. Michael positioned himself alongside, sword drawn. Israfel kept her eyes riveted to Gabriel as she sang—but it was Satan who wanted to reach her and breathe strength back into her soul.

Gabriel lay boneless in Raphael's arms, wings splayed, head back. Satan kept reaching for her, but the emptiness echoed. She was gone, gone—just gone. Now, when Satan finally needed her strength, she was extinguished—one last way for God to spit in his face. Gabriel could have sorted his thoughts and fed him the words, and then powered him up to get through the most odious performance of his life. Except—

—Except maybe she still could. Satan reached through space to his hotel room and summoned Gabriel's gift to him, that sigil-like cocoon vibrating with her power. Knowing God as she did, Gabriel would have prepared for an end-run around the Almighty. There wasn't enough time to unspool it like a silkworm's thread. Instead, with its cool surface pressed to his palm, Satan cracked it open to receive her power.

It wasn't her power.

Instead, it was her year.

It crashed through his awareness like a comet. He hadn't been able to feel her in Raphael's arms, but now she was everywhere, drowning his senses. She'd designed the cocoon to uncoil her journal in his mind, but instead he got it all at once. Overwhelmed, he couldn't even sort it chronologically, but momentarily it straightened before him. With Cherub thoroughness, she'd added an author's note explaining how it should have worked, how with her perfect memory she'd re-created every entry, even the places with an imprecise word scratched out or clarifications added into the margins. She'd also footnoted it with cross-references.

Her year began with guilt and anger, followed by self-recrimination, but next the loneliness. The frustration. The clenched teeth. And then—the support.

The unexpected friendship.

The shame in how all the angels thought Gabriel needed their help, and even worse, the way Gabriel actually did.

A letter written under compulsion to God the Father imploring an earlier return.

Months of struggle during which humiliation became humility...

...and then the moment when obedience became participation.

Finally, the realization when strength became not something Gabriel did, but something Gabriel could receive from God.

Feeding all that: community. The thing Satan had walked away from and never re-created for himself.

Gabriel in that one disgraced year had been directionless until crash-landing in a home, and that home had been the place from which all good things flowed. Until then, Gabriel had been primed for Satan to knock from the branch like an overripe fruit.

A home. A family. Care. The safety from which Gabriel had reached for the Father. The place Gabriel was when God reached back.

Worst of all was Gabriel's recall of Satan's temptations: his pursuit, his deception. Gabriel's confused longing. Gabriel's shame and horror. Gabriel's grief. He could see himself again through her eyes, only now Satan was urgent to reach through time to protect Gabriel back then, to step between them and scream at his former self, *Leave Gabriel alone. Gabriel is learning the thing you're going to need far in the future because you never learned it in the past.*

Satan pressed right up against the Guard but couldn't get through, couldn't reach her, not through the barrier and not with his spirit. Every time he tried, the absence echoed louder. He tried to push energy into her, but it only ricocheted back into his soul where her heart should have been. Or rather, where God should have been, except she'd filled that space so neatly.

"Let me get to her!" He glared at Michael. "I'll help her."

He'd breathe his power into her until she revived. He'd comfort her, no matter what it took. She'd ask him to repent, and he'd do it as a grand gesture for her. That should satisfy God. Satan would protect her and nestle her recovering spirit, and then he'd fill her with his own strength until she could look back at him. Everyone would see what he'd done. They'd praise it as self-sacrifice.

Eyes brittle, Michael squared his shoulders. "Gabriel doesn't need you."

Raphael had settled to the ground, wings covering her. Although he could have flashed her off level, he wasn't moving. It was a mockery of Satan for misjudging his resources. Jesus had warned the humans to figure out if they had enough stone to complete a tower so they didn't build nine floors and half the tenth.

Satan said, "Gabriel wanted to be with me."

Michael glowered. "She also wanted you on your knees before the Throne of Glory. I don't see either one happening."

Except Satan would need her to do that. If she wasn't here to show him—to straighten the ways—then how could he help her when helping her required her to help him? They'd both go down in flames.

Uriel flashed to the edge of the Guard, so much like Gabriel on the opposite side of the hotel door. Reassurance flowed from the Throne: Satan didn't require Gabriel to steady him. There were other strengths. Satan's pride wasn't the master of him. Instead, he could be the master of his pride.

The pair of songs had passed into their third iteration—no longer in sync because his was longer than Israfel's, and yet still woven together in counterpoint. Now a third song had joined the polyphony—Hell's anthem, only with all the words and the key changed on the fly so it was supporting the other two. That had to be Beelzebub's doing.

Satan recognized all their work and all their skills, and now he didn't recognize himself.

He reached again for Gabriel, but she wasn't there. He'd have pulled all of Gabriel inside if he could, dam her up in his heart and keep her there to power him. She could clarify the world for him, safe and trapped.

The thing Satan hadn't wanted to be for God: safe and trapped.

This was how Gabriel had chosen to use her freedom, in un-safety and vulnerability. She'd revealed the thing she'd never felt secure enough to share with Raphael. She'd risked everything in pursuit of a fantasy.

Which of them was less trapped?

Uriel stepped through the Guard. A question. A repeated question.

Satan breathed, "I don't know."

Uriel glanced back at Mary, and when Satan followed the gaze, he found Mary with tears in her eyes. She had her hand on Gabriel's head, but with her focus on Satan. It bubbled up in him that Gabriel's condition was the result of Mary's meddling, but he squelched the words before snapping at her. He'd read humans for centuries, and that wasn't the look of a woman who wanted to win. She'd already won. This woman was the one God had chosen to be the mother of the Son and the enemy of the serpent, and for some reason, even she wanted him back.

Ironic. He'd wanted to be wanted, and now they did want him. Just—not this way. Not on these terms.

Still outside the barrier, Uriel thrummed with encouragement, with reassurance.

Satan closed his eyes. *No.*

He felt something pushed into his hands. Before him he found Israfel, still singing. With that silky-grey cloak slipping over her arms, she handed him a ten-stringed lyre.

Uriel projected, *Play.*

Without missing any of the words she sang, Israfel reinforced this, projecting that Gabriel had wanted to hear him sing.

Gabriel would never hear it. She would wake up long after he'd been ejected again, and they wouldn't be able to say goodbye. They'd never said goodbye the first time.

In her journal, though, she'd loved his playing.

He pushed energy toward Gabriel, but he might as well have tried to fill a sieve. Israfel projected, *I'll remember and share the memory with her.*

His song was about to complete a loop, and he plucked the strings. Not quite right. The lyre he'd used back then was drawn from his soul material, so it resonated longer and allowed for more options. Nevertheless, he joined as the lyrics started over, and Israfel sang with him.

He hadn't played the melody the first time. His passage had fallen into counterpoint with Israfel's, so he changed what he was doing.

Uriel urged him to add the words, but Satan couldn't do it all at once. Even simplified, the piece was mind-bogglingly complex. First he had to remember the music—except someone was feeding him the notes. Israfel? Or was it Mephistopheles?

As he played, he remembered the other aspect of the instrument, how he'd infused all the notes with light so the song shone like a star, every musical phrase shifting with color, shimmering, expanding.

Uriel urged him again to sing, and this time, he did. He'd lied about so many things for so many years that he might as well lie one more time, singing words of love he didn't mean and never had meant. As Israfel had judged, they were childish, the point of view of an angel who knew nothing at all. Mercy? Nothing about that because the angels had never needed mercy. The song said nothing about what God would do to snatch back a child standing on the edge of a precipice. God hadn't needed yet to show Himself patient or persistent or willing to conduct a centuries-long rescue mission behind enemy lines. This was a schoolyard rhyme about God. God is big, and God is good. God made me. God made me to be with Him.

When Satan had sold Eve on the apple, he'd told her she wouldn't surely die—she'd just know good and evil. Which, one bite later, she did: knew evil in the only way it mattered, that now she was evil, and good irretrievable.

He hadn't known good and evil when he'd written this, either. Not the way he'd know it after inventing it and perfecting it and sloshing the whole of creation with its indelible dye.

Back when he'd given this song to God, he'd signed his name so God would always remember it as the thing Lucifer had done for Him that no one else could do. Back when he'd written this, he hadn't for a second considered his song a gift of love. It had been a tool created to astonish everyone with something more beautiful and more complex than anything they could come up with. It was a way to shame them, a way to say to God, "Recognize that I love you more than these." He'd emoted like a child, but at the end of the ages, everyone else had grown up.

Except it wasn't only the angels who'd learned more about God. For thousands of years, Satan had studied God, learning all His tactics, all His tendencies, all His traits. He'd needed to be able to predict what God was going to do next in order to outmaneuver Him. Beating God at His own game meant needing to know God just as well as the angels who still loved Him. Every time God had revealed a little more of Himself, Satan had thrilled with the new revelation. Hating God had meant endless contact with God.

Reeking of perfume and road dust, Jesus had said a certain woman loved Him with her whole heart because He'd forgiven her so much. Back when none of the angels had needed forgiving, did that mean there was no love? Or was it love unripe on the vine, tight and tart?

Israfel kept singing, but Lucifer stopped.

He'd thought it was love. What he'd sensed Gabriel feeling this week was so much richer than anything he'd ever felt, though, even at the height of Seraphic zeal. At the time, this song and these feelings were the best Lucifer had to give. God had accepted it, but had God accepted because that was all He'd get from this one? Had Lucifer been incapable of love all along?

Uriel projected to keep singing, but the words were gone. Lucifer couldn't even lie any longer. Perhaps it had always been a lie.

Gabriel should be sorting his thoughts so he could figure this out.

Uriel projected peace, followed by something more. Lucifer couldn't rely on Gabriel to repent for him. Gabriel was out of the equation, but once it came to this point, Gabriel was always going to have been out of the equation.

Lucifer's wings spread, but Uriel regarded him without distress. Or rather, confidence. Confidence that Lucifer could do this? Or was it confidence in God?

Gabriel couldn't ask on his behalf. Everything needed to be detangled between Lucifer and God.

Could he repent?

Lucifer closed his eyes. No. But he wanted to.

Uriel thrummed all around him: that was a start.

Lucifer flinched. That was what Gabriel had said.

Uriel moved closer. Perhaps it was a continuation, then, but still good. Then, in a low voice, Uriel breathed, "What's stopping you?"

What stopped him was the same friction that had stopped him at the beginning of time. God had made Lucifer this great, but then wanted to stuff him back into the same role as every other angel. Nothing had changed. Going back after all this meant it all had been a mistake and a mirage—or worse.

Uriel projected urgency, and Lucifer's thoughts collided into one another like uranium atoms in a reactor core. Although Gabriel couldn't make this decision for him, still Gabriel would have been able to detangle his ideas so he didn't have to deal with everything at once. Gabriel would have broken the problem down into the humiliation of admitting he was wrong, followed by the shame of abandoning everything he'd clung to, and then guilt of the suffering he'd caused. Gabriel would have teased apart the damage to creation from the damage to individual souls and the damage to entire societies.

Lucifer focused harder. As before, just remembering how

Gabriel sorted his thoughts helped to sort them. Objecting to worshiping God with a human nature had been an excuse. It would have been difficult, but Lucifer could have done it. In the intervening millennia, he'd done things far more difficult. Gabriel had immolated her pride enough to subject herself to God-made-man, and since Lucifer was stronger than Gabriel, surely he could have as well.

Being just another voice in a chorus of billions couldn't suffice for an angel strong enough to lead choirs and compose their songs. He'd been created specially, so he needed to do something special and be acknowledged as someone special.

Uriel took his hands, projecting peace. Lucifer hadn't realized he was vibrating, but he didn't quell it. Again Uriel pushed the question: what was stopping him?

What stopped him was the enormity of what he'd done. Every sin ever committed came back to him. Even factoring in free will, Satan was the cause of the angelic rebellion and then the human rebellion. Without him, none of them would have been brave enough to start.

Uriel sent, *You don't know what would have happened.*

Lucifer knew what he'd meant to happen. He'd meant Eve's temptation for the destruction of the human race. First she'd know her own evil, and then she'd know death. He'd believed death would mean Eve's un-creation, not death as in God stockpiling a billion human souls in a block of stone until the Word slipped inside as a dead human and blew it to rubble.

God had retroactively turned the snake into a truth-teller on both counts. They hadn't died...immediately. They had known evil. The sinners Adam and Eve had survived to have children who sinned, and later nations that sinned, and finally billions of individuals who sinned. Lucifer owned a share in each of those sins. God's mercy was an ocean, only there were miles of shoreline that needed to be covered, and the waves kept rolling back. Lucifer would try to carry the water, but then he'd look up to see the Son of Man sitting on a boulder, only to realize that needed to be covered, and the fields, and beyond them, the mountains required immersion, too. He couldn't cover it all.

Lucifer couldn't feel Uriel's hands any longer. He'd vibrated into an immaterial state, overflowing with energy and again overwhelmed by questions.

What was stopping him?

Even dissociated, he burned, and with nothing left to burn, his fuel was his own soul. Gabriel was right on one count: with her, he'd experienced joy. He'd experienced friendship. He'd experienced the fruit of someone else's prayers. He'd experienced unconditional love from the receiving end.

He'd seen his Earth destroyed. He'd seen everyone abandon him.

He'd prayed. God had answered the prayer.

He'd lied, and God had turned it into truth.

He felt hands again in his own. When he opened his eyes, Uriel had gone. Holding his hands was the Word.

Lucifer pulled back, but Christ clamped down on his wrists, looking him right in the eyes. *Not this time.*

Lucifer started vibrating again. *How can You stand to touch me?*

Jesus didn't let go. The important question was, could Lucifer stand to be touched?

Lucifer didn't have the wherewithal to tamp down his fire. Jesus before him was weak, the blood on His hands now smearing Lucifer's. His forehead was bleeding, and Lucifer could feel without seeing that the body had been pierced five times.

It had always been about being touched. Being touched meant being known, being vulnerable. Meanwhile, in front of him stood the Second Person of the Trinity, weak as He'd been the day they'd killed him, touched by nails and whips and human rejection. It was embarrassing and awful and frightening all at the same time because repenting meant being overpowered by weakness.

Lucifer sent, *If You reject me, You're hurting Gabriel.*

Jesus replied, "I'll take care of Gabriel. Let's talk about you."

Lucifer averted his eyes, fighting the urge to cover himself with his wings. *You can't forgive me.*

Jesus said, "How many times did you tell other people their sins couldn't be forgiven? Were you right about them?"

But Lucifer was different. Wasn't he?

Again, the thing Lucifer would have to let go of was being different. He'd have to subside into one voice among millions. Either he was different and couldn't be forgiven because he was so different—or else he was exactly the same as everyone else. God could wash him off, polish him up, plunk him into the multitude, and then forget him forever.

Jesus tightened His hands on Lucifer's. *I've never forgotten you.*

Christ's blood covered both of them. Lucifer couldn't hear past the flames, but it felt better to be talking to God in that same way he'd been talking to Gabriel. If their thoughts merged and mingled, it was conversation as close as it used to be, back before love turned into betrayal—when Lucifer had felt first loved and then betrayed, and reacted with a betrayal of his own.

God had never forgotten him. If God had forgotten him, he wouldn't exist.

So God would love anything He made?

No, he had it backward. God had loved him first.

Jesus said, "I made you because I love you, and in all of time, nothing you did has ever stopped me from loving you."

Lucifer shuddered.

Jesus continued, "I loved you enough to set you free. I love you enough to welcome you home."

Except, of course, Lucifer had to ask. He had to want it. He had to accept the consequences of being wrong.

Lucifer shivered. *I don't love You.*

Jesus sent, "Is Gabriel right, that what loved once can love again?"

I don't know.

He closed his eyes, and Jesus released him.

Gabriel's gift had been so small in Lucifer's hands yet so large in his heart. Gabriel had given him a story that was more than a story. The year of God's punishment had been Gabriel's own path home, fortunately before Gabriel had stepped too far from the road. That could also be Lucifer's path. Although sprawled on the ground, Gabriel under punishment had stood again with the help of community, and Gabriel had accepted that friendship only through humility. After being blessed by God, *You have nothing to offer me* had become, *I have everything to offer.*

The flames were lower around Lucifer now. He could hear his own hymn perseverating. Another strain had worked into the polyphony: the holy Trisagion of the Seraphim. Another song he used to sing, and one he could sing again.

Between his hands, Lucifer spun up his own cocoon, using flames instead of silk and memories instead of a story. As he spun, he sang his own lyrics. Israfel was right: time had changed the unchanging because creation had shifted around them. Lucifer's song was no longer beautiful or clever. At the shift of one line into the next, he defaulted back into the holy-holy-holy. Simple, repeating, endless. Undeniable. Forever and ever.

One at a time, Lucifer encoded into his cocoon all his decisions and actions, and all his works, and all his lying promises. He spun them into the shell of the cocoon, as slippery and repulsive as Hastle's egg had been, heavier than Gabriel's token, but as textured as Gabriel's journal. Into it he emptied out all the glamorous evil he'd ever done and all the structures he'd ever built. Inside his soul was now a catacomb of empty spaces.

Holy, holy, holy is the Lord God Almighty, Who was, and is, and is to come.

Then, with everything packed into that one bundle, sealed and coiled and glimmering with revulsion, Lucifer pressed it into Jesus's wounded hands. Everything he'd ever done, smeared with fingerprints of Christ's blood.

Holy God. Holy Omnipotent. Holy Immortal.

Jesus set it on fire. Smoke rolled out from His palms, and ash rose in a cloud. Lucifer went to his knees, hands crossed over his chest. All his work, passed through fire, was now revealed for what it was.

Have mercy on me. Lucifer closed his eyes as ash covered him, drifting over his hair and over his wings. *I have sinned against the Father, and I sinned against the Spirit, and I sinned against You.*

Eyes closed, he waited for condemnation and mockery, but instead came only silence as ash settled to the ground. The songs had ended.

Creation was an indrawn breath, a hesitation, and a question.

He was sin. He was weakness. He was destruction.

God was eternal and immeasurable, almighty, unchangeable, incomprehensible, and ineffable. Father, Son, and Holy Spirit, three in one. Three persons, one God, one love. One lover, and all creation the beloved.

Christ embraced him.

Forgiveness.

Here.

Here was where he belonged. Here he had belonged all along. Here, at the end of everything, a beginning. God had everything to offer.

The mockery never came. Instead, the relief. The acceptance. The welcome. The wick for his flame. The earth for his roots.

Here he could be small, could be a seed, could grow again—grow the right way. All things were possible with God. Over and over, he'd seen God doing things that were impossible, and now, God had done one more.

Christ shifted away. With a frightened protest, Lucifer reached to pull Him back when instead he felt Raphael laying Gabriel in his arms.

Jesus met his eyes. He wasn't leaving. They were a community. They could become a family. And someone needed him.

Vibrating, Lucifer pushed power into Gabriel. Power, but also gratitude. Though she didn't move, the candle of her heart sparked to life.

In his own heart was a similar spark. Tiny, but it could grow. God would feed it like a shoot with its roots deep in the ash, and Lucifer could let it reach for the light God offered. What loved once could love again. Likewise, what had been loved could still be loved. A fallen star could be rededicated.

Jesus took his hand.

Love is. The Father's voice whispered in his heart, filling that space with sound for the first time since the fall of the angels. *Love is, and love was, and love ever will be.*

Amen. Lucifer closed his eyes as he pulled Gabriel closer to his heart. *Forever and always, amen.*

Epilogue

As far as Michael could tell, Gabriel had been triangulating locations and measuring and remeasuring different positions for a solid hour. While she did this, she sang.

She would drop stakes of light into different points on the ground, then flash to other locations and drop new shafts. She'd then measure between them and either knock out both stakes to try again, or else move to yet another point and set up a light stake there.

She did all this to the backdrop of her voice, a tune that meandered as if she were talking to herself, changing languages midstream and then reverting back to lyrics Michael knew.

Raphael prompted Michael from a very long distance.

Michael sent back a negative.

Raphael sounded amused. *To get her attention, you're going to have to forcibly interrupt her.*

Michael flashed to sit atop one of the light posts. *If I break her concentration, she's going to be unamused to an incredibly high degree. Besides, this is fascinating.*

Raphael replied with bright laughter.

Cleaning up the Earth had begun in earnest a month prior, with human souls agitating to return to their former home and the reformed demons looking forward to the challenge of the cleanup. This, Michael could understand. Ataf had said it one night, looking down at the planet from the moon. "Considering the total devastation of my soul, I see myself reflected in the world.

Cleaning it up will feel symbolic."

Michael had leaned back on his hands, saying, "I like the parallel."

Ataf huffed. "Well, there are a lot of parallels, because there's no way the Earth could have healed itself."

Having everyone home—or home again—left Michael dazed, but dazed in the best way. He would approach Israfel with a question only to hear her in an intense discussion with Lucifer about whether the Holy Spirit "renewing the face of the Earth" meant "exclusively" the Holy Spirit or the Holy Spirit in partnership with created beings. Of course, two Seraphim in a hot argument had triggered Gabriel to show up, Mistofiel in tow, to lob a conversational grenade about whether "a new heaven and a new earth" meant actual new structures, or whether God would renew those in the way He did upon giving someone "a new heart and a new spirit."

After getting the Cherubim's perspective, Lucifer made the decision. The Earth was still, after all, technically his. "God didn't transplant actual hearts. Let's jumpstart the process so the humans can go home."

It kept leaving Michael breathless: *home*. Everyone had come home.

He reached for God. *This is amazing. Thank you.*

In his heart, God smiled. Michael trained his attention on God and the wonders God was working in the souls of all those who'd returned.

Gabriel had begun yet another set of measurements when she turned toward Michael's light post and jumped, abruptly re-engaged with reality. "I was about to move that! I'd have dumped you into the dust."

She blinked as she detangled from her thoughts. Michael said, "Don't let me disturb you."

She put her palm to the ground. "When are we—?" then started. "I didn't realize it was so late. I'm sorry I kept you waiting."

Michael shrugged.

Gabriel frowned. "An earthquake must have folded up the

terrain. Nothing's matching where I thought it would be, but it's not consistently off. This was definitely the Temple Mount. There should be anchor points between here and Heaven."

Michael said, "As things clear up, will it be easier to establish?"

"I'm able to get decent readings already on most of what should be under here. It's the distances between that are all wrong." Gabriel folded her arms and tightened her wings. "What did you want to talk about?"

"Just getting updates." Michael looked up. It would have been nice to spread his wings in the sunlight, but there still wasn't much of it.

Gabriel caught the thought. "Atmospheric conditions have improved to an average AQI of 712. I project breathable air within the next six weeks. Sunbathing?—that's going to take a little longer."

Michael said, "And the temperature?"

"Still inimical to life, but a perceptible rise." Gabriel nudged the ash with her boot. A month after the banquet, she'd finally stopped wearing armor, but her clothing resembled a uniform—something Michael could understand, given how hard it had been on her. She'd slept for five days after the banquet, and although it had finally slowed down, her power had kept rising. "I dislike how unsettled this feels. It isn't fitting that the Earth be anchored only to Hell."

In the next moment, her eyes brightened. "You're back."

Lucifer landed alongside Michael. Michael's feathers spread, and he fought the tension in his shoulders.

Lucifer didn't do more than nod to Michael, then said to Gabriel, "The Irin are on my case about restarting the trade winds."

Gabriel sighed. "I told them it's not time. Mistofiel told them it's not time. You told them it's not time. I guess that means it might be time."

Lucifer snickered.

Michael leaned against the light post, hoping something would require his presence away from here. It wasn't that he disliked

Lucifer...well, other than not liking him—but that was a lack of positive feeling rather than the existence of negative feelings. Michael still carried a lot of baggage, so he and Lucifer tended just to talk past one another. Lucifer did want all the damage undone quickly—as in, now-now-now—but realistically speaking, some of it just wasn't going to go.

Take, for example, the Irin. It kept being painfully obvious that they were two angels: Remiel, and a Camael who was trying to look and act like Remiel. While it was good they were together, they weren't identical and never would be again. To talk to them meant you knew which one you were talking to. They were, now and forever, merely complementary angels.

Yet Lucifer, every time, called them "the Irin," as though he could speak away the damage.

Similarly, although Michael and Ataf had discovered a mutual affinity for strategy games and discussing history, Michael hadn't encountered Hastiel more than a couple of times. He didn't wish Hastiel any harm, but now he knew what Hastiel was capable of. Their friendship had disintegrated, and they couldn't wish it back into existence.

Other situations, however, Michael found baffling. Until Gabriel first awakened, Lucifer hadn't left her side, and neither had Raphael. Apparently Raphael had spent that time talking to Lucifer and working with him as he re-aligned his worldview. Fair enough, but then Israfel had joined. To help, to heal, and not to argue. That had been the world that met Gabriel on opening her eyes.

There were dust-ups and arguments and hurt feelings that needed resolution. Thousands of years away from God didn't vanish from a demon's heart and mind. As with renewing the face of the Earth, though, prayer and hard work would smooth the rough edges. To unlearn the tactics they'd created to survive those graceless ages? It couldn't happen all at once. Just after the banquet, Raphael had joked that Gabriel would never forgive Lucifer for repenting while she was unconscious, and Lucifer had startled. Obviously she would "forgive" him—except it wasn't obvious. Ataf had a full-blown panic attack on remembering a tremendous evil he hadn't asked forgiveness for, and he'd begged Michael to come with him before God to confess it. Asmodeus had recused himself into the inner sanctum to pray, and he still hadn't emerged.

Former demons still deferred to Lucifer automatically. Immediately. Fearfully. For that matter, Lucifer still tended to issue orders, then hesitate, as if rifling through his mind to figure out whether whatever he'd just said were "allowed." If he got pushback, (and to her credit, Gabriel gave a lot of pushback,) his eyes would glint, but he'd catch himself before reacting. He seemed to catch himself frequently.

Their templates were broken. As with the Temple Mount, nothing mapped the way it should, but given time, God could straighten was was bent.

That wasn't even to mention the injuries. Mistofiel avoided Belazael. There wasn't anger between them, but in Belazael's shadow, Mistofiel always carried a faint flicker of fear.

Mistofiel also hadn't formed a bond with Lucifer, which Michael had figured would happen within the first two days. Of course, Belior had bonded him, but so far, Mistofiel hadn't even approached the already-bonded Seraphim he'd abandoned upon joining the Maskim.

(Interestingly, Rahab had begun warming up to Lucifer. Michael wasn't sure where that would lead, but it was heartening to watch.)

Even so, despite all the strain, when Mistofiel prayed, there was joy in having returned. When Michael prayed with Ataf, it took Michael's breath away how astonished Ataf was at the way God loved him. Ataf was shocked by the way he could love God, too. Right before he'd come back, Ataf had said he thought he could love God again—and he did. He did so much.

Lucifer had told Jesus he didn't love Him. Michael wouldn't ask if that had changed. Michael's only business was to make sure Michael loved God, and God would handle His relationships with everyone else.

Then there were the names. Some demons kept their fallen

names. As Ataf said, if that was the name God had used to pronounce forgiveness, then that made the name sweet. Many had reverted to their pre-Winnowed names. A third group had emerged, though—the ones who wanted new names to reflect their new selves. Rahab looked to be turning up as one of those. "His original name doesn't fit him any longer," Ataf had explained, "but 'Rahab' means 'Destruction,' and that doesn't fit, either."

Michael returned to the present as Lucifer gestured at the light posts. "These are the markers?"

"These aren't anywhere near close to the markers." Gabriel winked them out. "I cannot imagine what you did to obscure them —"

Lucifer raised his hands. "Not me."

"Oh, then I guess Michael did it." Gabriel's eyes glimmered with humor as Michael arched his brows at her. "I've triple-confirmed the location of the altar." She drove a light stake into the ground by her feet, then shot out a line of light and cast down another stake. "Okay, but then I measure to the gates, and it all falls apart."

Lucifer wrinkled his nose. "This is quite an obsession."

"Wanting to do things correctly," Gabriel replied in a sing-song while measuring another string of light, "is not being obsessed."

In his heart, Michael felt Saraquael project, *I'm sure they haven't had that conversation at least twenty times.*

Michael replied, *Be precise, or Gabriel will clarify it's been twenty-two times.*

Michael turned toward where he'd felt Saraquael, only to see that Gabriel's mapping expedition was drawing a crowd. Then Mistofiel was with Gabriel, driving different colored lights into the ground and debating locations. Michael backed up, and now there were far more angels helping Gabriel mark out the temple floor plan beneath the dust. Remiel and Camael sent a plume of grit into the air and drove it off on a high-atmosphere wind, which seemed counterproductive until Michael realized they were clearing more of the landscape. The Temple Mount should, after all, be a mount.

A dozen Cherubim had planted stakes, and now Gabriel started dispatching the others. You, mark the site of the Crucifixion. You, stake the location of the burning bush. Stake the home in Nazareth where Jesus became incarnate. On and on, and the longer it went, the more other angels and human souls gathered.

Mary and Uriel appeared beside Michael. "This is exciting," Mary breathed. She, at least, knew what was about to happen.

I'll wait and find out with everyone else, Michael prayed.

God teased, *Are you sure?*

No one needs protection now, so all surprises are by definition good.

Jesus appeared at the site of the altar. Lucifer whipped his head around to look at Him—and smiled.

That was a good surprise.

It was the light in his eyes, the way his breath caught just a little, the way his wings lifted. That was love. Whether Lucifer realized it yet wasn't a given, but if Michael needed any confirmation, it was in the way Gabriel stopped what she was doing and closed her eyes, relief wiping out the concentration on her face.

A very good surprise, indeed.

Jesus spoke to Gabriel, and then Michael felt himself tugged. He flashed to them, joined by the rest of the Seven as well as the heads of the angelic orders and dozens of pivotal humans. There were Abraham and Mary, and Moses and David, and Peter and Paul, and John the Baptist and John the Beloved Disciple.

An excited Gabriel was telling Israfel, "I'm certain now that the Earth contracted once the Presence of the Lord withdrew from it, like an old, wrinkled orange, and that's why the measurements weren't coming out right."

Jesus said, "Are we ready?"

The angels snapped to attention. Jesus continued, "My dwelling place from now on will be among you. I will be with you, and I will be your God, and you will be My people. I am the Alpha and the Omega."

Michael shivered. Jesus gestured so all the light stakes shone through the sky, solid at first and then diffracting as they speared the heavens. The whole sky flamed with their light. There, in the places Gabriel had placed stakes, the anchor points popped open, and power flowed from Heaven into Creation, renewing the world. Beneath their feet, Michael felt the planet begin to breathe again, like a dead heart once more pulsing.

Above the gathering of angels and humans, the outlines of a city appeared. The borders of the city shifted into the streams of light the angels had laid out, and the Earth swelled beneath them as it filled with the glory of God.

Gabriel had her hands to her chest. Michael craned his neck to watch the Heavenly Jerusalem settle into the plane of Creation. Light sparkled from the walls and the rooftops, but cities are made of people, so it was the human souls surrounding the area that sparkled brilliant as jasper and rubies and diamonds.

As the city firmed up, water began to flow. Michael could feel its spread, could feel the purity as it rushed over the face of the Earth.

Jesus turned toward the angels. "See? I'm making everything new."

Behind Michael, Lucifer's voice sang out the opening notes of a song—Dedication of the Stars.

Gabriel and Israfel joined. Then Michael sang, too. Sang with all the host. All the morning stars sang together again, and all the human souls. The air continued to clear, and the water flowed, and the city's foundation burrowed its feet deep into the earth.

In the next hours, Michael juggled multiple requests and continuous needs from every part of the Earth. This was the best kind of multitasking, and occasionally he was bilocating or trilocating to keep up with it all. Daisy-chaining his crises, indeed. Finally, he ended up back at the New Jerusalem. Lucifer and Jesus were on the other side of the river, so Michael joined Gabriel and Raphael before a tree.

The Tree of Life, growing here. Growing now.

Raphael smiled. "Isn't this amazing? This is where it's belonged all this time."

Gabriel hadn't stopped projecting awe at the fractals of the branches, the lighting on the leaves, and the tight buds that would erupt into flowers and finally into fruit.

Michael said, "You said it was too cold for plants."

Raphael gestured to the water. "It's warm, and it's keeping the land warm."

As Lucifer and Jesus joined them, Michael said, "Are you planning to bring down the Tree of Knowledge?"

Murmuring, "My personal Tree of Knowledge took the form of a cedar," Gabriel furrowed her brow. She paused. "A good argument could also be made for a pomegranate." She turned to Jesus. "May I plant a garden here, at the feet of the city?"

Jesus gestured, and she flashed away.

Raphael said, "Which will she bring first?"

Lucifer huffed. "That isn't even a question: one of the cedars. My question is, will she bring a cutting or transport a whole tree?"

Michael thought toward God, *My vote is the pomegranate.*

Gabriel returned holding Lucifer's heather.

Lucifer raised his hands. "What? You were supposed to bring a cedar."

Frowning, she said, "Supposed to? Is there a law of which I was previously unaware?" She raised the potted heather. "This plant was your road home."

Lucifer folded his arms. "Your cedars were your road home, and you brought me home. That makes them the road home for both of us."

Her expression didn't change. "This heather was the first plant to return to the Earth, so it's fitting to maintain that precedent."

Raphael sent to Michael, *While they're debating, should I plant a whole grove of pomegranates?,* and Michael choked on a laugh.

Lucifer gestured to the terrain. "It's not fitting at all. The heather would put my mark on the world."

Gabriel tilted her head. "Your mark is appropriate. The world was given to you."

"Good point." Lucifer turned to Jesus. "The world was given to me, and I can give it to anyone I want to. I want to give it to You."

Gabriel held out the heather toward Jesus. "This was likewise given to me, and I want to give it to You by planting it here, in Your world."

Jesus kissed Gabriel on the forehead. "I accept your gift." He reached for Lucifer's hand "And likewise, I accept yours. You may plant your garden."

Brows contracted, Lucifer folded his arms. "You didn't settle the argument."

"I didn't intend to settle the argument." With a spark in his eyes, Jesus added, "I've given you a new Heaven and a new Earth. Now that you're all home again, it's yours to decide what you're going to do with them."

Author's Note

Ironically, I'm not a universalist.

Universalism, or the belief that everyone automatically goes to Heaven, was branded a heresy early in the Christian tradition. The Bible seems to make it clear that not everyone ends up in Heaven, and Origen, who endorsed universalism (aka, "apokatastasis," or "universal restoration,") is a Church Father who never got named a saint.

As such, I wasn't even sure I wanted to write this, except that whenever I re-read the other books in the series, they all wanted to harmonize this way, with this one specific ending and one intention.

Most denominations do not believe in universal salvation, teaching that hell is a one-way trip. They say the natural outcome of free will is that some souls will choose isolation over love, and selfishness over generosity.

We can quote Bible verses to one another all day long, but I start to second-guess tradition when I hear things like Peter preaching that the Messiah "must remain in Heaven until the time of the universal restoration," (Acts 3:21) or Paul writing that Christ came "to reconcile to himself all things, whether on earth or in heaven" (Col 1:20) or "we trust in the living God, who is the savior of all humanity" (1 Tim 4:10), among others. While the Bible is very clear about the possibility of souls falling into hell, I'd like hell to be empty.

I'm not entirely alone. Gregory of Nyssa, a canonized Church

Father, wrote, "No being will remain outside the number of the saved." Then there's the conclusion C.S. Lewis reaches in *The Great Divorce*, that maybe some souls do emerge from hell, and for them, we call it purgatory.

When people talk about hell, they focus on the lost human souls, but how can we not keenly feel the tragedy of losing so many beautiful and bright angels? A third of them, according to the Book of Revelation. A third of those brilliant and unique and amazing hearts, each one created lovingly by the hand of God as if they were all individual species. What if they could turn back? What if they could love God again?

As Gabriel asks, "Can't? Or won't?" That's the fulcrum: free will. It's up to us to decide whether we heed the warnings: whether we obey, whether we serve, whether we respond, whether we love.

I write fiction and am hardly qualified to give spiritual direction. If you're not sure what your own denomination teaches, talk to your pastor, priest, deacon, or other spiritual leader.

Here's another perspective, though: the one put forward by Hans Urs von Balthasar in *Dare We Hope That All Men be Saved*? Von Balthasar posits that if we can legitimately hold out hope for *any* individual soul, then it's not unreasonable to hold out hope for *every* individual soul. He then takes a hundred fifty pages to break down all the Bible verses about an eternal hell and the limits (or lack of limits) of Jesus's salvific work. It is possible, von Balthasar says, to read the verses about hell as a dire warning of what *might* happen and the urgent necessity to choose right.

Put it this way: I taught my children not to touch the stovetop because they might get burned. None of them did. I hope it's the same with hell—that hearing the sharp warning of loss/isolation, and directed by the merciful love of God our savior, maybe everyone's soul might avoid touching the eternal stovetop.

I would like to thank everyone involved in the writing and publication of this novel, especially the ones who gave the encouragement to dare writing it in the first place. Special thanks to those who suffered through the earliest draft of the story. I'm indebted to you all, and I'm grateful for your inspiration.

Did you know there are six other full-length novels in the **Seven Archangels Saga**? Did you know there's also a novelette, **Once Only**?

Well, they're all available on Amazon in Kindle format, and the full-length novels are available in print, as well. Even better, the full-length novels are being released as audiobooks, so check Audible, Overdrive, Hoopla, Chirp, or wherever you pick up your audio. You also can ask your public library to pick up a copy.

A number of my other books have angels. If you want some humor, check out **Honest and for True**. Lee considers New York City her personal playground. She dates for fun, loves her job as an auto mechanic, and can see her guardian angel—a wisecracker with a strange fascination for the Rumours Album. (I love this story. It's so much fun.)

If you want drama, there's **Relic of His Heart**, the story of an angel who's trying to locate a relic stolen from an Italian church at the end of World War II—and the midwife who seriously does not have time for this.